Linda Grant was born in Liverpool and now lives in London. Her first novel, *The Cast Iron Shore*, won the David Higham First Novel Prize and was shortlisted for the *Guardian* Fiction Prize. Her second novel, *When I Lived in Modern Times*, won the Orange Prize for Fiction. *Still Here* was nominated for the Man Booker Prize. Linda Grant is also the author of *Sexing the Millennium: A Political History of the Sexual Revolution*, *Remind Me Who I am Again*, a family memoir, *The People on the Street: A Writer's View of Israel*, which won the Lettre Ulysses Prize for Literary Reportage, and most recently, *The Thoughtful Dresser*. Linda Grant's latest novel, *The Clothes on Their Backs*, won *The South Bank Show* Literature Award and was shortlisted for the Man Booker Prize 2008.

Find out more at www.lindagrant.co.uk

'Witty, stirring, formidable, above all readable.' Angus Calder, *Scotland on Sunday*.

'This super-subtle work is like a delicately spiced dish whose aftertaste testifies to the chef's skill: more striking in retrospect.' *Time Out*

'Linda Grant's remarkably accomplished first novel is piercingly sad.' *Guardian*

'Intelligent and ambitious . . . *The Cast Iron Shore* is a novel of ideas, and it aspires – almost passionately – to address questions which can only be called metaphysical: of freedom and identity, of purpose and becoming . . . fascinating.' *Times Literary Supplement*

'A remarkable choronicle of the second half of the twentieth century . . . Grant's outstanding novel demonstrates a commendable ambivalence towards its utopian socialist characters. She offers us big ideas and a clever plot, along with some truly fine writing.' *Daily Telegraph*

ALSO BY LINDA GRANT

Fiction

When I Lived in Modern Times

Still Here

The Clothes on Their Backs

Non-fiction

Sexing the Millennium: A Political History
of the Sexual Revolution

Remind Me Who I Am, Again

The People on the Street: A Writer's View of Israel

The Thoughtful Dresser

THE CAST IRON SHORE

LINDA GRANT

virago

VIRAGO

This edition published in 2010 by Virago Press
First published in 1996 by Macmillan Publishers Ltd

Copyright © Linda Grant 1996

Linda Grant has asserted her right to be identified
as the author of this work in accordance with the Copyright,
Designs and Patents Act 1988.

A CIP catalogue record for this book
is available from the British Library.

ISBN 978-1-84408-648-1

Typeset in Goudy by M Rules
Printed and bound in Great Britain by
Clays Ltd, St Ives plc

Papers used by Virago are natural, renewable and
recyclable products sourced from well-managed forests and certified
in accordance with the rules of the Forest Stewardship Council.

Mixed Sources
Product group from well-managed
forests and other controlled sources
www.fsc.org   Cert no. SGS-COC-004081
© 1996 Forest Stewardship Council
FSC

Virago Press
An imprint of
Little, Brown Book Group
100 Victoria Embankment
London EC4Y 0DY

An Hachette UK Company
www.hachette.co.uk

www.virago.co.uk

'As our hours of leisure shorten, it is essential that they should be made as charming as possible, and you can't have charm without women who have learned to conceal the iron in their characters.'

Lois Long, *The New Yorker*, 24 January 1942

'The text is home; each commentary a return.'

George Steiner

Acknowledgements

I owe the deepest of debts to Vivian Gornick's landmark study *The Romance of American Communism*, and in particular for the interview with 'Diana Michaels', who was the initial inspiration for Sybil Ross. I have also drawn on Lawrence Lader's *Power on the Left: American Radical Movements Since 1946*. Grateful thanks to Jonathan Raban for his hospitality, for directing me to the right part of the Washington coast and for some extremely interesting remarks about surfers. Finally, my gratitude goes to my agent Derek Johns for his long and invaluable involvement in the writing.

To Imogen Parker and Ronald Frame

1989

Suppose I were to die in a hotel room? Would it really be so bad? The maid would find me in the morning, my body still warm. There would be no pets to have gnawed my corpse as it lay undiscovered. The more I think of it, the more I pass my time collecting in my mind hotels where this death could take place. The Metropole is not one of them.

I sit out my days stinking in the heat, under the great chinoiserie chandeliers, iced like a grey wedding cake with dusty cobwebs. There are frequent power cuts and when there are, the fans grow torpid, then still. We are hot and sightless in the gloom for hours. The claustrophobia torments me.

Sometimes my cyclo man takes me for a drive through the night streets where the air is thick with the smell of pork fat. In the market women are weighing out puppies by the pound but still the dim red bulbs, like fat glow worms, which hardly light the coffee ladies' little establishments, lend a kind of enchantment and I say, 'Stop! Let's have coffee.' I want to sit at one of the kitchen chairs they place on the street but my cyclo man says they are not for that. '*Madame, c'est pour les messieurs.*'

The city is coloured ochre and burnt sienna and umber. The lovely houses that the French built lie in roofless ruins, a dozen families in each, save for an occasional restoration. You can go to the most elegant street in any city and find the most beautiful building and it will be the Italian embassy. So it is here.

After these futile excursions I come back to my room, labour up the stairs (the lift has not worked since 1957) and find that a rat has eaten another paperback, right up to the glued spine. The wooden frame of the mosquito net has rotted and crumbled. The Soviet air-conditioning unit has a fungus. It splutters out a little cold air, two or three inches around itself, as if designed to cool only its own mechanism. The ceiling rose flakes. The claw-foot cast-iron bathtub has rusted. I have already cut my foot. They say that that laughable liberal Jane Fonda stayed here, indeed in my very room.

Outside, skeletal men hang about, as if just looking at us, feasting on our fatness, will nourish them. When I come back to Hanoi they will be dead. But I would rather be dead myself than return to this place.

Finally there is a permission and a release. We are flying south a thousand miles, to Saigon. I feel much happier now for all ports are the same – Liverpool, Belfast, Hamburg, Marseilles, Barcelona, Genoa, Naples, Palermo, Piraeus, Odessa, New York, San Francisco, Vancouver, Manila, Shanghai. I understand ports. Through them come an infection of new ideas, a virus of difference. The races contaminate each other with the sudden vitality of new blood groups, the DNA runs rampant. No one who was born in a port knows who they really are. The line of ancestry terminates at the pierhead. Beyond the sea we know only a country from which a venturesome man or woman once made a journey. Neither that country nor this is our home.

Nationalists fear ports, their dirt and insubordination. There's no respect. Easy to come, easy to go, the sea is always there to offer an escape from the binding of the land. Stan was murder like that. He had jobs but he would never settle. One word out of place and he'd be off, down the dock road looking for a start. The next thing you would hear was a postcard from the Orinoco River. Ports don't inhabit the country they are in. Our backs are turned against the land, looking out for the stranger. Traders, traders all.

My room at the Caravelle is a considerable improvement. Nothing much has been done to it or the city since the Americans left, but that was only fourteen years ago; the French had not been in Hanoi since 1954.

Here, there is a line of ants making a progress up the walls of the shower, but everything works. There is even a clumsy attempt to imitate the lavish fruit bowls that are routinely provided in every Hyatt or Sheraton in Bangkok or Kuala Lumpur.

And a black Bakelite telephone by the bed. After all the fatigue and frustration of the last weeks, suddenly I am alert, thinking, calculating, my trader's brain doing sums in my head. How many rooms are there in this hotel? How many phones? And how much would they take for all of them? It's a windfall and Vietnam will not be a wasted journey, after all. Cool at last, sweat washed off and legs freshly shaved and talcumed, moving around my room in a miasma of Madame Rochas, I am light-headed with optimism. What does Vietnam want with these old phones which can't work properly? The Vietnamese need new technology, they're communists, they know that. They see progress in a line of pylons marching purposefully from the Mekong Delta to the Red River in the north: electrification, hydraulics, dams, bridges – they follow the Soviet Union into the industrial revolution. Faxes, modems, satellite dishes cannot be far behind. Give *me* your Bakelite telephones, let me bring them home!

I dress carefully in navy linen and make up my face for my meeting with the Trade Representative whom I have arranged to meet in the lobby. My face is not as bad as it was. I have had a few nips and tucks here and there, though not the full lift. There are a couple of Western women sitting in the lobby in khaki shorts and T-shirts with slogans on them I do not bother to read. Aid workers.

The Trade Representative looks like every other Vietnamese woman I have ever seen in cheap brown slacks, the white thread showing through at the seams, a cheap brown checked shirt, plastic shoes, an East German briefcase she's very proud of and a smile filled with broken teeth. I know from the briefing in Hanoi that she is a high-ranking Party functionary with a notable war record and so, as is customary with such initial meetings, green tea is brought. With these formalities she explains that she understands my mission. She has a programme for me. In Saigon there are many antiques available for export.

The country is full of *objets*, left behind by the French driven from their colonizers' villas on the high ground of the rubber plantations. Listen. She takes me down to the old rue Catinet, the street that runs down to the river. In the time of the French it was a place to shop for fashions from France, for lingerie and cigars and books. Then when the Americans came it was where you went to buy sex. Now, renamed something like Renunciation or Victory, it sells the debris of its colonial past back to the colonizers.

We stop first at an antique shop that has nothing but Art Deco lamps, the kind where slim girls stand on tiptoe holding globes which light up when a button is pressed on the base. All made in France or Berlin in the twenties and thirties. In my shop in Holland Park I will not sell replicas, but one must travel far to find the originals.

Every day I go out with the Trade Representative. Every night I push my way through the assault party of beggars at the door. Some of the children have the most extraordinary defor- mities – gargantuan heads, pure white eyeballs with no iris, no lens, like sightless angels. Agent Orange in their mothers' wombs did this to them, the Trade Representative says. They want money. It's no good giving them a fist full of dong. They want hard currency. 'Madame,' they cry. 'Gimme dolla.' 'Gimme fi' dolla.'

Every night I make my entrance. Tonight I am wearing a deep pink silk *aio dia*. I'd seen the young girls wearing them as they rode their bicycles about the city, their slim arms and hands protected from the sun by elbow-length gloves, like debutantes.

We sit together, me and the other Europeans, high above the city, canopied and protected from the sudden violence of its tropical storms, an advance platoon from Vietnam's next invasion. Fourteen years ago the Vietnamese won a great moral victory. As for the next war, the economic one, they are like babies. They cannot win. I see no class divisions here. Everyone is poor or poverty-stricken or starving.

We, on the other hand, have booked dinner at Madame Suzanne Dai's private restaurant, famously for years the only vestige of capitalism and the free market in the whole country, tolerated by the authorities. The restaurant is in her library, the chef was her children's nanny. There are portraits on the wall of her ancestors, mandarins in fancy dress and funny moustaches. A film of brown grease covers the glass. The whole country needs a good clean.

Course after course is brought, prawn wrapped around sugar cane, great fishes whose eyes still stare at us. We've had nothing like this since we have been in Vietnam. We get drunker and drunker. No hand brushes my leg under the table, tonight or any other. I realize that I am fifteen or twenty years older than the oldest member of our party. This, and the whole of south-east Asia for that matter, is no country for old women. With our coffee Madame Dai appears. She wishes to present us with invitations to the French ballet. It is not far. Her own cyclo man will take us. 'It was the French who first brought us ballet,' she says. 'They gave us everything, their civilization, their sophistication. They laid out our streets like boulevards. I still smell their perfume.' She suddenly stops and changes tack. One amongst us must be a spy, it stands to reason. 'But of course the Russians are now the greatest dancers in the world,' she continues, as if teetering on points. 'They take our best dancers to train at the Kirov and the Bolshoi. Perhaps you have been to the Soviet Union and seen them?'

Only I accept the invitation. I climb into a cyclo and the thin man pedals me along, past children carrying water from a standpipe in an old American helmet. He pedals past the women selling black-market cigarettes, gum, condoms. He pedals past a video booth where a large crowd inside is watching *Rambo*.

I arrive at what I think is a school auditorium. Inside a crowd of proud mammas and a sprinkling of elderly balletomanes eagerly await the curtain's rise. There is one other European, someone I have not noticed at the Rex or at the Caravelle, and there is something in his face that makes me start. He is very old.

His blue suit is good but it was made a long time ago. He will look at me again and again, at my black hair like a helmet, my nose curved like a saracen's sword. I will look at his, again and again.

The evening's programme starts with a spirited romp by a dozen or two little girls in tutus, which renders their mammas into ecstasies. It seems a shame that none have cameras to record this winsome moment. Indeed, how did they afford the tutus?

The old plush curtain closes and there is an interval. A middle-aged woman approaches me and explains what is to come. We are to see a performance of 'The Dying Swan' by the prima ballerina. Afterwards there will be a stirring and emotional tribute to the spirit of the French Revolution. Why? Because this is the bicentennial year, she reminds me. The ballet company, which has struggled, banned and underground, since 1975, has recently been able to restore performances due to the patronage of the government's Soviet advisers. There is a revival of interest in classical Western art, she explains. Recently a ragged but enthusiastic orchestra put on a public performance of *Madame Butterfly*, officially sanctioned because of its clear message about dangerous liaisons between East and West.

The curtain parts again. I know very little about ballet, but I see the dancer's movements are unsteady. Her limbs are not quite in the right proportion, really she cannot dance for toffee and her costume is cheap and preposterous, as if it had been made for some turn-of-the-century, end-of-pier concert party. Yet someone had laboured so hard to get it right. Someone knew what it should look like. And now I see this girl has the face of a great ballerina, the huge tragic eyes, the etched, tender red mouth. Death comes. I feel a spasm somewhere.

There is a curtain call, even a garish bouquet of flowers and the ballerina gestures to the wings. An old man with rouged cheeks comes out, diffidently, trembling. 'Mon mari,' the middle-aged woman says, proudly. On stage the dancers perform the French Revolution; the fleur-de-lis gives way to the tricolour. How do you express Revolution? By noble gestures, athletic leaps, the depiction of the masses – there are plenty of roles, even for the youngest, clumsiest member of the primary school corps de ballet.

Madame Dai's cyclo man pedals me back to the Caravelle. As we reach the square he stops at a café. He speaks a little English. 'We wait,' he says. 'Bad people. Go later.' I have no patience with this sort of thing. We are only a few hundred metres from the hotel. I'm tired and, as every night in Vietnam, I'm drunk. I want to sleep. But in the square, this Saturday night, is something I have never seen before. Ten thousand, maybe more, kids on motor scooters, bicycles, anything with wheels, girls in miniskirts perched on handlebars, ghetto-blasters on handlebars, blazing out rock and roll. They ride round and round the square. You can see they will mow down anything that comes in their path. No one can cross the road. These calm people with their scented tea and their endless bureaucratic formalities have turned aggressive. It is not a pretty sight and I am frightened. A cop on a white chromium Harley-Davidson rides in, using his baton to plough through a path. Girls are screaming, rock and roll is getting louder.

I know what this is. It's a demonstration.

I wait forty minutes for the kids to disperse; some are beaten and bloody, others ride defiantly off into the night. I stumble into the Caravelle. As I pass the dining room a girl singing 'My Way' accompanies herself on the pink electric guitar. I find that in my room, in the fruit basket by my bed, there's a green coconut, already slit, with a straw jammed inside. I prise apart the flesh and pour in a jigger or two of Scotch and drink this disgusting concoction.

Woozy, I go up to the roof where the journalists once gathered to watch the rockets fall on the outlying suburbs and hear the mortars' thud. I listen to the World Service on my little short-wave radio. I have been away three weeks and this is the first time I have remembered to turn it on. Here, we are held in time. I don't understand history's clock. Something has been going on in East Berlin. Gangs have knocked great holes in the Wall. Thousands are driving through in their Trabants. Honecker has fled.

A girl is being interviewed in English. 'Is reunification the next step?' the reporter asks her. 'What else would we want?' the girl replies. I begin to cry. All those years, everything we tried to do. The struggle, the marching, the dreams. What had it all been for? What the fuck had it all been for? Who are you when you have nothing left to believe in?

In bed, as I drift off to sleep, I think of my fantasy. Suppose I were to die in the Metropole? The maid, I suppose, would strip me of my clothes, look in my mouth for gold, sell my carcass at the market, where I would appear on stalls as an unfamiliar meat from a distant province.

I wake late the next morning and the Trade Representative is waiting for me when I go in to breakfast: salty coffee, a baguette, yellow jam, a tasteless slab of Soviet butter.

'Today there is no programme,' she says. 'It is good for you, you must be tired. You were out late.' I knew there were spies.

'What was going on last night, in the square?'

It is the children. They don't want war memorials, they don't want Ho, they don't want formaldehyde bottles filled with the wildly-deformed foetuses of Agent Orange babies, they don't want Party Congresses, they don't want Five-Year Plans, they don't want the Russians and they don't want to remember the war. They want ghettoblasters, air-conditioning units, electric guitars, Hollywood films, fun.

The Trade Representative and I sit there, two women, no longer even in middle age. 'Who were you?' I ask her. She answers at once, pleased at my attention.

'I was a novelist. Then when the war began I became a member of the bomb-disposal squad on the Ho Chi Minh Trail. I think you understand the fate of our nation and that all intellectuals had to make their contribution. Once, during the war, I saw an illustrated article about a football champion and I was so surprised that there was a happy life going on somewhere.

'When I was young we had to wear green and brown clothes, the colour of the trees. When I walk the streets and see how the young people have the right to be with their boyfriends and to wear beautiful dresses and go to dances I feel very sad for me.'

'Do you still write novels?'

'That was long ago.'

'Are they still in print?'

'Yes. Some. But they were not translated, you cannot read them.'

'Were any translated into Russian?'

'No. My novels were about the time before the war. They were love stories, and stories of how the peasants lived. There was nothing about politics or our struggle. They are not of interest outside Vietnam. If you want political art you must meet my niece. She was a singer in the anti-war movement. She was very famous during the Americans' time – we called her the Joan Baez of Saigon. She dressed like her and sang barefoot, which was a great shame for my family.'

'Describe your novels to me, then.'

'I wrote my first story when I came back from my studies in France in 1951. I had been very influenced by the French writers of that time, Cocteau and Sartre and de Beauvoir and Camus, and I tried to write such alienated, existential stories as theirs but my imitations were very poor. In Vietnam we had so little feeling of aloneness. I was a young girl during the war – not the Americans' war or the French war but the same war your people fought. We were occupied by the Japanese. I had never known much about peace. But my mother would tell me about her own youth and it all seemed so ordinary. I particularly liked her tales about young girls who loved a boy but the boy was not thought of by the parents as suitable. They had another boy in mind for her. My generation laughed at our parents who tried to inflict these old-fashioned ideas on us. We were Resistance fighters and we thought this kind of morality did not apply to us. But when we took up arms against the French and I lay with my comrades in a hole somewhere in the countryside I thought of those times and of those girls and their little problems. It was a comfort to me to think that one day that was all little girls would have to worry about. Sometimes I introduced an evil French landowner into my stories because there were several such examples in real life. But mostly I wrote about the many difficulties girls face when they are young and in love.'

'You could have stayed in France and saved yourself all those years of fighting.'

'Yes, of course I could. There was a Frenchman who would have married me very quickly. But you should not abandon your country because it is unhappy. That would be like abandoning your parents when they are suffering. And culture must have a land which nourishes it like a plant has to have a piece of land. All these questions, Mrs Sybil. Questions, questions. You never speak of yourself.'

'I'm thinking about myself all the time. Since I've been here, that's all I ever do.'

'You have never said if you have children.'

'No, I don't have any children.'

'How sad.'

Later, I will meet most of her family. Her husband is a journalist, also an interpreter, for the Foreign Press Bureau. Her daughter is a doctor and her son an engineer, presently in East Germany undergoing training. Do they all go to Party meetings together, I wonder? They stare at me. 'We are not communists,' the daughter says. 'We have never been members of the Party. We are nationalists. And Buddhists. We have no expectations. He who goes with the river must flow with the river.'

In my company the Trade Representative will develop a new insouciance that I find almost European, as if she was thinking back to her years in Paris after the war. To my surprise, she asks me if I remember the dresses we wore then, romantic frocks that grazed the ankles like ballerinas. 'The New Look,' I say.

'Yes. I had such a dress,' she says. 'It was greeny-blue, the colour of sea-foam. I wore it when I went out with my French boyfriend. He was quite rich because he worked in the aviation industry, making the calculations for Caravelle aeroplanes.'

'So you were not without caprice, not always serious?'

'Of course not. I was a girl and it is every girl's duty to be carefree unless they have problems of the heart. But you. I would like to ask about you, Mrs Sybil. We are all perplexed by you. How did you come to be a member of the Party?'

I told her. 'So you come from what the Chinese call the Middle Kingdom, those comrades who are motivated by conditions of the spirit rather than of class history.'

'Yes.'

'But you are no longer a member.'

'Oh, no. Not for a very long time, not since the mid-sixties.'

'A strange time to leave.'

'There were other circumstances.'

But this is in the future. On this day she has other business. 'A man was asking for you. I have a message. He wants you to meet him, here.' She has a map; it is from the Americans' time. On it is marked the abbreviation Syn.

'Who is it? Who is this man? A dealer? He has antiques for me?'

'No, he is a librarian. I know him, I think. But the message comes from my office. He has sent his cyclo.'

She lets go of my hand and stands up. 'Tomorrow there will be a programme for you. You will be pleased, I hope.'

How does Saigon look in the light? Like Nice, cream and pink stucco buildings lining the broad streets planted with palm trees. A city that once must have been like a *glace*. There are docks, and sailors of many nationalities walk there in their tropical whites. Everywhere, I notice, are signs of the return of free enterprise. On the pavements everyone has something to sell. The cyclo man pulls me beyond the market into the suburbs where the French once lived, suburbs I remember from my own childhood in a different port. Solid houses, large gardens. Houses for families.

The street is a long one and at the end of it I see something I had not expected to see in Saigon, *never*, not in the whole of Asia. A shut-up building. And, set in a stained-glass panel, a star.

The elderly European I had seen at the concert is waiting for me, with the keys. Close to, I can see what a superior cut his suit is made of, what good fabric. Unmistakably French tailoring. He unlocks the door and we enter. It is all as I remember it, the wooden cabinet that houses the scrolls, the women's gallery above.

'Who are you?'

'My name is Etienne Goldstein. I came here in 1937 to take over my father's company; we were traders from Marseilles. If I had stayed in France I would have been deported.'

'But you didn't go back when the war was over? Not even after the French had left?'

'Because of Vietnam, Saigon, I survived. I owed them something.'

'But after 1975? Under the communists?'

'I am a communist. I was a Party member from the age of fifteen, in Marseilles.'

'I was also a communist once. I was a member of the Party.'

He looks at me, at my dress, my hat, my belt, my shoes, my gold bracelets, without belief.

'Believe me, all kinds of people were communists, even me. I was a communist and being a communist made me better than I was. I tell you it could all have been so much worse.'

But I could see he had come to meet a fellow Jew, not a fellow communist. 'Where did you find your congregation?'

'There have always been Jews in Asia,' he said. 'In China from before Marco Polo. There are Jews all around you, wherever you go.'

'How can that be?'

'Do you think that to be a Jew you must only be born in such-and-such a place? That every Jew has a nose like ours? There are blonde Jews, Jews of every colour skin. Ours is a complex identity and Jews have always done what they had to to survive. Black Jews, Asian Jews, what's the difference? We carry our identity not in a place but in our story. There is no religion here now, of course. We are communists and have no need of it. But shall we remember?'

He draws the ram's horn from its velvet bag and raises it to his lips.

He stands at the window and blows, his cheeks hard and red below the thin strands of hair on his white scalp. I think the effort is going to kill him, but by God he's got it quite right, and his breath makes that sound that tells us who we are and what we must do. Against this, we are tested.

TEKIAH One long blast of alarm. The *shofar* sounds and a voice is heard, our own, waking us from self-deception.

SHEVARIM Three long blasts, like wailing in the desert.

The *shofar* sounds and those who are in chains hear, for it calls us to struggle for our freedom.

TERUAH Nine short blasts, like broken sobs. The *shofar* sounds, calling even the most distant traveller home.

And even I am summoned back. Of course, you cannot forget the past, it is with you all your life.

PART ONE

Chapter One

'Sydney, darling, a shrimp?' my mother said.

It was Easter Monday, 1938, and I was fourteen. We were on the front at Parkgate, sitting in deck-chairs under a tartan car rug in the wind. It was the seaside, but not the seaside.

My mother had gone off to buy an ice-cream cornet, Daddy and I had hoped, at least we hoped it was not something worse. But she had reappeared along the windy front moments later, vibrant in pink Schiaparelli checks, holding in front of her and clasped between one forefinger and thumb a paper tub of shrimps and a wooden fork. She bore them like a chalice, smiling.

My father looked at the shrimp, embedded in a lump of butter.

'Sonia, not here, please. Someone will see.'

My mother waved a lilac suede gloved hand at the empty marshes. 'Really?'

'At home, yes, but not outdoors, you never know who might be passing.' He was blushing, a dense shade of dusty rose.

'Everyone eats shrimps in Parkgate. It's a perfectly smart thing to do.'

'Put them away.' Pink turned to angry, livid maroon.

'You're being ridiculous,' my mother said lightly, the three words dissolving like vapour as soon as they left her lips.

In retaliation, to stop his mouth, my father removed a cigar from his inside breast pocket, which he prepared and lit with the numerous gold, silver and chromium gadgets he always carried about his person, carefully, so that the ash did not fall on his suit. He puffed and the brown smoke, smelling of acrid burnt spices, vanished in the fresh breeze as soon as it left the smouldering tip. He was about forty-five then, and as handsome as a movie star under his Homburg; in fact he was one of the few men who was even better looking when he took off his hat. Like Ronald Colman, he had a long, fleshy face and a moustache above full lips. He had a dark charm and an accent. Your eyes were held by the smooth white bank of his forehead on which I sometimes imagined I could stretch and lie as if it were a bed of marble. My nose, worst luck, I claimed from him.

In truth both my parents looked distinctly odd out of doors. Normally they only left the house, other than in transit, for medicinal motives, in the belief that carefully timed doses of fresh air were as beneficial for growing girls as certain patent medicines they bought at Timothy White's cash chemist. To this end I was walked, like a proud and strutting poodle in a jewelled collar, on an indulgent leash.

It was strange to know that here we were so close to the sea, for despite the open sky and the wide space and the tang of salt, the illusion of being inland was strong. In front of us was a vista of half a mile of short, coarse salted grass, stretching towards the gritty hills of Flint on the Welsh side of the estuary. A tidal wave ran through the marshes on the back of a north-west wind, turning them into a waste of sands riddled with gutters in which you could sometimes catch sight of drowning sheep. The Dee was not our river; it raced along the cut up to the landlocked port of Chester, and this weekend drive over the water (or under it, for the Mersey Tunnel had recently opened) was made largely out of a sense of duty. In secret we deplored the emptiness of the landscape, the desolation of the view, and in our imaginations we tarmacked the front, erected warehouses, sunk wharves, docks and piers and peopled them with heaving, sweating men burdened by heavy loads.

My father and I wore almost matching camelhair coats, mine with a Locke's label on which was embroidered in red thread the words Sybil Ross. My hair was cut in a black shining helmet, ending in a straight fringe above my black eyebrows. I did not like the style, but I did not know why. Looking back, I can see now that it was too severe for my face, which was heart-shaped, and the dense fall of hair shadowed my narrow eyes. In turn that drew attention to my nose, making it a hook or claw set above my lips, themselves inconveniently shaped as a rose-bud, a contrived Victorian mouth, just saved by little upturned points at each end. Only my chin was perfect, uncleed, rounding my face off to a soft but definite finale. My neck was proportionate and satisfactory. From the shoulders down, my figure was as yet to be determined. So far it was, on inspection, inconsequential, the hips and waist and chest still considering their final arrangement.

Even as long ago as that spring afternoon before the war, I had noticed that the fashions of the period did not really suit my mother. The short, sleek hairstyles, parted to one side in two smooth and lustrous caps, did not flatter her face, they made it harder. She had Wallis Simpson looks, angular and over-dieted, the jaw very pronounced, the blue eyes pale and deep-set, with faint matching bluish circles beneath them, and this however much she slept in, in the mornings, her breakfast tray growing cold on her lap. But then again, when her photograph once appeared in *Lancashire Life*, she was judged a great beauty by those who noticed it, like all the haughty, Nordic blondes they admired in that period. I was her daughter, her only child, yet I could never see it myself. I knew there was a coldness in her that she was not at liberty to do anything about. That her passion, such as it was, was purely acquisitive for she saw no other reason to expend it.

Both my parents were foreign. Daddy was from Belgrade, my mother from Rotterdam.

Of course normally Mother would not have been seen dead eating in the open air, insisting as she always did on afternoon tea in a smart hotel, a waitress lifting pastries with silver tongs, tiny triangles of sandwich, China tea drunk with a sliver of lemon, *never* Indian, which she understood from one of her magazines was 'not the thing'. (I think she may also have been worried about the social gaffe involved in pouring the milk in at the wrong stage before or after the tea? She could never quite get it right, so easier to avoid it altogether.) Now, in 1938, she hadn't the slightest idea in the world of the deprivation that was awaiting her in the future, with citrus fruits stranded on their hot little islands and she making do with powdered milk and tea sweepings like everyone else.

But buttered shrimps were what everyone ate at Parkgate, what Parkgate was famous for, and even our local gentry had been known to enjoy a tub or two and graciously agreed to lodge a testimonial at a cottage which immeasurably improved its trade by this recommendation from a member of the Stanley family. Had Greta Garbo herself deigned to sample the merchandise, she could impart no greater providence than the scrawled word or two from Lord and Lady Derby who, as far as I knew, owned everything on the Peninsula from Mockbeggar Wharf to Ince Bank. Parkgate was the Dee's final doomed attempt to assert itself as a carrier of navigational traffic, its last link with the sea before sand and silt choked the estuary. Every schoolchild in our part of the world learned of it: first a port for the Irish packet trade, finally this impossibility, an inland fishing village. The people made their living wading out into the marshes with shrimping nets, and the fruits of their labours my mother was now ramming down my father's throat, so to speak.

At home my father indulged in all kinds of what he called *chazerai*, one of his few words of Yiddish, which, though never explained or translated, seemed to speak eloquently, and with contempt, of the *cheapness* of the food, its contamination as well as its ritual uncleanness. I knew what it meant all right. It included rubbishy sweets made in unpleasant factories, sweets in which one may well find embedded some insect. It was fly-blown cakes in dingy windows, stale ham rolls. You would not want a morsel to pass your fastidious lips. But my father did. At dinner we began our meals with grown-up little hors d'oeuvres like angels on horseback while everyone at school drank a brown soup.

My mother went on eating her buttered shrimps. Their coating of grease never seemed to touch her lips.

I guessed that in his pocket my father had a letter from his sister in Belgrade. Correspondence from home always made him anxious and difficult, for he became temporarily conscious of the betrayal of his family, of the terrible thing that his beautiful wife was, sitting there beside him, picking a wooden fork at buttered crustaceans. I watched her finish them with unconvincing relish, screw the cardboard tub into a crumpled ball, walk a few feet and deposit it into a litter bin.

Then everything was all right again. We talked about me.

'You dress Sybil like a terrible frump,' my father complained, scrutinizing my camelhair coat and fawn socks with a professional gaze.

My mother did not have to look up at me to agree. 'Yes, she is certainly ready,' she said. 'We'll take her in hand the next time we go to London. There we will lay the foundations. You'll start giving her a dress allowance, of course?'

My father took out a little notebook in a gold case and inscribed some figures with his propelling pencil. He passed them over to my mother to inspect and she gave me an excited little nod. 'Oh yes,' she said. 'I think we'll do very well with that.'

'I'll think about a coat for her for the coming season.'

'Fox?'

'No, she's too young for fox. It's a middle-aged woman's fur.'

'Persian broadtail?'

'Too sophisticated. Chinchilla.'

'*Divine!*' my mother exclaimed. 'Witty, young and chic. A real statement.' She rested a long hand lightly on my shoulder and touched my cheek with her lips. I caught her scent before the wind cut it away and drove it across the marshes to Wales. Who would not be proud to be such parents' creation?

The bright, cold sun faded and a shroud of grey rain passed

across the Peninsula. The wind from the Atlantic scissored though our camelhair overcoats and my mother shivered in her unseasonable ocelot jacket. Before we left, my father got a passer-by to take a photograph of us with his Leica. I still have the picture somewhere. You can tell that we were happy as we walked back to the Wolseley singing.

Oh, how my mother sang, you had to hand her that, and it was the one thing she was never vain about. She sang only for my father, to my father. She would hear all the latest songs on the wireless then sit down at the piano, play the tune by ear and sing her own versions, sometimes even changing the words a little to make them sound as though they had been written just for him: 'Dear Mr Gable, I'm writing so you'll know . . .' became 'Dear Sydney Ross, I'm singing so you'll know . . .' Neither my father nor I were at all musical and we were entranced by her talent. My own attempts at piano lessons had failed dismally. I could not play my father the simplest of tunes for his pleasure. My mother knew how to take care of the things she loved. As for him, he loved beauty too, it was his great weakness, but he loved things for their beauty alone; that was where their value lay. My mother, on the other hand, naturally thought expensive flowers in florists' shops lovelier than the seaspurge that grew on these wasted marshes. And so did I. So did I.

I loved my mother. I know she loved me, of course she did. She kept her shoes wrapped in black or gold tissue paper in their boxes, her handbags in linen bags of their own; her ornaments were dusted personally with her long white fingers banded in gold and tiny emeralds. On me she expended the most exquisite care, like a gardener with a silver trowel forcing a small new variety of orchid.

*

Almost before I was conscious that I was a girl not a boy, that my hair was dark and my mother's was fair, that the high wooden fence around our garden was the boundary of my world, I knew that I was not a real Jew.

On Saturdays I stood alone in the ladies' gallery looking down on my father's head in his skullcap, his shoulders shrouded by his prayer shawl, while my mother shopped or did exercises for her figure or submitted to the torture of the permanent wave. Was I my father's or my mother's daughter? Each tried to make me theirs. And did I, with my black hair and curved nose, try to keep a low profile?

It is dark in the synagogue, the light is very old. The past is a ruffian that seizes us by the throat and squeezes out our misery. Although contaminated by his marriage, my father is still of the tribe of Cohen, the priestly caste from which he cannot abdicate. In a back room his hands are washed by Levites and his shoes are removed. When he reappears he stands with three other men, their prayer shawls over their heads like ghosts. Beneath this opaque veil he holds his fingers together in the way Moses did when he blessed the Children of Israel, the index and the little fingers joined.

My father shudders and his voice rises to a piercing wail, drops to a sobbing moan, in imitation of the priests blessing the sacrifice. All four rock backwards and forwards, possessed and tormented in the old light. Who had my father become when I could not see his face?

It is a savage and an antique spectacle, from the desert, from our nearly pagan roots, from the time of the Temple. Afterwards, when he is restored to his Austin Reed suit, men press forward to shake his hand, congratulating him on this *mitzvah*, on being so close to God and bearing so much pain.

Once a year, on the Day of Atonement, I leave for the saying of *yiskor*, the prayer for the dead. Through a crack in the door I hear them screaming and I leaf through my prayer book to discover the source of their grief, their desolation, not understanding how there could be so much pain in the world, let alone this ark in which we were all of us here floating, adrift in God's sea. 'Lord,' they cry, 'remember the souls of all my relatives, both male and female, whether paternal or maternal, whether they have been killed, slain, slaughtered, burnt, drowned or strangled. For the Sanctification of Thy Holy Name, for that, I offer charity for the memorial of their souls: in reward of this may their souls enjoy eternal life, wrapped in the shadow of Thy wings.' Secretly Jews embarrass me with their ostentatious sorrow, the reciting of these implausible calamities. The names of the dead are read aloud, my father's grandparents among them, and in Belgrade, at this moment, my father's name is also spoken, for to his parents he is dead and I was never born.

I knew the others only by sight, the Hafts, the Ginsbergs, the Glassmans, the Rosenblatts, all proud in their holiday shoes. I knew their occupations: tailors and cutters and bakers and cobblers, like characters in one of my books of fairy tales as if they had just stepped out of the Black Forest. What had they to do with me? Nothing.

My place was with the misfits, next to Lilian, the outcast daughter. Of course I knew who *she* was, who on Saturday nights stood like a sentry on Huskisson Dock guarding the ships, having sex with a small, rigorously selected clientele of sailors who gave her in payment each time a cellophane-boxed doll of the world in national dress: bold Spanish dolls in mantillas; Scotch dolls in kilts and tiny sporrans; Russian dolls, arms akimbo, legs crouched and crossed, frozen dancers. Lilian who sat madly in her felt suit and angora beret and mumbled expertly through the text I could not read, occasionally blowing kisses to the stone figure of her father down below.

I did not understand the square black letters of Hebrew. Unlike Lilian, no one had ever taught me. I looked at the translation on the other side of the page, telling me to exalt the Lord in dreary repetition, on and on for a thousand pages or more. All I knew was that my father stubbornly believed in God, in the God of his ancestors. He bowed his head every Saturday in observance and worship and righteousness. He couldn't stop himself, not even for my mother. He could not deny what was there by the evidence of his senses. God *was* in that place, in the *chazan's* voice and the strange writing and the six-pointed star, so that he believed, as I did, that God lived not in the sky but in the cupboard where the sacred scrolls in their velvet dresses and silver jewellery were housed. Capped in their silver bells the Torah was carried about through the congregation and the men raised their prayer shawls and touched them to the velvet skirts of the Law and brought them back to their lips and kissed them. (Or the Torah wore white satin on High Holidays.)

He did not hear the women in the ladies' gallery mutter in the shadow of their spectacular hats, like a flock of birds perched on the ascending branches of a tree.

'I wouldn't have had Sydney Ross if you'd paid me. He's a nasty man, stuck-up, a bully.'

'My sister-in-law went out with him. She said he could

never stop looking at blondes. He gave her a beaver muff in the end to break off the engagement.'

'I saw the wife once in Cripps.'

'What's she like?'

'Cold, very cold.'

'The first time they have a row she'll call him a dirty Jew.'

My parents had been married for seventeen years and there had never, to my knowledge, been an argument of any consequence. My parents rarely raised their voices, they did not have to. They revolved around each other like mechanical dancers on top of a musical box. Their sophistication was exactly matching, self-made. *These* people were ghetto Jews for whom the world was a place of terror stalked with ancient enemies. They heard the Cossacks' hooves in their dreams and in the corner of their minds there was always a suitcase packed and ready. To my father, the soul of rootless cosmopolitanism, theirs was a peasant mentality which sprang from the dark heart of Slavic Europe.

My mother's avariciousness, it should be said, was always pragmatic. She had never hid from me that she looked to marry money and my father's religion she simply ignored, as if it was some sort of quirk or habit, as that of other women's husbands who spent long hours playing golf or watching cricket. It did not interfere with her primary activity, which was to shop, and of this my father entirely approved. After all, it was he who paid. He willingly financed adornment in all its forms.

Every Saturday, at lunch-time, my father and I would walk home from the synagogue to our empty house, a large, four-bedroomed mock-Tudor semi-detached villa built just after the last war. A little later my mother would come home to supervise the maid in the preparation of our light meal.

Small panes of coloured glass inset into the windows, depicting medieval helmets and coats of arms, poured pools of red and blue and yellow light on to the carpets. My earliest memories are of my bedroom, lying in my little bed in the umber atmosphere cast by the small orange bulb in a toadstool-shaped night-light under whose frosted glass wooden goblins played. Next to me was the ottoman and in it all manner of toys: a golly with an eye missing, celluloid arms and legs adrift from the torsos of the dolls that had once possessed them. I would drift into sleep, but often woke when the hands of the clock showed some fantastically late hour, such as half-past ten, aroused by a single hoarse foghorn on the river. In the morning I would open my eyes, run from the bed to draw my curtains and look out on to all the gardens beyond, across the city, to where it ran out of gardens and the people who lived in those houses had only a yard.

Beyond the back path which housed a black creosote coal shed there was our own walled garden, for we lived on a corner and were shielded from the prying attention of fellows walking with their pipes in the evening and other people's children who regarded the intertwined wrought-iron initials of us three – 'SSS' – with awe and suspicion, as if the letters were some magic code that could be cracked. The garden, had they seen it, gave no clues that *they* might unravel. It was planted with such formal things as rose bushes and those curious, quasi-sexual flowers called antirrhinums that my mother adored and into the purple mouths of which I poked my little forefinger, opening the lips to find its secret heart of stamens and pollen. There was a rockery made of strange white glittery stone that I grazed my hands against when I was a child and fell off my tricycle. Once a week some men came to weed and dig and mow and my mother brought them tea in an old enamel pot on a tray which they drank in the garage. After dinner on summer evenings my father, a cigar in his mouth, would walk around the lawn under the heavy trees inspecting the beds, or sit on a bench sketching designs for the autumn's furs. There were only the three of us. No other child ever appeared. I do not think my father wished for a son: it was always women that he liked about him and the other two rooms were used as a boxroom and a dressing room for my mother, furnished with a chaise-longue upholstered in canary yellow. Inside the fitted wardrobes hat boxes rose as high as the ceiling.

On one of these Saturdays I asked my father, What does it mean to be a Jew? as he squirted a stream of soda water from the chromium siphon into a glass of Haig and Haig. He mixed me a small, very weak tumbler and sat back in his favourite, mock-Louis Quatorze chair, upholstered in pale blue velvet, the only interior decorating solecism in the whole house, otherwise furnished by Maples and Waring and Gillow.

'When we were slaves in the land of Egypt,' he began, 'and our forefathers toiled for the pharaohs with the blood of their hands and the sweat of their backs . . .' He ranged through history, ancient and modern: Masada, pogroms, King Herod, the Inquisition and the exile from Spain, Kristallnacht, our expulsion from England in the Middle Ages after the Norwich blood libel. There was no chronology in anything he said. Our slavery in Egypt could have been yesterday, the growing menace in Germany a thousand years ago.

'But every year is the first year of Creation,' he reminded me. 'Every year we wipe the slate clean and begin again. The *shofar* is sounded to announce our freedom and raise the banner to collect our exiles and gather us together from the far corners of the earth, the outcasts of the people of Israel.'

I did not want to be part of the world of pain he described. I did not want to be an outcast; I wanted to *belong*. And what I really wanted to know was what he *did* under his prayer shawl. 'What does it feel like? Why do you shake like that?'

'It's not for you to know.' He looked away.

'Because I'm too young?'

'Because you are not a man. And the other thing.' The technicality. That the two women in his house were excluded from the central purpose and mystery of his life. 'The only thing you need to understand, Sybil, is this. You start life as an animal, a wild animal. Your job is to become a human being.'

'But I am a human being!' I cried. 'What else am I? A frog, a house cat, a pigeon?' I heard my mother's key turn in the lock.

'Not in the eyes of God. You're still a savage.'

'So what do I have to do to become a human being?'

'It's difficult. All I can tell you is that you must be humane and follow in the paths of righteousness all your days.'

'Have you done that?'

He sighed. 'There are terrible distractions,' he conceded. 'I do my best.'

I was lithe and light, crouching on the leather pouffe at his feet. The top button of my blouse was inadvertently undone. He looked at my cleavage. 'Cover yourself up,' he said. He brushed his finger along the rim of his moustache. I noticed, not for the first time, that he was unbearably handsome.

'How will I know when I am a human being?'

'A darkness will grow in you, Sybil,' he said. 'You will never rid yourself of it.' Then my mother passed through the room carrying a tall blue Wedgwood vase of white asters and my father's face lit up. He took my hand. 'We're the Chosen People. It's the price we have to pay.'

'Is Mother Chosen?'

'Only by me.'

'Does she have a darkness in her?'

'No, thank God.'

My mother came back, empty-handed. 'Thank God for what?' she asked.

'That you're not one of the Chosen People, Daddy says.'

'Oh, that.'

After lunch she unfolded the green baize card table and we all played gin rummy for money. My father usually won.

Chapter Two

My mother had married Ross the furrier, not Sydney Ross the Cohen in his socks, dressed up in a white sheet, wailing.

Inside Ross the furrier's on Bold Street was enchantment, my father's principle distraction. The frozen wastelands of North America brought us mink, beaver, muskrat, opossum, ermine, silver fox, blue fox, red fox, white fox, raccoon, otter, sable, lynx, seal and wolverine. There were muskrats, marmots and martens from Siberia, the steppes of Tartary and the Pribilov Islands. Kolinsky came from the plains of China, ocelots from India, leopard from Ceylon, flying squirrel from Japan, chinchilla from the wilds of Peru, Persian lamb from Asia Minor. My mother and I did not drape animal skins around our shoulders like Neanderthals shivering in their caves. Far from it. My father's belief was that these were primitive, dumb creatures that willingly laid down their lives for us and not only to make us beautiful. They gave up their wildness and in death we civilized them, they became extensions of our humanity when we put them on.

My father was a god to me, he was the sun. I can't remember a time when I did not know his story. How his family had sent him in the summer of 1914 from Belgrade to Montreal to buy silver fox skins in the days before anyone knew how to farm them. And how, while his ship made its way back across the icy Atlantic waters, war broke out. How, arriving in Liverpool, speaking an English confined largely to the names of fur-bearing animals, he was mistaken for a German and his cargo was seized. How, by the time the skins were released, he could get neither permission to ship them out nor a safe passage across Europe. How he made the best of a bad job, sold them, put the money in the bank and went to work for a German furrier who died in 1917, whereupon my father bought his business, prudently changing his name by deed poll to avoid misunderstandings, proudly watching it blocked in gold letters above his shop front: *Furs by Ross*. And there was the photograph of him in our thin family album, younger and more handsome than I could bear. He was standing in front of the premises, a coat with an astrakhan collar hanging almost to his ankles, insouciantly holding a silver-topped cane, pointing with it at his own name above him. By his side was an anonymous woman with braided coils of chestnut hair covering her ears.

His parents were pleased. Why not have a branch of the family firm in England? To be so well situated on the principle Atlantic port could only be advantageous, and they dreamed about becoming new Rothschilds, commanding an empire of fur stretching from the Baltic to the Americas with such distant outposts as Vancouver and St Louis. Names to me, just names, but charged with a special meaning, for I imagined them as cities inhabited not by people but by animals, who kept shops and taught in schools and drove motorcars until they trooped off happily to ships where mysteriously they lost their insides and became pelts, then skins, and finally the furs that hung from satin hangers in the glass-fronted display cabinets of my father's shop.

His marriage, in 1921, ended his parents' fantasies and in the years that followed, his country, Serbia, became swallowed up in the dissolution and rebuilding of the new Europe. He was stateless and twice in exile from those he loved.

Yet he drew people in. Even those who bought their furs in London came to him to put their garments into his new cold storage warehouse, the first in the city. Lady Derby came, the Lady Mayoress came, the Cunard managers' wives came. My father knew them all. They arrived in the spring and returned in the autumn and my father put their furs on their shoulders and sent them forth to cold journeys on the train to culminate in dinner dances at hotels which always, as I knew, finished with plates of tiny petit fours that my parents brought back for me, wrapped in my father's handkerchief, from their own excursions into the night.

A woman is not a woman without her furs, my father said. A man in evening dress slips a sable from a woman's back and they drink cocktails together. Taking off a fur is a sexual undressing. Under the fur, satin or crêpe de Chine, cut on the bias. Emeralds. Diamond clips.

My mother didn't have a story. She came to Wallasey from Holland before the war, she said. Her parents had died when she was young and an aunt had brought her up. She was dead too. The past was nothing to my mother.

When I was a small child I became friends with a Jewish boy who lived along the road and in his garden there was a swing which he promised I could play on. He led me through the back gate and pushed me down as we passed the sitting-room window. He did not want his mother to see me in their garden, for I was regarded as an unsuitable playmate.

I spent most of my childhood at home upsetting face powder or trailing around the house in high heels and a mink stole with only my father, my mother and their terrible loneliness for company.

Which my mother assuaged at every possible opportunity. We shopped hard and I was apprenticed to her good taste. While other girls' mothers read *Woman's Own* and *Good Housekeeping* and ran up their own frocks, mine was totally impractical (we were always the first to have shop products; later she would live almost exclusively on fish fingers). She made a close fortnightly study of *Vogue* but the costumes depicted in it rarely appeared outside the Home Counties, however much she inspected the list of stockists. She would wander through the Bon Marché and George Henry Lee on Church Street with her nose turned up. Even in Cripps she could never find what she had seen in magazines. She wanted to be a Kensington wife, a society beauty, ideas so absurdly far above her station that once a year she would go to one, board a train and with my father travel down to London, he to attend the April fur auctions, my mother to swan about the West End and Knightsbridge pretending she did that sort of thing every day. She never sat in a London taxi with an air of excited expectancy, but always one of languid indifference.

This expedition, in the spring of 1938, was particularly significant. My mother and father were not to know it but the auction of that year was to be one of the last great fur sales before the war. More important, I myself was to be outfitted by my mother's own hand, my new dress allowance spent.

'*From the moment she enters the room the head waiter is her slave and the flagging violin takes new heart,*' I read in *Vogue*, on the train, while the countryside flashed past unremarked. Once we had pulled out of Crewe, that was what Down South meant to me, endless fields, a blank space until one reached London. '*Exquisite in every detail, she chooses for her perfume the Yardley lavender to which fashionable women instinctively turn for daytime and formal wear. The winsome beauty of this lovable fragrance gives that air of refinement and charm which adds so much to the enjoyment of every occasion. 2/6d to Two Guineas.*'

This was all I ever read. I wanted nothing more in life than for a head waiter to be my slave and to revive the spirits of a stringed instrument.

A taxi took us from Euston Station to the Cumberland Hotel, near Marble Arch. The Cumberland was nearly new, only five years old then and the last word in that decor called *moderne*. The chambermaids were barely teenagers and all from Ireland. When we came home at night we passed them, chattering softly on leather window seats at the ends of the corridors, in their chocolate brown uniforms with cream Peter Pan collars and cuffs. There were other young people there, I saw them sometimes, lonely girls from Johannesburg and Cape Town, for the hotel was particularly popular with South Africans. But in my green Moygashel dress (a very nubbly fabric, that) I ignored them. I thought of nothing but a world of sophistication my mother and I discussed endlessly: of arrogant ateliers and chromium night-spots, town cars and turbans, jewels like embers and chimerical costumes that fracture the rainbow.

We saw little of my father during our stay. He spent his time, like the other buyers, dressed in a white coat roaming the warehouses and inspecting pelts, piled in heaps, scraped of their fat and dirt, treated with touchy chemicals and shaped on wooden blocks to resemble a parody of the animals they had once been. The smell was terrible.

And so my mother and I were left alone for nearly a week. She believed in beginning at the beginning, which commenced with a visit to a discreet little shop off the Edgware Road to purchase a foundation garment. The whole of my trunk was encased in patented elastic tricot. 'It will massage away the young lady's unwanted flesh, tone the muscles and wake up the circulation, madam,' the sales lady told my mother. 'Of course the fit is not perfect, but we can make one up to her individual vital statistics.' Which were 32–25–34, the result of too many sweets on the way home from school. 'The young lady will find it restrains without constriction.'

Despite my fawn socks and the suspenders which flapped against my bare legs, I saw in the mirror the figure of my dreams.

We took the bus to Mayfair. 'Divest your mind of the cobweb of old ideas. Turn a fresh eye on the fashion front,' my mother advised me. She was not reading from *Vogue*. I believed later that a form of personality disorder overtook her when she shopped, which made her entirely unable to distinguish reality from advertising copy. Fashion is her soul's métier, I thought. What I know now is that fashion was all there was for her. Its amnesia suited her down to the ground. She had to have the

new to obliterate the past. 'I don't remember,' she would say
later. 'I only lived for today. I really don't remember.'

What *I* recall of the wardrobe we bought that day was a
Digby Morton suit: a coral pink tweed jacket banded with lamb
in the same earth-brown shade as the skirt beneath. It was
clean-cut and young, my mother said, and it cost a fortune.
Suits were everywhere that season. There was a hat, too, like a
pixie's which someone had maliciously snipped off halfway up
the crown. To complete the outfit we bought shoes with butterfly bows tied around the ankle. They were not Patou, my
mother said, but a good imitation. We spent for ever looking at
tweeds. Whatever I liked my mother vetoed. 'Oh, Sybil, you'll
be dismayed to see how soon the fitting-room chic disappears if
the material is not good, and this' – she rubbed it between her
fingers – 'is not.' Tweed bagged in the seat. We used to laugh at
women whose bottoms did that. I pined for a black crêpe
Maggy Rouf afternoon dress, jokingly buttoned with porcelain
vegetables but my mother was horrified, not by the black crêpe,
which was universally considered wildly unsuitable for a
woman under thirty, but because a dress was not an amusement
but a matter of drop-dead seriousness.

I remember, too, a Weil lipstick – a gold case with a scarlet
coolie cap. Rejected, too flashy. I was bought instead two pairs of
Mirrasilk stockings packed in a cardboard golden casket and
finally what my mother called 'a synopsis of your boudoir' – a
crocodile vanity case, filled with jars and bottles with chromium-
plated tops. It cost an enormous amount, eight guineas, and I
kept it long after my boudoir consisted of little more than a suc-
cession of plywood closets in some Mid-Western . . .

Normally we dined together, as a family, in restaurants where
my mother could make an entrance in her furs, commanding

attention. She was truly at her happiest when she felt herself to be the best-dressed woman in the room; to be the most beautiful was not her aim. Beauty belonged to Nature, that smelly realm. Chic, élan, taste – these could be acquired only by diligent study and long pockets. Beauty was nothing: vulgar, transient, animal in its origins. An animal died, decayed; a fur, enhanced by my father's art, endured. Fashion was timeless; it laughed scornfully at the wrinkles that formed and the sagging jowls and the mottled hands and the powder that lodged in cracks – all the pitiful vestiges of *beauty*.

But one night my father had to make a pilgrimage to Folman's to eat those greasy, unpleasant foods that never emerged from our own pantry, which eschewed starch and fats. Despite the habitual presence of stars from the London Palladium who would come in after the show finished, my mother would not accompany him. She stayed in our rooms with an egg mayonnaise which she bought from Maison Lyons next door and read the *Tatler*. So he and I went together.

He was waiting for me downstairs in the bar. I had been to the hairdresser's and my helmet of hair was at last cut, cold waved and set. I was poured into a nigger-brown cocktail dress with fur-trim hem, and dabs of Joy had been applied to my pulse points. I slid down beside him into one of the tub chairs, smiling with my red lips, smiling at him through my lipstick. I think he swore when he saw me, or something at any rate seemed to have happened inside, and I believed for a moment that he would send me back upstairs to wash off my cosmetics and change back into my camelhair coat and fawn socks, but it wasn't in him to do that. He held out his hands and admired me. As we revolved into Oxford Street I contained my grief that I was not, like my mother, a blonde.

It had long been agreed that it was my future to follow him into the fur trade as his secretary and he wanted me to meet Joe Kauffman, a broker who would bid at the auctions for a number of provincial craftsmen-retailers like my father. Kauffman's cigar was rammed into the side of his mouth like Popeye the Sailorman's pipe. His hair was crimped in tight, brilliantined waves. He looked at me, in my nigger-brown dress, with a professional eye. Glossy hair, supple leathering, sleek finish. A superior pelt.

He bent low, took my hand and kissed it, winking at my father as he did so. 'Well, Sybil,' he said. 'You've come to learn how we put the clothes on your back?'

Away from our house on Queen's Drive, away from the shop with its rickety gilt chairs and atmosphere of varnished opulence, away from the dim tortured light of the synagogue, my father took on a different cast. Bred into him (and, I suppose, into me) was that skilled mercantile sense of knowing how to get yourself out of any situation and even turn it to your advantage. His courtesy, European manners and Austin Reed suits only barely concealed his what's-in-it-for-me smile. Together, he and Kauffman dealt cursorily with the subject of the refugee furriers who were flooding in from Leipzig, spent more time on the desirability of jackets or coats in an air-raid shelter in the event of war (a coat would be warmer but a jacket more practical). They went into close detail about the forthcoming Paris collections. Names of couturiers flew about and there was an argument about the ideal dimensions of the mannequin. Models were tall but my father, who was only five feet seven, preferred petite women of my own height and that of my mother, five feet four or less. Then they discussed the mechanization of leathering and whether a machine could do what a man did, stamping on skins in a vat like a grape presser. Mostly they argued about money.

Across the room a table of Tiller Girls competed for the attention of the young band leader Joe Loss. Elsewhere mink stoles enhanced huge bosoms that glittered with diamond necklaces. A fat wrist hung with ruby bracelets would come up, the fingers gripping legs of boiled chicken, fat dripping on to tight satin laps and I saw no darkness there, although it was present, of course, only one generation removed from fear and starvation. What had my father bought? What had he instructed Kauffman to bid for?

Beaver, blue, red and silver fox, Persian broadtail, leopard, mink, mole, monkey, musquash, otter, rabbit, sable, seal and squirrel.

Kauffman picked up a chicken's foot from his soup and sucked the flesh from the bones. Hunting around he found a wishbone, crooked one half in his little finger and offered the other to me. My end snapped off, leaving him the flat joint. As I wiped my hands on my napkin he told me my lipstick was smudged and that I should retouch it, winking again at my father. I looked at the wing of chicken in my own soup plate, the fatty skin disintegrating from the flesh. I started to think about those strange cities inhabited by animals and I wondered again what happened to the beasts inside the pelts when the skins had been loaded into ships. And what about me? How had I been dressed and processed? What had been discarded beneath the skin?

Chapter Three

If I was being fashioned as a beautiful object to be looked at, then by whom and for what purpose? In that place without history, where my mother lived, it was entirely feasible that I could have made a noteworthy marriage and devoted my life, with her, to shopping and dinner dances. I had no implicit objection. But whom exactly was I to marry? No thought had been given to that. My parents' social life was active, but limited to formal dinner dances with business acquaintances. Once in a while my father would play a round or two at the Jewish golf links and he was a member of various organizations which he thought would enhance his business interests, such as the fur trade association and the Jewish Freemasons' Lodge. But people rarely came to the house. My own friends from school tended to be those who felt themselves outsiders in some way:

the daughters of consular officers temporarily posted in the city formed a large part of my circle. They did not gain me admission to a large and stable social set of brothers or cousins. On the rare occasions that I went into the houses of the English middle classes, I was overwhelmed by the smell of dogs.

Knowing that I would be unacceptable as a future wife to the sons of any of the men he prayed with on Saturday mornings, my father avoided the subject of my future. I don't know what he thought. Perhaps, like me, he was waiting for some imaginary Prince Charming to come and claim me. He was the kind of man who dreamed that his daughter might marry the Prince of Wales (now accounted for). I was still very young but there had never been anything particularly childish about my childhood. To the extent that I imagined adult life, I thought vaguely that I would be in London, a faceless man lighting my cigarette between rhumbas at the Ritz. I decorated the sets of my fantasies and planned, in fine detail, my many costume changes, but the older I grew the more I became aware of the city about me and it penetrated and dispelled my lovely visions.

I understood that everything came from the sea: my mother and father had come from the sea. The Mersey estuary was bottle shaped, the river forced through a narrow neck and so it could never silt up as the Dee had done, destroying our prosperity. We lived by the tides and the weather. At night I lay in bed and heard the sounds of the ships' horns on the river in the fog. We went to see someone off once, the daughter of the Cuban trade attaché returning home. It was late, close to midnight when they sailed, with all the lights on the liner blazing, turning the river into a piece of gold jewellery, and the tugs running all around the great ship and the orchestra playing and the passengers dancing as the engines drove them out past Ireland into the cold Atlantic.

Liverpool shipped cotton, Manchester spun it. Manchester needed factories, their foundations dug into the earth, and a stable workforce. Liverpool had a huge shifting population of casual labour, dependent on the port, sailors, dockers, prostitutes. They were savages, or so we believed. I was more susceptible to their glamour than one might think.

I first saw Stan one Sunday afternoon outside the Palm House at Sefton Park where statues of Columbus and other famous navigators gazed out towards the Atlantic. I loved the heat in there, seeing people blinded as they entered, their glasses temporarily steamed up. And now I noticed a dark boy of about twenty, with what I immediately recognized as a touch of the tar-brush, as we used to say in those days. He was arranging passers-by into groups and taking their photographs. It wasn't enough for him that they linked arms and smiled into the sunshine, they had to submit to all his poses. I watched him for a while as he took down their names and addresses in a little notebook and ran around looking for change from a ten-bob note.

It was late summer, 1938, and I wore a lilac shantung jacket over a mauve box-pleated skirt. My hair had grown, was parted to the side and fell across one eye before brushing my shoulders, a style that was, as usual, years too old for someone of my age. He saw me through his viewfinder and pointed the camera towards me.

'Have you got any film in there?' I asked him knowingly.

''Course not,' he said.

I laughed at that, not thinking of the poor people who

watched every morning for the post, sweethearts hoping for a picture of their loved one to remind them, when *he* was at sea, that once it had been summer and he had held his arm around them.

I liked the way he looked and I was prepared, for the moment, to ignore his common voice. Boys of my own age, even older, on the rare occasions when I met them, were intimidated by me, by my clothes and my cut-glass Kensington accent, expensively installed by elocution lessons which appeared on the end-of-term bill as an extra. Stan was not frightened. He was bold. He took my arm and led me into the Palm House and I walked along beside him, willingly. He was not even a real photographer but commoner than I had suspected, a ship's baker in the merchant service, a trade he had inherited from his father and grandfather before him. The old man, I was to discover, was a lascar seaman all the way from India, which accounted for Stan's dark good looks. He had just got back from a run to Famagusta and he entranced me with his stories of all the lands he had seen during his six years at sea, especially of Cochinchina where mandarins paid for flights of herons to be released against a crepuscular sky, watched by an admiring audience of guests.

As for me, I told him that my father was Ross of Bold Street, that I longed to go abroad but that Daddy had no passport and so we spent our holidays in Bournemouth, toiling up and down the zigzag path to the beach or riding briefly on the small funicular railway that ran up and down the cliffs. My mother had grand plans to go on a cruise one day, perhaps to Madeira.

'I'd advise against that,' Stan said. 'Those stewards are a randy lot.'

I did not know what randy meant. 'Stop being satirical,' I

responded, with a calculated degree of archness, knowing, from school, that this was always a sophisticated gambit.

He stared at me. 'What did you eat for breakfast, a dictionary?'

I really did not know what I was doing, looking at tropical trees with this common boy who, had I had a cigarette in my handbag, would surely have failed to light it but would have reached into the packet and taken one for himself, without asking. In my mind's eye I could *see* him in evening dress, his dark skin against the white of a starched shirtfront, but standing in front of me in his American-cut suit, his camera swinging, his hat twirling on the end of his finger, he was a picture of insubordination. It was all wrong.

'How old are you?' he asked.

'Eighteen,' I replied.

His older sister, a woman on the verge of middle age, sold ices from a Corporation wooden hut in another part of the park and we strolled over there to buy a pair of icecream sandwiches. As I was unwrapping my vanilla brick to insert between two wafers, Stan spotted a courting couple, the man in tropical whites, just off his ship. He left me for a long time with cold fingers as he took their portrait.

His sister called me over while he elaborately transcribed the name of the vessel and its master into his book, promising that the snaps would be delivered straight to the docks.

'I saw you with our kid,' she said. 'I hope you don't mind me saying this but you shouldn't pay him any attention. He only wants to park his shoes under your bed.'

It was strange to feel his tongue in my mouth and see my lipstick smeared around his chin. His skin smelt of his sister's

Camay soap, his breath of beer, that slightly sulphurous, egg-sandwich smell. I felt his erection press into my hip, very solid like the Dunhill lighter my father kept in his trouser pocket.

He was a tearaway. 'Whatever it is, I'm against it,' he always said. 'Liverpool is narky and I'm the chief nark. It's the bog Irish, on my mam's side.' I suppose he was kissing me, the boss's daughter, because he thought nothing was too good for him. He saw me as a figure not unlike a fender ornament on an expensive motorcar. 'I'll have that,' he thought.

We spent most of the month of June going round Liverpool on the tramp as he showed me off. We set out from the Pierhead to Otterspool along the cast iron shore. Wind blew from the docks, freighted with the stench of oil from the engine rooms of ships, of rotted cargoes from the warehouses. At night I heard seagulls crying in my dreams. We kissed, pressed in shop doorways, or him lying on top of me in the long grass at the park, his hand progressing towards my stocking top, yet he demanded that I be perfectly groomed at all times. His eye was sharp. He saw a scuff on the heel of a shoe, the almost invisible origins of a ladder, lipstick reddening a tooth. I felt as if I was a baton that had been handed from my mother to him, though I kept his very existence a secret, of course. I would have been ashamed to tell my parents where I had been – dancing at the Grafton Ballroom, for example, where the quality of my underwear created a sensation in the ladies'. I was AWOL. I suppose I could have been anybody's, but it had taken Stan's audacity and acquisitiveness to capture me. Sometimes I would look at him through my mother's eyes and I turned away. 'What's up?' he'd say. 'What's come over you all of a sudden? You're not going all moody on me, are you?' We nearly bumped into her in Bold Street once, clicking out of Cripps with a Cresta box under her arm. I pulled Stan into another shop where we waited until she'd passed. She didn't see us but Stan saw her and was impressed. 'When are you bringing me home for tea?' he demanded. He didn't mean cakes and sandwiches, he meant meat and potatoes and gravy and pudding. Obviously it was out of the question.

Yet I liked him because he did not make me feel neither one thing nor the other. It was of no interest to him at all that I was partly Jewish, a religion which he considered to be an irrelevance. As a Toxteth Catholic, a beleaguered minority around the Dingle, he had been brought up to go out on Saturdays nights in search of Proddy dogs, to give them a thrashing, and he told me about the time his sister went down to watch the Protestants march on Orange Lodge Day and lifted her skirt to reveal green knickers. His grandfather had never converted from his Muslim faith and so Stan was more willing than most to overlook the fact that, as I had often been taunted, my people had 'murdered Our Lord'.

Three or four weeks after we met, waiting at the Pierhead for a tram, he made an announcement. 'I've got a start. On the Bibby Line, Liverpool to Rangoon, stopping at Marseilles, then Port Said, Port Sudan and Colombo. It should be a good run.'

I knew that the funnel of the Bibby Line was pink and black, the flag depicting a gold hand holding a dagger against a red ground. I thought Mr Bibby himself had plunged it into my chest. I couldn't breathe.

'When do you go?'

'Friday. But there's something I want you to see first. It means stopping out all night, though. Can you try?'

'Certainly not. What do you want to show me?'

'Chinatown.'

'Why at night?'

'It has to be at night.'

I met him at eight on Wednesday on the steps of the Adelphi Hotel, a flight of stone stairs I had walked up with my parents to a function of the fur trade association, dressed in a chic little cocktail dress and on my arm my first lightly beaded evening bag. It was warm and on this occasion I wore a floral frock and olive-green cardigan over my shoulders. Stan appeared after a minute or two in a cream linen suit and a panama hat pushed to the back of his head, like a Cunard Yank, the men who took pictures of American styles to Liverpool tailors to be copied and made up. He reminded me of the Liver Building. Both of them had bags of swagger.

He took my gloved hand. We walked up Renshaw Street to St Luke's Church and, turning into Berry Street, plunged into the Chinatown night. I had been here before but only to the Far East restaurant where the waiters were conscientiously Oriental, giving their patrons souvenir packets of chopsticks and Chinese dolls. It was no stranger in his company.

'We'll stop in for a bevvy at the Nook,' he said. He bought himself a pint of Guinness and me an orange squash. We sat by the empty fireplace and drank in silence. He was moody.

'Tell me a joke, Stan.'

'I don't know any.'

'You know loads.'

'I've forgotten them.'

I watched the Chinese lanterns slowly turn in a perpetual procession of animal silhouettes and thought that this was turning into a washout. I had no idea why I was here.

'Is this it?' I asked, indignantly. 'Is this what you wanted me to see?'

'What were you expecting? Opium pipes and white slave traders?'

I had not known what to expect, only that if Stan was showing it to me it would at least be interesting.

'Why do we have to stay out all night? It was very difficult making the arrangements. I had to tell a lot of fibs.'

He didn't reply.

'*Why? Why?* Answer me.'

'Because. Because I want something.'

'What?'

'I want you to do it with me before I go.'

The world reduced to a button on the corner of his jacket sleeve. Now I was silent.

'Come on, Syb, speak up.'

'I don't know.'

'I won't hurt you, you'll like it, promise.'

'I can't.'

'Oh, yeah, give us a reason?'

'There are thousands of reasons but something might happen, that's one.'

'That's the general idea but I know what you're driving at. It'll be OK; I'll use something.'

'What do you mean?'

'I've got something in my wallet.'

'Oh.' I tried to picture the interior of his wallet. I saw banknotes, a picture of his mother and gran, a spare shirt button, his discharge book. Nothing else that had any bearing on the enterprise he was proposing.

'Go on,' he urged. 'What do you say? Don't you really want to be my woman?'

He'd spilt a puddle of beer on the table and I turned my

finger in it. The glove's tip stained. I drew patterns of beer on the wood. I didn't say anything, he didn't say anything. Nothing was as I had imagined, no man in evening dress, no cigarette lighter, no gown. We sat in silence for ten or fifteen minutes. I couldn't bear, when I looked up, his cold face. If I didn't go with him the evening would be finished there and then. I knew very little about sex. There were things nice girls did not do, but how nice was I? I wasn't sure. In an adolescent way I 'desired' him, not thinking about what desire meant. I just wanted us to go all the way, to see where it would get us.

'All right, if you want,' I said ungraciously, hoping that he would change his mind, declare it to be a joke or a mistake.

'Good girl,' he said. 'Drink up, we've got something else to fetch.'

We walked towards Upper Parliament Street. Until now I had only seen it from the top of a bus; I had never walked its pavements. The Georgian gentlemen's houses were all going to ruin, the stucco flaked, and the hallways smelled of piss. Coloured men and women sat on the steps smoking, listening to music from gramophones in upstairs windows, a music I did not recognize.

Up an entry near Faulkner Square Stan knocked on a back door. An Indian in a red turban came out into the yard. He looked at me.

'Nice girl.'

'Yeah,' Stan said. 'Are you carrying?'

'How many do you need?'

'Just a couple.' He gave the Indian half a crown and received back two thick cigarettes. 'We're set, Sybil. Do you want to hear some music first?' I felt like I had stepped into the sea from a pebble beach that shelved precipitously. I'd abandoned any idea of keeping my head above water.

The pubs were turning out. Men full of beer were roaring on the pavements, the amateur whores circling them, calling out their prices. We stepped through a green door into a club. The bouncer had pale skin, light-brown frizzy hair and a flat nose, that neither-one-thing-nor-the-other look. Liverpool was full of them, the descendants of escaped slaves and African and American seamen. We didn't know anything about immigrants in those days.

The room smelled of damp, of rotted vegetables, sweat and bad perfume, *not* French. A few pieces of fried chicken lay on the bar on a cracked blue plate under a glass dome. A huge gramophone was playing Erskine Hawkins, Duke Ellington and Cootie Williams, what Stan called race records, brought over by American sailors on the transatlantic runs and commanding big prices along the dock road. White women were dancing with coloured men on the tiny dance floor. The men slung the women over their shoulders or between their legs, like savages in the jungle, I thought. The women were flushed, their eyes hectic, swinging from limb to limb.

We sat at a table covered with red oil-cloth and Stan ordered us both rums. I took a sip of mine but it tasted like poison. The music thumped and crashed. A coloured man came over and shouted at Stan, 'Is your missis dancing?'

'You'll have to ask her yourself.'

The man pulled at my hand. I recoiled. 'Tell him to go away, Stan.'

Stan did nothing. 'He just wants to dance with you.'

'I don't want to.'

'You're not prejudiced, are you, Syb?'

'Come on, love, take a turn with me.' The man led me on to the floor and pulled my waist into his. I could feel his breath on my cheek. He smelled strange. I could not do the steps of the dance. Stan sat at the table drinking his rum and watching. My partner let go of my hand and squeezed my breast. Stan got up.

'OK, pack it in, we're off.' He stood at the door with my handbag. 'It's time, Sybil, it's time.'

He had a room, a house, in fact, off Smithdown Road near the hospital, which he had borrowed from a friend who had taken his wife to New Brighton for the weekend. The light was on in the hall. There were signed photographs of Dixie Dean and other Everton heroes to guide us up the stairs and into the bedroom. Inside was a double bed with a walnut headboard. The mattress was covered with a pink counterpane, an eider-down folded at the bottom. The dressing table was bare except for a cheap, cut-glass perfume bottle with a rubber bulb to spray the scent and a coconut carved to resemble a shrunken head. All the sailors had them. You could get one in all the pawn-shops. Stan took his shoes off and lay on top of the counterpane. He lit one of his cigarettes. I lay down beside him. We did not touch. He passed the cigarette to me; I knew how to smoke, my mother had taught me. 'You have to inhale real deep,' he said.

'Why?'

'It's a Mary Warner.'

'A what?'

'A reefer, hasheesh. It gets you high.'

'Nothing has happened,' I said after a while, slowly.

'Syb, you've been staring at the same bit of wallpaper for the past five minutes. Come here.'

He reached round and unfastened the zip in the side of my

dress. It bunched up around my hips. He pulled my slip above my head. I was naked apart from my brassiére and my patented elastic tricot foundation garment.

'Jesus, what the fuck's that?'

'It's my foundation garment; it was very expensive.'

'You mean it's a corset, like my mam wears?'

'No. It's nothing like that.'

'Well, whatever it is, let's have it off.' Naked, my skin was lined with red ridges from the seams. Stan stood up and got undressed, folding his suit carefully and hanging it up in the wardrobe, putting his shirt over the back of a chair and lining his shoes up under the bed. There were a few black hairs on his dark chest and a single darker mole under his right nipple. Curiously the nipples were indented. Round his neck he wore a silver crucifix, slightly bent in one arm. He stood there, his penis slowly rising. I had never seen one before. As it grew, I saw two pendulous, wrinkled sacs of skin emerge from behind.

'What are they, Stan?' I asked nervously. I believed they must be a terrible deformity, unique to him.

'What are what?'

'Those things, behind your . . . thing.'

'My balls, you mean? Haven't you ever seen any before?'

'No.'

'Hasn't your dad got any?' I did not know. I had never seen my father naked.

Stan's fingers tried to prise apart my locked thighs. I was more rigid than he was.

'Come on, Syb,' he whispered, 'let me in.' I was wondering when he was going to get his wallet. At what stage of the proceedings would it be necessary?

'What about your wallet?' I asked him.

'Oh, yeah, well, I don't actually have anything. But I'll get out at Edge Hill, I promise.' Edge Hill was the last-but-one station before the Lime Street terminus. I didn't understand. I began to cry and my mascara ran. Tears made rivulets through my rouge and fell off my chin. Stan lay back against the pillows and waited for me to finish. 'Go and wash your face,' he said. 'You look a sight.'

I stood in the bathroom as it turned and turned about me. I washed off my lipstick and my eye-shadow and lay on the floor for a long time, my cheek pressed against the coolness of the bath. After a while I felt him touch me on the shoulder. 'Are you all right?' he asked, not without tenderness, and hope flared. I looked up at him, stretching my hands out to his bare legs.

He started. 'Jesus fucking Christ, Sybil. How old did you say you were?'

We lay on the bed until it was light, smoked another hasheesh cigarette and began to scream with laughter. I said he smelled of Camay and why did he use a girl's soap? He said it smelled better than the carbolic the other sailors used. He didn't mind being a sissy. We got hungry and went into the back kitchen and he showed me how to fry eggs; he told me about some French rolls he could make called croissants.

We took a last walk along the cast iron shore. I knew he would sail away but he said he would come back for me when I was older. I wished the Mersey was like the Dee and he could not navigate the sand and the silt.

Then he went and that was that. The world closed down again. I shopped and went to the pictures. I left school and learned how to be a secretary. I mastered the arts of shorthand-typing and simple bookkeeping. I crossed my secretary's legs and manicured my secretary's nails. I grew another half-inch, then stopped. Stan was set in my heart, only a faint red glow visible above the horizon. He came and went, buying me a gift from each run – carved sticks, a hand of lace, a silver-plated locket, inlaid boxes that played tunes, once, absurdly, a fan made of parrot feathers. Once, a very small uncut opal. As for sex, he did not press me. 'We'll have you when you're good and ready,' he said. 'I can always sort myself out.' And so it could have gone on indefinitely but the war years intervened.

Chapter Four

After the Blitz started, my mother went out less and less. My father called in the doctor who diagnosed neurasthenia and told her she was not the only one of his patients who thought the bombs were specifically aimed at her. But my mother said she was not afraid, that she did not think there was one with her name on it.

Every night our neighbours would go to the communal air-raid shelters, but my mother affected to be horrified by the idea. For once, she raised her voice. 'Sydney!' she cried. 'Think of your daughter. Who knows who she will have to mix with down there? Children with . . . yes, I *will* say it, that ugly word, *lice*.' Nothing would do but an Anderson shelter. My father's hands were unused to labour with a trowel or a carpenter's saw and he got a man in to install it. My mother's spirits leapt. She stocked it with magazines, chocolates, tins of smoked oysters, and would clamber in, in the afternoons, to view it with an eye to interior decoration.

My father sized up the situation. He could see that my mother would have happily sat out the war at the bottom of the garden. He didn't believe in the shelter himself. He had watched it being built and he could not accept that it would protect us, so he had it bricked up and every night we caught the tram to St George's Hall to camp out in the cellars with a picnic basket and a silver hip flask of brandy. It was a ludicrous decision. The city centre and its enormous neo-classical assembly rooms were far more likely targets for the Luftwaffe than the suburbs, but my father quickly got into the spirit of our nightly life underground. He joined in the sing-songs, the quizzes and the games and out of his own pocket he paid a crooner from the Adelphi to sing a medley of carefully selected songs from the current hit parade while my mother and I, huddled together in our furs (myself all too conspicuous in my chinchilla), looked glumly on.

Conscious of his foreignness, and that he was too old to join the Pioneers, he enlisted in the Home Guard and took his turn defending the docks. He joined up with other furriers and flung himself into efforts to convince the government that fur was an essential commodity and should be given space on the convoys that navigated the submarine-infested Atlantic. But he went further than the rest in the shelter, humming 'I'm sitting on top of the world', he designed a fur waistcoat for our boys to wear to protect them against the bitter winds of the Canadian waters. I pictured Stan in one of these disastrous creations, looking bulky about the middle.

The more absurd, touching ways of doing his bit for the war effort that my father invented, the more my mother seemed to try to make herself invisible. Eventually, he brought in a specialist from Rodney Street, the Harley Street of the North, complaining, as he later wrote out the cheque for the fee, that this was what he should have done all along. The doctor concluded that my mother was suffering from diabetes. I had been called up for war work and spent a few interesting weeks in the wages office of a munitions factory, where I learned all about sex during the tea breaks from the sort of forward girls who had once admired my hand-embroidered camiknickers at the Grafton. (I had no doubt, now, what I would do when the next opportunity presented itself.) But after my mother's medical bombshell I was given leave to stay at home and administer her injections.

She would sit in front of her kidney-shaped dressing table, brushing her ash-blonde hair. She tried on all her costumes in turn. My father sat, hands in his lap, on the edge of the canary-yellow chaise-longue, watching her, shuffling her as if she were a pack of cards. 'The Jaeger suit now. Yes. Now the Molyneux evening gown.' He hung her jewels about her neck and, glittering, they descended the stairs together to waltz to the accompaniment of dance bands on the new radiogram, lost in each other's eyes. I occupied the uglier side of her life, stabbing her with needles on a timed basis.

Our lives disintegrated around us. I got used to seeing spaces in the streets, a short-cut to the shops. Then there were the human spaces, the pain of which you did not think about if you could. We followed the news about Yugoslavia in the *Daily Express*. The country had been partitioned by the Axis, and

Serbia and Croatia were now puppet states. There were no further letters from my father's family.

The whole of Liverpool was beginning to feed and clothe itself on the black market. Entire cargoes melted from their holds and disappeared down the dock road and there was a rumour that a Spitfire, in parts, had been offered for sale in a pub.

We feared the landmines the most, which drifted silently in from the river on green silk parachutes and produced craters that were eighty feet across. In November the public air-raid shelter in the basement of the school at Durning Road was destroyed and a hundred and sixty-six people were killed. The next day there were no buses. I walked along Smithdown Road as if it were an avenue of glass. At Wavertree, near the Mystery, I passed some dead cows lying on the pavement. In town a gang of civil defence men sat drinking bottles of beer on a three-piece suite that had been blasted out of a bombed furniture shop.

There had been nothing on the wireless that morning about the raid. There never was. You had to tune in to Athlone to find out what was going on. Everyone knew that details of the Liverpool Blitz were being suppressed by the censor because of the port's strategic importance, while the bombing of London was reported in what we sullenly began to feel was almost orgiastic detail. In a way we were jealous of the reputation the Cockneys were gaining for being able to 'take it'. What about us? We could take it too.

I sat down on the sofa to pick glass out of my bleeding ankles. There was a little rumour mill busily grinding out facts. 'What are you up to?' I asked.

'Guarding the stock against looters,' said a man eating a cheese roll.

'I saw some dead cows near the Mystery.'

'Was it near that Welsh dairy in Wavertree?'

'Could be.'

A little girl stopped. 'I heard that thousands are dead, *thousands*,' she contributed, like a miniature gossip over the fence post.

'Listen to the gob on her,' one of the civil defence men said. 'Right little defeatist we've got here.'

'Yeah, and there's trains that leave every day packed with bodies. It's true, it is, cross my heart and hope to die.'

A woman stepped up to claim her. 'Out of the mouths,' she said. 'They cremate them in secret.'

We all knew there was supposed to have been a peace march with white flags along Scotland Road. It might have been the communists or a German fifth column, according to where you heard it. You used to wonder what form the Germans' disguises would take.

The war had made Stan narkier than ever. He spent most of his time at sea, a cook on the convoy vessels that brought food and raw materials over from New York and Montreal. He could no longer come and go when he pleased; someone told him which ship to take and when. The tropics were off-limits and the fact that he was engaged in one of the most dangerous branches of the war-time services failed to spice up what he regarded as a monotonous routine.

The last time I saw him in Liverpool was during the May Blitz. We met at the Philharmonic Hotel near the university and art school, a pub where he sometimes sold on drugs to the handful of bohemian students who grew their hair over their collars, wore green shirts and listened to jazz with a sense of heightened duty. We sat under the stained-glass windows of Baden-Powell and other Victorian heroes, the air full of the thin, stale smell of bitter ale and ham sandwiches and Stan's American cigarettes. He looked much paler than when I had met him first, straight from the Mediterranean. There was a little gold ring in his left ear, impaled through a freckle.

By now I had forgotten that I had been brought up in the luxury trade and that I was a luxury item myself. I was seventeen and war had made me old in the head, a hard-faced bitch. Under-age but looking twenty, I sipped my gin and tonic. I was bold. Remembering my lessons, I took off my glove and slid my hand under his jacket. I pulled his shirt up and ran my fingers along his warm, bare back which wore not a vest but an American garment called a T-shirt.

'I'm ready for you-know-what,' I said. 'But you'll have to use something. When did you last go to the barber's?' I giggled. My hand glided round to his chest and pointed downwards. He pulled it away.

'We'll have to give it a miss this time, babe,' he said. 'I've got a dose.' I only just knew what he meant. 'That shut you up.' He smiled to himself. 'But anyway, that's the way it goes.' Far away we heard the thud of a landmine falling, maybe in Birkenhead.

We were used to the fright, as you got used to toothache. We stayed drinking in the Phil in the dark not from bravado but because we constantly juggled the odds. Everyone carried maps of the city in their heads: they hit *there* last night, stands to reason they won't come back that way tonight.

Later, around nine, we went to the pictures to see some cartoons and a newsreel of plucky Cockney sparrers strutting around in the debris of the East End. 'Nothing about us, of course,' Stan said loudly, in disgust. There was a smattering of applause in the surrounding rows.

When the Donald Duck came round again we got up to go. 'There's a wedding on in Everton Brow. Fancy looking in?' he said. It was nearly ten and there had now been a two-hour lull in the bombing.

We were most of the way up London Road when the siren started. 'Let's keep going,' Stan said. 'Take a chance. Fuck 'em.' It was all right at first, as if it had been a false alarm. The streets were deserted and Stan and I, holding hands, were alone in the dark world. I could hardly see him, just feel the pressure of his fingers and the sweat of his palms. As we got to Harker Street he stopped me in the middle of the road and kissed me, pushing his hand up my slip to the tops of my stockings.

'Aren't we the wild ones?' he muttered into my shoulder as he kissed it. 'Why don't we do it in the road?'

'But you said . . .'

He pulled back. 'You'd do it, too, wouldn't you? There's nothing to stop you, is there? You wouldn't give twopence what anyone thinks. We're the same, you and me, however it looks on the surface.'

To be like Stan, not an outsider but an individualist. 'You mean I'm an anarchist of life?'

'Where did you pick that one up?'

'From you, I think.'

'Anarchists of life. OK. Just don't let on to the ARP warden.'

Now I could see his face from above. The sky was a bowl of glowing red. Bombers cruised across it like dark fish. We began to run but my knees were buckling. Before it happened there was an enormous tension, a great unbearable calm that lasted for a second or two, then a huge force that knocked us back against a fishmonger's van abandoned in the middle of the street. I found that I was on my hands and knees. I could smell motor oil on my dress. I felt Stan's hand pulling me to my feet, then he let go. It was pitch black and I suddenly had the sensation that he had run away and left me alone in the darkness, so I had to say something, a nonchalant phrase to let him know that I didn't care whether he was there or not.

'Are you with the angels, Stan?'

'Yeah,' his voice came back, from a foot or two away. 'Only someone's stolen my harp.'

I took a step forward in the direction of the joke that had just died in the air and bobbed up and down like a puppet. A heel had come off my left shoe when I'd fallen under the van. I got down on my hands and knees again to look for my handbag, my arms sweeping the ground, but they only stumbled against cobbles.

'Let's push on,' I heard him say. I took both shoes off and held them in my hand, walking barefoot on the pavement in my stockings. In this fashion we reached Everton Brow, about fifty yards away. A social club seemed to have been hit, though not badly; it had been damaged, not destroyed. 'That was the wedding,' Stan said. 'They've copped it. The groom's going to have a job tonight, giving his missis a surprise.' We stood together, giggling and shaking. He began to kiss me again for the sheer relief of it all, I suppose. We were alive not dead, ha ha. Two bridesmaids staggered out. Their skin was a strange colour, a sort of beige like a mac. One was sweating all over her face, holding on to her head. They walked past us, disappearing into the world.

We had to go in, you couldn't stop yourself. You had to see.

It was totally calm, completely silent, a dream time of partial light as if we were underwater. The bar had blown out towards the door. Lying under the rubble was the bridegroom with a green face, stiff and straight like a plank. I was sure he was going to die but he didn't, he was just suffering from blast. He looked totally relaxed lying there, except for his head, which was moving from side to side.

The bride in her parachute silk wedding dress was covered with blood. She was dead.

I felt this was the world now, peace and terror at the same time and my mouth full of the taste of soot. It was awfully difficult to move. As Stan steered me out I seemed to be growing iron legs that sank themselves into cement holes in the floor. I took root in the street outside. We couldn't have been indoors for more than twenty or thirty seconds.

I stood there planted, seeing my father lead a small impromptu band of musicians through their most up-to-the-minute repertoire, smelling the familiar fragrance of my mother's scent in the sooty air. I heard their softly foreign voices telling me that I was special and beautiful and nothing bad would ever happen to me. I needed no one but them, their company would last me the rest of my life. I couldn't wait to get away from the spiv, the hooligan who had brought me here.

'I'll take you to St George's Hall,' Stan's voice said. I hated the sound of it. I wouldn't take his hand. We walked along the streets without speaking, passing a baby's blanket smouldering in a privet hedge. Bedlam was breaking over the city. The gutters were flooded with ruptured water mains, and fires were raging from one end of the docks to the other. The air smelled sweet and charred because Rowntree's chocolate factory, on

Picton Road, was burning down. We came to the great façade of St George's Hall. It was not calm in there but full of noise, the scream of near-misses, the whistle of the stick bombs, the continuous thumping of the guns, the ringing of fire engines and ambulance bells and the insufferable sound of hundreds of people screaming.

Towards the edge of the great crowd my parents were sitting, stiffly and a little apart. My father looked debonair, he was smiling. My mother was wearing an old squirrel cape, her fingers tightly clenched around a magazine. My father reached out to put an arm about her but she cringed. There was another massive explosion.

'Mein Gott, warum habe . . .' she cried. Which was odd, because she always told me she couldn't remember any Dutch. Or was it German?

When the all-clear finally sounded, close to four o'clock in the morning, we walked in silence home to Queen's Drive. Bombs had fallen in the suburbs but the house we lived in was untouched. My mother was very white. She went straight to bed. I looked at the carpets from Waring and Gillow, at our eau-de-Nil walls, at the row of bells to summon our now non-existent servants. I looked at a copy of Vogue. I looked at myself in the mirror. So, as it turned out, I had Nazi uncles and Nazi aunts, Nazi cousins. The enemy was in me, Nazi blood pumping my empty heart.

She had come with her mother and brother from Hamburg before the Great War. Like my father, they had changed their name. What was history for her? Name-calling in the street, the traction of nationalism that pulls us through wars. She didn't need it. Her mother and brother had returned to

Germany in 1919. She had never got on with them anyway. She set herself up to be English. She couldn't see any point in being anything else. But she had never achieved better than a good pastiche of English society. If you had hung her on the wall you would have seen a collage of magazine cuttings. She never fooled a real Englishman in those xenophobic days and she had to settle for another foreigner, someone as deracinated as herself. She couldn't account for falling in love, for finding that together they could live an exquisite imitation of life. Now she thought Germany was going to win. We all did. Then, something crude inserted itself between her and my father. Shackled to him, what was her future? Deportation? Worse? Or would she have denounced him to the occupying authorities? And what about me? What would she have said about me, her daughter, not a real Jew in even my father's eyes, but real enough by some other system of classification? Germany lost in the end. I would never find out what she would have done and the shadow of that unmade choice would hang over her for the rest of her life.

Hours later, my father made a soft-boiled egg and took it up to her on a tray. I passed the dressing-room door. She was in an ecru ballgown from before the war. She was wearing all her jewels, every necklace, every bracelet. Diamond clips weighed down her hair. 'Now the Schiaparelli,' my father said. My mother changed, obediently.

I had no chance to discuss any of this with Stan, for I did not see him until after the war was over. His letters were short, full of jokes and information, much of it obliterated by the censor unless he used the coded language of the Liverpool docks which I struggled to understand. His last letter came from New York in 1944. He had already been torpedoed twice.

Hotel Algonquin
20 July

Dear Syb

Well I've been hit again. We didn't do so well as last time when the Germans picked us up and took us on board and gave us a case of ciggies. When your ship goes down your whole world goes down with it. You haven't got a deck under your feet any more.

It wasn't a load of fun but at least when they found me they dropped me off here instead of that dump Montreal where you can't understand what the Froggies are going on about half the time. I had to report to the New York Pool but they say there's nothing for me yet. Right now, I'm working – don't laugh. There's only gimpies left, you can get any kind of job and even the bastards at the Pool think you're contributing to the war effort. I'm on nights at this hotel, baking. They've locked up the posh writing paper so I can't prove it. Pity, you could show it to your Mam.

Syb, you should see New York, it's hectic. A film star took me out for cocktails. I won't tell you who, but I know what the dirty bastard wanted. Maybe he'll get it if his luck's in.

Anyway, the War won't last forever. You'd better come here. You won't see me in England no more. When they tell me they've found me a ship, I'm backing out. Don't tell anyone.

All the best
Stan(ley Maguire)

The war did end eventually. We went down to St George's Plateau where there were bands and thousands of people dancing. We did the dance which we knew now as the lindyhop, which I'd seen in the coloured club so long ago. There was boating on the lake in Sefton Park until midnight. I rode on the Illuminated Tram. As he had hinted, Stan deserted in New York. Two or three months into the peace my father received a letter from his nephew Jasa in Belgrade, who had fought with Tito's Partizans and had never been captured. Before the war he had travelled extensively in the Soviet Union on family business. His contacts in Leningrad were excellent. But now he was a journalist on the Party newspaper, travelling back and forth between Yugoslavia and Moscow. He signed his name with a red hammer and sickle stamped next to it.

Jasa wrote to say he was sorry to have to tell my father that his family were dead. He, Jasa, was the only survivor as far as he knew. He supposed they had been rounded up by the Cetniks and sent to camps in Germany or Poland. No one who had left had returned, so it was impossible to say what might have happened to them and worse to try and guess. But they were all gone, except for himself and a small branch of his mother's family in Sarajevo. And, Jasa reminded us, six hundred thousand Serbs were dead too, murdered by the same hands.

Everyone my father knew was receiving letters like this one and my father took the news no better or no worse than the next, but something had changed and he was not the same man. He lost his easy suavity and his trader's smile, that what's-in-it-for-me look fixed and hardened on his face. He despised the post-war Labour government, hated its puritanism, the extended rationing, the dreary subdued greens, browns and greys of the clothes, loathed the Utility Fur they forced him to make. He withdrew into that distrust and self-righteousness that so characterized Jews of his generation and my own, who were survivors but not intact.

Home was different. He no longer spent his evenings among the antirrhinums but held secret meetings raising money to arm the Zionist terrorists in Palestine, a country which before the war had existed for him only in distant mythology, the imaginary land of every religious Jew. He must have struck some deal with my mother for now she underwent conversion to Judaism and wore a rather vulgar diamond-crusted Star of David around her neck, and wheeled in coffee and cakes on a hostess trolley to him and his friends.

If you re-invent yourself perpetually, you are unburdened by morality. I have said my mother lacked an inner life, but now I wonder if my father only had his because he inherited it, as a lord is left his family's estate. You could not blame my mother for being impoverished, down there.

When I asked my father if I could emigrate to America there was no objection. I half expected him to urge me to wait. Everyone was talking about going home, home to the Promised Land that would be ours again in just a matter of time, two, three years at the most. The pictures in my Junior Bible would come to life. Young hands would be needed to build our new country. But he never mentioned it.

I sailed off in a green jumper dress with red rib stockings and gloves. My head was swathed in jersey. I sat on deck with my hands buried in a fur muff, holding my vanity case with its precious cargo of lotions and creams. In my mind I waved a handkerchief at the places where Stan and I had strolled. I waved at what was left of the cast iron shore. From the ship, Europe was a dark continent, lined with the skeletons of burnt-out warehouses. They looked like broken teeth.

Chapter Five

On the ship going over, the ship on which I finally, at twenty-one, lost my virginity (to a steward from Normandy who secretly brought me saucers of champagne with fragments of sugar cube at the bottom), I leafed through a magazine and saw a picture of a mannequin picking her way through the rubble of Paris in a pencil-slim suit and no hat, and I thought that it was, after all, just possible to be entirely reborn.

January 1946. Cold. Sleet in New York harbour and only making out the shape of the city at the last moment as we steamed up the Hudson and docked at the end of our ocean crossing in the days when everyone came to America from the sea. Disappointment that the Statue of Liberty was muffled in fog. The dim shapes of freighters, of liners stacked up in the piers from the Forties to the Sixties. Idling in the Narrows behind a battleship bringing home deck after deck of cheering, hooting men, their individual voices carried in the echoing white silence over the water. Then the weather lifted and what I saw: an empire of light, light in the shop windows, puddles and sheets and rivulets of light glimmering on the sidewalk in the rain, masts of light rising from the street cut up into irregular patches, light making words, light making pictures.

And the odour of rotted cargoes in the warehouses, oil from the engine rooms, iron and cement, construction workers' sweat, hot-dog carts' steam, gales of Chanel Number Five blowing out from department stores. The smell of work and the smell of money.

Traffic, slide trombone, languages I don't know anything about, and more traffic.

Shops. A store that sells nothing but ties, a block of stores that sell nothing but wedding gowns.

The Chrysler Building like an armadillo's penis, at Times Square a billboard of a giant airman smoking a Camel and blowing out real smoke. Smart women in red hats, pausing on corners to straighten their seams. Discharged servicemen everywhere. Cowboys in uniform and Puerto Rican marines sitting on steps playing mamba. A frozen city on heat.

A city between two rivers that I wander through all agape. Of the Hudson and the East River, I choose the Hudson.

I had a job and a place to live. I was a mannequin and sales clerk at a Fifth Avenue fur store. By day I modelled coats and stoles and capes for women whose husbands sat beside them on the apricot leather banquettes and who, no doubt, wished they were going home with me inside those expensive skins and not their Amazonian wives, none of whom, I thought, had an iota of my mother's taste. In every way I enhanced the merchandise. To me, American women seemed grotesque creatures, with their bright, strong teeth and shiny hair like horses and their great feet on which they strode along the boulevards. I could not believe how many of them wore trousers in town, topped with sweaters, garments which at home Mother and I would have expected to see only on a land girl.

At night I took the subway to lodge with the furrier and his wife in Brooklyn Heights. I was happy at first, inspecting such marvels as a portable wireless and a waffle iron. The kitchen was my playground and I overfilled the machine the first time I used it, creating a monstrous pancake with a life of its own which threatened to overwhelm the kitchen. My employer was dismayed by my brittle looks. Rationing, he believed, had made me over-lean, and in comparison with the women around me I saw in the mirror the beginnings of a blueprint of my mother's looks, but, fed on pot roast and apple pie *à la mode*, I began to curve and fatten. I felt released from tragedy to a country where tragedy had been banned by the founding fathers and I was at home in that city-state which gave no hint of the loneliness and the emptiness of the continent it inhabited.

As soon as I stepped off the liner I had started to look about for Stan, half-expecting him to be there to meet me. In the store it was sometimes thought that I had a distant, haughty look but it was because my eyes were always focused out of the window, fearing that he would pass by and I would miss him. It had been eighteen months since that letter from the Hotel Algonquin but I tried the kitchens anyway, running my fingers through sacks of flour wondering if *his* hands would later knead it into dough. The cooks said he still worked there sometimes but they had not seen him for a while. He had good luck these days. They could not or would not tell me where he lived and I thought that they were surprised that I should be asking for him.

At last, one morning in February, stopping off on my way to work to buy a pair of nylons to replace the ones I had laddered on the subway, I saw him coming out of the St Regis, no longer a Cunard Yank but the real thing. His hand was cupped over a Zippo lighter in the wind, and a Broadway matinee idol, whom I recognized from pictures in the *Post*, had his hand cupped over Stan's. I tapped him on the shoulder.

'I'm here,' I said.

He looked me up and down. 'Nice get-up, kid, love the mink.' It was my father's parting gift. He kissed me on the cheek. It was too cold to detect his smell. The matinee idol stood waiting with a cab.

'You're very hard to find. Are you pleased to see me?'

'Sure. This calls for a drink. What do you say to a bevvy tonight?'

'Love to.'

'Good. You're in with a promise.' He smiled. I could see he wasn't a boy now but, if he was older, age had made him slightly shop-soiled in his looks. His self-assurance was wearing thin. A cold shaft of sunlight struck him on the face and he flinched. As he blinked, I noticed how transparent his eyelids were, delicately traced with blue veins.

'You've got an American accent.'

'I wish.'

It turned out that he drank in his own neighbourhood, at the White Horse on Hudson Street in the Village where merchant seamen mixed incongruously with poets, like the

Philharmonic Hotel back home. It was Dylan Thomas's time and I suppose I must have been there sometimes when he was, but I'd never heard of him then. With me, Stan's American accent was more pronounced. Still a Cunard Yank, I thought, after all these years. Immediately, I began unconsciously to imitate him.

We only had one drink before we walked round the corner to his apartment in the meat-packing district. Even in the centre of Manhattan, even where Broadway skirted Central Park, you still felt that New York was a port in those days when at the end of every street you could glimpse the glitter of water from blocks away and skid across the icy intersections to avoid giant trucks thundering down to the piers, or be jostled by handcarts pulling fruit and vegetables transported by scows across the river from the farms of New Jersey. Where Stan lived was only a block from the shore, Sailortown, full of gossip about ships' movements, stolen goods changing hands for a pittance, grudges of the sea paid back with knives and baling hooks, a lifeline for him to the great diaspora of the Atlantic. He liked it there, liked walking in the cold early morning along the Hudson, past the shipyards and the cranes, past the shivering longshoremen numbly picking at ropes. He said there were secret places you could go to in the summer where every kind of pervert hung out, laughing and strutting, some in dresses, some just in their shorts, whistling and calling out and pointing at their parts. I had forgotten Stan's habit of perking up conversations with some cameo from low-life like this.

'Congratulations, Syb,' he said as he unlocked the door of his room. 'You're the first dame to have seen the inside of this place.' It was small and bare, papered with a pattern of bamboo leaves and twigs, a narrow room with a single bed. A few suits in the closet, ties everywhere, no photographs (though I'd sent him one of me, care of the Algonquin). A little kitchen, a closet with a shower that didn't work. An uncurtained window with a view over the fire escape and a glimpse of trucks parked in a loading bay. He'd swept some cigarette butts into a dustpan but hadn't emptied it. We undressed. The silver crucifix was gone. Under his shirt-sleeves he wore a heavy steel slave bracelet on which his name was engraved, and there were a few more hairs on his chest. On his forearm was a tiny, banal tattoo depicting an ink-blue anchor. And so, after eight years, we made love, me primed by the deft hands of the French steward, knowing what to do, not knowing how to fake a response, or needing to.

'Pity I wasn't the first,' he said when we'd finished and I lay, dreamy against his ribs, his fingers resting on my breasts. 'I heard Liverpool was chocka with GIs. You must have had some fun with them.'

'Oh, yes, lots.' I looked at the room and tried to remember the last one we had lain in together. I recalled an eiderdown, a bottle of cheap scent. 'How do you know that actor?'

'Who do you mean?'

'You know perfectly well who I mean. You were with him this morning.'

'Don't ask.'

'I want to know.'

'Are you jealous?'

'How could I be jealous of a man? It's not as if I . . . Oh.' As I have explained, the war had exposed me to much that was improper and, besides, who had not heard of Oscar Wilde and his mysterious misdeeds? And I was aware of a pub in Liverpool that queers frequented. It was called the Magic Clock.

'Get it?'

'I think so.'

'I hope so.'

'Why?'

'It's just the way I am. I've always swung both ways. I'd have thought you would have caught on by now.'

'Did they make you do it at sea?'

'Why do you think I went to sea?'

'So you're a sissy?'

'Well, what do you think? I mean, babe, you should know. Did you think you were making it with a girl?'

'I suppose I could put up with it as long as I'm your girl-friend.'

'I don't operate like that.'

'What about the way I operate?'

'Syb, I'm twenty-seven. This is the way it goes. I'm glad you're in New York and I'll show you round and we'll do it, I'll fuck you silly as often as you like, but you're on your own.'

'OK. I'll do whatever you want. I don't care.' He drew me to him and kissed me, very gently, all over my face, as if everything he had just said had been a lie. He moved his head down to my breasts, to my stomach and beyond and he parted my thighs and I was surprised.

We had breakfast early, uptown at Walgreens: coffee, bacon, eggs, potatoes for him; Hollywood lunch – cottage cheese, canned pineapple – for me. We ate in silence; my fork went in and out as I tried to think of something to tell the furrier about my overnight absence. With each mouthful, I swallowed the hurt of it. Why, I had a perfect little world – New York, Stan, money in my purse, the spring collections right around the corner and who knows what new, post-war look?

He searched my face for the hollows that used to be there under the cheekbones. 'You don't need to finish all that, you know,' he said. He finished his, got the check and paid it, slipped my mink on my shoulders, walked me to work and kissed me on the cheek. 'I'll be in touch,' he said.

'How can I reach you?'

'I haven't got a phone. You can always leave a message at the bar. Don't worry, I'll see you right.'

I have never been good at making new friends. I sat at home in the evenings with the furrier and his wife listening to the Bob Hope Show, Bing Crosby and the Benny Goodman Orchestra on the radio or turning the pages of that season's bestseller, *The Egg and I*. I forget names a lot but I still remember theirs: they were Louis and Ida Max. Louis was like a child's drawing of a man, executed by joining up a number of circles. He was bald with a tonsure of hair round the back and sides of his head and the odour of Havana cigars clung to his suit as it had to virtually every grown-up I had ever known in my life. He was American-born and, yes, he had lost relatives in Europe and cried out their names on the Day of Atonement, but they were great-uncles and great-aunts, people he had never met, and his expansive trader's smile meant no more than it said.

Ida overdressed and didn't care. She seldom made it over the bridge to Manhattan. Her days kept her busy playing cards and doing charity work to raise money for refugees. At lunchtimes Louis would often send me out to pick up some little trinket from the bargain counter at Tiffany's which he would bring home and hide about him. When we got in, Ida would run over and pat his pants pocket and feel something hard, and squeal.

The game they played was that he would run away from her and she would chase him round the room until she got her trophy – a pair of little pearl earrings or a charm for her bracelet – and she would tinkle into the kitchen, adorned, to serve up dinner.

They were warm, happy, easy people, like loose slippers. No one ever called me back before I left the house to point out that I had not blended my foundation over my jawline properly so as not to leave an unsightly mark. The streets of Brooklyn were wide, and even on the coldest evenings, as Louis and I trudged up the drive on our tired and sodden feet, the light from the brownstones turned the dirty snow banked in alps and ranges against the sidewalk a deep and promising amber.

The winter passed. I made it my business to discover the shops and the stores. I did not find in them the restrained elegance I was used to. The wealth of the city, unharmed by bombs, astonished me. Nothing I had seen in London could compare with Lilly Daché's dazzling store on East 56th Street, a cathedral to hats, with its round salon upholstered in leopardskin, its silver and gold fitting rooms for blondes and brunettes accordingly, the entire creation topped off with Lilly Daché's own penthouse. When I sailed from Liverpool, Utility's shoestring silhouette still dominated the clothes that were available in exchange for the coupons in our ration books. But in New York I saw everywhere the symptoms of a deep and satisfying frivolity – leg-of-mutton sleeves, side-swags, panniers and even *bustles*. Shoes were spikier, stockings were sheerer, busts were higher and my own hair had been cut into a short, delicate page-boy bob. First I bought a wasp-waisted corset, a Mainbocher copy, then, for the first time, I entered Lilly Daché not to gape but to buy and, confronted with her two perfumes, Drifting and Dashing, I bought – both!

Then I felt all my mother's little fashion tyrannies fracture, and their dictatorship was overthrown. I saw their ruins in my mind's eye as if from a great distance. I bought my first pair of saddle shoes, a polo coat and B. H. Wragge velveteen trousers, like the college girls wore, and in this outfit I went to the Margaret Sanger clinic to have a diaphragm fitted. In March I had my photograph taken at the Photomaton to send home to Liverpool; there was a softness in my face I had not remembered noticing in the mirror. In the picture I was laughing and the pose, with my head to one side, was more casual than was fashionable in England at the time. I was beginning to look like an American.

Stan was more attentive than I had expected, though when I presented him with a copy of the photograph he did not have it framed and I never saw it again. Much of how he spent his time, how he earned a living, who his friends were, remained a mystery. Since he had left the sea, ducking and diving had become a way of life with him. Sometimes he was flush and we would go to the Diamond Horseshoe or the Hawaiian Room at the Hotel Lexingon to drink cocktails from coconut shells, or the Astor Roof to dance to Harry James and his orchestra. I aspired to the Stork and '21', El Morocco and Sardi's, where the celebrities of the day could be spotted, particularly El Morocco's zebra-striped interior and though Frank, the Maître d', had a sharp eye for mobsters, the overplastered and the overdressed, my class was Stan's ticket. The impoverished and dowdy English were not exactly in vogue that season but those in good furs could once or twice dodge through doors that would otherwise have been closed to us, in the very grand shadow cast by the Windsors, though we did not manage to do better than the Arctic tables for nobodys and out-of-towners.

When we took to the dance floor, Stan waved at people and greeted them by name. They nodded at him and stared at me. Occasionally the men would come over to ask me for a dance or take their partner back to her table and return to cut in. But Stan hung on to me tightly.

'Why do they want to dance with me?'

'I guess they think you might be a movie star,' he said, confidently, into my shoulder.

'Oh, give me a break. Who are they, anyway?'

'Junkies.'

'The women too?'

'Some of them.'

'I don't believe you. That woman there, she must be forty-five and she looks like Eleanor Roosevelt.'

'No, she's not a junkie. She's into delivery boys, preferably from the butcher's. She likes dark meat. That guy she's dancing with, him too. He's a dinge queen.'

Other times he had no money and we spent the evening in a diner, sharing a blue-plate special and a Coke, but wherever we went Stan was never anything but impeccably dressed and even in snowstorms he would insist that I went out in heels. He disapproved of my new, rather mannish American look, which I reserved for loafing about Brooklyn at weekends, and my wasp-waisted faux Mainbocher corset made him laugh. He liked me best with nothing on at all or dressed with a sophistication that to his hustler's eye spelled money. The room off Hudson Street was freezing and we made love under my furs. Afterwards I would get up and put on my mink to make coffee.

'All fur coat and no knickers, that's you to a tee,' he said, watching me from the bed. When the temperature dropped even further we would let ourselves into the furrier's store with my keys and spread the coats out on the apricot leather banquette and fuck underneath them. Our million-dollar fucks.

But as the excitement of New York wore off, I began to feel lonely again. I was at Stan's beck and call. Like a dog, I always came when he whistled. There were days when I missed him and I would hang out outside his place, hoping to surprise him, but he never turned up. By the spring the intensity was passing. I supposed that he grew bored with sleeping with one sex for too long and boredom was certainly his enemy. I knew I bored him, and his own glamour was tarnishing for me. I had never been much of a reader but even so it embarrassed me that often, when I met him at the Horse, he was engrossed in a comic or a cowboy novel. He was very smart in one way, but I think he had what the head doctors would call a limited attention span. I was no longer sure if he was an anarchist of life. Possibly, as I had once suspected, he was just a spiv.

We couldn't keep things up as they had been going and I decided to expand my social network and find a friend. Other girls worked for Mr Max, but my special status as his lodger forbade any intimacy and invoked outright jealousy. So my strategy was to start to take my lunch breaks in the same cafeteria every day and pretty soon I spotted another girl who did the same thing. In a new first for me, I struck up a conversation. She said she had seen me too but was intimidated by my fancy way of talking when I ordered my meal, and my chic outfits. I had to be rich to afford that mink. I pointed to the small diamond studs in her ears. It turned out that, like me, she got them wholesale, for she worked at a jeweller's four blocks away. She pushed out her hand and said she was glad to make my acquaintance, that her name was Thelma, she was twenty-five and her sweetheart had died in the Pacific.

It was nice to have a bosom pal, to take turns about Central Park together guessing the labels on the fashionable women's outfits, to play that old game we thought we had invented: 'Suppose you had to lay the very next person you see . . .' Now we walked around with linked arms and discussed who we liked at the movies. I said I had a shine for Ronald Colman. I showed her some pictures of my parents. 'Your poppa looks like him,' she said.

'I know.'

In the days when I heard nothing from Stan I took on my mother's role, instructing Thelma in how to dress. I pointed out how waists were diminishing, a very early storm warning, had I known it, of Dior's sensation the following year. I filled Thelma's head with the names of the bright new British couturiers who had emerged since the war ended: Edward Molyneux who designed in Paris until the Occupation; Angèle Delanghe, a refugee from Belgium; Bianca Mosca; Norman Hartnell; Elspeth Champcommunal; Hardy Amies; and last but not least the brave Digby Morton, who, in 1940, had set out for New York with an export collection but had met a torpedo mid-Atlantic and had spent twenty hours in the inevitable open boat. I told her of Paris, and of the first collections since the war ended, of Balenciaga, of Patou, Pierre Balmain, Lelong, Piquet and the milliner Maud Roser. Thelma was attentive and fulsome in her thanks. I had given her, she said, a proper European education and it was obvious that she felt more assured, tripping down Park Avenue under a green hat formed of a stove-pipe crown on a head-hugging cloche. She no longer spoke of the dead boy in the Pacific.

Within a month she had found a new sweetheart, a clerk at Tiffany's, and after going out as a threesome for a while we went our separate ways. I think I might have been a lure or bait to win him, her friend with her fabulous clothes and her classy British accent who taught her that she could be reborn.

When I turned twenty-two I looked at everything that was going to waste inside. It seemed that all around me the entire population of America, home from the war, was getting wed. To marry, that was the thing to do. I now categorized Stan as an interlude, a product of wartime. There *was* a place for me in America, a situation which would justify all the fastidious efforts that had been expended on my upbringing. I would marry some boy that Ida would no doubt fix up for me and I would have my own home in Brooklyn Heights, joining the women of my generation in morning charity work and after-noon bridge, as life was lived in the movies.

I dreamed pleasantly through April. Summer would come to Brooklyn and I would sit on the porch and drink iced tea with my beau. Ida would bring out pie and withdraw tactfully. My past was nothing; everyone had been crazy during the war and girls of my age had been forced to grow up too soon. Under the cover of the blackout mistakes were easily made, you took people at face value and acquired friends you quickly discarded in peacetime. I practised these words until I believed them. My beau and I would have a short engagement, then a small family wedding (his family, not mine). There would be an apartment at first, then a house and I would shop at the A&P, unmould jello salads and budget carefully. I would resist all suggestions to furnish my home in the hideous style known as American colonial. This time next year I could be a mother with a nursery nurse to take care of the unpleasantness. In five, ten years, there would be no trace left of my cut-glass Kensington accent, only a slight clipping of the vowels on certain words. Oh, the war was over and the dead, if not buried, must have been granted their eternal rest.

At the Jewish tennis club I met Marvin Green, blond, round-faced and cheerful, implausibly nicknamed Poppy, a copywriter with one of the new advertising agencies set up by young veterans, one of those that took on Jews. I was a poor player and he was a good one so I deliberately flattered him for his expertise and inevitably it was not long before we sat close in the club house, two straws in one bottle of Coca-Cola. Poppy was at first mystified, then entranced by me, at how quickly – it had been only months – I had arrived in the USA and yet could so thoroughly convey the impression of being an American. Without effort I had down all the brand names of the products he represented. I was a prototype consumer. He tried out his jingles on me and I listened carefully and made informed, thoughtful comments, always trying to place myself in the position of those who might be tempted to purchase, and my remarks were conveyed back to his clients.

Poppy himself was divinely uncomplicated. These were days of drive-in movies, trips out to Long Island or cheering the Dodgers, the time during which I observed the ways of those about me and sought to become just like them. His room at his parents' house was hung with his college pennants, for even with the quota system he was a Columbia man, and I marvelled at the thought of me dating a boy with an education.

I was called on the telephone, picked up in his car. In short, I led a normal life and liked it, one that I could never have lived at home, saddled as I was then with the burden of the past. Nor, I found, was he without passion.

Poppy had been to war, enlisting the week after he graduated, but he had not seen much action. His unit always seemed to come in after the event, the housemaids of the US military effort, tidying up the mess. It embarrassed him that he had never heard a shot fired or sighted the enemy. I spoke a little about the Blitz. I evoked the dead bride in her parachute silk dress, the groom with his green face, the beige bridesmaids, the shelter bombed in Durning Road, the blitzed cows. I told him one day about a story we had all heard: a lady, a lecturer at the university, had been walking along Catherine Street when the sirens started. Looking around for a shelter, she heard a couple calling out to her from their doorway. She followed them into the cellar and stayed there until the all-clear sounded. They drank tea and sang songs together; the old woman knitted a balaclava helmet for her grandson while the old man looked through his seed catalogue. The lady lecturer opened her briefcase and got on with her marking. The following evening she returned to thank her protectors and found a fragment of wall and a pile of cold, damp ashes. When had it happened? she asked the ARP warden. The previous week, he told her. I had believed the story once. I didn't now, but Poppy did. The whole war and all of us in it had started to seem vaguely surreal to me, and this new life in America made its memory much stranger, yet mischievously I peddled these old stories, all the better to entrance him.

No one likes to enquire too deeply into horror. Only those who were there scratch away at the memories like a scab.

Poppy held my hands and told me that the past was a closed book; it, not me, was on the shelf.

What I liked about him, as the summer and our romance wore on, was that he believed ferociously in the peace and in the consumer boom that he predicted was coming. He talked about the wartime industries that were re-tooling, manufacturing automobiles and vacuum cleaners and refrigerators. He described miracles that were in the making: coffee you didn't need a percolator to make, you just put a spoonful into a cup and added water. All the drudgery would be gone from housework. Oh, I really *wanted* to be a housewife.

Everything was perfect except for the time we drove out of the city to Fire Island. We stood on the beach watching the ocean. 'Look!' he said. 'Isn't this something? I've been coming here since I was a kid and it still gives me the same thrill. It's so *beautiful*. How would you describe it?'

The sky and the sea were indistinguishable colours. My feet stood on sand; behind me were clumps of grass. The sun shone. The sea seemed quite small, really, the whole landscape just an emptiness. 'I don't know – big, I suppose.' Was this right?

'Yeah, but how does it make you feel?'

'Bored. Can we go back to the city?'

He stared at me, hurt and angry. 'You don't like Fire Island? That's impossible. No, wait, maybe you're a mountain person, you like mountains.'

'I've never seen a mountain.'

'I'll take you to the Rockies on our . . .'

'Can we go, please? Can we go to a roadhouse for coffee?'

The visit to the ocean was a setback. I had not prepped for an admiration of Nature. But Marvin soon forgot about it. 'Sybil,' he said when he proposed, 'this is the best time in

human history for a girl to marry. It's the age of the housewife.'
When I watched him drive a ball across the court with his
miraculous backhand, a triangle of sweat deeply indenting his
chest, I felt his soul was full of light.

I was formally presented to his entire family at a Saturday
night dinner. We got no further than the meatloaf when his
grandmother began the interrogation.

'And who is your father?'

'Bubba, her father is a furrier in Liverpool, England. A well-
respected man, he works for the Promised Land.'

'His name?'

'Please, Marvin. His name is Sydney Ross.'

'And what was it before?'

'Izidor Roth.'

'From?'

'Belgrade.'

'I will enquire. Your mother?'

'Sonia Ross.'

'And what was it before?'

'Mrs Green, I don't think she ever said. I never knew any of
my grandparents.'

'From?'

'Hamburg.'

'German?'

'Yes, German.'

'German Jews, we don't know much about them. When did
she get out?'

'A long time ago, during the first war.'

'So you must have relatives on your mother's side in
England?'

'No, none.'

'No uncles, no cousins? How come?'

'My mother didn't have any family. Her aunt brought her up. She never—'

Marvin's mother dropped the serving spoon into the creamed potatoes. 'Sybil, your mother is Jewish?'

'No, she isn't Jewish.' They stared at me in shock and horror and perhaps pity. But there was nothing that could be done. Marvin took me home before dessert.

Chapter Six

My two or three months' absence from Stan, during my abortive engagement, had renewed him sexually and made me suspect that at least there was no other woman in his life. I no longer doubted his bisexuality. I saw him start when he saw a man whose arrangement of limbs, or way of walking or of combing his hair, caught and held him in some place I did not understand. Once, I suppose off his guard, he remarked how a fellow on the subway's blue tie matched his eyes. Homosexuals, I believed, were promiscuous on principle, but there were those who needed lovers as a point of order and stability to come home to. Stan used me as a wife. He was a sailor returned to the woman who waits for him in his home port and who never asks and would not wish to know the other arms in which he has lain in other cities. But the days when he had been young and had the kind of simple beauty that would grant him the care of a rich protector were coming to an end and he was cast loose in the city again, bruised perhaps by love and given a freedom he was no longer sure he wanted.

After the fiasco with Marvin, with some regret I left the Maxes' house and my job. I wanted a break with what had gone before, a second chance at a new start. I went to work as a sales girl in the third-floor couture salon at Lord and Taylor, where my detailed knowledge of Hartnell and Molyneux overrode the anxieties, in the personnel department, about my morals. For I had now moved in with Stan, to the narrow bed and the slight stench of meat drifting up from the warehouses along the sidewalk. We would sit on the steps in the mornings, drinking paper cups of coffee, watching labourers swing dead frozen cows and sheep and pigs along rails from refrigerated trucks. Then Stan would go back to bed and I would take the bus uptown to enter the premises by the back door, punch my card in the clock with a thousand others and beneath the vaulted ceilings hung with gold-tasselled lamps spend all day on my feet deploring the taste of Mrs Average, USA, convincing myself that I was glad of my lucky escape.

Living with Stan, I got to know him in many of his guises: the cocky half-caste, the Cunard Yank, the hustler, the marginal modern who took for granted his welcome in the many submerged worlds that every city harbours. He was more than a spiv. I admired the way he put up his front and took what life dealt him, but as I grew familiar with each persona I wondered if he did not hang on to them so determinedly to protect an inner fragility whose origins I could not even guess at.

Having made an effort to fling myself at the American Way of Life, I had been surprised at how it had pitched me back

again. There were no two ways about it, Stan and I were foreigners, we hung around the edges of things. This puzzled me
at first, since America was the country of immigrants, but
when you saw the Puerto Ricans and the Poles and the Jews
and the Irish all barricaded into their little enclaves, speaking
their own languages and eating their own food, you could
understand that becoming an American was a slow business: it
began with finding work and a roof, then, and only maybe,
learning the tongue. The food was the last to go. Stan and I
were indistinguishable from Americans on the surface; they
could understand us when we opened our mouths, for example, but when we looked back we shared no memories with
them.

Stan, I realized, didn't understand their sports. He had actually shaken the hand of his hero, Dixie Dean, and had his
autograph on his programme, but this souvenir, carefully kept
locked up in his suitcase, could not be produced to any effect at
the Horse. On his uppers once, he had tried to sell it and had
hunted all day for an Englishman who would recognize its
value. In his failure, he knew that he had been run to ground.
At sea, landfall was only a temporary respite from the company
of men. There were sailors who never got further ashore than
the first pub at the end of the dock road and, though he would
have hated to admit it, Stan was one of those. In the two years
he had been in America, he had never left New York, never
even gone as far as New Jersey, let alone Boston or
Philadelphia. He made his living in the place he felt most
comfortable, the waterfront, sticking close to the margins,
petty trafficking, his own kind.

I stuck to Stan because—

Sex.

I liked sex, very much. I had liked it with the French steward and with Marvin but in both of those cases it could not be
obtained without some complicated procedures to do with, in
the one instance proximity, and in the other my being someone
who it turned out I was not. So sex was offered and withdrawn.
In the rhythm of my life with Stan in the single bed, it was just
there, take it or leave it. If he was not in the mood and I was,
he would always find a way of obliging, though admittedly with
a rather absent mind on occasions. He didn't bother taking his
clothes off if he wasn't feeling horny. He would bring me to
orgasm with one hand while holding a Zane Gray with the
other, and could become so engrossed that he didn't notice
my sighs and spasms that should have indicated that I had
achieved my climax. But I had no complaints; I thought it was
very good-natured of him to bother at all. Me, I was always in
the mood. 'It's just a little itch,' he would say. 'I'll unzip and you
can give me a hand job.' But I'd have my dress over my head
and pull him down to the bed, smelling Old Spice and covering his chest with lipstick kisses.

I kept the room clean – there wasn't much to it – and
ironed his shirts and polished his shoes and picked dust and
lost dimes from the cuffs of his pants. In return he never made
me cook. We went out to diners or he brought home a bag of
hamburgers to eat in bed. We were never short of bread: he
would go into the little kitchen and bake – dinner rolls, Parker
House rolls, brioche, cup-cakes which I iced. His shaving
tackle took up a few inches in the bathroom; the rest of the
available space was where I installed my crocodile vanity case.
He cleared out his closet for my clothes and waited for hours,
lying on the bed reading 'Little Rich' or 'Sad Sack' while I
dithered about what to wear. Only when I said that I was ready

would he look at me carefully, noticing things that I had missed – a stain invisible to my own eye, a loose button. Unlike my father, he had no great colour sense, nor did he know the names of designers or what was in vogue. He trusted my taste. But when he was satisfied he would nod quickly and bring his thumb and index finger together to make a circle. 'You look grand,' was his final verdict. We didn't even talk much. I felt that we had entered a time out of time, both of us waiting. I didn't know what I was waiting for. He didn't tell me what he hoped or expected.

I took my clothes off sometimes, when he was out, and looked at myself in the mirror. 'You're still young,' I thought. 'Something could happen.' I started to think of my naked body as clay. I made Stan rub me down with creams I bought on discount at work. Every morning I touched my toes, pumped my upper arms like windmills, grimaced at the sink to prevent the hair-like lines above my upper lip that waited to jump out at me in the future. Over the Labor Day weekend, after Stan had been absent for nearly a week and admitted casually (to my shock) that he had missed me, I made him cut my pubic hair into a heart with nail scissors. One day he brought home a camera and took pictures of me while I slept. For days he practised with no film until he showed me a box of prints and I saw myself, my face and my body, through his eyes. I thought I looked like an exotic pet such as a Siamese cat or Chihuahua dog.

The euphemism that would later become common to describe Stan's line of work was import/export. He bought from longshoremen who pilfered cargoes from the port and he had a line to the Indian seamen who brought in cannabis, which he sold in clubs uptown. Harlem was another country. You didn't need a passport to get there but it was like the Arctic: everyone knew where it was but no one wanted to go. In exchange, he exported small quantities of heroin which he dealt *downtown*, occasionally arranging to satisfy other tastes if he could oblige and he felt like it and his own cut made it worth his time. He never used heroin himself. He said it was a mug's game, along with gambling. Harlem was a good place for foreigners. The people who lived there were the only ones in America who weren't immigrants.

He would take me with him sometimes on his forays uptown. As I crossed the line at 110th Street that divided the neighbourhood from the rest of the city, I came to see that Upper Parliament Street had only been an echo, a mirage on the other side of the ocean, that this place for Liverpool Negroes was *the* place, from which everywhere and all time was a deviation. After the scented wealth of Fifth Avenue, the elevators at work swagged in velvet, the chic little sundresses at sixty dollars, Harlem was a brown world – uniformly decrepit brownstones, boarded-up stores from which the money had fled, all the names on the businesses recognizably Jewish, for the Jews were the last white people to leave there. There were no skyscrapers. The light was different. The accents weren't the same. An army had tramped up to Harlem from the bus stations of mid-Manhattan since the war, and nearly all of its numbers were from the South. The food was a little like the food I'd seen in the club back home: fried chicken on a plate with strange grains and odd vegetables coated in something syrupy. Men strolled across 125th Street and Lexington Avenue in buttoned-up coats, elaborately knotted neck-ties, their faces shaded by the brims of their hats, but there were others who dressed like nothing I had ever seen before. I called them clowns in their zoot suits with watch chains hanging to their knob-toed two-tone Florsheim feet.

Of course he took me to the Apollo Theatre where, in their dying days, we heard some of the great swing bands of the era: I loved the showman, Cab Calloway, his conked hair flying about his head as he hi-de-hied across the stage in his pure white suit, singing the song about the Man from Harlem, and all the references in it that I caught to dope, him lasciviously winking at us white girls in the audience, while we laughed despite ourselves and loved the way he called us frails. All his horns made a sleazy, sexy sound and all his horn players held their big gold instruments slung low round their hips and shook them at white women, *particularly* white women. When we got home and Stan would light up a final reefer as we lay in bed I wound myself into sleep thinking about Minnie the Moocher and puzzling over her and the King of Sweden: a Negro girl and a man with a pointed gold crown on top of his yellow hair, sitting on an ermine throne like Old King Cole as Minnie mooched and smooched in circles round the pile of things she had been needing. I saw her behind the platinum wheel of her diamond car and the piles and piles of money she was forever counting with us all dressed up for Minnie's wedding day in our fine threads as 125th Street inexplicably adopted the dressed windows of Lord and Taylor.

And I remember one night, after I had seen Duke Ellington for the first time and had heard him play, for the first time, the sublime 'In a Sentimental Mood', when we did not take the A Train back home to the apartment off Hudson Street but stayed drinking until four at Small's and rode by cab the whole length of the island in which I lay, half sleeping in the crook of Stan's arm, with all the lights of Manhattan streaming past us into blackness, as if I was waking out of dreaming and my dreams were pulled by gravity back into sleep. And when we came to Sheridan Square impulsively I told the driver to drive on until we reached the very tip of the island where we drank coffee in the new light and then walked through the double-arched, eau-de-Nil gateway to board the Staten Island Ferry, which was, on this particular run, named *Miss New York*.

For the first time I saw Stan at sea, noticing how his hips rolled and how he placed his feet flat and far apart once he had a deck under them. 'You're a sailor,' I said sleepily, stupidly. He explained all manner of seafaring things: our speed of fifteen knots and hawsers and tackle, and pointed out the cranes of the naval shipyards at Brooklyn with an unfinished troop carrier lying below. He showed me what a sailor saw – how the city was reached by a network of bays and waterways and in what manner it was protected by the drawn-out span of Long Island against the wilder weather. After twenty minutes or so our boat docked and we turned around. *Miss New York* filled up with commuters on their way to Wall Street. People had brought on their breakfast and sat inside drinking coffee and eating bagels or Danish or just plain, unglamorous toast. A woman wrote a letter, balanced on her knees. A college kid in a sweater read his books. A man in Air Force uniform held the hand of a child dressed like the Princesses Elizabeth and Margaret when they were little, in double-breasted coat and round angora hat. We stood ahead watching the city take shape and come into luminous view as it had not done when I had first arrived ten months before. Stan identified the Cunard Building. The sun rose and shone and, inexplicably, out of the blue sky there was a sudden hail storm which left my hair wet and sparkling.

'You look like the Statue of Liberty,' he said.

It was our starry moment.

And then the ferry docked and we tramped ashore with all the other commuters.

Chapter Seven

Stan was always out in front of me. Now I'd learned to appreciate jazz and the swing bands, he had moved on to something else. He said that swing had become smarmy, like syrup dripping off a hot sidewalk. It was finished, it was dead. I couldn't decide whether he actually knew anything about music or if it was just that he liked being ahead of the game. Or maybe this was him forever drawn to what was new and marginal. Or was it that race music spoke to that portion of him that felt itself to be doubly an outsider? I'm talking of a time when anyone would be white if they could help it; there was no percentage in shouting about being anything else. A century ago, during the times of slavery and perhaps now in the segregated South which even I could not help knowing something of, Stan would not have 'passed', with his Indian grandfather. But here in New York, though the Maharajah of Jaipur had been turned away from the Stork Club under the colour ban, Stan was assumed to be – well, what? Usually a wop until he opened his mouth when his Limey accent aided a confusion he relished. Despite my big nose, no one ever thought of me as a Jew and I sounded, softly, more American than he did. We made a good-looking, largely unclassifiable, déclassé couple.

Now he was into be-bop. Fifty-Second Street between Fifth and Sixth Avenues was a street of run-down brownstones then, with clubs on the ground floor and flophouses up above. Harlem's grand days were over since the riots three years before and the whole section was off-limits to servicemen. Fifty-Second Street, or Swing Alley as the papers called it for a while, was close to Times Square and it was here that you went if you wanted to hop across the race fence for a night. Dizzie Gillespie lookalikes in flashy suits, berets with bass clef pins and chin whiskers swarmed into the area, buying a drink and hiding it under their coats while they jumped from club to club so that one drink was good for several bands and lasted all evening.

I hated be-bop. Charlie Parker, in particular, drove me nuts. There was no rhythm, no melody, nothing to dance to, nothing you could sing. It began nowhere, went nowhere and ended, very suddenly, nowhere. The notes flew about all over the place and there seemed to be too many of them. The music was a cool frenzy that reached me from a cold star, far away.

'You've got to get into it,' Stan said. 'It's easier when you've had some blow.' So we would find an alley and smoke some weed and come back when we were stoned. Everyone stood around, just listening, intent in their little worlds, hardly drinking, not talking. The music floated through me as if I was the

Invisible Man without his bandages. 'Now are you in the groove?' he asked. Stan had lately discovered how to talk jive, like the hipster he now aspired to be, and he was full of these incomprehensible phrases, calling white people ofays or pinks. Everything good was righteous, every time I did something he didn't like I was his 'chick', coming up on the wrong riff. 'What's your story?' he'd ask when I got home from work at night in a new outfit bought with my staff discount. 'What's the line on that drape?' he'd demand. At times like this he reminded me of my mother.

It was a long time, months as far as I knew, since Stan had been with a member of his own sex. He didn't talk about it any more and I didn't like to ask. His sex drive had periodic highs and dips and it was never as strong as mine, nor could he fully satisfy me, which made me suspect he was not such a great lover as he made out. But I felt that I had bound him to me and though there had been no signal that would tell me he returned my infatuation, neither was there any suggestion that he might be thinking of leaving or that he wanted me to go. Far from it. I guessed that he had lapsed into laziness, that his wandering was done and he had settled for me, for the usual, for the easiest option. And though we lay, night after night in the narrow bed, shaken by the thunder of trucks from the slaughterhouses, and though I was only a working girl like any other, he was never going to forget that I was the boss's daughter and I was a prize. Besides, who else did he have? What else?

The men in the 52nd Street clubs made no impression on him – he said he never had been a dinge queen – but they did on me. At the Apollo, at the coloured club off Upper Parliament Street, I was an outsider, a voyeur allowed admission because I was young, pretty and white. But here the races mixed with greater ease and in closer proximity. It wasn't like the old days of Harlem when limousines pulled up with their society cargoes to be unloaded into white-only night-clubs while Negroes in blackface did antics for their amusement. There were no minks on 52nd Street (I left mine at home), nothing from Tiffany's. It wasn't smart to come here, it was – the new word – cool. We were the pioneers, the Beats in the making, and I could have become one too, if only I'd liked the music.

What drew me back to 52nd Street, what had kept me with Stan, again, as usual, was sex. I wasn't afraid to dance with a Negro now, if only one had asked me, if only there had been dancing. Until I got close up, I hadn't known that so many shades of black skin existed. The sailors in Liverpool from Nigeria and the Gold Coast had very dark skin which absorbed the light. There were Negroes in America with skin so pale that they were called 'yellow' or even 'high yellow'. Everyone straightened their hair painfully with lye and so they hoped to 'pass'. Some of the women who were 'yellow', who had their hair permed and elaborately set might have got by, seeming to be merely of Spanish or Italian descent or even Jews, had it not been for their flat, wide noses. When I had played tennis in Brooklyn I had discovered that girls my own age were beginning to have their noses operated on to make them smaller, upturned, retroussé. They lowered and modulated their voices to match their new noses and were unrecognizable as Jews to their own grandmothers. And had the darkness grown in them as they got older, to stand in for the shadow that had once been cast by their old noses? I didn't think so.

Though I hadn't had a nose job, neither did I have the name

my father had been born with. Like everyone else, I was trying to 'pass'.

Yet best of all I liked the men who were really *coloured*, skin a mixture of gold and cinnamon, Negro but not too Negro, but more 'coloured' than Stan. I didn't care to think how they had got like that, I just saw them as good-looking fellows, whatever angle you considered it from.

Stan did nothing to stay in shape, as I did. Physical labour belonged at sea and when he was on a ship his muscles bulged and his body was taut. His forearms were still strong from kneading dough and I loved him best with his shirt sleeves rolled up, counting the fine black hairs and the five or six freckles that made a shape like the Plough in the sky from his left elbow to his wrist. But most of the time he just lay around in bed all day smoking dope and eating peppermint candies, listening to the radio, so his naturally thin chest was developing a bulge below his shirt and I could pinch handfuls of fat from around his waist. In a year or two, Stan would be thirty.

The men in the jazz clubs were younger, their bodies tighter. And there was this oddness: Stan was always tense, on the ball, even when he was stoned and lazy. I suppose that being bisexual he was never sure what it was that he wanted and in any situation he would always be on the lookout for something else. He had felt the land pushing behind him all his life, and though he found himself stalled and idling on shore he was still in a state of nerves. Maybe he would grow out of it if our being together was more than just an over-extended leave, if he could admit that he had left the sea for good and prepare to settle down. I thought about us, moving a few blocks further inland, to the heart of Greenwich Village which would still be bohemian enough for him. And I had thought, too, that he might some day get a job, possibly as a photographer on *Life* magazine, why not? I had no plans for him to remain a baker all his days.

And while I was busy dreaming our future, I looked at Negroes in the jazz joints of 52nd Street and noticed their *looseness*, how every limb hung with its own precise weight, how the heaviest and oldest of men and women had their lightness, how they moved with grace and charm as if the centre of gravity of white people was wrongly placed. How uncomplicated they all seemed in their sex. Beyond this constant seeing on my part there was nothing. I knew nothing about them. I never spoke to a Negro; I was always with Stan and he did his deals with them in private. He respected them for their music and he never called them niggers (I cringed when I remembered I had once possessed a 'nigger-brown' cocktail dress). The narkiness in him had seen how they were treated at sea, getting worse pay than white crew, and the family had a long memory for what had been done to the lascars who had been indentured to a ship for life to pay off some trifling debt. He'd tested me once, long ago in Liverpool; he'd wanted me to know that no one stood over him and no one stood over anyone else. And if I was his woman then I was good enough for any Negro, and any Negro should be good enough for me. Coming to America at the end of the war, I had been shocked at what I had read of segregation in the Deep South. No, I wasn't prejudiced. Stan had made sure of that. And who was I, with my own secret history, to lower people for what they were born to be and could not help?

While I was looking at Negroes, Stan was looking at me, looking at them. He said one night we should go up to Harlem, dancing. We had hardly danced together since before the war, at the Grafton Ballroom, when he was dragging me round town as his prize new acquisition. There's something about sailors and dancing that doesn't mix; perhaps they're always moving to a different rhythm below them.

'What will you put on?' he asked, as we got ready to go out. He'd selected for himself a dark tan suit, a peach-coloured shirt and bitter chocolate tie which were now hanging up waiting for me to press them. They were all my gifts, bought out of my paycheque on my staff discount, but chosen by him. I was in my slip and bare feet.

I had nothing special in mind, probably a wool and taffeta dance dress a la Pauline Trigère that I found dramatic without being fussy. Stan had never said he did not like it.

'Nah, that's too plain,' he said from the bed. 'What else have you got? Look for something with a bit more sauce.'

There was a narrow, short skirt somewhere, flecked with silver. I got it out and showed it to him. 'Righteous. Have you got something red to go up top?'

'*Red*? Are you out of your mind?'

'Well, whatever you've got.'

There was a white crêpe de Chine blouse somewhere. It was plain but very low cut, sewn for a woman with a broader frame than mine, so it made a kind of wide tableau of my breasts. It had come in as a sample and I had taken it home without trying it on. I'd never worn it.

I put the ensemble on to show him and he nodded. I got undressed again to do my last chore. He liked to put on a fresh shirt every day and sent them to be washed at the Chinese laundry across the street, but I nagged him about the expense. The weather was cool now and the peach shirt could survive a second wearing, I had argued. I pulled it on to the ironing board. It did smell, not of sweat but of him, Old Spice and a faint whiff of cigarette smoke. I thought it was a sexy combination as I stood there in my lingerie, ironing.

Just before we went out, he knelt and began to straighten my seams. His fingers, always slightly swollen (perhaps because of the cold, perhaps from a tally of years of physical labour), delicately pinched the dark brown nylon ribs until he had reached my stocking tops. Then he pulled gently into place a tape on my garter belt that was stretched at an odd angle across my thigh. He began on the other leg, the slow detailed execution of a straight line up a curved surface.

'Walk forward,' he said, when he had finished. I stepped a few paces towards the door. 'That's it, we've got it now.' He stood up and swore as he looked down at his dusty knees. He asked for the clothes brush and scrubbed away at pieces of lint and cobweb strands. 'You're not much of a housewife, are you?' he complained.

It should have been an erotic moment, him kneeling behind me, his hands working their way up towards my thighs, but it was unarousing. Clad less smartly, he might have been a window dresser. God knows how long it would have taken us to get out of the house if he had worn stockings himself.

That night was the first night I danced with a Negro – properly danced. Stan brought his camera with him and in the corner of my eye light flashed, illuminating my partner for a moment in a sudden dead white glow. He had come over and asked me and this time Stan had told me I should decide for myself, but I was already on my feet. 'She can dance,' Stan shouted after us. 'She taught St Vitus.'

I'd long ago got the hang of the lindyhop; I was light enough to be thrown about and I flew through the air and under legs and over shoulders with ease. You couldn't get Stan to do it. He wasn't any good at that sort of thing and he had too much cool to expose himself behaving poorly. The lindyhop reduced the world to a blur, everything turned upside down and inside out. I felt like I was in a milkshake. I found out a part of myself on the dance floor, something to do with me and sex. I could go on and on and on once that music was inside me, jumping and jiving, everything lost, the past lost, the future immaterial. I could feel my calf muscles tighten by the minute and I got it into my head that if I pushed hard enough my waist would bend round at one hundred and eighty degrees. I kept having to lick my upper lip and my hair was plastered to my forehead. God knows what I looked like, I couldn't have cared less. I don't mean to say I was a great dancer, heavens no, I wasn't, not compared with the rest of them, but at least I got into it, as they said in jive talk.

I danced with a dozen or so men under a mirrored ball in a cheap dance hall to the swing jazz I'd grown to adore. It was a place with 'atmosphere', as they say. The flash lamp occasionally exposed and lit up other white girls dancing with Negroes. Some looked like cheap amateur whores and others were obviously college co-eds, but the rest told a different story. Then the music slowed. Someone was holding me tightly. He said I smelt very strange. I had dabbed on Dashing, the perfect scent for the evening, and I offered my wrist to his nose but he said he wasn't calling attention to my perfume, it was something else, and I didn't know what he meant.

In the ladies' powder room I repaired my make-up (I had smooched with Stan between dances to show my partners I was really taken). I smelt my wrist and there was a faint trace of

Dashing still there, beneath a smear of perspiration that had made my whole body slide around in my partners' arms. I found that the armpits of the white blouse were stained and even my silk underwear was damp. My face was like a red spotlight in the glass. A white girl stood next to me in a leopardskin print skirt. She was well below five feet tall and very thin with sandy hair. When she spoke I could see she had lipstick on one of her teeth but, unlike me, she didn't seem to be sweating at all. She was pulling a comb through her colourless hair. She looked at herself and if she didn't like what she saw she did not show it. She seemed to get thinner as I watched, but the stinking bathroom failed to diminish her. Girls like this, hard as nails, girls who threatened to cut you because they knew how. Girls who formed the crowd scenes in my New York, perpetual extras in my own little drama. Who were never going to 'pass' for more than what they were – white trash.

'Is this your first time here?' her reflection asked me from the mirror.

'Yes, this is my first time. I came with my boyfriend.'

'The guy with the camera. Does he work for the papers?'

'No. He just likes taking pictures. He always has. I suppose it's a kind of hobby.'

'Has he got a regular job?'

'Oh, he's in business.'

'I can guess which kind. You work?'

'Yes, in a department store.'

'Me too. In Macy's.'

In the basement, I bet. 'Which floor?'

'I work with special lines.'

Bargains.

'You?'

'I'm with Lord and Taylor.'

'A Murray Hill girl. Which floor?'

'Third.'

'You sell fancy dresses?'

'Couture, actually.'

'Cooty what?'

'Imports, from France and England.'

'You're foreign yourself, ain't you? Now I can hear it, you have an accent. Where you from?'

'England.'

'Londonengland?' She said it all as one word, as Americans did.

'No, the North.'

'I'm from the South myself. A hick town in southern Alabama, Monroeville. You heard of it?'

'No.' When I got to know the white girls who hung out with Negroes, I found that very many of them were from the South and they all told the same story. When they were growing up, black men were off limits; segregation defied their desires. They could see that Negroes were, for the most part, better looking than the inbred boys with the ferrety teeth that they were supposed to date. Then the war came and those very boys were sent away and the Negroes stayed behind until they were needed, being eyed hungrily, until enough Caucasians were dead for them to be trusted with a gun and shipped overseas. Some girls took the chance and made their great leap into danger, but it never worked out. Someone would always call out that these women had been raped, drugged or ambushed. The Negro's animal nature made him prone to lust, the reasoning went. Women, *especially* white women, were supposed to have a distaste for sex, beyond the chastity of premarital kissing.

And so they came north and endured the loneliness of the cities, of rooming with others who weren't their kin, of poverty and the bullying I knew went on on the lower sales floors. All their earnings were sent home or went on outfits like these, for they believed they had to smear themselves with plenty of honey if they were going to catch a bear. They went without enough to eat and the only place that seemed familiar was Harlem, where they recognized the food, and dark faces on the street brought them back to who they were and where they had come from and, finally, gave them courage to get by from day to day. Southerners needed Harlem. Without Negroes the poor were lost, for only Negroes gave the measure to their precise place in society.

Those little girls in their cheap dresses, almost on the edge of malnutrition, living for Saturday nights and high heels, so far from home and yet so bold. For as they missed the intimacy of the old world they had left behind, so they had a freedom for what they had never dared before: to try a Negro, to *taste* a Negro, to transgress. There was nothing political in what they did, no legacy of guilt they came to settle. They just finally satisfied a deep and ancient want in their kind that was like a fault line, like a seam of black coal runs inside the mountain and is exposed when a road is finally cut through and reaches at last the claustrophobia and torment of a town that settled in the wrong place and, turning its back, lost sight of the rest of civilization and was itself lost to sight.

The incalculable risks these girls took, and how few I ever met who succumbed to drugs or sold themselves. The brave little girls who danced on Saturday nights in Harlem so long ago and what became of them no one knows, for they faded fast back into America, to become invisibly old and unremarked on, or perhaps they moved to California to live off air and oranges in the sun.

We left at around two and took the subway. It was still early for Harlem but I had to work the next day. I looked down at my shoes and they were almost broken. The rubber tip on the right heel had come off and worn down the wood almost to the bone. I walked like a drunk. My nylons were literally in tatters where two long runs had met at the knee. The silver flecks in my black skirt had pulled all over the place. The white blouse wasn't going to be made good at the laundry, it was finished, irredeemably stained with a mix of spilt beer and sweat. I stank. Nothing left of Dashing. Stan was still as cool as a cucumber, pulling out a handkerchief and polishing the lens of his camera.

In our room that night I had it out with him about the photographs. 'You could at least have *asked* me if I minded.' I wanted to provoke him, I wanted a fight. After all the dancing I was feisty, I reckoned I could take him on like Joe Louis. I balled up my fists when I thought that we could begin some resolution of our aimless life.

'You've never said anything before. I've taken loads of pictures of you.'

'Not nice ones, though. Why are they always dirty pictures? What happened to that one I got done at the Photomaton? What did you do with that?'

'I've still got it somewhere. I didn't throw it out. What's bugging you tonight?'

'I don't want . . .'

'What? What don't you want?'

'Why did you bring me over here?'

'Where? Bring you where?'

'To America.'

'Me? Bring you to America? You brought yourself. You just turned up. I didn't do nothing to you, you know your own mind.'

'But you wrote, you wrote and said . . .' Wrote and said I should come and see everything he had seen: a transistor radio, a waffle iron, a skyscraper, Harlem.

'Are you going to wash, Syb? You stink.'

'Yes, of course, in a minute.'

He pulled a lump of hashish from his pocket and applied a match to it, shaving off burnt fragments with his pocket knife. I held my breath then let it out. 'Stan. Why not get a job? Let's find a bigger apartment.'

He giggled. 'What kind of job?'

'I thought you could be a proper photographer. Maybe one day you could work for *Life* magazine.' He didn't giggle again. He took his usual sharp inhalation from the reefer and handed it to me. I shook my head. 'No. I don't want any.'

He sat on the edge of the bed staring at his shoes, leather shoes that housed his narrow feet. I knelt down and untied the laces and eased them off. I put them away in the closet. He let the reefer go out before he had finished it and he did not light it again. I went off and showered. I took off all my make-up with cold cream. I came back smelling of Dove. We undressed and lay down together. He held my hand and we went to sleep that way. I used to wonder what he dreamed about as he slept beside me. Did he escape into his other life where men courted him and gave him money and he did whatever it was he did with their bodies that I did not want to think of or imagine? In that world was he happy, fed on tasty and expensive trifles at a suite in the St Regis, given gold wristwatches he always lost? Was his true love lost back there in his times of dreaming?

All over the city couples lie sleeping together. Some have just made love and called out each other's names, and then turned over, closed their eyes and betrayed them.

And now I dreamed and in my sleep I also danced in other arms.

Chapter Eight

In mid-December, when our room was so cold that I came home from work every night and got straight into bed beneath my furs, and we lay together like a pair of spoons in a drawer, sometimes turning to puff cannabis smoke into each other's mouths, Stan received a message from the Algonquin about a big party in Washington where catering crew were badly needed. Wires had been sent to all the hotels looking for relief cooks and bakers to lend a hand, but their own kitchens were busy that festive season. So Stan had an offer – five days' work at three times the union pay. The note was pushed under the door one evening by someone who didn't bother to knock. Stan put on my musquash jacket, a kind parting present from Mr Max, and walked on blue feet to retrieve it. He was having nightmares. In them, he thought that one of his eyeballs had fallen out of its socket and when he'd tried to push it back in he'd botched the job, the axis was wrong or something. Everything he saw was distorted. Tables and dogs had three legs. People were the wrong colour. He said that in the dream he always knew he was dreaming but when he tried to wake up, he was paralysed. He'd lie there believing he was awake but unable to move until finally he started and shrieked and sat up, his eyes wide open, sweating heavily. It was plain to me he was taking too many drugs. There were things he experimented with while I was out at work and which he didn't say much about, mushrooms from Mexico and pills that kept him awake for days.

He came back to bed with the note and sat up against the pillows still in my musquash jacket. I stroked the sleeve and begged him to take the job, though I never expected him to listen to my advice on anything. I thought about and even hinted how with the money we would have enough to move out, to a place where we could have our own carpets, heat, even perhaps a phone. He just nodded and pulled my head to his shoulder and kissed my hair. What was he thinking? That it was cold enough and I was right? Or was it in his mind that once the cash was in his pocket then he could decide what to do with it? All his deals went on splashes – our night at El Morocco, an expensive suit for him, a Parisian dress for me – and it was, after all, one of these deals that had kept my three furs in cold storage for the rest of the summer after I had left Mr Max.

He went off a few days later. 'What will you do while I'm gone?' he asked while he was packing. He was the greatest packer I ever met. He could fit two suits and three shirts into the smallest valise and they'd emerge without a crease. He stowed shoes by magic. Things came out of that suitcase like all the paraphernalia of a conjurer's hat.

'What do I ever do when you're not here?'

'I don't know, what do you do?' At the last minute he'd decided to take a pair of shoe trees and they seemed to dematerialize into a single unbulky dimension beneath his shorts and a couple of comics.

'Nothing. Wait for you.'

'That's not necessary. You can go out if you want to.' He didn't even look up. That was the trust he had in me.

'Where?'

'Wherever you want.'

On the subway uptown he suddenly asked me for a mirror. I handed him my compact and he took his comb out of his pocket and ran it carefully through his hair, combing hair oil into drier strands. He looked at himself again and smiled. His hair was freshly cut and though it had started to recede a little at the front, the loss only accentuated a slight widow's peak which I liked but which he felt he had to hide by pushing his hat further forward. At least it was a journey and he had a girl to wave while his train drew out of sight along the track, like in the movies. I was glad for him.

In fact I wasn't sure how I was going to get through those few days on my own. For months Stan and I had lived in such a little bubble together. I went to work the next morning, and, hardly even remembering the earlier part of the year when I lodged with the Maxes and walked out with Thelma, I wondered what other people did with their spare time. My problem was that I had no very obvious milieu in the store given the imperative need to be fairly secretive about my domestic arrangements, and while I was certainly not ashamed of Stan (at least most of the time I wasn't), too much about him and our relationship required impossible explanations. It *was* bohemian to 'live in sin' as we did. Our forays up to Harlem and the jazz clubs were at best unorthodox and his means of earning a living I positively had to keep my mouth shut about. I didn't care much what others thought of all this but I did have the capacity to see how it looked from the outside, to those who did not share our common origins in that city across the Atlantic, who had not witnessed what we had in the darkest hours of the Blitz. How could I tell them that with Stan I felt beyond harm, conjecture, criticism, that when he was there he resolved what inside me were my deepest, most hidden divisions? I loved Stan. I was certain we could make something of ourselves. We were each other's destiny and I mysteriously believed that our meeting at the Palm House was due to more than chance. I had saved him from his homosexuality and he had saved me from the void into which my queer ancestry had cast me.

Every day I took my breaks in the staff cafeteria, where I ate a modest little lunch – a chef's salad or a tuna fish sandwich and a soda. Since I had joined Lord and Taylor in the early fall, I had been quickly promoted and my peers had become the college boys and girls who were recruited to go straight into management and who hung out in a social group after work, intimidating by their graceful manners and a certainty about what was, in their in-crowd jargon, *comme il faut*. As Marvin predicted, we were poised on the edge of a great explosion of retailing, the beginnings of the golden age of shopping, and from all over the country graduates were converging on New York to make their careers in the great department-store boom at a time when America had been released from the war into a new confidence created precisely out of being cut off from the superior intelligence and culture of Paris and London. The members of the college set were all of a class, all from good families uncontaminated by any frisson of distaste for 'trade', and photographs were passed around of beloved mothers and fathers, brothers, sisters, cousins, Gramps, so many relatives! – all *doing* things: playing tennis or lounging on the beach throwing balls, or at the wheels of small boats in nautical caps. They seemed to spend their entire lives out of doors, sometimes even engaging in activities normally reserved for labourers, such as cheerfully manhandling armloads of logs across a snowy yard. More amazingly, they also kept in their wallets pictures of their pets with names like their own – Muffy or Scout or Tip – and when they returned to the store after Thanksgiving weekend the smell of animals still clung to their clothes and shoes. Nothing the matter in those arrangements of relationships, I enviously believed. *They* had nothing to hide. When they asked to see a picture of my own family, I showed them one of the Burrell and Hardman studio portraits of my father, in various shades of milk chocolate, now pre-war and rather dated. They didn't seem to notice the resemblance to Ronald Colman, I supposed because they did not go to the movies much but actually, as I later guessed, they would have thought that making such a comparison was a little vulgar. In the evenings they went to theatre openings together and discussed not the private lives of the players, as I would have done, but their acting techniques. I couldn't tell a good actor from a bad one. But rapidly surmising, despite my now mid-Atlantic accent, that I was English, they assumed I was cultured and sophisticated.

They would have had me in their group – a girl called Fizz
did her best to cultivate me on their behalf, as if they had put
their heads together, drawn straws and sent her to carry out the
task. At first I was caught off my guard and flattered by the
attention they paid me, how they used my name in every sentence and asked tactful but intelligent questions as if they were
actually interested in anything I said or did and really needed
my opinions. I was fascinated by how naturally, within a few
weeks of meeting each other, they had so cohered together,
inventing their own special slang and packing their social lives
with an endless variety of engagements – drinks parties, dinner
parties, costume parties, plays – and still they put in long hours
at the store and found some minutes after midnight to study
the latest texts of retail theory. There was a period of a week or
so in which I considered that I might at last have found a line
to that imaginary land of faceless men who lit your cigarette
and took you dancing, a richly furnished domain that had held
me in its enchantment for so many years. But it wasn't dancing.
And it was Fizz who invited me to a concert at Carnegie Hall.
I can't remember the name of the composer. I was bored stiff.
We went for a cocktail first at a bar her daddy visited when he
was in town and where she was known and hailed across the
room by other girls and boys. She had one of those absolutely
open American faces, heavy, honey-blonde hair in a French
pleat, flat hands, clipped nails, square teeth, blunt cheekbones.
She carried the breath of the country club with her wherever
she went. Her parents had had all the children painted in oils
by a local New Hampshire artist and she carried photographs of
his efforts, of herself at nineteen depicted in a white organza
dress with a puff-blue sash and a double string of pearls about
her neck, holding in her lap a Siamese kitten. Behind her was

a hazy window and, beyond, a sense of woods in the early morning. In the painting she had little feet that tapered to nothing and slender fingers, which one did not exactly find in life. In the photograph she was standing in front of a large carved fireplace at her parents' house, dressed in pants and a letter sweatshirt, the painting above her.

'We're all so excited that you're working with us, Sybil,' she said. Were they? Why?

'It's just a job to me really.'

'Come on, Sybil, you're a great saleswoman. You have such chic, everyone thinks you're headed straight to the top.'

'I've not been at the store that long – how can they tell?'

'Oh, Sybil, of course we can tell, you stand out.'

'That's not my intention.' She was eating the olive in her Martini, working her way round the middle with her two front incisors like a beaver; it looked as if she'd start on the stick next. I put mine to one side. She ate too much. She was going to have to be careful about that.

She laughed, quite loudly as it happened. I was surprised no one turned round to look. 'Dearest Sybil, that was what we call a *compliment*.' She said the word slowly, sounding each consonant and vowel. 'You're supposed to accept them with grace, like flowers from an admirer.' Marvin had sent me flowers, usually rather insipid pastel roses which I detested. The longer I spent with Fizz the more I had an uncomfortable feeling of being got at, which was less her fault than my own for not being charming, for having no smalltalk. I lacked her sunny disposition and I was certain it was too late to acquire it.

I couldn't think of what to say next so I excused myself and went to the bathroom to wash my hands. In the mirror, even in the kindness of the dim light, my skin still looked sallow so I picked up the cake of soap and lathered it about my face a bit and retouched my lipstick, drawing the outline of my mouth first then filling in the centre like a colouring book. My narrow green eyes were hardly more than slits and my pupils slightly large, though smaller than Stan's, which were permanently extended. I was watching my intake of pot. One of us had to earn a regular living. Then I powdered my nose again. Fizz didn't get it. I couldn't give a fig about the world of merchandising, it was the clothes that drew me. When by some mischance I'd put the wrong thing on, I'd spend the whole day feeling exposed, like a snail without its shell, and yet in the right outfit I defied the world. Tonight I was wearing saffron yellow and a boat neck. It was a disaster.

I walked back through the tables where girls like us, in jaunty hats, meeting after work, their shopping stowed on unused chairs, drank their drinks and gossiped and opened their lives about them like a bullfighter's cape. Another Martini was waiting, Fizz's half-finished already and headway made on the olive. I sat down again and felt the cold drink slide around my tongue, anaesthetizing it. Fizz was waving to the waiter for a second bowl of peanuts as if her finger ends weren't salty and greasy enough. I'd only eaten one. She'd finished the whole bowl on her own.

'Listen,' she said, leaning across the table, her arms folded on it, her blue eyes shining and her lashes making shadows on her cheeks. 'Can you keep a secret?'

'No one better.'

'It's not official yet, but I think it's OK that you know. We want you to be one of the first. Ryan and I are engaged.' I knew who Ryan was. He was an undistinguished sandy-haired fellow with a beaky nose above a small flabby mouth, though apparently the great-grandson of a general. His build was slight, his waist not much more than a hand's span when he took his coat off. I judged he weighed less than his fiancée. His domain was furniture, which others, more brawny than he, had to move about.

'That's nice.' She waited for more. I did my best. 'Great. When's the happy day?'

'June! June, beautiful June – when else does a girl get married?'

'Of course, I should have thought.' The way she was looking at me I could tell she thought my lukewarm response was due to jealousy. She picked up my hand and held it in her own soft one, warming me. I looked down at it. No ring. She caught my glance.

'I'm getting his grandmother's engagement band but it's a little old-fashioned so we're having it reset.'

'How lovely.'

'Don't worry, Sybil, it'll happen for you, I just know it will, and soon.'

'But you don't know anything about my private life.'

She took my other hand. 'Oh, yes, we do' – notice it was always 'we'; they didn't just go about as a group, they *thought* as a group – 'we've seen your beau.' It was the first time in my entire life that I was sufficiently distant from my usual self-absorption to contemplate that others might talk about me behind my back. I could not bear the idea of it. What on earth did they say?

'Me? I haven't got a beau.'

The smile wiped from her face like a hand passed across a frosty pane of glass. She was only just hanging on to my fingertips. 'Oh, I'm sorry. Was that your brother?'

'*Who?* Oh, OK. I know.' Stan had once met me after work. I'd come out and found him lounging against the wall, smoking a Camel, looking everyone up and down as they streamed through the staff entrance. It was interesting how I separated him off from the social world of fiancés, how I would not let him through that door.

'The attractive fellow, dark hair, like a model from the Sears catalogue. Oh, gosh, I didn't mean . . .'

But I was laughing at that. 'Yes, you're right, he'd love it, to be a model in the Sears catalogue. I wonder how much you can make as a male model? Oh God, that's funny.'

'*Is* it your brother? He does look rather like you. I don't want to pry, but . . .' She tried another smile – in fact she couldn't help it, it was the natural set of her face.

'No, don't pry.'

I'd wiped the smile off her face again. I couldn't help that either. I was no good at conversations.

So we were back to talking about her and Ryan. I wished that Stan would fly in on powerful silver wings like a steel eagle and bear me away. That would have made them stare.

The gap in the circle of hands closed after that evening and they were wary of me now, puzzled perhaps, but cool and formal. Fizz still waved wanly from the other side of the staff cafeteria but I just nodded and ate with someone else whose presence at my table sent them an unignorable message about my rejection of their world. I could see the point of beautiful manners but I wasn't going to be able to get the hang of them myself. I'd been more at home with Marvin's crowd but if that hadn't worked out this was surely not going to. Actually, I guessed that the cooling off would have started once they'd discovered I was a Jewess; not that I'd planned to tell them, but it was bound to come out.

There had been one or two disparaging remarks about the conductor Leonard Bernstein as we sat in our seats at Carnegie Hall, waiting for the orchestra to file in with their instruments. Had I gone to the wedding in some New England Episcopalian church I would have been lost, not knowing the tunes to the hymns or when to stand or sit. On the whole I never gave God a second thought but still the name of Jesus stuck in my throat.

My lunchtime pal was Morris, a window-dresser who, it was blindingly obvious to me, though apparently to no one else, was as bent as a nine-dollar bill. He knew I couldn't give a damn about that kind of thing.

'My mother sent me to a psychiatrist,' he admitted, the first time we spoke. 'He couldn't do anything with me.'

'Oh, screw the psychiatrist.'

'I did.'

'Not really?'

'No.'

He knew about Stan and was keen to meet him, though I wasn't stupid; I wasn't having that. Morris was also Jewish, like Marvin, but he had as little to do with his parents as he could. And so we ate our tuna fish sandwiches. We were both watching our figures.

Morris was as close to a confidant as I had had so far and, although I did not tell him everything, I told him enough for him to be going on with. In turn he confided in me about his secret loves. He'd not yet 'done it', but he was only twenty and he was sure he would very soon. He had everyone down as a homosexual and he even saw something in Fizz's compulsive hand-holding with all her girlfriends. 'Watch out, Sybil,' he'd stage-whisper as she swung past with a loaded tray. 'She's angling for another date.' And this:

'What's your favourite canine, Sybil?' he'd say loudly in the elevator.

'Oh, poodle, I think.'

'Makes for a nice collar.'

'If you can't afford astrakhan.'

He lived not that far from Stan and me, deeper into the Village, and apparently he spent his weekends practising his violin and daring himself to go out to one of the homosexual bars he knew existed.

'But I can't risk leaving the house in case I miss him, the man I *love*.' He meant the dancer across the hall who had, he told Morris, spent the war exempt from duty portraying dancing servicemen in those stage shows in which a unit put on their own show, but without women some had to dress in women's costumes and don wigs. The dancer was always one of those. Privately, I thought Morris was going to have to move fast or else he would miss his heyday. He was going bald at a rate of knots, his fair hair not just receding, as Stan's did, but thinning all over. He fretted about his teeth which stuck out rather and he was saving to see an orthodontist yet simultaneously terrified that he would be told to wear a brace for two years. He began to say something utterly awful about the effect of this on his imaginary sex life, but I went bright red when I saw the point approaching and told him to shut up.

'Stan has gone to Washington,' I said, as he was speculating about the calories in a small cup-cake. 'I'm on my own for a bit. What do you think I should do?'

'Do something with me. We could go to the movies. Or you could come round and see my apartment and I could play you a sonata. It would be awfully cosy. I could make us a salad and you could bring a bottle of wine.'

'That sounds nice.'

'And you sound lukewarm.'

'Do I?'

'I think so, yes. Don't worry, I don't mind being rejected, I'm used to it.'

'I didn't mean . . .'

'You can't possibly know what you *mean*. Only your id knows that.'

'My what?'

He explained about the ego, the id and the superego. It wasn't that hard to understand and I felt suddenly rather brainy.

'So there are these impulses I'm always keeping in check but they define what my real desires are? Is that what it's all about? I thought it was to do with having a complex and talking about your dreams.'

'You should pay attention to your dreams. That's how I found out about myself. Sybil, Sybil – she was a surrealist woman, she was like a figure in a dream – I want to dress you in a smoking jacket covered with shot glasses like Salvador Dali made for the window of Bonwit Teller.'

'Who's Salvador Dali?'

'A man who believes that his dreams are possible. Like me. Hands will come out and clutch you, your head will be a wing.'

'Or an anvil.'

'Or a hammer.'

'Or wool.'

'Or a musical note, a semi-quaver.'

'What are we talking about?'

'The absurdity of dreams.'

'Are they absurd?'

'Oh, yes, of course. You must believe that. You do promise me that you do?'

'I'll promise you anything.'

'Your lover? For one night?'

'No. Not that.'

'Tell me your dreams, Sybil.'

'You first.'

'No, I asked first. What about you? What makes you wake up in a sweat?'

'Well . . .'

'Come on, I'm dying to hear.'

I told him about the dance halls in Harlem and the men I'd danced with there and how I thought about them and what I wished for.

'Ooh. Now that does sound more sexy. You could go there on your own, to Harlem, while Stan is away.' I thought of the white women I'd seen in the dance halls and of what it might be like to join their shifting, marginal population. The idea terrified me. I only dipped my toe into the water's edge when Stan was with me, protecting me; it was a game I played with his connivance. Him watching me dancing with Negroes was part of our own sexual relationship. For each of us there was an Other whose shadow sat at the end of our bed. Morris was too young and inexperienced to understand any of this. Yet – why not? It was possible that I could step, for a moment, out of the binding of my sex by Stan's pale indolent body.

Fizz and the college set were together as usual, radiating cleanliness. She was now wearing her sparkler. Gold clawed a central diamond surrounded by amethysts. From this distance Ryan looked as if he was from impoverished, watered-down stock. Fizz was going to beef up the family line. She might have told him she was descended from good old English yeomen but I'd not have been surprised if there was closer Polack blood. If I was going to be charitable, I'd have said she had child-bearing hips. A sudden wave of hatred for them all came over me, followed by real nausea. I could have been part of all that if I'd had a proper start. They didn't know they were born.

'Just promise me one thing,' Morris was saying from very far away. 'I want to know *everything* tomorrow and I mean I want to hear it all.' His face was lit up with curiosity. He looked at me and saw a wing.

Chapter Nine

I went out that night. I went to 52nd Street. I would have gone
to Harlem, where I could have danced and where I would have
liked the music, but it seemed so far away, light years off at the
end of the subway line, while 52nd Street was not even much
of a distance from work. I didn't dress flashily. I wore a wool
skirt and a short, matching jacket and to its collar I pinned a
small brooch in the shape of a leaping jaguar. There were
plenty of women out at night alone, but none were going
where I was. I looked at the people around me on the subway
and for the first time I wondered about them. What jobs did
they do? What, for heaven's sake, were they thinking? I'd
never noticed old people before. This woman of, oh, say, fifty,
riding uptown in a cloth coat with a fur collar, a hat with a red
feather and ringless fingers, what kind of life would she have?

I couldn't guess. And here was a very old woman of maybe seventy with hands that might look like birds' feet beneath their gloves, her own swollen feet pushed into what could only have been crippling shoes. She too was riding uptown, dressed for an evening out. I calculated that she had been my age at the turn of the century when waists were small and bound with tight belts, and bosoms were trimmed and veils floated to the shoulders in that era when women were nothing but mystery. The woman in the red-feathered hat pulled out her compact and dabbed at her nose. She smoothed rouge on her cheeks. The compact was finely engraved gold and you could tell it was heavy in her hands. Who had given it to her? I could drive myself mad asking such questions.

At 14th Street two boys got on the train, one white, one Negro. The white one reminded me of Morris, pale hair standing out around his head like the fuzz on a duckling. The Negro was wasted. I recognized the look in his eyes. There were traces of blood on both their faces. The Negro clutched his buddy's arm. Everyone in the car was staring at them. 'I got it coming to me, man,' the Negro kept saying. 'I can't fault her for what she done.' He started crying.

'I should have said something,' the white boy said, and began to cry too.

'There was nothing you *could* have said.'

'Oh, Christ, it didn't need to turn out like this.'

'I know it, but . . .'

The Negro was sobbing now. I was sitting with my mouth open. He looked up at me and wiped his face on his sleeve. 'Your eyes got enough to eat?' he shouted. They both stopped their tears and took me in. I turned my head and saw that everyone was sitting unnaturally still, their eyes pasted to the opposite window. The white boy softened his voice. 'You want to come to a party, baby?' The Negro smiled. 'Come with us, little girl. We'll show you the town.' I was feeling the rails drag on the wheels, and the speed of the train diminishing and the lights of the approaching station flood the car. Someone shouted, '42nd, all change for Grand Central Station.' The boys stood when they saw their stop. The white boy grabbed my hand as they waited for the doors to open and pulled one of my fingers to his mouth and sucked it quickly. 'How did that taste?' the coloured boy was saying as the doors closed behind them. All of this was very fast, the space of two stations.

The woman in the red-feathered hat and the old lady turned to me after we pulled out. 'They belong in jail,' the older woman said. I nodded. I was only shocked, not upset. I could feel the palpitations. Now they were gone, it was kind of funny. 'Where I come from, we don't bother with jail,' Red Feather contributed, in a soft voice. 'The white boy might turn out not so bad after a spell in reform school, but the nigger needs teaching a real lesson.'

I looked back at her coldly. 'My boyfriend is a Negro,' I lied, and saw her face sharpen into an axe.

I rode the train a stop longer than I should, to 57th Street, and walked back five blocks. Nothing was going to stop me tonight, not that, at least not when I'd found a diner where I could, on the excuse of a cup of coffee, wash my hands. Life in New York had its risks and a couple of stoned kids weren't going to put me off. If they thought they had imprinted themselves on my skin they were wrong. It was their words that bothered me. What were they talking about? Who was 'she'? Wife, girlfriend, sister, mother? And of all three of them, who was it who was in danger?

The diner, which mainly served the lunchtime trade, closed

early and the waiter was standing around with his coat on as I finished my coffee. Most of the lights were off and the glass cabinets that usually displayed revolving pies seemed as empty as dark aquariums. The waiter polished the counter stools with his cloth and they span away into the silver night. The cash register was covered with a piece of sheeting. All the food was stowed somewhere, in the back in refrigerators.

'You going home, kid, or going out?' he asked me kindly. He was burly, in his forties, a few strands of hair slicked back over his head.

'I'm going out.'

'Where's your date?'

'I don't have a date. At least not tonight,' I added quickly.

He pulled himself alongside me on the bench seat. 'You shouldn't be out on your own. Bad things can happen to you.'

'I'll be OK.' I pushed a nickel tip towards his folded arms, outrageous for a cup of coffee. See, it said, winking up at him. I have money. I can look after myself. The cook, a Greek, came out of the kitchen with his coat on and sat down too.

'Come out with us,' he said. 'We take you home. You come and meet my momma and I make you dinner.'

I smiled at that. 'Do you live with your mother?'

'Of course I live with my momma. Come to our house and we'll feed you.'

'It's not what I had in mind for this evening.' They looked at me closely, examining my clothes and hair, and looked at each other. Later it occurred to me that they might have thought I was an expensive prostitute, or maybe not even that expensive. They ushered me into the street and tried to walk my way until I went down some subway steps, doubled back, and shook them off.

The street was choked with music. I went into a club Stan and I had been to before. The sound cracked out and wrapped itself around me, yanked me in from the door like a whip, like a lasso. Smoke stung my eyes before I had reached the bar. Standing with my drink I did not lack for attention. It was honey this and honey that, invitations to go out for some blow, to go back to a room, to go for a walk or go for a taxi ride. It was the first time I had felt the power of my looks, of my sex. I had always stumbled around oblivious, thinking only, as ever, of one man. Both Paul, the steward, and Marvin seemed to have conjured themselves up from nowhere. Tonight I kept count of my conquests, on my fingers, on my toes and when I had out-numbered them I began to tick them off against the bottles ranged against the back of the bar, which winked back at me in return. I was held there in my place, swaying slightly, smiling slightly, feeling alone and unfrightened, conscious only that here I was meant to *be* as the room turned and turned about me, and I could have anyone I chose, though I would choose to have no one at all.

This is how I met Julius.

'You reel them in then throw them back again, don't you?' he said in my ear.

'Pardon?'

'Why do you white girls come here to torment us poor coloured people? You get a kick from this?'

'No, it's not like that at all. I just came here for the music.'

'I've seen you here before, with your boyfriend. Where's he tonight?'

'He's gone to Washington, to work for a few days.' He was much taller than me. I had to stand on my toes to shout at his bent head.

'I know his kind of work. He's a dealer, am I right?'

I didn't know if there were Negroes in the police department. Maybe there were. 'No, you're mixing him up with
someone else. He's a baker, he's gone to Washington to work at
a party, a political party.'

'Which party?'

'I don't know who's holding it.'

'I mean the Democrats or the Republicans.'

'Oh, that. I've no idea. I don't think Stan has any interest in
politics.'

I'd made him smile but it didn't bring any warmth to his
eyes. 'And you? Are you interested in politics?'

'I don't know. I've never given it a moment's thought.'

'Do you work?'

'Yes, at Lord and Taylor.' I was still gauche enough to be
proud of this, status by association.

'You in the union?'

'I don't think so.'

'You don't even know if you're in the union?'

'I don't believe there is a union there.'

'There is at Macy's.'

'Oh well, *Macy's*.'

'What's that supposed to mean?'

'Haven't you ever heard the expression, I'd rather work in
Macy's basement? Meaning, I'd as close to rather being dead?'
This was a cake-walk, having a conversation with a Negro,
plenty of the cut and thrust and back-talk I was used to with
Stan.

'Yes, I know that. You have an easy life at Lord and Taylor?'

'Pretty easy. I work on the third floor. I sell haute couture
from Europe. The skill is in keeping up with what the designers

are doing in Paris and London. You need to be knowledgeable and advise the customer.'

'So you spend your life telling rich people what to wear, fat old rich people who don't have the taste to know what to wear for themselves.'

This struck me as very funny. Had the college set thought of that?

'You have an accent, don't you?'

'Yes, I'm English. From England.'

'I've been there, I went to England.'

'During the war?'

'Yes, during the war.'

I remembered trains pulling in at Lime Street, their contents who had come to save us pouring into pubs, spilling out on the streets on summer evenings. 'There were Negro GIs in Liverpool, where I grew up.'

'I was stationed near Liverpool. Burtonwood. You know it?'

'Yes.'

'I was glad to get sent to Liverpool.'

'Why?'

'I always wanted to see that place. It was where they shipped the slaves from. Did you know that?'

'No, I didn't.'

'What do they teach you in those schools over there in England?'

'Not that.'

'I'm going now. I have someone to meet. Want to walk to the subway with me?'

'I wasn't leaving.'

'Maybe you should.' So, as I had stepped into the Palm House with Stan when I was fourteen, now I turned and followed Julius into the street. He was going uptown, I was going downtown. We shook hands under skyscrapers that flared, his face lit by cabs which were moving lines of gold. He took something from his back pocket and handed it to me. It was a copy of a newspaper, the *Daily Worker*.

'What's this?'

'Read it some time.'

'Isn't this a communist paper? Is that what you are, a communist?'

'No, I just buy their paper. It makes sense to me, it might make sense to you.'

He ran down the steps of the subway, leaving me alone on the street. Where was the sex in any of that? He'd reeled me in and thrown me back.

'What's this shite?' Stan asked when he got home, throwing a wad of money on the table. Our room was spotless, the ashtrays washed, all his shirts laundered and hanging, colour-coded, in the closet. I had stood on a chair to take down the nicotine-brown drapes and poured boiling water on them. It was only the cold that beat us, our breath clouding the air, but the stove was on and its door open, letting a little heat out.

'It's a paper someone gave me. I haven't looked at it.'

'*Daily Worker*. I used to read that on the ships. They're worse than the government, that lot, they want to keep everyone in their place. Share everything out so nobody's got nothing. That's another mug's game.'

'I didn't buy it. Someone gave it to me. A man I met on 52nd Street.'

'What were you doing there?'

'I went the other night, on my own. Aren't I brave.' It was a statement, not a question.

Stan seemed bemused. All of New York, except the little acreage where I worked at Lord and Taylor, was *his* territory as Liverpool had been his, excepting the tiny spaces he allowed my parents to inhabit. For the first time I saw that he did not really believe I had an existence separate from himself. I had worked my way into becoming an extension of him, of the room, of his suits. He hung me in his closet, so to speak. And now I knew why he might come to accept that we would stay together, move out to a proper apartment and that if he did not get a job he might leave the old life of hustling. His *secret* life – he did not have that any more. But I did. I had a secret life.

On Christmas Day we ate out at a hotel. He dressed smartly, conservatively in a dark suit and an almost funereal tie. I wore one of Hattie Carnegie's little black dresses. I took only one course, watching my figure. Stan drank brandy after the meal and smoked a cigar.

'A sort of celebration?' I asked.

'Your manicure's got a chip.'

I had started to think of experimenting with a lighter shade of nail polish, one which did not show the wear and tear as did this fire-truck red I had on at the moment, which tended to age my hands, making them look like talons.

'What will we do for New Year's Eve?'

'I've been meaning to talk to you about that. The hotel in Washington has asked me back. I'd need to go up on the thirtieth. I'd get done by the evening on the thirty-first but it's an all-night job. I'd be pretty knackered. They're laying on a bus for us the next morning. I'd be back before evening on New Year's Day. What do you think?'

I was amazed that he'd consulted me. 'Same pay?'

'Yeah, same rate.'

'We could move?'

'We could think about it.'

'Then you should go.'

'What will you do?'

'Would you mind if I went back to the club?'

'Yes, I would mind.'

'Then I won't go.'

But when New Year's Eve came and the hour drew on to nine and then ten and I thought of the revellers in Times Square, I put on a cheap little party dress under my musquash jacket, the most unostentatious of my furs, went to the door, came back, put on the little jaguar brooch, went to the door again then turned with my keys still in my hand and walked into the bathroom and took something from its little case and pushed it inside me and then finally I left. And the direction of the traffic urged me on, further north, block after block until I came to 52nd Street and once again the whip cracked and the music drew me in.

He was there, Julius.

'Did you read the paper I gave you?'

'No. My boyfriend said . . .' I offered him Stan's observations on politics.

'Your boyfriend sees himself as a rebel. He likes to kick against it. But there's nothing up in his head. He doesn't know what he's kicking against. He doesn't *have* anything to kick against.'

'I don't think that's true. He comes from a poor family. He's not even properly white, you know, his grandfather came from India.'

'But white enough, he passes.'

'Yes, he does pass.'

'But now he wants to be a phoney Negro like the other white boys here, talking jive, trying to be a hipster.'

'You don't talk like that.'

'No. I don't.'

'What did you do in the war?'

'I was there.'

'Where?'

'Europe.'

'I had relatives in Europe that were killed, on my father's side. In Yugoslavia.' I did not normally speak of these misfortunes for fear that more would be asked, more demanded. But he didn't seem interested. He changed the subject, spectacularly.

'I like that little dress you have on. And that's a fine piece of jewellery.' He reached over and fingered my leaping jaguar. Now it was real, now those brown fingers were on my skin and I was afraid and excited. My head felt like a heavy wing that had started to beat the air and a bluster was blowing around me.

'You're very pretty, but you know that.'

'I suppose I do, but I don't have much luck in romance.'

'What about that boyfriend? Are you going to marry him?'

'I don't know. I don't know if he wants to.'

'He's a loser. He's got it written all over him. He's going nowhere. He came to mind the other day. Have you ever thought he might be a queer?'

My glass was empty. My eyes were stinging from the smoke and my skin was slippery and sweating. 'What makes you think you're a winner?'

'Oh, I am. That much I know.' He tapped his head. 'I think, you see. That's what pulls you up front, whatever they do to you at the starting gate.'

'What do you think about?'

'Do you want to come some place and I'll tell you?' I did, yes. I wanted to. What did I think I was doing? I thought I was being bold and modern. How did I feel about it? Panicky, like I was being kidnapped but I'd fallen in with my abductors, they'd made me their friend. We rode the bus uptown, careful not to touch, not talking. His clothes were shabby and didn't fit properly. They looked as if they had been bought for a younger, smaller man. He seemed to be uneasy out of uniform, for he had the rigid back and authoritarian stride of the recently discharged serviceman. And his hair was not processed but short and nappy. 'Like a home boy just got into town,' he said, when I asked him about it. Since we met he had hardly smiled, not even when he touched my little silver and jet jaguar and his hand accidentally? – brushed against my breast. I saw then that his fingernails were manicured and carefully clipped, unlike Stan's which were left to grow until someone noticed them and he became embarrassed, hiding them in his pockets or behind his back, when I would cut them with clippers I bought specially for him from Woolworth's and massage cream into his calluses when I thought he wasn't looking.

I liked the width of Julius's shoulders, I liked the size of him. I liked it that there was nothing evasive in his sex. I liked his colour.

I saw how as we got higher and higher in the island the white people got off and the black people got on, until we reached the line Central Park drew above the city and I was the only white person left riding that bus. It wasn't midnight yet but everyone was drunk, even the women in their stoles and jewels who stood in the centre of the street in front of the oncoming traffic, flagging down prowl cars and shimmying their hips to an invisible band.

His apartment was better than ours, less tidy but more like a home. It had what ours hadn't, books, newspapers. Photos of people smiling against a background of fields or lazing in back-yards. A framed military citation hung on the wall.

'It's homely here,' I said.

'Homely like an ugly woman?'

'No, homely like home.'

'As long as I have my own coffee pot, I've got a home.' I thought he would offer me a drink or some weed but he didn't; he made two cups of coffee. When he went to the refrigerator for a bottle of milk I looked past his arm and saw that it was full of food – cheese, eggs in a bowl, chops, an opened can of peaches, a blue jug that had the word cream written on it, a plate covered with wax paper. He turned round. 'You want something? You want to eat?'

'No, no thanks. Nothing for me.' Dimly, I thought that I was hungry and that I had a sour taste in my mouth. I'd eaten noth-ing since lunchtime. Stan usually brought up the idea of food before I did and when he wasn't there I forgot about it.

'I think you should have something anyway.' He pulled the plate from the refrigerator and took a jelly donut from it and put that on a smaller plate. 'Here.' He pushed it towards me. I'd been holding my purse tightly on my lap like a small shield designed for the protection of ladies. I had to put it down to take the plate. I took a bite from the donut and now there was sugar round my mouth. Crystals fell to the carpet and his eyes followed them. 'I'll get that later,' he said. He was sitting opposite me, in an easy chair, while I sat strategically on the couch, allowing him the option to make a move.

'Do you hate white people?' I asked. 'For what they've done to you?'

'I think they're weird.'

'Do you think I'm weird?'

'I don't know yet.'

Julius installed air conditioning, though ironically he couldn't afford to have a machine himself. He thought he might be the only Negro in New York to have that qualification. He saw into the heart of white people's lives and he judged them. He told me a story of how he'd put a unit into a man's apartment who had called him back a week or two later to tell him that he had a woman friend who was also interested in air conditioning. The man gave Julius the number and told him he should call her. He did call a few times. She wasn't there. Or he woke her out of sleep and she said she would call him back, but she never did. Then one hot night when he was in the shower he heard the phone ring. It rang and rang before he reached it. The man said that he was over at the woman's apartment and she'd decided. She wanted Julius to come over right away; at least he could make a start.

Julius did not rush to get dressed. The man called several times while he was getting ready. He took the bus from St Nicholas Avenue where he lived, way up in the hundreds, downtown to Murray Hill ('where you work'). The doorman sent him up to her apartment. The man opened the door. Inside he could see the woman naked on a couch, bruised and bleeding. She had only just taken a terrible beating. What happened here? he asked. Do you want me to call the police? I hit her, the man told him. She's no good, she's a tramp. Julius swung at him. He told the woman to grab her clothes and run but she didn't move. She just sat there, watching Julius beat the living daylights out of her boyfriend, beat his white face and kick in his lilywhite head until blood oozed from his nose and he lay on the floor panting, not moving.

Then Julius felt badly afraid and he ran. They had his phone number and he knew the police would be waiting for him when he got home. He walked the streets that night and all next morning until he found a bar in the Village and alone and exhausted, blurted out that strangest of stories to the bartender.

But the bartender had heard a similar tale before. He told Julius he thought he had been set up. That the pair were perverts, into sadomasochism, and that he had been used to provide the man with a beating his girlfriend's weak fists could not have given him in return for her own.

'So what do you think of that?' he asked. 'What white people do. Are they all there?' He tapped his head.

'I've never heard anything like that in my life before. I don't know what to think.'

'But is it right or wrong? Do you know the difference?' He took his coffee cup for the first time and drained the contents in one swallow, like a glass of beer.

'I don't know. I think I do.'

'What did your parents teach you?'

I tried to remember. Those Saturday lunchtimes came back, the taste of whisky, the weight of cut glass, the back of my father's clipped neck as he leaned towards the bottle, the smell of wet fur quietly drying on a satin hanger in the hall. 'My father taught me that I was born an animal and my job was to turn myself into a human being.'

'Your father said that?'

'Yes.'

'I don't think you've done what he told you, have you? I don't see you as a human being at all.'

'So what do you see?' I thought of the pictures Stan had taken of me while I was sleeping.

'Some kind of monkey, maybe, the organ grinder's monkey all dressed up.'

'You're very rude.'

'Do you think so?'

'Yes.'

'So that's what you think about. About a rude nigger.'

'You're just . . .'

'Yes?'

'This isn't fair.'

'Oh, OK, not fair. So you have a sense of justice?'

'I don't . . .'

'What are you?'

'What do you mean?'

'What are you doing here?'

'You invited me. I thought . . .'

'All this thinking you say you do.' He took a packet of cigarettes from his shirt pocket and pointed at it. 'Do you want a smoke?'

'Yes, please.' I had my own pack in my purse but I was too nervous to get it. Anything here could be a wrong move.

He took two out and passed one to me, not standing, just extending his long arm. His cuff was frayed. He lit his own, not holding it between his lips but clenched lightly in his teeth. He didn't light mine. I sat there with it in my fingers. He looked at it. 'You need a light?'

'Yes, obviously.'

He came over and clicked his lighter then returned to his chair. We both smoked in silence.

'So, let's hear it. What do you think about?'

I thought about myself a great deal. I was absorbed in that very interesting topic. I thought about Stan, trying to figure him out, watching his moves, trying to second-guess the next one. Only by thinking myself *into* Stan could I have what I wanted from him and that meant he sort of absorbed me, like moisture coming into his skin, my own essence always depleting. Why was I here? Well, partly to make it in Stan's world on my own terms so I would become more a part of him, not less. But I didn't want to talk about Stan. And I did have a thought, if you could call it that: 'Well, what I'm going to wear, what I'll eat. And . . .'

'Yes, and?'

'Who I'll sleep with tonight.'

'You want to sleep with me?' His expression hadn't changed. No slow leer, no movement towards me. I was going to have to sweat this one out on my own.

'Yes. I do.' It was ridiculous us talking like this. He was yards across the room.

'Where's your boyfriend?' The lover or the loved one, who sins the most? My heart was pure, it was Stan's that was full of deceit and evasion. So I reasoned.

'He's in Washington again. He won't be back until tomorrow.'

'You don't care that you're cheating on him?'

I smiled, I hoped seductively, smiled at him through my lipstick. 'Do *you* care?'

'No, I don't care. You'll reel me in then throw me back, is that the way it goes?'

'Yes, that's about it.' There was a little flurry of triumph in my chest as I assented.

'So you want me to fuck you.'

'Yes. I want to . . . fuck.' I'd finished my cigarette and stabbed it out with too much energy in my fingers. The paper on the stub split and crumbs of tobacco fell into the ashtray at my feet.

'So you can say you've made it with a nigger.'

'You can think that if you want. I can't stop you, but it isn't true.'

'You're just curious?'

'Yes, I suppose I am curious, it's true. But it's more than that. My boyfriend isn't . . . He lacks *drive* sometimes.'

'I got him, didn't I?' he suddenly shouted. 'Got him in one.' Then he lowered his voice to a whisper. 'Just an old stud, that's me, out in a field servicing the hot little mares whose own stallions can't give them any action.'

I blushed. This was too coarse for me. 'If you don't want to, I'll go.'

'Maybe you should go.'

'I'll get my coat. Will you come out in the street with me and find me a cab?'

He didn't get up. I stood at the door, pinning my hat to my hair. All this banter, this back and forth, it didn't mean anything. When you have looks, you find that out. Either they want you or they don't and he wouldn't have brought me back there if he hadn't known what was bound to follow. Later, when I knew his pride better, I saw that the balance could easily have tipped the other way that night. But I had been wise and didn't answer back and so he saw me as a blank sheet of paper he could write on and fill out all his thoughts that ranged so far beyond what he could possibly know or imagine. He was an arrogant young man and he had a hunch that *he* could make me human. So he came over to me and took my hand and pulled me towards the bedroom and in I went: in heat, in joy, in triumph, with no idea where sex was going to lead me.

Oh, yes, he did have the 'drive' Stan lacked. He pulled me on top of him and I rode through the night. He looked at my body as if he was memorizing it and I did the same with his. Sex went on for hours, without languor. He didn't speak once while we were doing it. Stan and I would giggle and lark about and, because we were often stoned, would sometimes fall asleep in the middle or get up and have something to eat. 'That was fine,' Julius said afterwards. 'You needed that, didn't you? I know *I* needed it.'

I lay awake the next morning thinking about what I'd done, trying to recall the unfamiliar room's dimensions and track my exit from it. I could smell the ashtray on the bedside table and when I moved I felt his sperm trickling down inside me. I wanted badly to wash but I did not want to stay. Julius seemed to be a very heavy sleeper, unlike Stan who stirred if I touched him. His big shoulders heaved and he snored. Now it was over, I felt alone and desperate, not sorry for what I'd done but bereft of it, like that downer Stan sometimes got after taking certain pills. The bedroom was so full of stuff, Julius's stuff, it didn't need me there, it wanted me to go.

I left while he was still sleeping as I knew a man leaves a woman. It was eight a.m. on New Year's Day, 1947. I rode the bus downtown through empty streets smelling his special smell on my skin and on my clothes. The closer I got to home the happier I felt. 'Just the once was enough,' I thought. I got off

the bus and I saw my dishevelled reflection in the mirror of a
truck and smiled at it. I stood on tiptoe and freshened my lipstick. By the time I reached the meat district I had forgotten all
about Julius. I bought an issue of *Life* magazine at a news stand
and looked at the pictures as I walked up the street home. The
Chinese laundry opposite our apartment was open and I passed
through a white cloud of steam and cleanness that billowed
through the door keeping that few feet of store frontage free of
the slicks of dried blood and crumbs of raw flesh that stained
the rest of the sidewalk. The meat labourers were already at
work. In the winter they were frisky, holding snowball fights
and stuffing cows' tails down each other's pants. Most of them
were hung over this morning but an Italian was waving around
a pig's tongue on a stick. He called out to me in his own language, which I didn't understand. I waved back and laughed,
dodging a snowball, caught in the crossfire. 'Wait, *bella*,' he
shouted. 'Wait, wait.' He ran inside and returned with a brown-
paper package. I looked in it and there was a slab of raw liver
and something covered with fat and veins. '*Fegato*,' he said,
pointing to the liver. 'And this is heart.' I thanked him and
shook his bloody hand. He made to kiss me on the cheek but I
turned slightly, and it landed clumsily on the left-hand side of
my mouth. He smelled of blood and sweat and spunk.

   I climbed the three flights of stairs. Something was wrong.
The apartment door was swinging. The light was on. Two of
Stan's five suits were missing from the closet together with
most of his shirts and a few of his ties. His suitcase under the
bed was gone. The box of photographs he had taken of me
weren't there. Neither was his camera. There was no sign of the
picture of Dixie Dean. I felt I'd had a great blow to the back of
my head which had loosened my brain from its pan and thrown

it back in a jumble of confusion, grief, disbelief, fear. I was a nothing, moving through the room, turning over the mattress, looking on shelves for anything he had left behind and that I had missed. I lay down, a little nothing, and trembled myself into even more nothing. There was nothing there. I was too frightened to look at myself in the mirror. I knew I'd vanished. My throat and nose were too dry for me to cry. I got up and pulled the dark tan suit from the closet, still on its hanger, and draped it carefully on top of me as if he were in it and we were making love, him still dressed. After many hours I put his empty suit to lie down beside me, where together we passed the long, long night.

The next night I slept with another of Stan's suits and I dreamed I was sitting on an unanchored rock in the middle of the Atlantic Ocean and it was so cold I sang to keep myself warm. The fish that swam had fur instead of scales, it was that cold. Stan and Julius were ships which sailed back and forth on a sea that was full of vessels which could never land, and none of them stopped. None of them came near my rock and lowered a lifeboat to take me up into the warmth. My rock drifted past Newfoundland, past Montreal with its lights shimmering through the ice-haze, but still my rock floated along, sometimes bumping into icebergs or hearing the laughter of a great transatlantic liner in the form of my mother and father dwindle in the fog.

I looked for him for two months.

I traced another cook through the Algonquin. He said that Stan had arrived in Washington on the thirtieth with the rest of them. Some time in the afternoon the next day he had gone out for a smoke. The cook said he had heard two men talking to him. Stan had come back into the kitchen, taken off his apron, hung it up, put on his coat and his hat, picked up his bag of overnight things and left. He hadn't come back. That was the last he had seen of him. Stan had said nothing to anyone in the kitchens before he went – anyway, they were working flat out, too busy to notice.

I sent a note to the matinée idol, backstage at a show. He sent a message to me at work and I met him one lunchtime at a coffee shop off Broadway.

He called Stan a greasy little chiseller, he called him all sorts.

But he put me on to an old flame, a banker, at whose party he had first met Stan. He was a middle-aged man, gravity was affecting him. His eyes and his jowls were falling. His suit was very, very good and he smelled of something discreet and expensive. He didn't remind me of my father but it was like being with him. The smell of his cloth soothed me. He would only meet me out in the open, where he could pretend he'd just started chatting to a stranger, and so we sat in Central Park in the blistering cold on a bench watching the skaters twirl and pirouette on the newly frozen surface of the lake while the snow lay fresh upon the trees all around us.

He remembered Stan when he came first to New York in 1940, a sweet boy, an innocent boy, he thought, though I found that hard to believe. 'He did have a sweetness about him. Didn't you see it?' He looked at me, sitting beside him, shivering in my mink. 'Women miss that in a man. Maybe it was all those women who brought him up – his mother, his grandmother, his sister. Did you know his family?'

'I met the sister once. She was a lot older than him.'

'Yes, he often said he felt he had three mothers. He needed

men in his life, that's why he went to sea. He was looking for an older man. I don't think he really was homosexual. He just had a need, an emotional need, that only an older man could fill. He talked a lot about sex but he didn't *do* much. He wanted to be petted, that was the main thing. He wanted someone he could show that vulnerability to. Did he tell you about his time during the war?'

'I knew he was torpedoed.'

'He'd had a hard time at sea when he was younger, always sick, getting diseases on shore and not knowing how to avoid them, let alone cure them. But he had a terrible time, an awful time, on the convoys. Women have no idea what men suffer and men never tell them. I was in the cavalry in the first war; I know.'

He looked at me. I was crying, not for Stan and his ordeal but for myself. He patted my knee once or twice. 'Were you going to get married?'

'I thought we might. He was making a lot of money over the holidays and I wanted to move us into a bigger apartment.'

'Money he made from narcotics?'

'No. Proper work, in the kitchens at a big party in Washington.'

'He was always hanging out with niggers. I don't know why.'

'Stan would never use that word.'

'Oh, he had this idea about them, he made them out to be more than what they were. It was all about the Atlantic and how it was a sea they were all made to sail and the kind of traffic it carried: spices, slaves, that kind of thing. The niggers didn't like him, though. They knew what he was really about. They never could stand him touching them, though they were wrong there. He would have married you. You were the ground under his feet. He told me that. But do you know something?'

His hat had been on his lap; now he put it on. 'The ground is what sailors fear the most. It's only the land that can wreck a ship. Do you belong at land or on the sea? Now, looking at you, I think I know. You're a surfer, aren't you? You like to roll in on the big waves that crash on the beach, you belong in the shallows. Neither the land nor the sea, neither fish nor beast.'

He got to his feet. 'I hope you find him. If you do, let me know. I'd like to see him again, though he won't let me suck his cock any more.'

And this. 'Was he the guy with a kid by a coloured woman in Tryon Park? I don't know, it might have been him.'

Chapter Ten

In the early spring Julius took me in and made it his mission to turn me into a human being, a fully paid-up member of the human race. I sensed that there had been another woman living there, not long before, for sometimes I found, in unnoticed corners, small pools of scented face-powder or a clip or a comb. I had learned from Stan not to be jealous, never to enquire, but I did not make the mistake, this time, of allowing Julius to be mysterious; about the other woman, I would find out in due course, for I wanted to know everything about him, to devour his history.

Our life together was uncomplicated. Only in bed were we on equal terms, equally demanding. We met in bed, outside it we were strangers. Dressed, I was diminished in his eyes and my own. He talked, I listened. He told me his story all in one go, one Saturday night, until three or four in the morning, smoking and talking, smoking and talking, as I listened in astonishment. That night was to be a turning point in my life, for it put into place much that would later come to be defining characteristics of my 'philosophy', and it prepared the ground for almost everything that was to follow. I had to ask many questions, but in its essence it was this way with Julius. He was one of those disillusioned Negroes who had returned home from the war to find that nothing had changed in America. He was born in Chicago, where his father worked on and off in bars and speakeasies washing glasses and mopping floors, occasionally doing errands for Negro mobsters. The father, he said, hated the sight of books. He tore up Bibles when he could find them, cursing the Scriptures. The house was godless, thoughtless, and the children were treated with cold contempt whenever they spoke, or laughed, or played.

The mother was very young when she married, barely fifteen, and her husband was twenty-five years older. According to the only photograph of her Julius had ever seen, taken when she was thirteen and just on the verge of stopping being a child, she was destined to be exceptionally pretty and the father had spotted and chosen her. She cried when he told her a wedding picture was a waste of money. Then she became good at holding her tongue and the marriage lasted, even prospered. But after a number of years she fell foul of the law in one of the countless accidental ways that, it was explained to me, beset poor people. What? It could have been a misunderstanding over a bill in a store, or a bar of candy transported through the door by one of her children, unpaid for. It might have been nothing more significant than a wrong kind of look. But she went to jail and when she came out she finally found her voice.

From then on she turned her back on her family. Julius last saw her when he was ten and she would have been about thirty-five but looking, he said, about a hundred, her cloche hat with a purple imitation silk flower pinned to it all askew on her head, bawling loudly in the streets of the city, running up to men in smart suits with high collars and derby hats, pulling her dress down over her bosom and exposing her unbound breasts.

There were five children, and Julius's father did what he could to raise them but it was a silent, sullen household and they knew little but fear, and outside it they ran wild. The oldest were the three girls who fell pregnant and married as young as their mother had done. Where were they now? I wanted to know. They disappeared into the oblivion of poverty and hunger at the beginning of the Depression. Julius remembered that the middle sister, Priscilla, had once entered a competition on the back of a can of beans and won a paintbox. The box was the marvel of the street and she achieved a kind of stardom whose light reflected on her brothers and sisters.

'She never used that paintbox,' he said. 'She kept it wrapped up in newspaper and buried deep down among her smalls, and sometimes I used to get my hand in there because I wanted a good look at that paintbox with all these weird names like Prussian blue and indigo that I couldn't make out. I got a thrashing when my father found me – he thought I was trying to get my hands in her panties.' He smiled at this and I was, for a moment, radiated by the little warmth. 'So. When she got married she took the paintbox with her to her new home and one day, while her husband was out working, I guess she had the urge to paint a picture. Except I bet what she turned out wasn't a picture, I bet it was a mess. There are no artists in my family.

'When her husband came home he found the table all wet and blotched by colours and paint water was dripping over the sides. There was no dinner cooking and, Jesus, that made him mad. He took the metal box and cracked it over my sister's head, with all those little squares of paint rattling around and falling out of the tin and scattered all over the floor, under the stove and down through cracks in the floorboards. Then he put the empty box in the garbage, snapped the brush in two and hit her across the face.' I saw that Julius was unconsciously clenching his fists as he came to this awful climax, but who his anger was directed at I could not tell. Was it a desire by a kid brother for revenge against a man who had hurt his kin? Or a rage against useless women?

The two boys, Julius and his brother Julian, were vicious creatures by Julius's own admission, stealing whenever they could, dreaming of becoming real mobsters, saving what they made to buy a gun which they planned to share between them, to start their business as serious hoodlums. Julius said he loved the gun and spent hours taking it apart, polishing the metal pieces and reassembling it. This insight frightened me. Throughout the whole of the war I had never seen a weapon, apart, of course, from various undetonated bombs that some-times fell harmlessly into someone's back garden and had to be dismantled by the army. Outside the movies I had no experi-ence of physical violence. But Julius said he liked mechanical things. His brain understood them. Like the paintbox, their gun was kept in a drawer for best. They fancied themselves as contract killers and the bosses they most wanted to serve were not other Negroes but white men in grand cars with peroxide blondes who resembled Jean Harlow beside them. They went to all the gangster movies of those days and this connection enabled me to see where he had been. I glimpsed them for a moment in my mind's eye, strutting through the ghetto, their hats pulled forward shading their unlined teenage faces.

White mobsters did use them. 'They saw us as expendable niggers whose lives weren't worth the matches they used to light their cigars,' Julius said. The brothers took terrible beatings and in a strange way, he admitted, they even relished them. They stopped believing that they would make it as mob bosses in their own right and came to feel that their lives would be short, violent but glamorous.

His brother died in the dark night, clumsily, falling through the rotten stair treads of a brothel and breaking his neck at seventeen. Julius thought he had to die his death all over again for him, he had to die twice, but this time in a blaze of gunshot wounds in full daylight, on the steps of City Hall. In reality, he said he now realized, there was little chance of it. He wasn't important enough to merit such a killing. He went on stealing, menacing small shopkeepers, getting beaten by other gangs' errand boys, always called the nigger kid by the people who paid him.

Then one day he went into a barber's shop. 'I had this knife lying warm and comfortable and snug in the waistband of my pants. When I stood at the door looking hard and menacing, the barber laughed at me. I pulled the knife and the barber looked at it. And then the barber said this.

'He said, "What are you doing? What are you doing and why are you doing it? Take your time. Think about it before you answer."

'Christ, nothing had ever surprised me so much in my life. In truth I had nothing to say to either of the questions but the biggest surprise was that I'd been asked. All my life I had been yelled at and now I was being required to take part in a *conversation*.

'It was like time had slowed down. I remember staring down at the haircuttings on the floor, at the photographs on the walls of Macassared heads, gleaming like they were patent leather. I took in the customers lined up in chairs waiting for their haircuts. I saw boys my own age and grown men, fathers and sons together. I could smell and distinguish each of the many preparations a barber uses to straighten and dress a Negro's hair. I felt paralysed, the haft of the knife was growing colder between my fingers. I just wanted to die there and then.'

I shifted about in my chair, hoping that I understood but knowing I didn't. I wanted to cross the room and take his hand but I sensed it was the wrong moment to do so. Yet he kept *looking* at me as he told this story. This was not just an act of remembering. He wanted me to know. This was part of my education.

He walked out of the shop but returned a week or two later to have his hair conked and cut. As he felt the lye burn into his scalp, he told the barber that he had been thinking, or trying to but nothing came. No thoughts at all. In his head he saw Jimmy Cagney's face snarling at him from the movie screen. He saw his brother's body lying beneath broken balustrades.

The barber told him there was someone he wanted Julius to meet. She was a woman in her fifties then, the grand-daughter of one of the great orators of Negro emancipation from the previous century, and every Wednesday night she gathered together in her house the best and the brightest of the local Negro community. For the first time Julius came into the home of a well-to-do Negro. I wanted to know what it was like, I wanted all the details about the interior decor. This was hard for him but eventually he described to me a circle of men (and a handful of women) sitting in a pool of undulant muted light cast by innumerable shaded lamps, their silk fringes disturbed by the air from an overhead fan. There were dried grasses in vases in the empty fireplace and above them, on the mantel-piece, a clutter of porcelain figures – imported from England, he thought ('Wedgwood?' he asked. 'Does that mean anything to you?') – depicting coloured children holding fishing rods or wearing strange, old-fashioned clothes and bearing small trays, importantly. The whole house smelt not of old food or the sourness of dirt, but scented by things he could not name. The drapes, on this summer evening, were still open and beyond the windows he could see a garden and the dark forms of cats pass-ing and re-passing across the lawns. Tobacco plants were growing in pots on the porch and their perfume made him feel dizzy. He said he broke out in a sweat and felt the knife in his waistband begin to slither down his leg.

Some of the people there that night were so prominent, even he had heard of them: doctors and lawyers and professors, one or two actors from the Negro movies he rarely bothered to see. The other guests were introduced: he's a painter, she's a poet, this man is an intellectual, and he was dazzled. Later he found out that the painter was a sleeping-car attendant, the poet a cook and the intellectual a hod-carrier. But *here* they were somebody, they were what they really were.

A maid, dressed in a real maid's uniform, brought in coffee and pie. On the very edge of his consciousness Julius knew of the Garveyites and their plans for everyone to return to Africa, and of the communists who wanted to redistribute all the money so everyone had fair shares. In Chicago he had walked past picket lines, had petitions thrust into his hand to sign. But he was too angry to hear them or read, lost in death's romance.

Now he stopped daydreaming and the claustrophobia lifted. In the woman's house he discovered ideas. 'Looking back, I can only see myself then as an animal, an inhuman savage creature roaming the city, a danger to myself and everyone else. But now ideas intoxicated me. The people there wanted to know all about me and they listened to what I said. My life felt as if it had been seen and acknowledged. At first I thought I might be an artist of some kind myself, but like my sister before me I found out I had *no* talent, none whatsoever. Whether I wrote or painted, I just made messes. I don't have an eye,' he said. 'I see that you have an eye. But I don't.'

The woman noticed during their weekly discussions that his brain had a recognizable logic. It followed lines of argument; it reasoned. She had it in mind to send him back to school and perhaps even put him through college. 'I think you could be a scientist,' she told him.

They talked on through the summer that he turned seventeen. 'I learned of Plato, Aristotle and Spinoza,' he said, ticking them off on his fingers. 'I read through speeches from plays by William Shakespeare. I learned about gravity and the positions of the planets, about hypotheses and empirical methods, the speed sound travels at and the speed of light. I committed to memory the periodic table. Do you know that?' I shook my head.

He worked his way through much of Dickens, then Engels and *The Ragged Trouser'd Philanthropist*. He learned, for the first time, of W. E. B. DuBois and of Richard Wright and Langston Hughes. Finally, as his mentor always knew he would, he came to Marx and Lenin. Through words and language, Julius told me, he discovered a life in which he could become bigger than himself, a life bigger than he had ever known existed. 'I looked around and I saw patterns. I understood for the first time that my pain was not only inside me, but in the world, that it connected me to all the others who felt the same pain and, most important, that it has a name and it's a condition of the way things are ordered.' The death wish lifted and left him, though the hurt stayed – it even grew, but now he put it into the harness of his anger and it was under his command and had a direction. He felt he was an historical entity, living through history.

As for me, I barely knew what Julius was talking about, but I did not forget his story and it would come to mean more to me when my own little soul, as shrivelled and as dehydrated as a dried pea, began to sprout and shoot.

When the war began he enlisted but he had to wait for one of the segregated units to form. Over in Berlin he saw right through the American political system, saw it for what it was. Every day in his jeep he rode past the Soviet sector and looked at it. He wanted to talk to fellow soldiers in the Red Army but they had no cornmon language.

He did not return to Chicago, though he wrote fitfully to the woman who had opened his head as if she was an old-fashioned surgeon letting light into the darkness of his cranium. Now he only half believed that at the war's end, having defeated injustice on foreign soil, having freed the Jews from their terrible slavery, Americans would come home and see their own country differently and the old evils would be removed. 'Denying Negroes their rights and keeping the African people in the slavery of colonialism is the same argument as fascism – the exaltation of a Master Race,' he said. I nodded, on more familiar ground. Discharged from the service in New York, he stayed and waited and watched but nothing happened. He could have taken advantage of the GI Bill and gone to college, but the woman had made him arrogant. The Ivy League schools would never have accepted him and he thought the Negro universities were second rate.

He saw that the demobilized white GIs took all the best jobs for themselves, leaving the Negroes with the shit they had had before the war began. 'I saw that we still couldn't vote in some places but we'd bought war bonds. We couldn't get jobs, yet we'd played our part, salvaging paper and metal and fats. We'd faced the Ku Klux Klan at home then gone off to die to free the Jews. When are we going to free ourselves, Sybil? When will *we* be free?'

I sat in stunned silence. I thought of my father's sermons about when we were slaves in the land of Egypt. I understood! I understood!

In the year after the war ended, he told me, my own first year in America, when I idled on Fifth Avenue or lay in a doped stupor in Greenwich Village, there was a new reign of terror in the South aimed at the uppity Negro veteran – a lynching in Georgia, a police riot against Negroes in Tennessee, a vicious beating of a Negro soldier at the hands of a police chief in South Carolina which Truman had done nothing to prevent or punish. 'If the President can call out the Army and Navy to stop the striking railroad workers and the maritime workers' – but I had finished his sentence for him – 'why couldn't he unleash troops to stop the lynchers?'

'*Yes!*' he cried in triumph. 'You've got it.'

He jumped from his chair and pulled me to him. 'The monkey's interrupting the organ grinder.' Daylight was coming to Harlem. It all made sense. I understood. 'You're crossing the Red Sea,' I said and he, who remembered as little of the Scriptures as I did myself, knew what I meant. We went to bed and I received my earthly reward.

He found in be-bop something I could not hear, though I caught it sometimes, out of the corner of my eye. It was a hard, unromantic music with a cold metal heart, a pure, cerebral sound, which gave its musicians a freedom to go anywhere, do anything, be anyone they liked. It took them to the stars.

He wanted me to dress as plainly as possible. He couldn't see the sense in fashion. But there again, he liked the way I had what he called 'class'. Like many Negroes of his generation, he believed that Europeans were more sophisticated, more lib-eral, that they belonged to an older and wiser society to which it was possible to escape from the mindset of American racism. We were walking past a store once which had an illuminated globe in its window. 'Look, Sybil,' he said. 'See the Mediterranean? See the countries that are all around it? See that one at the bottom? That's Africa. See how close Italy and Greece are. Spain nearly touches it. Europe and Africa are that close, just separated by one little sea.'

I still lived with an ache I couldn't speak of. Before, I had dreamed of Julius, now I dreamed of Stan. In this dream I was always at some starting place, somewhere familiar like our old apartment or the store, when someone came up and told me where I could find him. I would set off, following the directions I had been given as the city grew less and less familiar and then I was lost. Stan never appeared, nor could I ever find my way back to the beginning. I would wake, sweating heavily, and reach out to touch Julius, sleeping beside me. Sometimes he would wake up too. 'Are you having that old dream?' he would ask. 'You'll never find him. You don't need to find him.'

But if Stan had sometimes vanished for days on end, when he returned he made up for it. Julius was always there but he would ignore me for hours. I would say something to him and it was as if I wasn't in the room; I was the nothing I'd felt myself to be the night Stan left. He would sit in his easy chair reading books, his big back bent over them and the bottle of ink he always kept beside him very blue when the sun reached through the smeared windows and caught it, dazzling me with indigo so intense it seemed like a scent. He used an old-fashioned dip pen, the kind they hand out in schools when you graduate from pencil, and with it in his hand he *talked* to those books, telling the margins all his secrets.

I had nothing to do. I didn't sew, couldn't cook. He frowned when I brought home a magazine and after I'd looked through it I found it next morning in the garbage, the faces of the movie stars peering through coffee grounds and egg shells.

I wanted to try a new style of make-up but when I took out my vanity case and looked at myself in its inset mirror he put down his book and lay it in his lap. 'Isn't the bathroom the right room for fixing yourself up? Anyway, we're not going any place, are we?'

No, but I was going mad with boredom. I spent an evening or two a week with Morris of whom Julius disapproved more than he did of Stan. 'Another fag friend,' he called him. I'd go over to Morris's place after work when it was his day off and he'd spent hours the night before simmering bones for that evening's chilled consommé, swirled with cream and sherry and decorated with parsley.

'What's the difference between parsley and pussy?' he asked as I put in my spoon.

'Don't know.'

'You don't eat parsley.' It took me until mid-afternoon the following day to get the joke. Julius was far too uptight to go down on me.

Then, when we had shared a Babe Ruth for dessert, which he cut into bite-sized sections, he played the violin so sweetly I thought my heart would break watching him standing there so young and fair, the little linen cloth draped over the shoulder of his violet shirt on which his fiddle rested. And all his music was directed at the door always held ajar in the hope of a certain knock, for he played half turned away from me and I knew that the honoured place was empty at his feast. He said he loved me but the words only came from a loving nature. We were just a temporary plug in each other's lives. I asked him why he hadn't studied music at some conservatoire.

'Oh, no money,' he said.

'Aren't there scholarships?'

'Sure, but you have to have your father sign.'

'Yes, I see.'

'But we soldier on,' he said, putting the violin away in its plush-lined case. 'And we think of other things. We do our best to make the windows of Lord and Taylor look like stage sets with all the actors stopped just so for the pleasure of those who have to walk by. We take our little paycheque home and our thoughts, at least, are free.'

Suddenly he rolled up his sleeve and looked at his arm. 'Pathetic,' he said. I looked at it too. It was.

'I do exercises for mine.'

'*Really?* Show me, do.'

I went through the motions of my windmills and he followed along, both of us waving our arms about like French
traffic cops.

Then we heard the dancer's step and we stopped and
became the dummies in Morris's windows, our arms in the air.
And the unbelievable happened. The dancer knocked. Morris
couldn't speak so I had to do it for him. The dancer came in.
He *was* a good-looking man, in blue jeans and a red shirt. I
looked down and noticed that his flies were undone.

I might have courted a great deal of trouble, living as I did with
a Negro, but how was anyone to know? Julius never touched
me outside our bed. We never went out to dinner or dancing.
Our social life was at first restricted to the clubs on 52nd Street,
but once he realized that I did not actually like the music he
preferred to go alone and our only outings, then, were walks
round Central Park together on Sunday afternoons or visits to
the various art museums where, despite the fact that it was me
who was supposed to have the 'eye', I was lectured in his dry,
precise way about schools of painting. Like all autodidacts, he
was a bit of a bore.

There was only one way I could get under Julius's skin, and
I couldn't do that very often. If he was sitting next to me on the
couch (and I had to find some pretence to get him there) and
if the radiogram was playing some race music and he was sitting
back and relaxing and tapping his toe to its rhythm, and if
he'd had a beer or two that sent the blood running to his face –
oh, and if there was an R in the month because there were so
many intangibles that had a bearing on this – then I could
take a risk – and tickle him. He'd go spare, he really lost it. He
would cry with laughter. 'Oh, no,' he'd shout. 'Oh, Jesus, not

that, no, stop it, get off me, oh, shit,' and he'd be *howling*, tears running down his face, his arms flailing about trying to grab my hands but they were too nimble for him and I'd have his shirt open and my fingers would be burrowing under it to his belly. He'd laugh so hard it was like all the laughter in him which he'd hoarded until this moment came running out like cats from an alley and spent itself. And I'd stop when his whole face was wet and he was sprawled on the floor where he'd wriggled to try to get away from me and I'd sit on the edge of the couch looking down at him, giggling in my triumph, shaking off a shoe and starting all over again on his exposed stomach so he'd grab my foot and squeeze it and sit up and try to land some kind of fly punch. Then I would be on the floor and he'd be tickling me until it was me that was screaming for mercy, biting the back of his hand or pulling his hair to make him cry out in a mock falsetto: 'Oh, noooo. Not that. Not hair-pulling. Call the cops, she's murdering me. Get those night sticks out, man. Bring out the paddy wagon and take her away.' We were at our best together in these tickling sessions. But they didn't happen all that often.

Mostly, I sat in that big expanse of couch with the radio turned off, listening to the clock ticking until he'd look up from his books to see me yawning and say, 'OK, honey. Time for bed. You seem ready.' And I would nod and he would fasten the top on his bottle of ink, wipe the nib of his pen with a rag, mark his place with a fringed leather book-mark and rub his tired eyes. After we'd brushed our teeth and I'd massaged in my creams, we'd go into the bedroom, climb between the sheets and he'd put his arm round me. If we did not have sex, then we'd each stare into the darkness alone until one of us fell asleep. But if we did, then he would thrust himself inside me as deep as he could and lie there for a moment or two before he'd start to move, and in this temporary stasis I experienced a sense of *fullness*, of my body made whole, and it was in the stillness rather than anything else that we were together. I think it would have been enough for me if he had not moved all night long.

When I wrote my dutiful fortnightly letters home to my parents I did not say with whom I was really sharing my new address. I told them I had moved in with another girl from work. My mother replied more often than my father. She complained a great deal about the rationing and the amount of time it seemed to be taking to clear the bomb sites of rubble. Reading between the lines, they seemed to be living in rather straitened circumstances. The fur trade had not returned to its pre-war production levels and throughout the austerity my father's old customers were having their furs remodelled rather than buying new ones. My mother said he spent nearly every night at meetings. Belatedly he had discovered a cause from which she felt excluded and their old, perfect intimacy in which even I was not entirely welcome, had gone. 'He used to know how much I love him,' she wrote once, unguardedly. 'But I think that now he has forgotten. I have to win him back and I know that my only weapon is my unreserved loyalty. I will *never* leave your father, no matter what he does. Not even that terrible thing.'

I wondered about this for many weeks. What dreadful action could my father have possibly committed? In a later letter she enthusiastically recommended the new Max Factor pancake make-up which hid, she said, the most obtrusive blemishes. My mother's skin was the kind that aged badly, prematurely wrinkling, but she never had any blemishes, unless she meant some kind of bruise.

Did I love Julius? I was afraid of him. Despite learning more about him in a month or two than I had managed to discover about Stan in eight years, I did not have his measure. If we talked at all, it was only because he liked to play with my mind. 'Look at this table,' he said. 'If there was a scratch on it just there, would it be the same table?' I did look at it, my brain collapsing. 'Yes,' I said. Then, 'No.' 'You're not thinking!' he shouted at me. 'Think.'

'Why is this important?' I once ventured to ask him and he picked up his coffee cup and hurled it against the wall. I just went into the kitchen, got a cloth and wiped up the mess.

'What the hell are you? A maid? You want to be a maid? I'm not surprised, that's all you're good for. Where's your respect for yourself? When are you going to start thinking with your brain instead of with your cunt?'

I wondered if I was to spend all my life being passed from hand to hand. I had been in America just over a year and if you included the journey over I had had four lovers. Each time I lost myself and became whatever they wanted me to be. My only certainty had been my good taste, my special knowledge which *was* valued, for I had been promoted at the store and even sent on a course to learn how to be a better saleswoman. But none of my boyfriends understood the effort it took, the close studying of magazines to keep up with what was happening on the Continent, the detailed examination of each season's line to try to predict what would happen in the next. When we went round the Met together, I would frequently stop to admire a dress in a painting. I would peer at the lace and curse brush strokes that in a slapdash way concealed the exact cut of the seams. I wanted to touch the art, or rather I wanted to rub together between my fingers the fabric it depicted.

The other thing I knew was my body and its responses. I was an expert in that. Perhaps I was further out than women of those times, for I came to feel more and more in control of my desires and what needed to be done for them to be met. I learned boldness and found the right words to tell a man what I wanted him to do. This astonished and unnerved Julius, who thought that only whores really liked sex. 'You sit there in your fancy clothes,' he would say as we ate our breakfast before we went our separate ways to work, 'but you're a whore in bed.' I took exception to this.

'I don't think I'm a whore. I think it's perfectly normal for a woman to enjoy making love, exactly as a man does. If all women got as much of what they wanted as me, you'd see a lot of changes, I can tell you.' And then I stopped, amazed at myself. For this was the first original thought I had ever had. You could say it was the closest I'd ever come to an idea. Julius put down his cup of coffee and looked at me. I looked defiantly back. 'That's what I think. I won't unsay it.'

'I don't want you to.'

'Good.' Then, 'Do you think I'm becoming a human being?'

'I don't see much evidence.'

'I don't know what you want from me!' I cried suddenly, in despair.

'Funny, I know what you want from me.'

Julius wasn't really cruel. He just saw me as an object for improvement, and where is the cruelty in that? I was able, sometimes, to give him pleasure when by chance something I said hit its mark. He was trying very hard to think of what I could *be*. He wanted the best for me. But later that evening he fell into one of his dark rages when he treated me with all the coldness he had learned from his father. He swore at me and called me a vampire bitch. He sat by the window looking out across the blackness of Central Park and hammered his fists against the glass until I feared it would shatter. I realized that for all his mystery I had known Stan through and through. I would never understand Julius, not in a million years. I didn't know if the woman who had been there before me was Negro or white. Our lives had just touched by accident and when he left me, as I believed he obviously would, I would feel relieved.

I've made it sound like my life with him was misery, but, you know, it wasn't. Once I bought some canary-yellow camiknickers. Canary yellow! What a colour! So I was in the bathroom one Saturday morning washing out my smalls, thinking I should wash my yellow camiknickers separately. I drained the water from the sink, squeezed out all my other panties and lay them over the edge of the bath to dry. Then I filled the sink again with hot water and ran the tap over a cake of laundry soap. I slid the camiknickers in and at once the water turned bright yellow, the colour of saffron, and as it did the sun came out outside and shone for a moment through the frosted glass. I looked at my hands in the water, the skin under the nails already as yellow as jaundice and I felt immeasurably happy for no reason at all other than the usual, that I was twenty-three and alive not dead.

Julius called out from the hall. 'Are you busy in there?'

'I'm just washing my smalls.'

'Do you mind if I come in? I'm desperate.'

'Come on. I don't mind.'

He opened the door and walked past me. He wasn't wearing a shirt. He undid his pants and urinated in the toilet.

Forgetting myself, I stepped over to him and kissed his bare back, rubbed it with my hot, soapy yellow hands. He jumped with surprise and the jet from his penis stopped. He looked down at it. 'Jesus, woman. What have you done? I'm going to have to get a plumber out to take a look at me.' But he was laughing. I pointed at the sink. We looked at the water in it. 'You've drained a couple of pints off the sun, there,' he said and splashed his fingers, and as I did too so our hands caught together in the folds of my camiknickers. He fished them out and twirled them on his finger.

'Have I seen you in these?'

'I just got them. I've only worn them once.'

'Well, let them dry and let's go out.'

'Where?'

'Just for a walk.'

It was spring and we did not need coats. People were shopping and going about their business. A few men sat on the steps of their houses drinking coffee and glasses of beer. The prostitutes and the drug-dealers were still asleep. Harlem temporarily belonged to women and their children. We strolled along Strivers Row. 'Do you think you'd like to live here?' he asked.

'Oh, yes,' I said, looking at the gorgeous Italianate terraces that would not have been out of place in Florence. And I began to babble about interior decor.

'You'd like to live there so you could do up the property?'

'Of course, why else?'

I turned my head to the sun's little warmth. It did not occur to me until years later that perhaps he was asking me to marry him.

I felt confident enough to ask something. 'There was a

woman living with you just before me, wasn't there? I don't mind, I'm just asking.'

'Yes, you guessed right.'

'Was she . . . white?'

'She was.'

'What happened to her?' He had his head bent, looking at his shoes as they marched along the street.

'She went back to her husband.'

'Oh, I'm sorry.'

He'd speeded up. We got caught among some Seventh Day Adventists coming out of church.

'Don't worry,' I said, panting. 'Everything comes round. I know you'll leave me.'

He stopped short. Coloured men and women in church hats were shaking each other's hands. '*You'll* be the one to leave,' he said.

'How do you figure that?'

'The way I see it, you're a foreigner. You've already left your own country. You don't have any ties.'

Suddenly I'd got it. 'Is that why you like me? Because I'm a foreigner?'

'That'd be one thing,' he agreed.

'What would be another?'

But I guess he didn't hear, because he just continued his upright march along the sidewalk, his fast pace which some-times tried to race the traffic when it was caught in the rush-hour crawl. His clothes were just the same as when I'd first met him, his expression was no different. A very pretty Negro woman passed in a russet linen dress (a cast-off? was she a maid?) and I saw him look at her, though she barely looked at him in his shabby coat and frayed tie. She did not notice me, for it could not have appeared that we were together. Then he quickly touched my arm and her chin twitched and she glanced at me with such rage, the features bunched up into a small fist. Now she saw that Julius was indeed a handsome man, despite his nappy hair and his cheap old threads. I turned to watch his face and he was just completing and discarding a smirk.

We were each using one another in our own different way and who was the most culpable? I had tried a Negro, tasted a Negro and for the moment I was content and waited to see into whose hands I would be passed next, who would conjure themselves up out of nowhere to take me.

Chapter Eleven

And now I close my eyes and I see myself in Julius's apartment. How pretty I was, my hair still in that curly page-boy cut, my waist the same as my age: twenty-three inches. I'm dreaming of the New Look, of a ballerina-length dress that brushes the ankles. There are six or seven people in the room, it's our Wednesday night meeting. I've rushed home from work, buying cookies on the way. Julius is talking about what a let-down the socialists have been in England. Have they swept away imperialism? Has anything changed in India or Africa? 'The British Empire is the biggest enslaver of the human race the world has ever known,' he says. 'Your government . . .' and I point out that I have lived in America under Truman for longer than I'd lived in England under Attlee. I don't tell him that in our family we had all dutifully voted for Churchill.

In fact I had become extremely interested in the condition of the Negro and I had begun to follow reports in the newspapers of the unfolding events in the South that would lead to a new awakening among Julius's generation. Half of me (my father's heritage) identified, the other half (my mother's bad blood) thought it bore the burden of the guilt.

On Wednesdays Julius tried as best he could to reproduce those gatherings in Chicago before the war and though he was in no position to form a salon he was highly regarded by many activists in the neighbourhood for his deliberation, his refusal to engage unless he was intellectually certain of his ground. His mind moved always in a linear way, from step to step, so that once he had come to a decision he had no need ever to question his premises again. It was all very different from the way I came at things, circling around them, making a sudden leap as if to drag them to the ground. He brought together a musician or two, guys from the clubs who had had something of an education and were prepared to lay aside their horns and their weed for a few hours to see beyond the hip little world in which they reigned supreme. There was another engineer like himself, a union organizer and her white husband, and a middle-class Negro from Strivers Row, the son of a minister who was working as a labourer to 'get back to the people'. The men flirted with me, the woman hardly ever noticed me. She looked me up and down and from then on she just looked through me. I didn't blame her. Negro women took enough nonsense from middle-class white women, whose clothes they pressed and whose meals they made, every day of the week. Her husband sometimes smiled at me, kindly, but only when his wife's back was turned.

They would take turns to pick a topic, then together we

developed an analysis. This analysis was, to Julius, the highest form of thought. He was always happiest when the darkness of human experience was suddenly illuminated by mental clarity. I would have been just glad to pass round the coffee but Julius wanted me to play my part. I had to make a contribution. I was to take a 'subject', speak on it for twenty minutes, then lead a discussion. It was impossible. I burst into tears.

'Just talk about something you know,' the engineer said, trying to encourage me. He was a very serious man who knew a lot about the atom bomb. I had never managed to exchange more than a few words of pleasantries with him.

'I don't know about anything.'

'Sure you do. Just stick to objective reality and you can't go far wrong.'

'Tell us about the retail sector,' the union organizer said with a not particularly pleasant smile. 'You must have an analysis of that?' I looked around wildly to Julius for support and did not find it. He said he thought that wasn't a bad idea. At first I thought he meant the minutiae of stocktaking but gradually I understood that I was, for the first time, to pay attention to the people who worked around me rather than the merchandise. For two weeks I kept a notebook in my purse and wrote down my ideas.

So it was my turn. I set up chairs in a circle. I was wearing a very plain navy suit and a white blouse. My audience sat and listened. I saw their faces relax from scepticism to interest. To my pleasure, I saw busy pencils and from time to time heads nodded.

Department stores, I argued, were difficult to organize because they broke some of the rules of classic theories of wage labour. In a factory, a worker sat all day hammering a widget and it made no difference if he was happy or mad: the widget still got hammered. But in a department store, selling was a social interaction, which the managers often found difficult to harness. A good saleswoman brought to the job many paths of expertise: knowledge of the merchandise, charm and a pleasant demeanour, the capacity to make the customer feel enhanced by whatever she was being sold, for even if it was the cheapest pair of gloves we were persuading her to buy, we knew what we were really selling was a kind of glamour. And if we harangued her into buying an outfit which was ill-fitting or didn't suit her, why, she could return the very next day and demand her money back. The best saleswoman had a lifelong *rapport* with the customers, who put themselves in her hands and as they married and had their own families they brought their daughters to her. And they in turn grew up knowing that if they were uncertain about the length of this season's hemlines or whether a colour was right to wear in town, then there was someone who would advise them and lead them, until they left the store with the confidence to step out on the avenues feeling smart, stylish, thoroughly feminine – feeling, perhaps, even a beauty.

A hand went up to interrupt me. It was the engineer. How, he asked, could the bosses apply scientific management to selling, dividing and regularizing the work process?

How could you standardize the mystique of the relationship between seller and customer? I replied. You could not. You could not even bawl out an employee in front of her, for there were still memories then of the early days of the century when well-heeled shoppers were outraged at seeing underpaid, overworked women toil long hours in unhealthy surroundings, and it was often these very shoppers who organized the campaigns for better conditions for store workers.

Yet still the bosses did find ways to divide and rule us. Department stores were popular places to work, for a start. Unlike factories they were clean, even scented. In these palaces of consumption, women felt at home among things they recognized and were familiar with: millinery, haberdashery, furnishings, bolts of fabric and notions, pots and pans and even the new, exciting scientific machinery of the kitchen, such as devices that washed your dishes or automatically shampooed the carpet. Staff discounts were accepted practice everywhere, so there was a chance to acquire goods at a substantial markdown. There was never a shortage of women waiting to get hired.

And one of the biggest ways the bosses had to keep us from uniting against them was by having two tiers of staff, full-timers and part-time. We full-timers earned more and got more staff perks. We were the lords and ladies of the selling floors. You would see the part-timers in their shabby suits *saying* they were only looking for pin-money because the word was round that this was what the personnel department wanted to hear, but *we* all knew perfectly well that these married women were desperate to move off the extra board and that some pieced together a hard living from bits of short hours here and there.

I explained to my audience that I had started to think that the department store was a microcosm of a tiny feudal society, ruled over by a distant emperor and governed by the managers and their barons, the designers, the buyers, the floorwalkers. And below them, forming their court, were first the salesmen, then the seamstresses in the workrooms who did alterations, the mannequins, and, last, the saleswomen. We in turn looked down on those who sold at bargain tables set up in the aisles or worked on the notions counter. Toiling at the lowest caste in this domain were the wrappers, the inspectors, the stock people, the message carriers and the lift operators, one or two of whom I judged to be possibly Negro, though stores would never knowingly hire coloureds.

But whatever the job, long hours (particularly during the sales), bad backs, sore feet, unpaid overtime (to attend store meetings, do inventories, replace stock, rearrange departments) were our lot and our paycheques were always diminished by the ever-present struggle to be impeccably dressed, for saleswomen, in particular, spent more money on clothing than any other working woman.

At this point my analysis had reached its end but I had not spoken for my allotted time and the audience seemed unwilling to ask questions. They wanted more. They wanted full value.

'I don't know what else to say,' I explained, my hand crumpling a paper napkin. My mouth was dry.

'Just go with the flow,' one of the musicians advised.

Julius turned and glared at him. 'Don't come up with any old junk, Sybil,' he said.

'Tell it like it is,' urged the minister's son.

So, emboldened, I went on, entering areas of my life I had *never* spoken of, speaking of things I was hardly aware that I had even thought.

When I was first hired at Lord and Taylor, I told them, every department had its long-tenure employee, a woman in her fifties, always ineffably smart, who had made the store her life-long career. These women terrified me. Their hair always seemed more beautifully coiffed than anyone else's, their suits never in need of pressing, a demure cameo at the throat their only jewellery. They knew their departments as a mother knows her baby's face. They could be gracious if, in some way, by your work you pleased them but on the whole they were petty despots whose life consisted of the small power they held in their tiny kingdoms. They had 'theories' about the psychology of the shopper, which were sometimes correct but always, once having been formulated, clung on to for decades. The 'flapper mentality' was one 'type' they liked to identify, girls who spent their money unwisely, bought the latest fad, irrespective of whether the fabric was 'good'. Our saleswomen would narrow their eyes as a customer asked for a particular garment. 'Very well, ma'am,' they would say and handle it between distasteful fingertips, and sometimes the shopper would be so disheartened that she would bolt from the store. Or else, brazenly, she would laugh and pay a fortune for some shoddy trifle that was a month's salary to the saleswoman, and turn her smart back swinging the parcel, maybe lifting the corners of her mouth at me as she passed – as if to let me know that the garment would be worn once or twice and then discarded, given to the maid, who try as she might could never press it so that it looked as it had done on her mistress, for the cut was so poor that only the stiffness of the 'dressing' had made it hold its shape.

But often these older saleswomen were right and it was perhaps the dated slang they used that misled the ear, for in that shrewd assessment was a *felt* sense of the Customer: what she would try and what she would not countenance; why she would spend half a day almost to the point of tears discarding ballgowns until she found the one that made her seem like a fragile ornament, for this was the ballgown she would wear to tempt or force a proposal; how she would pay more than she could afford for a certain dress to win back a husband whose eye was looking elsewhere; how a sadness could be assuaged by a hat of such insouciant caprice that it could not fail to make her feel gay. And the saleswoman's great gift was to sell to a poor woman just a scarf or a vial of cheap perfume so she felt that in the store she had entered a place of enchantment, and her down-at-heel shoes and shabby pre-war coat fell away into nothingness beneath the glittering new self she put on with that scarf wound about her or walking home scenting the air with her sweetness and looking for all the world as if she was a woman hugging to herself some marvellous secret.

These saleswomen, who were once thought so conscientious, stable and thorough, were now in the process of being discarded in favour of youthful 'snap'. Young men who returned from the war to begin their careers in merchandising feared them for they were reminded of their mothers, and who were these men, with their medals and citations, to be treated like small (and not very clean) boys? Week after week we would gather in a manager's office with one of our doughty *vendeuses* while they were given their presentation clock or silver-plate tray, paid for by a grudging collection among us junior staff, and they would all make the same speech. About what the store was like when they first came there before the Great War, how lovely the ladies were then in their feathered hats and floor-length street costumes, and there would always be a joke about short skirts and discovering that they were not the only women in the world to have *legs*. And then they would cry a little and take one or two of us aside to say we had always been the favourite and made us promise to come and visit them, which we never, ever would. So home, to a grey worn-out husband and empty rooms (some had lost sons in the last war). Or home to nothing.

When I had finished my talk the audience stirred and Julius

put up his hand to say that was there not an element of soap opera in all this? What were the balance of forces between labour and management? Why was there no union? And the union that organized my industry – were the staffers corrupt, or porkchoppers? How did we do in our last contract? What was the record of the union on racial chauvinism? What did I judge would be the response to a strike vote to desegregate the department stores of the city?

Needless to say, I could give him answers to none of these questions. What he called soap opera was the only way I knew to describe what I saw around me every day. I got up hurriedly and gathered up the coffee cups and went into the kitchen to make a fresh pot. One of the musicians came in behind me and put a hand across my shoulders. He squeezed. 'You're quite a chick, Sybil,' he said, smiling, looking me up and down. 'You should hang out more. Let me know when you've finished with Mister Serious in there.' He was very good looking. I would have liked to take up with him but I could not see how I would ever get the chance.

That night, in bed, Julius touched me and said I had done well, and this exasperated me.

'So why didn't you say so? Why do you have to put me down all the time?' Something occurred to me. 'You aren't ashamed of me, are you?'

He was silent.

'You are.'

'Don't be like that.'

'Oh, throw me back, for God's sake, throw me back. Put me out of my misery.'

'I won't kick you out. But you have your own free will. Do you want to go?'

'No.'

'Well, then. Quit bellyaching.'

But I had kept something back at the meeting.

When I first went to Lord and Taylor after I left Mr Max I noticed a woman who seemed very different from the rest of us. At that time the store was aggressively recruiting college girls and students; it prized amongst its staff a 'clean' look: clear complexion, even a light tan, American clothes with simple accessories. Our chief designer, Tom Brigance, turned out lines with a strong element of *le sportif*, play clothes like wrapped tops that bared the midriff worn with trousers, or soft sarong draping. This woman could have been any age at all, but I guessed she was in her late fifties, always dressed in a blue serge coatdress that never seemed to be properly laundered, and a sour smell came off her skin which she tried to disguise with a pungent brand of inexpensive eau-de-Cologne. Everything about her was colourless (I once overheard her being ordered to put on lipstick).

What drove everyone mad was the way she incessantly grumbled, in English and some other language which was thought to be Hungarian or Romanian. She muttered about her feet, about the customers, about the girls she assisted. The *sotto voce* mumbling beneath her breath was like something unpleasant stuck to the sole of your shoe that followed you about all day. She was moved from department to department, bagging or selling the cheapest sale lines, once even operating the elevator until the shoppers complained of her rudeness and that odd smell, like rancid butter, in such an enclosed space.

I assumed that she had been there many years, that perhaps ill-health had lowered her from a position of somewhat greater authority. To my surprise, I found she had been employed only a month or two longer than I had myself. Why was she kept on, I wondered, when the image of the store was so at odds with such an employee? The only explanation anyone could offer was that she could be a poor (very poor) relative of someone higher up in the company. Like everyone else, I avoided her, for the young always fear the stench of old age and failure the most.

One evening, just before we were due to close, when the last customers were still lingering over a hat or a pair of court shoes, for it was Thursday, the maid's traditional night off, I noticed she had picked up a silk flower and held it to her hair. As she looked in the mirror something changed. The doormen ushered out the last of the shoppers, the gold-tasselled lanterns dimmed and by a trick of the disappearing light she seemed to be standing in a parlour furnished like the photographs of my grandparents' house with my father's bare legs dangling over the edges of a dining-room chair: peach-coloured velveteen curtains and a fringed pelmet muffling the windows, palms with leaves shaped like daggers, armchairs dressed in Bruges lace anti-macassars, unlit gas mantles, a claw-foot mahogany table on which a silver candelabra was shining with the light of half a dozen rose candles. And I stood there transfixed, watching her smiling as she admired the sea-green silk flower in her hair, not fifty but eighteen, at the very moment she had finished dressing and someone was waiting for her at the door, so close I could hear his breath and his tread in the hall.

Then a floor-walker appeared. 'Merchandise can become very grubby if fingered,' he said, as he swept past.

The expression on her face as if she had been hit, turning as the blow came from young to old . . .

The floor-walker would never have said such a thing to me.

He said it because she was old and poor and ugly and he wanted to punish her for it. 'This is not right,' I thought. 'This is not just.' I sat down and hid among the skirts of the ball-gowns and wept. And that is how my passion was born, for while I wept for myself, for the father I had lost, I wept for her.

I had another secret. This passion grew in me. I had no way of expressing what I had seen or felt. It would have sounded – trivial? No, sentimental.

In time the woman became lost to view but something had been ignited which burned away my solitariness and connected me, tangentially, to the world.

PART TWO

Chapter Twelve

We were hanging out of the windows of the train, leaving behind the confining geometry of New York City, chanting back at the retreating rails: 'One, two, three, four / We don't want another war.' It was the summer of 1948, the summer of the presidential campaign, the summer, also, of Alger Hiss. I was not a citizen, I did not have the right to vote, but what did that matter? I was riding the Pennsylvania Railroad 'Common Man' special down to Philadelphia as an alternate at the Progressive Party convention, sent by my union. When I looked around me, the cars of the train were packed with housewives in their smartest dresses, veterans still in uniform, teachers and doctors in conservative suits, students in blue jeans and work shirts straight from the voter registration drives in the South, where a million leaflets against segregation had been handed out in Georgia *alone*. Apart, not because of our racism but because of our awe, were the Negro unionists from the Tobacco Workers of North Carolina and the International Longshoremen of New Orleans.

We got mildly drunk on beer and sang union songs and a song we made up specially for the Republican nominee, Governor Dewey: 'One thing I just cannot take / A moustache bigger than a can-di-date.' Three thousand of us were about to descend on the City of Brotherly Love, and as if we were on a country hayride we got out picnic baskets and ate. We were so young, hardly anyone over the age of thirty. Since VE Day, this was my first experience of a mass event and my first ever experience of camaraderie, the friendships forged, the romances that blossom. *Me*. Imagine *me* there, but I was and, worse, I was enjoying myself. For hours on end I forgot to open my purse, take out my compact and powder my nose. When I ran into a mirror that I thought was an open door and bumped my forehead I was horrified at my appearance – hair tousled, lipstick that was hardly more than an outline round my lips, two runs in my nylons and the buttons on my suit jacket done up wrong. I looked a fright, a horrible mess, which is how you wind up when your mind is in two places at once and you aren't paying enough attention to your appearance.

This degeneration had begun a year before. My study group had suggested I should switch from Lord and Taylor to Bloomingdale's. My old place of employment, the reasoning went, was not a useful base for organizing: a group of staff had just failed to get sufficient signatures to enable us to apply for union certification. The customers were not working women but the idle rich and, as I knew well, even the staff were recruited from middle-class college kids. Bloomingdales, on the other hand, sold to women who worried about how to make the family budget last the week, women who knew what it meant to make hash out of leftovers. The whole place was lacklustre, out of the way, in the gloom cast by the shadow of the Third Avenue El which rumbled right above its doors and that slightly louche district of seedy brownstones and rundown bars that surrounded it.

In vain I pointed out what everyone knew from the department-store grapevine – that there were plans to tear down the El, raze the brownstones and the bars and construct in their place commercial office buildings and apartments, housing affluent people who would be within walking distance of the premises. The management had decided that in order to maximize their gross profit performance they needed to sell higher-priced goods, and they set a course to turn that drab store into a chic and affluent fashion leader. But there was no arguing with the members of my study group, particularly Irene, the Negro unionist.

When I moved to Bloomingdale's and signed my dues check-off card, and said what I had been told to say – that I wanted to get involved – the organizer looked at me dubiously. 'Do you have any skills?' he asked me. 'Are you good at writing pamphlets?'

'No.'

'A speaker, perhaps?'

'I wouldn't have thought so.'

'Have you had any experience organizing?'

'None.'

'Office skills? I don't suppose you have any of those?'

'Yes! Yes, I do. I can type, I can do shorthand and double-entry bookkeeping, I can cut stencils. Everything. I'm trained.'

He looked at my fingernails, which were manicured and painted coral pink. 'I'll trim them. Tonight. Or now. You have nail scissors?'

'You I can use.'

So I had short nails and I needed to give myself a manicure every single day, touching up the polish. Of course I was there because Julius had sent me, because I was coming to care for him and I wanted what he wanted. He was only being like my parents, for all three of them, with the best will in the world, were trying to make something out of me. But that wasn't all. No, it wasn't just about Julius. There was something else that wobbled along on its own, shaky but independent of him. Sometimes I thought of the mad old woman at Lord and Taylor, holding the flower to her hair, and sometimes I thought of Red Feather, the woman on the subway, and what she wanted to do to niggers. Discovering my own capacity for compassion, I had surprised myself. I did want to be made. I wanted to *be* someone. I wanted to be part of the world, a member of the human race. It was curious, wasn't it, that my straying to the margins had taken me on a hairpin bend which led right back to the very heart of society, to the pulsing, ticking beat where we find out if we have any reason at all to be alive.

The way I learned about life from Julius, you were either for things or against them. What are you for, what are you against? That was what he wanted to know of everyone. And thus, are you with me or against me? There was a side to everything, everyone formed a line to the left or the right. You couldn't take a little from here and a trifle from there, it didn't work like that. People who sat in the middle of the road got run down, Julius said. People were neutrals because they had no heart, no guts. 'You must have had some spunk to get on an immigrant boat and make your way over here,' he told me. 'Now let's see if you have a heart or maybe what you have inside you is some big shiny piece of hard metal junk, like a bracelet or a ring.'

I thought a lot about racialism and I read about it too. I'd started on the novels of Richard Wright, for there wasn't much else to read just then, a year or two before Ralph Ellison and Jimmy Baldwin exploded into print. Race was an easy place for me to begin my political education because the injustice was so palpable. As a (part) Jewess I was bound to identify with Negroes, whereas the proletariat gave me more trouble. What did I know about the workers? Not a lot. Of course Stan was technically a 'worker', though I don't suppose he'd have thanked me for saying so and wouldn't have identified himself that way. He went into kitchens when he was short of a few bob and if he was in the union it was only because he had to be to get the work. So I ignored the proletariat and concentrated on the Race Question.

As Julius had pointed out in our study group, Jews were the niggers of Europe: had the Nazis gained ascendancy here in America instead of on the other side of the ocean, the Negroes would have been marched off first to the concentration camps. I said that Jews would have gone too and Julius agreed, but he argued that we wouldn't have been the first and that we would have had money and contacts, we would have been able to get out, at least most of us would. In the South the plantation owners would have delivered the Negroes straight to the gas ovens themselves. I wasn't sure. Wouldn't they have needed them as their workforce? Someone had nodded when I said that. I was very proud of myself. I was becoming a 'thinker', even though my point seemed to be no more than common sense. But Julius said no, I was wrong. Mechanical cotton pickers were on their way and the writing was on the wall for the old rural economy of the South. Why did I think there was a mass exodus to the North?

Still, the connection between Jews and Negroes was there. When I remembered what had happened in Nazi Germany and how my own relatives had died, what did I feel? I felt a mixture of fear and guilt. My sexual attraction towards Negroes was not the only thing that fed my outrage about segregation. For I seized on the Race Question as a way of burning out of my soul that diseased part of it which I had inherited with my mother's blood. So I threw myself into political work and I found that inside, it did me good. And though I barely understood, at first, the explanation for all the injustice there apparently was in the world, none the less a fire was in me and it lit up everything I saw.

In my study group, what I began to understand about communism was this: it was not just a matter of the opposing interests of the classes but of morality. Everything we did – even buying a loaf of bread – was a political act subject not just to abstract economic forces but questions of right and wrong. The bread was not only a commodity, it was the product of many people's labour. How much had the man been paid to make that bread? (I knew the answer to that.) And the truck driver who delivered it to the store? And the person in the store who sold it to you? How were they treated? Did they have proper breaks? Were they fired when they were sick? Was there a labour union to organize them and give a voice to their rights as workers? Was the bread priced so that the working class could afford it? Was it good bread, not made with adulterated flour? Was the store owner forced to pay into some mob-run protection racket? Socialism, Julius said, got you into the habit of thinking this way, so that even alone in a room, or, worse, alone in a cell, you were connected to the rest of humanity. Workers had built your house or your prison; the bed you lay on had been constructed by a person and even if it had been made by a machine, a man or a woman pushed its gears and oiled it.

I grew ashamed then of the other part of my inheritance, that trader's instinct that gave my father his place amongst the bourgeoisie. What was the first lesson of business? Buy cheap, sell dear. How could I tell anyone what he did for a living? That he sold luxury items to warm the backs of the idle rich. My furs stayed in cold storage. I did not pay the bill and eventually all but one that I reclaimed were forfeited. I wore a cloth coat like everyone else. Only my crocodile beauty case remained. I would not give it up.

Then, like a movie I was watching, the great history of our century began to unfold for me: I began to fit the names of characters to the roles they played, the lines of the plot grew clearer and politics came to seem like the most engrossing story, but one which I did not always have to view in muffled darkness for I could step into the screen and join it.

There in that room I heard of the Spanish Civil War and the brave people from all over the world who came to make their stand in the very first struggle against fascism. How could I have been so ignorant? Hadn't I watched the newsreels, sitting nestled between my mother and father? What had I been dreaming of during those months that led Europe into the grip of Hitler? Why had my father not alerted me? Why had he sat in his blue velvet chair drinking expensive whisky or dawdled among the flowerbeds, stupidly watching the light fail in the sky and admiring our pallid northern sunset? *Why* had he spoken, dismissively, of the *schwarzes* as we motored along Upper Parliament Street? Couldn't he see that they were immigrants just like him, or that many had even been born there, and for generations, going back as far as the eighteenth century? When he told me of our slavery in the land of Egypt, why did he never mention the slavery of less than a hundred years ago? And when we freed ourselves and went into the Promised Land, why was there no mention of the Africans and Indians who actually lived in their Promised Land which was made foreign to them by the invader? And if the Jews of Masada fought back, why shouldn't the workers fight back when the troops were sent to break up their picket lines? As for my *mother* – had she deliberately plotted to keep me in such a state of imbecility, like a prize cow with a ribbon round its neck? How could I have *loved* them?

So it began, my great romance with moral grandeur.

In the union, I excelled at what I later learned the Communist Party called Jimmy Higgins work. I was good at it – I was great at it! I worked hard and I worked late. Every evening I went straight to the union office and put the files in order. I dusted and got out a mop and a bucket of hot water. At every meeting I was there with my notebook taking the minutes and later typing them up, cutting a stencil and distributing them. Someone needed a thousand leaflets by morning? I would stay half the night pumping the handle of the mimeograph machine. I began to organize systems – suppose a speaker was coming to town and fifty people were needed to applaud him? I delivered those fifty people. I coerced the sick out of their beds to walk a picket line. And because I was always cheerful (and also, of course, because I was pretty) I was popular with the men who ran the union and they all agreed it was a good idea that I should come along with them to Philadelphia. I'm not sure that's what their wives thought.

So here we all were on the 'Common Man', and for the first time I was leaving New York and going somewhere. My union's delegates were back in the club car, informally caucusing, while I took time out to watch the view. The fellow sitting next to me introduced himself as an instructor at City University, an unmistakable Wasp, of the nervous, bloodless sort, his thighs, as sharp as scythes, pressed together beneath the folds of his pants. He produced from his pocket a single ham sandwich, wrapped in wax paper, and began to take a bite. The girl in the seat across the aisle looked at it. She was big, masses of black hair, huge bazoomas which she must have had to hoist into place hydraulically every morning, big cherry lips, a cotton dress smothered in loud red roses. Common as hell but you couldn't help liking the look of her. 'That's all you brought?' she asked him.

'It's sufficient for my appetite,' he said.

She indicated to the luggage rack above us. 'Would you be so kind as to reach for my valise?' He stood up, swaying with the motion of the train. His own weight and the weight of her bag seemed an equal match for each other. He pulled and the upper part of his body was driven back. His right foot lunged forward, to steady himself, and it landed, heavily, on her left shoe. The bag crashed to the floor of the car and the catch burst open. 'My God!' he cried. 'What is that?'

Inside were several loaves of long flat Greek bread, pounds of cheese and meats, bottles of olives and gherkins, a mason jar of oil, a bag of home-made cookies, a box of imported chocolates, apricots, russet pears, oranges, a vacuum flask of coffee and a bottle of wine. Underneath were a few clothes.

'You brought your food with you for the whole convention?'

'Just for the journey.'

'All *this*?'

She looked at his long, underfed face, his ham sandwich lying on his seat, and gestured to the rest of the car. 'Perhaps others would also like to eat?'

As much as I could, I palled around with these two until I worked out that I was turning into the spare wheel. He was like a chick in the nest, his mouth forever open being fed gobbets of food, sometimes direct from her own lips. He was enslaved.

For myself, I tried to steer clear of that kind of thing. I had a man of my own at home. Instead I took notes in my Pitman shorthand and typed them up to distribute to my fellow union members. I was the preferred choice for this as my transcripts were always scrupulously fair accounts of whatever was said, even when I was paraphrasing. I had no point of view that I could impose. I ran errands and passed on phone messages. 'Good girl!' they shouted after me as I raced through the hallways. I slept, oh, maybe two or three hours a night. The more I was on my feet and active, the better I could keep their hands off me.

On a higher level, invisible to my own limited view, editors at the *Marxist Review* had contributed to the Progressives' written platform. There was to be a disarmament agreement to ban the atomic bomb. The right to independence for Puerto Rico and a unified homeland for the Irish. The vote would start at eighteen. National health insurance and a pension of a hundred dollars a month for the old. Federal aid to public schools. Price controls. Legislation to wipe out the lynchings in the South and end race discrimination in employment and the armed forces. Public ownership of the banks, the railroads, electric power and gas. And, meeting with my puzzled approval, a pledge to raise women to first-class citizenship.

Disarmament was the point. You could hardly call it a radical programme, but my generation, assembled in Philadelphia, were the youth of the moment who had fought in Europe and the Pacific for our post-war peace and though I had not, of course, been in uniform, I knew the horrors of bombing better than most around me. An atomic war was unthinkable to us.

The Race Question was very big. I remember one caucus. A couple came in late. He was in his early thirties, dressed as if he'd come straight from the oil fields, in blue jeans, a blue jean work shirt with pearl snaps, leather jacket, tooled pointed-toe cowboy boots. No hat. Also, a dark-skinned woman in the coming-into-fashion peasant dress of dirndl skirt, low-necked blouse, a necklace of coloured wooden beads. His face was calm and impassive. *Her* mouth was set and sullen as if they had just broken off a row she was winning to remember that they were letting people down by their absence.

'We sure are sorry we're late,' he said, courteously.

We were talking about voter registration. When he raised his hand, other hands went down, deferring to him. 'Foy,' the chairman said. 'You want to intervene?'

He made a rather dry speech, mumbling slightly, but I could tell it was a good one. He knew the South. It was in his voice. He looked down at a note in his hand, written on a piece of card torn from a cigarette carton. 'I have some figures here,' he said. He listed the numbers of dead, killed trying to register. The room was cold and clammy, listening to them. He drove on through his points, modulated, reasonable. His voice would sometimes fall so low that we would all scrape our chairs forward to hear him. When he finished, he sat down calmly, putting the note in the pocket of his work shirt. He pulled a cigarette straight from his jacket and lit it.

I wondered who he was and at the exaggerated respect he commanded when he was not even a Negro, and though I found him attractive it bothered me that his words were listened to so attentively when Julius was stuck back in New York, confined by the need to make a living in the summer months when everyone suddenly felt the heat and our phone rang and rang with calls begging him to come over and install an air-conditioning machine right then and there, whatever the cost. This guy had the facts but Julius had lived it.

Then it was the climactic rally at Shibe Park with Wallace driven around in an open car, and we shouted and screamed for him until we could scream no more. Behind him was Senator Glen Taylor of Idaho, the vice-presidential candidate, who rode about the park on his horse followed by his wife, his brother and three small sons, who together formed the cowboy singing troupe by which the family earned its living, touring Idaho and sleeping in their car at night among the sagebrush and the jack rabbits, without whose roasted flesh, he admitted, they might have starved to death during particularly lean times. We sang along to his guitar and later to Paul Robeson, who performed 'Ol' Man River' and Loyalist songs from the Spanish Civil War. In the distance I saw the pair from the train strolling together, their arms around each other's necks.

It's hard not to be sentimental about music. Some people blub as soon as they hear the first bars of the 'Londonderry Air'. In the afternoon I drifted through the rally, relieved of my duties, biting into cobs of corn, the butter running down my chin and my neck, staining my blouse, and I didn't even notice. I sat with whoever called out to me to join them and we sang songs together. Those songs were my education. First I learned of the thirties. Homeless men sleeping under bridges in Pittsburgh, Chicago, Denver, everywhere. The Dustbowl. CIO organizing. Strikes in Detroit and the coalfields. Lynchings, as ever. The Communist Party at the height of its strength and its confidence. A portion of the working class shedding the long inheritance of its powerlessness. A working class with an identity and a destiny in the scheme of civilized life.

Then another America that lay beyond New York, the America of mines and mills and logging camps, of day labourers and skid roads, an America that was said to be vanishing then in the post-war period of full employment yet preserved in pockets of rural poverty in the Appalachians and the segregated South and in the ghettos of the cities and amongst the old.

And before the communists there were the Wobblies, the International Workers of the World, who tried to heal the pain and loneliness of hobo America until they were savagely beaten, and though they fought back and defended themselves (as if – although they were starving – they had *rights*, for God's sake), they were hounded and shot and lynched and massacred until they were no longer the Red Menace, but forgotten.

The glittering, dead plains of the Utah salt pans where Joe Hill rested in jail and wrote his testament before the copper bosses (forgotten) shot him in their own interests.

A thousand workers in Centralia who marched from nowhere in the night, in silence, to mourn the butchered dead, then dissolved back into the no place they had come from.

Suddenly, like a fever, I wanted to see it all, San Diego, Maine, the Grand Coulee Dam. For the first time I was touched by this great continent, this great country. *America!*

What was touched? Something in me, perhaps that place in the soul of every Jew who wanders. By the fire, a blanket wrapped round my shoulders, I talked to a man who had been there, been in Centralia, he said. He must have been sixty and he walked with a stick. He told me his right leg had been lost in a mill accident and in its place was a wooden prosthesis. He wore a hat like a cowboy's, and a string tie round the collar of his denim shirt and engineers' boots with straps across them. There was something wrong with one of his eyes – it swivelled around with a life of its own. I thought of Stan's cowboy books and how thrilled he would have been if he could have met him too.

'I'm not afraid to say I'm a communist, even though it's given me almost nothing but hard times,' he told me, taking my hand. 'The romance of American communism is like nothing else. Without the dream of communism what do you have? I'll tell you what. Barbarism. The wilderness, prehistoric, primitive. With it, what have you got? Civilization, a communal life. All romantics belong on the frontier. It's that place round the next bend where the hard and dusty road gives way to the fertile valley and the migrant rests and recognizes the place he came from and says *here*.'

Not the margins, then. Not the sea.

And then he broke the spell by bringing his face very close to mine and trying to kiss me. I could smell his old breath laced with liquor and I wriggled away from his arms and ran off.

Chapter Thirteen

For a number of months Julius had been inching towards the Communist Party but always holding back, not sure he could trust them, though they were desperate enough to recruit him, and I was dragged along in the great swell of his progress. Our apartment was suddenly visited by people of whom I had had no conception. Now I was among Jews again, in a world which thronged with them. 'Ideas!' they cried. 'Without them, life is nothing. With them, life is *everything*.'

'Are you listening?' Julius said. 'I hope you're listening.'

Those who had come to America as fully fledged socialists, the heirs of the failed 1905 Revolution, terrified the life out of me. There was a thickness to their existence. They had an explanation for it all. You could not stop them. They didn't talk, they gabbled, they shouted, they thrust forefingers into your face, they grabbed your arm and held it in a tight clasp. As often as not their spit would be in your eye and the odour of their most recent meal forced into your nostrils, but it was a small price for making sure you got the point.

This disjuncture between crudeness and intellectual sophistication was the clue to their origins. Ghetto Jews, just like the ones I had known at home, the scum of Eastern Europe. But ghetto Jews who were not interested in hats and who was married to whom and who had married out. They had a higher purpose. Marx, a Jew, was one of their own.

(One of my own, too: a Jew, a German.)

Like the Liverpool Jews of the pogroms, many were not native city-dwellers; they had been born into remote Polish or Russian or Lithuanian villages where the ground always seemed hard and rimed with dirty snow or which were wretchedly hot and plague-ridden in summer, the houses squalid and miserable, the rabbis ignorant, the neighbours hostile and the authorities prone to aimless violence. In such places, they told you, history was still stuck somewhere in the Dark Ages and in a single generation they had taken a great leap into not just the present tense but into the future. By the time I came across them, they were beginning to die off, killed by a mixture of hard work, poor tenement air and sclerotic attacks brought on by their volcanic rages, but a surprising number of their children had followed their parents and grandparents into the Movement.

I kept as far away from them as I could. In my view they were worse. They had marched out of the womb as fully formed Young Pioneers, and grew up into sexually inexperienced little puritans – self-possessed, self-important, self-righteous cadre who frowned on the slightest expression of levity. For sport, the boys enjoyed hanging about on street corners, baiting Trotskyites or sometimes even ambushing them and banging their heads against walls, which allowed them to inflict serious injuries without the inconvenience of carrying a weapon. The girls were the ones who were in charge of my reading programme. My ignorance and stupidity were a challenge they relished and like so many before them they positively glowed when they understood how blank a slate I really was, for my thoughts had not been distorted by any of the many 'deviations' to which I could have fallen victim.

So I was set to study as never before, to read, to learn, to soak my brain, to become someone. I was chained to print. Where once I had been apprenticed to my mother's fastidious claims to being a provincial fashion leader, now I was forced into the harness of a Higher Purpose and, by a little osmosis, something or other seeped in. It wasn't much but it was something. Night after night Julius and I sat, him reading. Me dutifully reading. It was not what I'd had in mind when I ran away one night to the jazz clubs of 52nd Street in search of sex and adventure.

And then in the fall of that year, 1948, my cousin Jasa arrived from Belgrade to take up a post as cultural attaché at the Yugoslavian Embassy. Julius had never met anyone from a communist country before and he was impressed that I, of all people, should form such a link to the international socialist movement. Jasa would call at the apartment and the two of them would go into the bedroom together and sit on the bed, talking, the door closed against me.

Of course I saw my cousin alone from time to time. We drank coffee together on the occasional Sunday in a variety of Viennese cafés, where he would try four or five cakes, truculently throwing each one down after a bite. Not as good as before the war, as the *tortes* and *kuchens* that were served in his father's house. And the coffee too thin, the cream too palely primrose instead of butter-cup. This distaste for American cooking – why should he care as long as there was plenty of it and it was nutritious? Discontentedly he puffed on a Camel. He was older than me, over thirty and his Partizan 'hardness' was inevitably bruising to someone as naive as myself. Yet once he had been a furrier like my father and he seemed to have retained the memory of the finer things of life.

Yet his constant complaints seemed less to do with a nostalgia for the *blintzes* and *schnitzels* of home, but a submerged craving for luxury. I liked to imagine that he had my father's look about him, but he did not. Even if the family resemblance had been there, Jasa – whose hair was a little red and sandy and with a moustache more unruly and less well-trimmed – had cultivated himself as a throwback to some distant peasant ancestry, a canny political gesture, I suppose. I sized Jasa up as one of life's main chancers: opportunist was not quite the right term for him, for he was not exactly a man who turns like a weathercock; it was more that he was vested with a greater share of the trader's survival instinct than anyone I had met before. Perhaps this was uncharitable. His father and mother, his grandparents, his two sisters, had all vanished into a premature nothingness. Who could live with that horror? But you ask – no, you think – so what did *he* do to survive? I felt that with Jasa his survival was a membrane that had hardened and formed a crust over his eyes so that he could no longer see out of them. He had with him in America a wife though no children yet. She was not Jewish.

What work did he do as cultural attaché at the Embassy? I

had no idea. There was no mention of foreign policy. He wanted to talk about America. Throughout those fall months we discussed the outcome of the November presidential election and what would be the effect on Henry Wallace's candidacy now the Communist Party put its weight behind him and the Progressives.

'Can he win?' he asked. 'With the Party's support he'll gain a hundred thousand votes and lose three million.' But the campaign was my first taste of *realpolitik* and I was awash with optimistic idealism. I had surrendered myself to study and for the first time I could confidently put forward a learned 'position', which I mimicked for his benefit.

'Of course he will. Don't forget Wallace was one of the architects of the New Deal and everyone remembers how, without it, capitalism would have broken the country's back.' (So they said.) 'When Roosevelt was running the war, and Wallace was his vice-president, who do you think was running the country?'

Easy. Study group stuff I'd memorized.

'He supports the Soviet Union. This will give him popularity?'

'Yes, he is a friend to Russia but not the way people think,' I pronounced. 'You have to listen to what he says. Truman is gunning for a new war, maybe lots of wars, not with the Soviet Union directly but in the small countries that it supports, and that way he wants to destroy everything the workers have built and dreamed of since the Revolution. Wallace is different. He says that if America accepted that there are two separate spheres, each with their own way of life, there could be friendly, peaceful competition between the powers and gradually, he thinks, America will become a little more socialist and

Russia will introduce some elements of free enterprise and democracy. The voters will understand that his programme is a recipe not for revolution but for co-existence and his election will do away with the threat of a new war. A vote for Wallace is a vote for peace.' I smiled at my cousin in a condescending manner, confident I had got my point across.

I had about me the shining, newly forged political armour of those who go into battle for the first time. Nothing had been dented or broken. My tanks were invincible, my small arms deadly.

'You don't think he's a little crazy?' Jasa said. 'I hear he writes to a Russian mystic and conducts seances. Maybe he'll start wearing a turban next.' We were, that late October afternoon, in a café in a street off Columbus Avenue, where the coffee was imported from Europe and reasonably priced, the pastries made at the back by a team of young Polish refugees, bright girls in scraps of cotton scarf tied about their heads who sang while they rolled out the strudel dough or read letters from home and cried, dropping their tears unseen into the currants and apricot jam. It was just around lighting-up time, when people hurrying along the street sometimes seem hazy about the edges, a time to slip into memory, or to summon all your powers to resist it.

'You shouldn't believe everything you read in the capitalist press. Wallace is a good man. When he's in the White House we'll move from New Dealism to socialism and then to communism, you'll see.' I waved my cigarette about, jabbing it in the air to make each point.

'I begin to think smoking is bad for women. It puts wrinkles on the face. I see it in some of our older comrades.'

A year before, I would have gone home and stared for half

an hour or more in the mirror. I would have bought a magnify-
ing glass and examined each inch of my skin. Not now. 'I am
answering your question. We're having a political discussion,
not talking about movie stars.' None the less, the next day I
made the first of my lifetime's attempts to give up smoking, this
one lasting four days.

'Don't take the Party too seriously,' he said. 'America will
never go communist, not in a thousand years.'

'How can you say that? When half the world is going communist how can America resist? There's no way it won't
happen. I give it, oh, ten years at the most. The red flag will be
flying over the White House by 1957.'

'Not America. America is different.'

I stared at him in dismay. 'How? And anyway, you hardly
know America. You've only been here a few months and you
haven't been anywhere but Washington and New York.'

'You've been further?'

'No, but in my study group there are comrades from all over
the country. They come from everywhere. I've heard them
talk.'

'And have they ever *left* America?'

I was hurt at this little attack. I sprang to the defence of my
comrades. 'Yes, some have, during the war.'

'Listen, forget their war stories, they never got further than
the PX. Europe is a separate problem from the United States.
But here, no. The leadership doesn't understand America, they
don't know how to make an American Party. They are too old,
there are too many European Jews. If a man like Julius could
get into the leadership, well, that would be better, but there's
another problem he would have to face, the race chauvinism.
It's all impossible, I'm afraid.'

I lit a second cigarette. The waiter had brought Jasa another pastry and he was interrogating its interior with his fork; a dribble of some kind of liqueur amassed in a pool on the plate. 'So why are you trying to persuade Julius to join?'

'For Julius, because it is the best thing that could happen to him. Where else is the poor guy to go, a thinking Negro? What other place is there for him? It's like putting him behind bars in a zoo but at least he's safe, his mind is fed. It was an act of mercy.'

'What about me?'

'That's what I'm telling you, you'll empty your head of this nonsense sooner or later. Eat something, why aren't you eating?'

But actually he was wrong about that. The election – well, there he was right: it was a disaster. A humiliating million and a half votes cast for Wallace nationwide. I couldn't believe it. Less than three per cent. A Truman victory that would overwhelm all dissent not just for four years but ten, fifteen. The inevitability of war in Asia. War, Julius assumed, of utter finality, an atom bomb war.

Once you have the trick of seeing things from another point of view, it changes you for ever. Simply put, I did not want to die in a mammoth explosion, then atomic fall-out. I dreamed mushroom clouds over Hiroshima. I wanted to live. The alternative terrified the hell out of me. I was a damned sight more frightened of a nuclear war than I was of the Reds.

Julius was at first deeply depressed, then resolute. 'That's it,' he told me, as we listened to the final results coming in on the radio. 'I'm signing up for the CP. To hell with so-called American democracy. There's nothing in it for the Negro when every ballot in the South is rigged.' He believed now that the

South was an oppressed nation in its own right but that even so there was no way that the Negro could be freed outside of a working-class struggle for a new Marxist world order. It was the Communist Party that supported his half-thought suspicion that two centuries of slavery and segregation and lynchings were an act of genocide against his own race.

What about me? I was to become a fellow traveller, he informed me a few days later; outside the Party but a sympathizer. 'They don't like us to have girlfriends outside.'

'OK,' I said. That would teach Jasa.

All it meant was that I had to study harder and Julius was often out at meetings. When he returned, he did not discuss what he had been doing or what he thought. It was crazy for him to have become a communist then, when the anti-Red scares were just about upon us, but who could have predicted what was to come, the depth of the ferocity? And, besides, what exactly did he have to lose?

New York had become for me a different city from the one at which I had made landfall, not even two years before. Accidentally, I had fallen into a way of life that was invisible to the casual eye, a submerged substratum of the city which did not appear to the newly arrived traveller: that city of light and rain, of icy pools of slush gathered at the sidewalk's edge in winter, the blast furnace of humid air that filled one's apartment in the summer, the shops, the skyscrapers, the restaurants you could read of in the society pages, the demi-monde that Winchell documented. The public face of New York hid another life which was *the* life for the people I now found myself amongst. Dirt and poverty was their heritage. They had grown up on the Projects, in the co-operatives, they haggled over shoddy scraps of nothing at Macy's. They bought herrings from a barrel in the Lower East Side and if they made it, they took a vacation in the Catskills. The only way out was through education, through ideas, through books.

'I'd be playing out in the park on a summer's day, getting a little fresh air and exercise, which God knows you needed,' someone told me, 'and my father would walk past on his way home from work and come and grab me by the collar and drag me inside. He wanted to know what I was doing in the open air like a savage when I could have been sitting at a table with a book, improving my mind.'

They believed that this was the real America and who was I to disagree? If I had thought, back home in Liverpool, that I was not a real Jew, imagine how I felt here.

Doggedly they kept me at my studies. I found the novels easiest. Political theory, which Julius devoured – yards of Lenin at a time, pound on pound of Marx – I could not get through. I always forgot the beginning of the sentence by the time I got to the end. Well, it was all above my head. I wasn't an intellectual. But I did my best. At least it brought Julius and me closer together. He would not read a novel. He was, he said, 'only interested in the truth. I don't want to read a book of lies.' So I used to recount the plots to him as we sat over our meal and he would show me how the characters were wrong or right in what they did.

Meanwhile I went to work every day at Bloomingdale's and braved the stares of the other workers when, as I left the store at the end of the day, I headed uptown, staying on the bus as the numbers of the streets got higher and higher and only maids were getting on. The maids got to know me after a while and sometimes we'd talk and they would tell me tales of the apartments where they worked, of vain, silly, bored women with nothing to do all day but change their clothes and pick faults in their employees' work.

'My lady made me iron the dress she's gonna wear tonight, five times, *five times*. I couldn't get it done like she wanted it. I said to her, soon as you sit down this dress will crease, I can't make it look how it came from the store, ma'am. You had it six months. Why don't you wear that new dress, you got last week? She tells me, "That dress don't fit me." I say to her, "Why you buy it, then, ma'am?" She says she's gonna diet right into it. I ask her why she don't just buy a dress that fit but she tells me to stop talking and keep ironing. Why do you white ladies like to be so skinny?'

I said we just preferred it that way. Didn't she? Anyway, all the movie stars were very slim. Didn't she want to look like one of them?

'All the movie stars is white. I can straighten my hair but I'm never gonna be Rita Hayworth however hard I try. My husband says he likes something you can get hold of in bed. What about your man?'

'He seems to like white women.'

'Yeah, they're all the same.'

'Do you have to be a maid?'

'It's work. No different from working in a store. You're still waiting on people. That's all it is.'

'My boyfriend waits on people as well, I guess. He installs air conditioning. Some friends of mine say that the only honest work is making things.'

'Like working in a factory?'

'Yes.'

'Sure, the pay's good. But that's not work for coloured people. The unions made sure of that.'

'Oh,' I said. 'I see. Tell me more.' They also serve who only stand and wait, I thought of this woman, serving me in her fashion.

And hence it was that, on an evening a week or two later at our study group, I was able to 'make an intervention' on the condition of the Negro working classes within the labour movement.

Julius came home late one night. I heard his heavy tread on the stairs, his key turn, his fingers clicking. I was waiting up for him, reading *The Grapes of Wrath*, which I was finding both interesting and engrossing. He crossed the room without taking off his topcoat and sat on the couch next to me. He was smiling.

'What's your book?' he asked, turning the cover towards him. 'Oh, a novel.'

'It's about migrants, grape-pickers in California,' I said. 'It's some book.'

'Coincidence. I'm being sent to California,' he said.

'Oh.' I gave a blasé, affected little laugh and went on reading my book.

'Just "oh"?'

I looked down at my feet, trying not to cry. So I was going to be on my own again. I should have known it would be him that would leave, not me. I felt deserted and abandoned. I got a lump in my throat. I saw the fragility of my purpose. I had scrambled up a little slope and there was a minute portion of dirt under my fingernails. Well, I was to slide back into meaninglessness again.

He got up, went into the kitchen and came back a few minutes later with a cup of coffee and a stale slice of bread spread with margarine. He ate the bread, looking at me, still looking at my feet.

'What goes on in your head? Sometimes you look like a brainless dope, other ways I see it you've got some angle going. You want to come to California or not? Speak out now, this is the only time I'm asking.' Was it a planned surprise? Or had he just thought it before that very moment? Had he thought of me at all until then? I don't know.

My shining face betrayed me. '*Really?*'

He turned away to the window, his shoulders still heavy under his coat. His back shrugged.

'I don't say things I don't mean,' his back said. Night beyond the windows, papers rustling under his feet. His shoes were always turned up at the toes. He was always claiming truth and authenticity, but always playing these little games with me, with my head. Stan was straighter.

'I would love to come with you.'

'Yeah?' It was a kind of sneer.

'If you don't mind me coming. If I won't get in the way. I promise I won't get in the way. No ties.'

'In the way?' his back asked. 'No ties?'

I meant of his political activity, but perhaps he understood it differently.

'No,' I said. 'Absolutely not.'

'And I won't get in your way,' his back replied. His back became his front at last, his cold front. 'So we have a deal, then. You come along, no commitments.'

'No,' I said. 'No commitments, of course not. I wouldn't dream of suggesting it.'

He thudded up and down the apartment, clicking his fingers, smirking to himself.

California, land of sunshine and oranges. Sometimes big changes come about just like that; you don't really make a decision, life carries you along. This was how I saw it. As long as I wasn't on my own, I was fine, anything would be OK with me.

A week or two later Julius returned with another piece of news. 'We have to make a stop on the way, just for a few weeks. The Party has a little work for me to do there.'

'Where?'

'Minneapolis-St Paul.'

'Where's that?'

He took out an atlas and we looked at America. The country was cut in half by the Mississippi River and on either side of it were two cities. I liked that idea, of a metropolis divided. I liked it that we would make the journey in two stages. I traced the route lines of roads with my finger and saw them spread like the lines on an old woman's face, across the wide grimacing countenance that was to me the shape of the USA.

Unknown land, our hearts' desire then as it is for others now. And the unfamiliar names of states and their cities melting on my tongue. Mysterious America.

Morris had just broken up with the dancer, with whom, it turned out, he was *not* in love. Now he had lost his virginity he wasn't going to be tied down by one man and so he let himself loose on the bar scene. He was happy, all right. Everything was going his way – he'd been picked up by a fellow from one of the big magazines who'd found him a job in the art department laying out pages and sometimes designing covers. *He* was stealing invites and gatecrashing parties given by Lenny Bernstein and the British couturier Charles James while *I* was typing at the union office. He was having a fabulous time.

I told him my news one night in a Greenwich Village café where – to hell with our figures – we drank hot chocolate with whipped cream and melted marshmallows. It was hard to keep his attention. Every guy who came in made him look up.

'I have relatives in Minnesota,' he said doubtfully. 'You'll find it a pretty quiet place.'

'Maybe I'd appreciate a quiet life for a change. Anyway, it doesn't matter, we won't be there for long.'

'The winters are bad. Lot of Norwegian stock, none of them too bright, dumb animals with the strength of oxes but stupid, like meat. I'd cut my throat if I had to live there.'

I passed this on to Julius. 'Don't judge a book by its cover,' he said. 'And be sure never to pay any attention to anything a faggot has to say.'

Still, I kissed Morris tenderly goodbye, certain that one day we would meet again, though in fact we would not. I told him to look after himself and he promised he would. He told me to listen to my dreams. 'Keep following the yellow brick road, Sybil. Be a surrealist woman, always be a wing.'

'Oh, go on with you,' I told him.

'Suck some cock for me out west,' he called from his window as I walked down the street.

I made one important contribution to our great trip to California. I sold my last mink and with the money I bought us an automobile, a brand-new Chevy. Julius had learned to drive in the service and he promised to teach me on the way. His books went into storage. The apartment was rented out to some other person. I scrubbed its every surface clean before we left.

So we set off with high hopes and I bade my farewells to New York. It was a clear, bright winter's day and the skyscrapers had a kind of burnished radiance in the sharp sunlight, like a city of castles in a dream Morris would design for the cover of a magazine. The streets had never seemed lovelier as women strolled about in their furs, sometimes with little dogs on the ends of leads running ahead, like tiny engines pulling great liners along. A young black hipster in a hat that Frank Sinatra would later make famous was clicking his fingers on a street corner, waiting for the *Walk* sign, and just out of the corner of my eye I believed I saw an impossible thing – a man dressed up as a woman, but I wasn't sure.

'I'll never see Stan again now,' I told myself as we passed out of Manhattan. But that was history and the future lay ahead of us as we crossed the city limits. I had a little lump in my throat as I glanced back through the rear window but I was young and looking forward to an adventure. Tentatively I put my hand on Julius's knee and gave it a little squeeze and he did not take it away. I let it rest there for a while until it got hot and sweaty so I slid it back to my own lap. I looked at his profile next to me. His eyes were on the road and his thoughts were somewhere else. I shifted towards the window and looked away, out to what was there, to be seen.

Chapter Fourteen

I can remember the route, in the way that you give directions, saying where you turn right, and at what point you turn left. But what do you pass as you go? Why do you make the journey in the first place? And who was that person anyway? So hard to recall. I said I saw myself in Julius's apartment in my ballerina-length dress, and I did. The mind can take pictures of itself, of the outside of things. But what about who we are inside? That's what I have always found so difficult to remember.

I know that we were driving along and I was wearing a grey costume with white cuffs and gloves and that in Pennsylvania there were grey clapboard houses adrift in wheat fields. That the clock on the cherrywood dashboard stopped almost immediately. And that a hundred miles from the city everything was silent. We kept to country roads. There were no spaces

between things, just a few things in the spaces. Rain muffled
the sound that crows make. The radio picked up and lost
intermittent signals; snatches of dance music, a hospital drama
and local weather squeezed through cracks in the glass and
drifted into fields rutted with frost. In Ohio and Indiana the
airwaves failed. Children shouted abuse at us at crossroad
towns but we never called back. We stopped from time to time
to drink coffee and eat pie.

Oh, I felt fine at first, on top of the world. It turned out that
driving was one of the things I liked, was good at, and Julius
was encouraged to find that at least there was something I
could do with ease. My hand lay lightly on the wheel and a
little inch in either direction could alter the course of your
life. A tiny pressure on the gas pedal tore you through towns
that would otherwise have detained you. I loved our car, *my*
car. Once I drag-raced some kid from a *Stop* sign. Another time
I raced another car through a storm. I was captain of our fate.
Julius was terrified. 'I created a monster!' he shouted out of the
window. 'What the fuck have I done? She's a hellcat behind
the wheel.'

We drove into Minneapolis three days later on a Saturday
lunchtime and I wanted to be sick at what I found there. 'Oh,
Christ,' I said to Julius. 'This isn't it, is it?' Despite what Morris
had told me, I had no idea, none at all. The Twin Cities were
still sleeping off the excitement of their discovery a hundred
years before. There was supposed to be water all around us, we
were at the head of the Mississippi, so why did these people
look like farm folk, the stench of cows sticking to their clothes?
The river didn't impress me, it didn't interest me. The place
seemed pointless. All the faces I looked at, paused at intersections, were ugly. You could lay place-settings for six on those

faces. After an hour I was sick of the sight of yellow moustaches. All the women were overweight. The department-store windows we passed were terrible, the stock dated, full of 'timeless' fashions in big sizes.

'Julius,' I said. 'Where the hell are we?'

'America,' he replied. 'This is it. What you see is what you get.' He was acting nonchalant but I could see he wasn't pleased either.

We checked into a hotel and he made a phone call. 'Good news,' he called out to me, in the shower. 'There's a meeting tonight. They say it's OK for you to come.'

'Great!' I shouted back. 'Just great.'

We set out for what was, Julius reminded me, a secret destination. It was a little while before the terror started and when it did it was to descend more lightly on out-of-the-way places such as this; even so, everyone was paranoid. We drove around in circles for a while, following directions deliberately plotted to mislead anyone who might be following us.

Finally Julius said, 'We're here,' and in we went.

Among the people assembled there was no resemblance to the political activists I had known in New York. Although there were Jews, of course (Jews get everywhere), the clamour of Yiddish did not fill the air. There were no Negroes at all. I was surprised to find that outside New York City the Party had little representation among the coloured population. Although I was a foreigner, at least *there* I had been among immigrants who remembered that there was something else than the country they were in. As Julius pointed out later, these people came from the heartland of America that was as alien to him as it was to me. The farmlands, the mining towns, the great interior drama of American life that had been played out for two

centuries on the Great Plains – I had sung along to it so senti-
mentally one evening the summer before, and here it was laid
out before us in an expanse of checked shirts and browbeaten
hats. Their faces looked as if they had been as formed by the
weather as the Presidents' faces on Mount Rushmore (which I
had seen in pictures in *Life* magazine) had been eroded by the
wind and the rain and the ice. They were not by any means all
proletarians: there were schoolteachers, librarians, clerks at
City Hall and of course a few college professors. But most of
them were much of a muchness, from the same Scandinavian
stock. I was later to feel that when immigrants came to
America they just kept going until they found somewhere that
looked like home and they stopped, and said *here*. The
Scandinavians saw in Minnesota, that watery, landlocked state,
an approximation of Norway and Sweden.

And they looked at *me*, in my grey costume and white cuffs
and gloves. Julius was greeted warmly, being a 'catch'. But to
those who were descendants of the pioneers who put the
prairies to the plough, I was just a johnny-come-lately, not
three years off the boat. What took you so long? they seemed to
say. So you come here when *we* have done all the work. You
don't like Minneapolis? Be grateful you have a city at all. Who
do you think made it? Us. Who built it out of nothing with our
own bare hands? They put out those hands and shook mine.
'Pleased to meet you,' they said. But I suppose to them I must
have seemed like a doll you place on a shelf, kept always
wrapped in its cellophane packaging.

When we got back to the hotel I turned to Julius, stricken.
'How long do we have to stay?'

He looked pretty shaken himself. He started to get
undressed. Then: 'Oh, don't worry, it'll be fine.'

'What do you have to do here?' I asked him.

'I'm sorry, but I can't say,' he replied, almost humbly. 'But I do promise that I'll try and get us out of this place as quick as I can. We're going to California, just keep that in the back of your mind.'

We went to bed and in the inky blackness which was that city at night, we made love. For the first time in whatever it was between us, it felt like it was him and me against the world, as we held each other in our hotel room, reminding each other of whatever name it was we had used to sign ourself in on the register.

Ten days passed. Julius was out most of the time. I stayed in the room and read. I tried not to look out of the window. At what? I got through a lot of pages, that week and a half. Books were now beginning to engross me. Hemingway, Steinbeck, Theodore Dreiser, Sinclair Lewis and Upton Sinclair, the kid Mailer. 'Just trashy novels,' Julius said dismissively. He saw that kind of thing as a phase you had to go through, like a child has big print and pictures before they go on to proper books, written for adult life.

It was so cold. We had arrived in early February when the ground was hard, white and bare and though there was a thaw a couple of weeks later, a few days after that another snowstorm blew in from Canada and the temperature dropped below five degrees. The apartment the Party rented for us after the first two nights had steam heating but I was never as warm as I had been in that freezing room in Greenwich Village with Stan, lying under the weight of my mink.

Here, cold was what you thought about. The sky pressed down on you. Sometimes I looked out of the window and saw the air glittering with colours, where the moisture had frozen and the light refracted off it in the sun. The liquid on people's eyelids froze over. A woman died, lost in a blizzard in her own yard.

One morning Julius woke before me and touched me out of sleep. He placed a hand on my shoulder. 'You feeling strong?' he asked me.

'I hardly have my eyes open.'

'OK, now don't get sore, there's a bit of a problem, a road-block, let's call it.' Something was seeping out of Julius, his arrogance, I suppose. His manner towards me had become conciliatory.

'What problem? What's a roadblock?'

'We're going to stay here for a while.'

'How long a while?'

'A few months, three, four, six, maximum.'

I sat bolt upright. 'You promised.'

'I know I did, but a promise I make to you doesn't have the same weight as a promise I make to the Party. You know that. I do what they tell me.'

'What about me? What am I going to do all day?'

'We've thought of that. You can get a job. There's a potato chip plant that's hiring. They have a lot of women workers there and I told them that you have experience organizing with women.'

'But in a factory? I wouldn't know what to do.'

'Sure you will. You'll be fine.' I could not believe he was being so encouraging, the man who had always put me down. I could see his embarrassment in his face. 'There's something else. They don't like that you're not a member. They think you should join.'

'Me? They wouldn't have me, would they?'

'Well I wouldn't have thought so, but it seems that they will. Security reasons, I guess. Better you're in than out.'

And that's how I came to join the Communist Party.

Something was happening to America, then. It was coming under the sway of mind control. Everything Red was bad. It was like Germany under Hitler. This time I watched out for the signs of war, I did not daydream. War was coming and men would have to fight it. Why should the Negroes have weapons pressed into their hands so they could go and bear arms against the Soviet Union – which in a single generation had raised mankind to full human dignity? Julius asked. And why should anyone point a gun at the soldiers of the Red Army who four years before had entered and liberated Auschwitz? I replied. I could not bear to live through another war when there was still so much from the last one I could not speak of. My generation does not talk about these things. That does not mean they are forgotten. The past is not behind us. It is with you all your life. My father came home one morning after his Home Guard duty and put his head in his hands and wept because he had pulled a child's blonde head from beneath a girder and it had come away without any body. He never said anything about it again. The last thing Mr Isaacs told his son Clive, before he went back after his leave, was 'look after your mother for me'. He was killed in Italy. Clive was only nine. I used to see him in his short trousers queueing for rations for his mum and sending for a man to mend a window after a blast. No more war, no more war. Please, no more air-raid shelters, no more firewatching. No more revelations in the dark.

In a few months a terrible savagery would be unleashed against us. Later that year we would be divided into cells and recruitment would virtually cease, links dissolved with the rank and file. But in the meantime I was sent down to the Party office and assigned to a woman called Joanne, whose task it was to turn me into a cadre. Some hope. I looked around and though I had been in rooms something like this in New York I saw clearly now the wrinkled posters advertising some kind of strike or other decorating the walls, the framed photographs of V. I. Lenin and Uncle Joe behind glass, the piles of unsold newspapers – only the Gestetner machine and the typewriter, the workings of which I knew so well, were there to remind me that there was a common thread between this place and the one I had left behind.

Joanne was in her forties and what looks she might have had were gone. I did not notice then that her eyes were sharp, that she took in everything, that she sized up life before it sized up her. I just saw her shapeless dress and threadbare knitted jacket of a style that would not even have been fashionable before the war. And the hair streaked with grey, tied up in a knot at the back of her neck, as if all she was concerned with was getting it out of the way.

'Oh,' she said. 'The girlfriend. How did he wind up with you?'

'Liked the look of me?'

'Men.'

People were bundling up copies of the press to be sold on street corners and the mimeograph machine churned out copies of leaflets.

'Is it usually this active?' I asked her.

'Yeah, most comrades like to come in early and get stuff done. They come straight from their jobs. You need to be fixed up, I hear.'

'Packing potato chips.' I made a face. 'Is it easy work?'

'It is if you're used to it. But I guess it's not the kind of work you *are* used to.'

'I had a job in a munitions factory once, during the war.'

'You were on the assembly line?'

'No, in the office.'

'I work in an office. What a fucking life. Take care how you dress or they'll make you a secretary. Put on some pants. I can lend you a pair if you don't have none.'

'I take a pretty small size.'

'Use a belt, they'll bunch up round the waist. How did you say you ran into Julius?'

'In a jazz club. In New York.'

'Jazz, it's degenerate music.'

'Tell that to Julius.'

There were a number of different jobs you could do in the factory, and none of them was at all pleasant. At the back, where you couldn't see them, men unloaded potatoes. By the time they got to the bottom of the pile, there were always a sizeable number that had gone bad and so the stink of rotten tubers filled the plant. When I was told I was going to the factory I imagined a bunch of us sitting around in a circle wearing turbans, peeling potatoes and telling dirty jokes while we were at our labour. But there was no peeling; that was done by shovelling the potatoes into a vat of some kind of acid that ate off the skins. Then they rumbled down a chute into a tank of freezing water to wash off the residue. Diagonally across the vat was a metal bar and two women who always had colds stood on either side in white rubber boots dipping their hands in to pick out oversize potatoes and smash them in half on the bar.

The potatoes disappeared for a while into a machine which sliced them, then they fell into the fryers. The next job was hateful. Fresh from the fat the chips cascaded lightly down on to a belt and there were four women this time to reach over and pick off the blackened ones, which were discarded. Some of the chips were blistered and full of hot fat, which burst all over your fingers when you touched them, drenching the white cotton gloves that were supposed to protect your skin. The best, most experienced workers burnt their hands only once or twice a shift. I burnt mine five or six times an hour.

The easiest task was tending the machines that drizzled a shower of salt and flavourings on to the chips as they passed, but the finer the powder, the more it got in your throat and eyes. The most complicated machines, the ones which packaged the chips, were operated by men. There was little for them to do until something went wrong, and they sat on stools reading newspapers and checking the sports results. Most of the factory's workers were packers. Eight of us sat on each side of the line and transferred forty-eight packs of chips off it into a cardboard box. Each time you picked up a bag you had to press it slightly. If the bag did not resist your fingers, there was an air hole and the chips would grow stale. You discarded them and they would be sold off cheap at the end of the day. If the line was moving too fast or we were working too slowly, bags of chips piled up at the end of the line and fell off on to the floor and soon they were rustling around your feet, and if you didn't pick up your speed then you felt them reach your knees.

Bashing, picking off and sprinkling were regarded as the élite occupations, not only because there were fewer of them but since you faced your fellow worker you could talk to her, whereas on the packing line you sat in rows, looking at some-one's back. Nothing had prepared me for the monotony of life as a packer. Counting out forty-eight packs of chips fully occu-pied my attention. It was impossible to think, or the boxes would have the wrong number of packs in them. You counted forty-eight for a shift of seven hours, plus half an hour for lunch and two coffee breaks of fifteen minutes. I would fill three boxes with one hundred and forty-six packets of chips and find that only a minute and a half had passed.

This was my city now, a metropolis in which rivers of dirty water ran and chemical clouds drifted over our heads. Man-made city of machines and alleyways between them, the sky obscured, the hurrying crowds three times a day rushing to and from their stools. City of the masses, only the masses, a city with no shops or glamour or nightclubs or deviant margins. A night-life the same as the day. No Statue of Liberty but the hooter that sounded to tell you your shift was over.

Three shifts were in operation and as I had the lowest sen-iority I was put on graveyard. I clocked on at ten at night and clocked off at six in the morning. In the parking lot, later that summer, I would come out of the plant, look at the saplings and fireweed and smell the lard on my skin. In those first weeks I slept all day, waking in the early evening, when Julius was out at some meeting or other. As for recreation, at any given time I had a mass of reading to get through, in fear of Joanne's bitter tongue if I had not completed my assignment.

I made an effort to put into practice what I had learned at Bloomingdale's, but at the plant we workers were just hands, nothing more. We were reduced to a pair of hands, and we knew it. The widget got hammered, the box got packed. That was it, take it or leave it. I could bring no other insight to bear

on the situation. So Joanne explained Marx's theory of alien-
ation to me and it made complete sense. The first few days you
ate some chips, then you developed a lifelong aversion to them.
The bags of potato chips had nothing to do with us. We couldn't
give a shit about them. You hated everyone you saw eating a
package of chips. You wanted to tell them how that package
came to be in their hands, what people had to go through to
get them there and you believed that if they knew, if you could
convince them, not another potato chip would ever pass their
lips as long as they lived. Though how things would be different when the workers owned the means of production, I wasn't
sure. Maybe potato chips would be abolished in a better world,
and other, more pleasant jobs could be found for those who had
to manufacture them. I know the Party said that the workers
made things, things which kept the country going, but potato
chips? Who needed them?

Most of the workers in the factory were women, but hardly
any of them were in the union. It wasn't that they were anti-
labour, they just said it was men's business. I tried arguing with
them at our breaks. I showed them how much better the men's
conditions were than our own because they had naturally
feathered their own nests.

'The union is in the pocket of the management,' one
woman said.

'So why don't you get active?' I cried.

They looked at each other and laughed.

'What? What?'

'Go and become a big shot in the union, Sybil. We'll vote
for you.'

'What about *you*? Don't you understand we're all in this
together?'

'And who will look after our kids while we're at the union meeting? Who'll get my old man's meal?'

I'd never thought of that.

It was nothing like the department store. I hadn't a clue what was going on. They were younger than me, most of them still teenagers, but they all had children, three or four by the time they were my age. They worked for a bigger icebox and a television. The older ones remembered hard times. 'I have six children, buried three.'

'My husband lost a hand in the mill. It's been four years and he's still waiting on compensation.'

'I lost my mother and father in a fire. The oil stove was tipped over and burned our house down. I'd hardly started grade school when I was put out to work by the orphanage.'

One time an Indian woman came to work there. She was from Baffin Bay with a stout torso, like a seal. The foreman couldn't get anyone to work with her. She wasn't much good at any of the jobs. She was slow like molasses in winter, they said, so they put her in with the men, hauling potatoes. Some kind of fight broke out, no one found out what caused it. We looked up and saw a guy marching into the main plant, holding her by the arm. He was screaming at her: 'Fucking squaw, fucking cunt!' He pulled her arm and stuck the hand into one of the fryers, into the boiling fat. She was screaming. The arm came out, looking brown and cooked, the skin peeling. He got fired. I don't know what happened to her. The union didn't do anything. I could never get any information.

Some union organizer. I took no comfort from the fact that it was the Party's fault for sending the likes of me into such a place. Who was I to make a critique of the recent turn to industry, which was forcing teachers and social workers and even professors into the factories to purge the Party of its petit bourgeois tendencies?

I hated everything about that place. I have never been a rebel by inclination (I don't have the strength of character), but it took every ounce of the strength I did have not to walk off the line in the middle of the shift, go down to a beauty parlour and surrender to a perm, a facial and my fingers in a warm bath of soapy water as my cuticles gently softened.

I lasted two weeks before I told Julius I'd had it, made a mistake. I would never do anything in industry. I would never be a proletarian, not in a million years.

'That's what Joanne says.'

'Oh well, she would. She doesn't have to work there.'

'I guess she wouldn't mind. She does what she's told.'

'I don't want to do what I'm told.'

'Tough.'

I looked at him. 'Is that it, no compromise?'

'Yeah, that's it.'

'This is murder. Can't you talk to them for me?'

'You said you weren't going to get in my way. Wasn't that what you said? You've got your life, I have mine.'

I had to concede him that.

'Yes, but you've never had to do this sort of work, it's demeaning, not just to me but to everyone. It's demeaning to the human race. We're just animals in there, worse, they have some freedom, we're just things. It rots your brain. No one should have to do what I have to do all day. It would be better to put a torch to the place.'

He shrugged. 'So now you know how the other half lives.'

'Yes, but I don't even like the city, maybe in San Francisco I could manage a little better, at least there you can go and walk about when your shift is over, instead of getting straight in your car and driving home. Here I can't even walk round a corner without being frightened that I'll freeze to death.'

'So what?'

'When are we going? Can we leave yet? How much longer? And there's another thing. I don't like the way people look at us on the street when we're together. I get nervous.'

He laughed out loud. 'Oh, *really*, nervous? Oh, how the little girl has suffered.' I went red. Race chauvinism was real in Minnesota. It was palpable. To my eyes Julius was handsome, his eyes burning with the ferocity of his intelligence and his rage. He was cultured; he listened not just to jazz but to classical music. He knew about fine art. He had hauled his way out from the primitive swamp of the ghetto. He was fully human. To our Italian neighbours down the hall in our temporary apartment, however, he was just an ignorant coon and I was little better than a streetwalker for going with him.

But perhaps it would all be different in California. 'How much longer?' I asked him again.

He turned away. 'I don't know. I'm not sure. Something is—'

'What? Something is what?'

'Nothing. We'll talk all this through later. Let's eat. What you cooked?'

I stood my ground. 'Meat loaf with creamed potatoes and corn. Talk what through later? What's going on? I'm a Party member, you can tell me, can't you?'

'I told you, it's nothing. Not yet, anyhow.'

I should have known something was up when Julius came home one day with a dog.

'What's that?' I said, when he brought it up the stairs to our apartment. I don't know what kind of dog it was: something biggish.

'Always good to have a dog about the house,' Julius said. 'It'll keep you company when I'm out.' I looked at the dog and the dog stared vaguely back. It bared its teeth and saliva drooled over its fur.

'Look,' he said. 'It's smiling.'

'How can you tell? I think it's sharpening its fangs. It's awfully big. And it smells.'

'Would you have preferred a cat?'

I tried that out in my mind. 'No, I don't think so.'

The dog ate noisily from a tin dish of smelly canned food that Julius put out for it.

'Take it away,' I said, recoiling.

'No, no,' Julius replied, 'you'll get to love it. You can give him a name if you want.'

'A name?'

'Yes, sure.'

'People have names. Animals are just . . .'

Julius and the dog were a new phalanx of power, opposing me. He assumed a kind of goofy tenderness towards it which I thought was beneath his dignity.

'Always wanted a dog,' he said, tickling it under the chin.

'This is the first I've heard of it.'

'Run!' he shouted, throwing a rolled-up paper across the room.

'I don't like pets.'

'Well, it's staying.'

'Yes, but we aren't.'

'We'll cross that fence when we come to it.'

'What do you mean?'

'Look, try and get to know the dog, it's good security. The Party suggested it and they're right. Go on, pat him.'

I touched the dog with two fingers. Its fur was coarse. 'Wouldn't make much of a coat,' I said.

Julius looked at me. 'This is a whole new side I'm finding out about you,' he said.

'And me you,' I said right back.

Chapter Fifteen

I did not know it then but I was to stay in Minnesota for two years. Every spring I would look at the white bare ground in the backyard of our building and know that nothing could ever grow there again, that all plant life was extinct. Yet every year the thaw would come and up would pop the grass, flowers, zucchini, tomatoes, pumpkins. A magnolia tree outside my window grew big flat white petals. Around us lakes unfroze and the prairies tried not to be too dull. And so on for the summer months until ice appeared once again. It was Nature doing its thing.

I was totally cut off from the past. I had been advised not to maintain any contact with anyone outside the Party from a former life. I could not correspond with Morris. From the time I left New York to a period many years in the future I had no further communication with my parents. I was warned that any mail I sent or received was bound to be intercepted. I wondered about them sometimes but their world was no longer the same as my own. I was ashamed to tell anyone that I had a father who made fur coats for rich people, for a living, and that my mother existed entirely as a clothes-hanger. Besides, was I not purging myself of their malignant influence? I had made, I thought, a decisive break with the past.

After we had been in Minneapolis for four months a strike broke out at a little community college on the outskirts of town where the support staff – the secretaries and the administration clerks – had recently certified as a union and were going for their first contract, largely through Joanne's leadership. When I had first met Joanne and found out more about her, I had thought, superciliously, that hers was an unenviable existence: a forty-year-old woman in a two-room apartment rented from fellow-travellers, a cup of soup and crackers after a long day, nothing to do but read documents or listen to the radio, then off to a narrow bed with hospital corners. I played malicious little games, trying to match her up with someone, always choosing the comrade with the worst breath or bad feet as her beau. Julius was startled when I mentioned this.

'She used to be married to . . .' He mentioned one of our most romantically handsome members back east whom I had particularly noted when I had seen him at the Wallace convention.

'What? How could that have been? She's years older than him,' I replied, staggered.

'Trust you to judge a woman on her looks,' Julius said. That was a bit rich coming from him. He had hardly chosen me for intellectual stimulation. 'They're about the same age. In fact they grew up together. They were married for it must have been fifteen years, since they were teenagers, I heard.'

'What happened? Why did he leave her?'

'You really do get hold of the wrong end of things, Sybil. She left him.'

'Why?'

'I couldn't tell you. You'd have to ask her yourself.' But he knew I would never dare.

Joanne, who typed stencils of course outlines and reading lists all day, found that if it had been tough enough getting the necessary signatures for a certification vote, it was harder still teaching the women who came to work every day in grey suits and little white gloves how to negotiate. At first they asked for a modest raise of six per cent.

'Are you out of your minds?' she asked them. 'Don't you understand, you have to have something to negotiate down *from*?' She tried to get them to see that they should demand an across-the-board increase of a dollar figure: unlike a percentage increase, it did not automatically widen the gap between the highest and lowest grades of worker. The secretaries were amazed. No one but us communists had ever taught them how to think like this. For the most part they were middle-aged, like Joanne herself, women who had married before the war and had not had to delay starting their families like those who had reached adulthood a year or so later. Try as they might, the college, who would have liked to replace them with shapelier, less homely types, found that younger girls would no sooner start work than they would get married and resolutely decide that their career would be as a home-maker and they would be off to one of the new tract developments outside town before they'd even found out the names of everyone in the faculty. It was the opposite of what had been going on in the retail trade back in New York, where it was the older workers who were pushed out on to the street. Here, middle-aged women were pretty well all the employers could get.

Still, the college's view was that it could starve these little secretaries out as long as it didn't take their pathetic union seriously; indeed it wasn't as if their husbands were union men, for they were more likely to be white-collar workers, like their wives, than blue – clerks, salesmen, public officials, maybe even accountants or dentists. The administration thought that if they just ignored the union, their girls would feel foolish and give up. A morning on a picket line in their suits and high-heeled shoes, when the temperatures were still struggling above freezing, would send them back to their warm offices and their coffee percolators and then a forgiving management would even go so far in the girls' favour as to invent the kindness of a college cookie fairy which would fill a fresh plate for them, every break.

It was late April when the strike started, the time of the spring thaw when the air was still cold enough to freeze and there was always a chance of another blizzard but the snow already on the ground was turning into rivers of slush. The limits of the campus were defined by the college as a road halfway up a small, man-made hill and it told the union that was the place they would have to set up their picket line. This was disheartening news. The first morning the thirty or so support staff turned up dressed for a day at work (a few cautious ones ornamented in pink or powder-blue ear muffs), wearing over their coats brown linen tabards with the words 'On Strike' stencilled in sticky black, shipped down from the union head office in Washington, along with some picket signs. Thus attired, they really believed, Joanne said, that their wan, pinched faces would move hearts of stone, that the strike would be over by lunchtime and all their demands acceded to.

By the end of the day they were very cold. They had stood gallantly in the middle of the highway with their signs, stopping each car as it drove up, handing a leaflet through the window to the driver and politely asking him or her to consider their grievances. A couple of instructors and a handful of students turned back. The rest roared through. It was the same thing three days running and the secretaries were more than ready to give in. Then Joanne asked them if they wanted outside support. She begged them to give it one more day. Reluctantly, they agreed: just another morning and then . . . well, they had been going over it in their minds and perhaps the college really did know what was best for them. The usual fights were breaking out, the usual 'I told you so's' when things go wrong.

There was a meeting that night which the secretaries didn't know anything about. I was not there, of course; it involved a higher level than my own. Joanne was there and Julius was. Julius came home late and told me not to go into work the next day. I was out of the potato chip factory for the time being.

'We want you to back this dispute,' he told me. 'It's going to need your organizing skills.'

'Mine?'

'Yes.'

'So you concede that I have them.'

'Well, let's just say we've got the chance to find out if you do or not.'

I rose in the dark and Joanne came by at six-thirty in her car to take me to the strike. She didn't say anything, just handed me coffee from a flask. As we sat at a set of lights she turned to me: 'Don't fuck up,' she said. 'Just don't fuck up on me.'

The Party was out in force. By seven a.m., when the cleaners came up the hill walking or in wrecked-out old automobiles, there were two hundred of us on the picket line. The sky had a bruised, oily look about it, like dirty fat in a pan, and there was no sun to burn away the patches of black ice on the road. Some of us stood on the central reservation, on hard, coarse grass, others on the sides, landscaped bleakly with straight lines of immature fir trees. Wherever you stood, icy water found a way into your boots. Although we were only five miles out of town, and the college just a walk away, I felt engulfed by the desolation of our surroundings.

But what a difference two hundred made. Some of us were Party members, others fellow travellers or unionists who had come along to lend a hand when our comrades put out the call. The Party could find a use for everyone: the Greek, Spiro, who ran a restaurant in town, drove up in a pick-up truck with a coffee machine and a tray of donuts at eight and came back at twelve with hot-dogs and fried onions. Someone else brought song-sheets and we cheered our spirits, arms linked, singing 'We Shall Overcome' and 'The Ballad of Joe Hill'. At two-thirty I heard a roaring and stamping from around a bend in the road and the sound of a labouring engine.

'It's the cops!' someone shouted.

The nose of a flat-bed truck appeared. We watched it in silence.

'Goons,' the same voice muttered.

'Pinkertons,' said someone else.

Then the driver pulled down his window. 'Reinforcements!' he cried and out from the bed of the truck climbed fifty husky union men. I thought, suddenly, of my father and his height, five feet seven inches, beside theirs. I don't think there was one man under six feet and many must have weighed over two hundred pounds. The secretaries were watching them as well. I don't know if they knew what to think. I suppose they had begun to realize what they had started and how it was bigger than them. They must have looked at these guys in their plaid jackets with their crude hands and faces, pure meat factories, and wondered what they had in common with them, beyond the fact that, inexplicably, they had come to lend their support.

All day our numbers ebbed and flowed as picketers took their stand for a few hours before heading off to their own jobs, or came straight from shift or between making their kids' lunch and picking them up again from school. Our estimate was that around five hundred men and women had lent their aid that first day. We turned back a supply truck driven by a Teamster with beer for the college bar and another with frozen sides of beef and bags of hamburgers for the cafeteria. We stopped the mailman and a guy from the Bell Telephone Company, who had come down to fix a faulty line. We had a long talk with the driver of a bus carrying members of a rival college basketball team, here to play a game.

'You get out here,' he told them. 'I'll see you back down here when the game's over.' The basketball players stared at him in disbelief and then looked down at the slushy road. 'That's right,' he said. 'You've got to walk the rest of the way.' The secretaries had no idea they could do all this.

The next morning the road was unnaturally quiet. Seven, eight, nine o'clock. Only a handful of vehicles drove up and some of those turned back when they saw us. Then we got it. They'd stayed away. The secretaries were breathless with exhilaration. The suits and nylons and make-up had gone. They were in blue jeans and boots and heavy sweaters and their perms were pushed down under caps and knitted hats. I was kitted out in an outfit a guy in the Party had bought me from the safety boot truck that called at all the mills and factories: jeans, boy's work boots, a boy's plaid jacket.

I'd like to say we won that strike by the end of the week, but we didn't. The college administration paid bonuses to any member of management that would do the girls' jobs. The instructors drifted back to work and got their wives to type their course outlines and reading lists. Very quickly the word was put out that the strike had been infiltrated by Reds and a number of the secretaries immediately marched across the picket line on principle. After the winter's final blizzard some students stood in front of us, pelting us with snowballs rolled round rocks. In the absence of supplies for the kitchen, everyone brought sandwiches and the school cafeteria was closed for the duration, the cooks and kitchen workers temporarily laid off: they *loved* those secretaries now. But we carried on. We walked that line for two months. I breathed and ate that strike. I showed them how to set up a telephone tree so that just one person needed to make two calls and in turn they would call another two, so we could have reinforcements there within an hour. Joanne had everyone organized into committees and subcommittees that met in a beer parlour every night where we'd drink Michelobs on almost empty stomachs.

I got to know those secretaries very well: Marcia and Laurel and Lynette and Fay and Hannah and Inge and Mary. Their names summon them. I had friends. I had whisper and gossip and camaraderie. I swapped recipes. I came over at weekends and styled their hair. I laughed with them. Although they were not proletarians, they were no class at all. They were women and they did what women do. Women are the same the world over. How will you ever convert a woman from an interest in fashion magazines and movie stars? Why would you want to? Even now in an American supermarket I cannot see one of those old-fashioned jello salads with pieces of ham and tomato and lettuce suspended in them without thinking of dainty Fay and *her* jello salads, those lime-green concoctions that we sat and ate on the grass verge of the highway, decorated in peaks with dabs of mayo. Or big blonde Inge and her fox-fur tippet which she insisted on wearing over her husband's letter jacket because, she said, 'I don't want anyone thinking I'm not a *female*.' How she made those truck drivers stare.

And they liked me. They helped me get my typing back up to speed. They enjoyed the rest. I thought it best not to introduce them to Julius.

A few of the secretaries went back to work because their husbands told them to. One or two found themselves in bed with those union men the Party had pulled out for them, and left home. One of them, sensationally, set up house with a secretary from City Hall.

And when the beer parlour closed and there were only a few hours left before we were due back on the picket line, then we in the Party would have our faction meeting and decide our tactics for the day ahead. It was very bold of us to organize them, in those terrible days of the Red scares, but our cause was so obscure it took some time for it to gain the notice of FBI. And anyway, who were they? Just a bunch of *secretaries*; who cared about them?

By June we assumed we had lost. The college was closing, exams were done. There was no one to stop with our picket line. And then, suddenly, the college made an offer: six per cent, exactly what the secretaries had first wanted to ask for. Actually, I think it was the publicity that did it: we always got the prettiest secretary to be photographed or go on TV, the one with the kookiest voice to do radio, and so they won the public's sympathy and the college found itself with letters from the mothers of prospective students saying they wouldn't be able to find the money for their son or daughter's fees if the administration didn't stop bullying those poor women . . .

It was my finest hour, that strike. I'd do it all over again tomorrow if I could. The secretaries went back to work in late summer to prepare for the fall semester and I lost touch with them not long after. As the campaign against the Red Menace rolled along, one of them snubbed me in the street and the rest kept their distance, which you couldn't blame them for, given what could be done to them if they'd been called before the Hearings. Not long after the strike Joanne was struck down with some sort of wasting disease in her legs. For a while she came to meetings on sticks, then we had to push her up the steps in a wheelchair. She couldn't organize any more so she had to organize herself: I heard she set up some sort of fighting group with other cripples.

I used to go and meet her sometimes, for coffee in a little place she knew wasn't so hard to get in and out of.

'You did good work during that strike,' she said. 'I was proud of you. We have plenty of comrades who can sit in a chair and read a document and tell you what's the matter with it and dash off a position paper. And we've got comrades who can give speeches, and comrades who can give you an hour-by-hour account of what happened in the October Revolution. But if this Party's ever going to make it with the American working class it needs people like you, who can get up in the dark and get themselves down to a picket line and know that that picket line's going to be effective because they know they've pulled out enough people to make it effective. Everyone is where they should be, not someplace else on some other day. It isn't glamorous work but someone has to do it and you do it better than most. I would never have believed it of you when I first saw you, but, fuck it, I was wrong. You should be proud of yourself.'

I reported this conversation back to Julius.

'Yeah,' he said. 'I was told.' But nothing else.

It is odd, isn't it, to think that during the time I was a member of the Communist Party I came closest to the true heart of the American way of life, which was not, after all, New York City and probably not California either. You have to leave the edges if you want to know what a place is really about.

Not by any stretch of the imagination was I a leading cadre like him, but I was what the Party needed then, a dependable comrade who, below the horizon of FBI attention, would weather it through those terrible times. I had a potential role: to help in my very small way bring into being a world without suffering and exploitation. What could be a grander design? What greater moral life? The revolution, I was assured, was just around the corner and even now we were turning that bend and would reach it, as long as we took the correct path and organized. These were the two things. Correctness. Organizing.

If I raised my powder compact to my face and looked in its mirror, what did I want to see? My mother's face looking back at me? The knowledge of *what* I was I had carefully buried away for a very long time, since that terrible night in the air-raid shelter and the strange, deadening morning that followed. A Nazi, a lousy Nazi, Europe's blood on my hands. What could I do to purge myself of that terrible legacy of slaughter and evil? I believed that I should grow another outer self, one that would in no way resemble the dark interior of my little world. If the inheritance that came through my mother's line was to kill and enslave and gas and torture, my choice would be the opposite. I would stand for justice and equality for all. By *doing*, surely I could not only make amends but transform myself if I was for all that was best and noble. If the Nazis had persecuted the Jews I would rescue the Negroes and the poor and the hopeless. The woman at Lord and Taylor who once was young and now was old and poor and lonely, I would be her champion.

I understood Marxist economics and Leninist revolutionary theory on only the most rudimentary level but I understood this, something that the strike had taught me: that action and intention is everything. It is the doing of something that makes it real.

Could I slough off my past in this way? For a long time I thought I could and really I wanted to go on believing. But recently I was watching a wildlife programme on TV and I noticed that when a lizard or a snake discards its skin to make shoes and handbags, what is underneath? Another skin, just the same. But that was later, another time altogether.

Chapter Sixteen

How quiet the prairies were. Traffic was a hum so low I hardly heard it. Sometimes I felt like the serpent after Eve's Fall, crawling around on its belly licking dirt and breathing dust. Land was everything, the lakes an illusion. 'You have the sky,' people told me, so I looked up and there it was, flat blue or high white and I thought I'd like to play there, kicking clouds around or hiking from one horizon to its opposite. But there was nothing to climb in Minneapolis. You had to get your views from bridges or tall buildings. It was that time at the end of the decade when you started to see planes passing over between the coasts. Hardly anyone I knew had been in an aeroplane, apart from the guys who had flown in the Air Force. The sight of something flying overhead only confirmed the pull of gravity that glued me to the ground. I never stopped missing the sea but the prairies held me down. After a while, as I say, I didn't mind.

But Julius always said we would go to California. He always told me it was a matter of time. I believed him. Six months became nine months, became a year. From a magazine advertisement for the Pan Am airline, I clipped a colour photograph of a beach between Los Angeles and San Diego and thumbtacked it to the wall. A figure – it might have been a man or a woman – in bare feet and rolled-up pants was walking, splashing in the surf. Some kind of palm tree was waving up in one corner. Off-shore there were islands I didn't know the name of. I would lie in bed and look at the photograph, and look back at myself from the vantage point of a breaker.

Then it turned out that the Party had other plans for Julius. He was being sent back east, further east than Long Island, even. He was being shipped over to Russia to be trained in their cadre school. I had not had an invitation, either from Julius, or from the Party.

There was nowhere to cry and no place to scream. Dumped again. Yet how could I have expected otherwise, for surely I had always realized that this liaison between Julius and me was temporary?

'How long have you known?' I asked him.

'Not long.'

'Before we left New York?'

'Not really – your cousin only mentioned it.'

'*Jasa* did?'

'Well, he just asked if I would be interested, if he could swing it.'

'If he could swing it?'

'Have I got my own echo, or what?'

'I don't understand. I don't understand what Jasa has to do with this, and why he didn't say anything about it to me.'

'Well, honey, I don't know either, you'll have to ask him.'

A week before he left he took me to a restaurant run by Party sympathizers. Ukrainian food, heavy on the stomach, meatballs, kasha, cabbage. Glasses of lemon tea to follow, like my father drank, and sweet little pastries. Julius walked into that place like a lion, like Robeson, and everyone smiled when they saw us. You could tell he would be taking the boat across the Atlantic to adulation and respect. 'I'm glad for you,' I said when we'd finished eating and he had shaken hands with another well-wisher. 'Really I am.'

'You mean that?'

'Yes, really.'

He got up and came round to sit next to me on the red leather banquette. I was truly melted by this public show of affection and we sat quietly together sipping our hot tea, my small arm resting on his. I thought of what a long road we had both travelled since we first met by chance on 52nd Street and I liked to think that if I had not been good for him, at least I hadn't done him any harm. As for all he'd done for me . . . There was no denying I was more than I had been, more curious, more serious, more judgemental about what mattered, less critical of what was essentially frivolous (though still a million times more superficial than anyone else in our circle). What Julius had achieved was to put into harness the one complicated part of myself. He'd harnessed my guilt. He did a good thing there. I could have died inside of its toxic poisoning.

'Do you think I treated you badly?' he suddenly asked.

I considered the question. 'I really appreciate everything you taught me. Before I met you I didn't know what I wanted, my old trouble. Everything is so random and haphazard with me. I was just drifting about.'

He choked on the slice of lemon in his hot tea. 'You? Drift about? Is that how you see yourself?'

'Well, yes, don't you?'

'Shit, no. You're a grasper. You have this will, you go for what you want.'

'What do you mean?'

'You wanted me.'

'Yes, I guess that's true.'

'And got me.'

'Yes. Did you mind being got?'

His voice softened. 'No. I didn't mind. You can be a lovely person when you put your mind to it. You eased my mind sometimes.'

'Really? Did I?'

'I liked to watch you sitting there while I was reading. You were good to look at.' How could I tell him I was bored to death?

There was something else he wanted to say, but he couldn't get it out. It was having a hard time coming. He drank some more tea to clear his throat to ready himself for it.

'I never wanted to tell you this, but you reminded me of my mother. When she was young, I mean. Not in looks, of course, just your innocence – ignorance would be a better word but you'd take offence at that. There were times you were there when you were the only thing stopping me from becoming like my father. Because you put me in mind of her, I couldn't do nothing bad to you.'

'Like your father in what way?'

'A drinker.'

'But you hardly ever drink.'

'Don't think I'm not tempted.'

'What happens when you drink?'

'I get angry. No, I mean really angry. I hit a woman once. But I never did that to you. I didn't, did I?'

'No, of course not.'

'You wouldn't have stayed if I had, would you?'

'I don't know. I can't imagine anyone hitting me.'

'You're lucky, then.'

What could I say to that? Nothing. We sat in silence for a while. The smell of meals was all around us. Silverware clattered on plates as portions of schnitzel were speared and chewed and swallowed. Sugar had fallen on to the table from our pastries and my fingers made patterns in its dust.

'But you don't want to waste your life,' Julius was saying. 'You have a meaning now, a moral purpose.'

'Yes, I know you're right. I think I'm getting there.'

'I should give you something; a keepsake.'

'That's OK. I have everything I need.'

'Still, I'd like to get you something. Maybe a phonograph.'

'Keep your money.'

But no, we paid the bill, I stood through a round of shaking hands, and we caught the bus and went down to a department store where we found a dinky little phonograph in a red and cream leather carrying case. Julius pulled the dollars out of his wallet slowly and put them on the counter.

'I got you a disc, too,' he said when we reached home. I cried out with pleasure; it was Duke Ellington's 'In a Sentimental Mood'.

'This is kind.'

'Your old boyfriend never gave you nothing, did he?'

'Not a gift, no.'

'You can keep the automobile, by the way.' I thought this was a bit rich, since it was me who had paid for it.

'I wonder what would have become of me if I hadn't gone down to 52nd Street that night,' I said, thinking aloud.

'You'd have come to a sticky end,' he said.

'What kind?'

'Drugs, maybe. You were doing dope. You could have graduated to smack.'

'I suppose, but no, I don't think so.'

'No, maybe not. Graspers don't do that kind of stuff.'

'Did you ever do drugs?'

'Only way back when. When I was a kid. Not since before I went into the service.'

'What *did* you do in Europe?'

'I don't talk about that.'

'I had a war too, you know. I was bombed.'

'Yeah?' he said without interest.

'There's something else I want to ask you. How come you don't go with women of your own race?'

He looked at me, surprised. 'Coloured girls? Are you crazy? They're only after one thing.'

'What?'

'My money.'

'You haven't got any money.'

'They don't know that. Compared with them, you're Little Bo Peep. They will *waste* a man.'

'Why did you come on to me that night, when we first met?'

'It was a bet.'

'Who with?'

'Guy I'd been drinking with. You don't know him. We always had those bets on when white girls came in.'

'I see.'

'It doesn't mean nothing now. That was just what started it. But when I start a job I like to finish.'

I looked at him and thought of all he had been through, of how complicated he was. I wondered if it was really possible to have a love affair across the race divide. All I was doing was dancing around in the shadow of his charisma. I had learned that word recently. That was what he had. I had fallen for him originally because he was exotic. Now I knew that the skin, the hair, was the least of his strangeness. They were nothing.

'What will you do now?' he asked.

'I guess I'll go back to New York. I'm not sure if I can imagine being in California without you. There's no one there for me.'

'Who do you have in New York?'

'Well, Jasa, and Morris.'

'Oh, yeah, the faggot. Well, don't bank on going back to New York. It isn't up to you.'

'What do you mean?'

'Just take it as it comes, Sybil.'

I was not sure what he was driving at so I dismissed it from my mind. 'I don't have a present for you. I don't know why. I just couldn't think of anything you'd like.'

I suppose it was our imminent parting and the embarrassment of the gift that made him withdraw from me, over and over again. 'No big deal,' he said, shrugging. 'That's the way it's always been with us. I give, you take.'

'But I've done everything you asked me! I pay my way, I do the housework. I make—'

'That's not devotion. You're like blotting paper, you absorb my essence.'

'I always thought it was the other way round, that I was absorbed myself.'

'Well, you should think on that.'

Yet on our last night together I couldn't sleep. I held him to me. I needed his weight.

'Oh, you're not going to leave,' Joanne said. 'We need you.'

'I want to go back to New York.'

'No.'

'But . . .'

'Are you refusing discipline?'

'I'm no good here. I have nothing to offer.'

'You did all right during the strike; we want to keep you. If you leave you'll be expelled. We'll have no choice.'

'So expel me, see if I care.'

'Well, there's a little difficulty for you on that account.'

'What's that?'

'You remember that study group you were in in New York?'

'Yes, what about it?'

'We just got word it was infiltrated.'

'Who by? Who was the agent?'

'Some guy, married to a Negro organizer. Everyone is under investigation by the FBI. You just got out under the wire, leaving when you did. We had a lot of grief getting Julius his passport. Look at Robeson – they've taken his away. People are being deported.'

'So what are you saying?'

'Well, you could go back to New York and the minute you make contact with your old friends they're going to be watching you. You could be on the next boat home. What do you say to that?'

I didn't know what to say. This terrible news was sinking in. (If it was true. Was it? She could have made it up on the spot. Years later, doubts would grow in my mind. One thing you could say for the Party: they were certainly smarter than I was.) I made another point. 'I couldn't stand going into another factory. I can't work in those places.'

'Who said factory life was a vacation? The workers can't leave, they have to put bread on the table.'

'But they have families.'

'The Party is your family now.'

I gave that a great deal of thought.

I called Jasa in New York. 'Remember me?' I said down the line. 'Your little cousin. I'm calling you from Minneapolis. Where I am on my own. On account of the fact that my boyfriend has been shipped off to the Soviet Union.'

'That went OK, terrific. So when can we expect you?'

'What the hell is going on?'

'What can I tell you?'

'I don't know. Tell me.'

'What were you doing, a member of my family, hanging round with *schwarzes*?'

'I don't believe this.'

'Well. Something to believe is that your boyfriend is out of the picture now, his head is down over his studies learning to be a top cadre and I'm sure he will go far.'

'Is that your doing?'

I could hear his shrug. 'Ask yourself what future could there have been for you with him? Half-caste children? You don't expect I should stand by and watch that? You should find a young man, a liberal; I mean, get married, have some children. Soon you'll both lose interest in politics, he'll make money, you'll have a nice life. This is just a passing phase.'

Outside my window the snow was thawing. Water dripped from roofs. 'I can't believe I'm listening to this. A race chauvinist. Worse than the people in Mississippi. How can you sit there, a communist, and be so cynical?'

'Cynical? No, I don't believe so. That's the fate of romantics and I have never been one of those. I'm a pragmatist.'

'I'm not. I'm in the Party now.'

'Oy,' he said.

'So what's your philosophy?' I asked him mockingly, wondering at the view he looked out on from his apartment. Did the spring wind still blow through Central Park, turning the island upside down like a maid airing a bed?

'You asked, I tell you. Why do we need governments? All the people require is an economy, trade, a market for their goods. Why should they care who buys as long as someone is buying?'

'But without them how would you raise taxes and build roads?'

'OK, those you nationalize, the coal, the mines, the railroads. Everything else can take care of itself.'

'You'd be at the mercy of the Mob, paying them protection money.'

'What's the difference? You still have to pay and it all comes down to the same thing in the end. Without governments people go on eating and having sex and going dancing.'

'Ah, so you're an anarchist!'

'Those? Babies. Never have anything to do with babies.'

I wished Joanne was there. I wished I could set her on him. 'These are just words, you're just using words.'

'What else should I use?'

Car doors slamming on the street, signs of life, the white world in retreat. 'And rights, what about those?'

'No one wants rights. They think they do but when they have them they realize that all they wanted all along was to have a good time.'

'Well, I believe in rights. I've seen what happens to those who don't have them.'

'Excellent!' he shouted down the line. I held the receiver a little way from my ear. 'Now you have a moral purpose, which is just as it should be, but I tell you it could have been any-thing. For me, it was getting the fascists out of Yugoslavia but I did not have a choice. I kill them or they kill me. With your father, well he's a crazy man. Something I don't get there. He sends me all these letters about Israel but I don't see him pack-ing. He just likes a cause. We're all the same, Jews. We have no capacity to live in the present, only the past and the future. So, like us, your father has learned that it's better to live in the future.

'Anyway, back to you. This is a terrible time for the Communist Party in this country. They're going to hunt you down, they're going to persecute you. Listen, come back. Forget elections. Forget economics. Eat good food. Wear good clothes. Remember what you forgot about being a woman. Bring your children up right, to respect their mother and father. You will have lived as a Jew should.'

He was offering me the gravitational pull of the old life, which according to him was there for the taking. Not to have to think, to be pretty, to empty my head of everything but dresses. He started to speak of how things were in New York City, of a new restaurant he had visited lately, of shows he had seen, and as he kept up the onslaught of temptation I thought of those old dreams of mine: marriage to a suave faceless Englishman, shopping in Mayfair for dresses. Marriage to Marvin, being a housewife, afternoon bridge, dresses. Marriage to Stan and dancing, smoking dope, dresses. Why should I not say yes?

'Have I convinced you?' Jasa urged. 'Shall I send you a train ticket?'

Well, I thought, I'll go. And then I began to think about Julius. When I first met him he didn't know what a diaphragm was, he'd never seen one before. I think he was shocked. He thought that using birth control was somehow making sex premeditated and it only felt right to him to do it outside marriage if one got carried away, if one was forced to abandon one's rational self, swept up by passion. He did not seem to feel, as I did, that he had any right to pleasure. I wanted to give him that, take him to the sweet, uncomplicated places where there is nothing to think about and nothing to get right or wrong. I believed that it was in my gift to make him happy.

And what he could bring me was no less worthy. There was another sweetness: to lie with arms around me in the centre of things when the Party was massed all around us, connecting us to the great wide world and all its inhabitants in every land under the sun.

'I'm thinking,' I said. I was thinking that one night we were sitting together, Julius and I, both of us reading. I looked up and saw him, a pen in his hand, making notes on some position paper or other. When he caught my glance, instead of frowning, instead of asking me some question of fact, some enquiry that would catch me out, he did something he had never done before: he winked and doffed an imaginary hat as if we were passing on the street. It was an act of utter complicity and I smiled back. Then he went back to his work. It was nothing, nothing, yet outside our house there were stars in the sky. Beyond the window you could see for miles, oceans of darkness under the heavens. I felt a sudden rush of expansion in my heart. I felt a peculiar sensation: that I had air to breathe and space to move about in. I know we are all looking for our freedom. Moses took his people out of slavery through the dry land the Red Sea made when it parted. The confinement of the places of the interior contained this paradox: that only in the centre of things – and it does not matter whether it is the land or the sea, each is its own territory, a law unto itself – only when we are most tied to something do we have the potential for being and becoming. Do you belong on the sea or on the land? the man had asked me. I belonged on the shore, he said, neither fish nor beast. I believed that I could prove him wrong.

I could get in the car and drive back to whatever uncertain fate awaited me, or I could stay. But I knew what the answer was. I had known for some time.

'I'll fix everything. We'll make you a homecoming,' Jasa said.

'You know something, Jasa?' I replied. 'Go to hell.'

'Sybil. Let me tell you something. It's all shit. Life is shit, too.'

'I know. But sometimes life can be great, or you can make it great. I believe that.' What choice did I have?

So I stayed in Minneapolis and in the Party. On my own, in the apartment Julius and I had once shared, I spent my little free time lying in bed listening to the radio, looking through the window watching the leaves break. I was getting thinner, my body felt brittle. I tried to keep up appearances but I watched my pretty looks coarsen. I was desperately cold without the furs I had sold or left behind in New York, abandoned out of principle. A cloth coat did nothing for you in the snow and, quickly reverting to being my father's daughter, I secretly vowed that one day, somehow, I would have another fur, though it might not be a mink. I would settle for musquash, cony, anything. I stopped reading fashion magazines. I could not bear to see how far I had fallen from their ideal of loveliness.

I would sit by my bed at ten in the evening and think of New York, a place where people were dancing and having a good time, where people were getting drunk and others were getting high. The city would be full of moving lines of gold, the taxi-cabs, the tail lights of cars, women in their evening gowns. There would be smells, both good and bad, of perfume and piss, bilge water at the docks and champagne in the pent-houses. Down in the poor neighbourhoods people would have finished eating and if it was warm they might still be sitting out on their steps, sipping beer.

Outside my house there were smells of earth and vegetation and quietness. Along the street, many lights were already out. Peace, perfect fucking peace.

Who could I call on the telephone? No one. The phones were tapped.

I had found out what a joke life could play on you. I had got what I wanted at last, a place to belong, people who wanted me, and I had never understood until now what belonging meant; that belonging robs you of your freedom, it puts chains about you. You can't belong and follow your own wishes at the same time.

I could see that that was the big difference between Manchester and Liverpool. In my home town you could live a life without attachments, easy come, easy go. The sea was always there to offer you a lifeline, an escape. You were always on the lookout for something better. You tethered yourself with ropes to the cast iron shore, but you could slip the knots and sail away, any time you chose. And come back, time and time again.

I had inadvertently committed myself to the highest of all possible goods, the fight to bring about a better world, to improve the lot of the human race. It was not a commitment to a place, but it was a commitment. I had willingly done so for my own sake to make me human, too. To pay my dues to humanity. But Julius had never told me that my life would no longer be my own.

All around me were those who understood everything there was to know about tying yourself down, attaching yourself to something, whether it be a place or an ideal. People here had worked the land, generation after generation and of course they wanted to up and go, but they didn't. They stuck with it because they belonged there and because they saw that sense of belonging as the heritage they would pass down to their children.

Once or twice I took Joanne a casserole I'd cooked from a recipe on the back of a tuna can. She got around in her wheel-chair, spinning her wheels in rage and helplessness.

'Have you ever had a life of fun?' I asked her.

'Fun? Sure we have fun. We have pot-luck suppers, we have socials, I used to go dancing before I lost my legs. We danced in people's living rooms and in their yards in the summer. You can always make time for that.'

'With comrades?'

'Of course, always comrades.'

'Did you never long to meet other people?'

'No. The Party has been everything to me, all my life.'

'When do you spare some thought for yourself?'

'I don't. Why should I?'

'What about your feelings?'

'Them. A petit bourgeois deviation. As if any one else was interested. When people say "I feel", what they mean is "I want". Are we all to fall down and worship the eternal veracity of their almighty feelings? Get a grip on yourself, I want to say when they come to me with their problems. Grow up. And it's the same for me. I don't have to tell you everything. You're not my shrink. Don't expect deep psychological insight. You won't get it.'

'You must have feelings about your legs.'

'Of course I have feelings!' Her voice rose to a shriek. 'Anyone knows how I feel, anyone. You don't need me to tell you what it's like. Shit, shit, shit.'

I was embarrassed. I did not know where to put myself. I changed the subject. 'But there is sexual chemistry between people.'

'Certainly,' she said, calming her voice, looking pale and exhausted. 'That has a scientific basis.'

'But how you feel emotionally about someone else, what about that?'

'You got an itch, scratch it.'

'Even if you're itching for someone outside the Party?'

'That's out of the question. How can you date a person who doesn't know what our real inner life is? What we're about is achieving objectivity, and to overcome the subjective conditions that thwart Progress is the strategy that will lead us to revolution. To fall in love, particularly with an outsider, is to get yourself bogged down in the subjective. I make only one judgement about people: their actions.'

'Intimacy?'

'You have it here. Look, in the Party there is no hierarchy of labour; a teacher or an artist is no better than a millworker or a store clerk. All our work has the same value, to bring about the new society. We're not the unquestioning robots the capitalists make us out to be. Remember the strike? Yeah, *that*'s intimacy, what you had then. Do you want to hear about their problems with their mother-in-law, with their husband? What they do in bed? You want to know about little Johnny and his teething? You want to listen to that garbage?

'You don't. The Party has given you a home. It's in struggle that you become a fully paid-up member of the human race. Struggle is what gives morality its practical dimension. The best-read comrade will never be a revolutionary until he has engaged in action.'

I filled up her plate from my casserole dish. Her plain face was animated. I had brought over my portable phonograph and I played her Julius's Bessie Smith and Ma Rainey records. Their voices seemed to break like pickaxes on to the bare ground.

PART THREE

Chapter Seventeen

Then it was 1955 and I'd had a message and I was driving to the sea. I was sitting in my automobile at the side of the road about twenty miles from the coast. It had taken me six years to get here. I was maybe a few hundred miles north of my original destination; the arrow had failed to reach the target. I had missed my mark. California lay two states below me but I had not yet given up on that dream. Dreams of a better life are all one has. If Julius had wound me up, why, then, I was still going. I whizzed on of my own volition.

On the way there was plenty of weather. Clouds boiled and hissed steam, and steam from the saw-mills dissolved into the clouds. Mountains appeared for a moment then vanished. Rain flooded the road and the railroad track that ran parallel to it. The sky was full of movement. Minute by minute the weather changed – sharp sleet, a hailstone bombardment, drenching rain, blue sky and high, scudding clouds. I revelled in all this sudden change, I delighted in it.

I looked first at my eyes in the rear-view mirror then my mouth in the mirror of my powder compact. I was not the same woman who had left New York; I hardly knew the little fool. I had utterly transformed myself. Over and over again. It had become my forte. My hand was hot round a nickel. The pay phone was only a few feet away and there was nothing to stop my opening the car door, getting out and walking over to make my call. There was nothing to it, I just had to dial. Still I sat. But you cannot stay in your automobile for ever so I rang Julius and I asked him, 'Is your house clean?'

There was a pause, then I heard that harsh–tender voice, the voice of Moses bringing his cracked tablets down from Sinai. 'Cleaner than you ever got it.'

I had crossed the Rockies, which gave me a headache, and then the Cascades and reached the lumber city of Seattle. On the map there was a rain forest which had wrapped itself around a mountain and beyond that a long unbroken line of coast from the Juan de Fuca Strait near Canada down to the Oregon border. It looked as if someone had put a finger in the edge of the country and, before it withdrew, the coastline almost closed around it. Two spits of land that didn't quite meet held a bay captive and in its mouth was a lumber town. Even on the map it looked as if it were in hiding and this is where I was to make my rendezvous with Julius after four years, home from Moscow.

'They say it isn't the end of the world, but you can see it from here,' he said along the humming wires and laughed, expecting me too to laugh at this worn-out joke.

'Oh, yes, yes, I've heard that one before,' I replied. 'I've heard it plenty.'

I got back into the car, drove for another half-hour or so, crossed a bridge and I was there. The town was booming, the mills were working full tilt. Plants were turning out doors and cedar shingles and floorboards and closets and shelves and furniture and houses. A workboat yard announced it was building bowpickers and seine skiffs. An orange mountain range of wet wood chips – cedar, fir and hemlock – towered above a line of Union Pacific freight cars in a waterlogged yard. It was feeding the livid fever of the rest of the country for construction, for the houses that contained all the housewives.

But for all that, town was only a main street and another street parallel to it, named for the river. There was nothing much: a tiny movie theatre tiled in blue and yellow like a Moorish palace, a Jewish-owned furniture store, alleys running between the two roads hiding the overhead telephone and hydro cables. Couples were strolling along, stopping to look in windows, having conversations, sometimes arguments, I suppose about what they wanted to buy and how much it would cost and when they could afford it. Their faces were shapeless with happiness. Prosperity was making them insufferable. Buses stopped but no one got on or off. I don't know who had settled the town. It was named after another port in Scotland but the Norwegians must have been quick to follow, for there was a Nordic Gas Station and Sven's Donut Shop. There was even a suburb, and I laughed when I saw that it was called Cosmopolis.

The sun came out so I parked my car and crossed the tracks through saplings and garbage to the waterfront. Downriver, planks were stacked on pallets, but apart from that there wasn't much to see, just a few stumps of rotting piers and the docks with an electric fence around them. I did not have to ask myself if I was apprehensive about seeing Julius, for my stomach was churning and I threw up my breakfast into a pile of weeds. I had spent a lot of time in the past few years controlling nausea. I wondered if he was thinking about me the same way, and if he had held down his own sickness. The light turned mother of pearl. I tried to retrace my steps back to the road but I couldn't find the path I had come down, though I could see my car only a few feet away, with men in plaid shirts and blue jeans passing it without concern, not even bothering to look or call out that I was trespassing. I stepped towards the road on what I thought was an orange path and my feet sank almost to the knees. I let out a little scream. Quicksand! But it wasn't, it was wood dust that had settled in hollows and gullies where the rain filled up and deceptively resembled dry land.

I had to remove my shoes and stockings and pick my way back barefoot to the car. The rain fell again before I reached it and I washed my legs and dried them on a towel.

I drove on, through the town to the sea. It was so odd to remember that back in 1949 Julius and I had set out in this very car to drive from coast to coast and that I at least had finally completed our journey, never knowing what I would find or who I would meet. The Pacific was rushing towards me, mile after mile devouring the road. I drove past cranberry bogs and a cranberry canning plant, occasionally glimpsing through the trees how the bay widened and became dense with shipping until at last there was no more land left. Then I came upon a strange, run-down little place, its mirror image just a tiny distance across from it, like Siamese twins that had been separated. I was now a good judge of towns and how they had come into being. Others I had passed through had been populated out of the exhaustion of the settlers but here they would have gone on if they could and, as if it suffered from some stunting mutation, the place seemed never to have got above a couple of thousand people. Maybe they came and stopped and said no, turned back or went south, having made some error in their calculations, thinking that they had reached some place that was warmer and drier than it turned out. Its size was lethal to it. It must have dreamed of becoming a port because there was a coastguard station built of white clapboard with green windows and a turreted lookout, but a woman in a coffee shop said later that the harbour was too shallow for serious shipping which instead navigated the deep trench of the Puget Sound. As it turned out, the coastguard station was only ever used to watch for enemy ships and bombers during the war. So crab stands were beginning to appear and little booths selling bait. The dock was being extended out into the sea to run salmon fishing charters. Two or three motels were under construction. The place was setting itself up to be a tourist attraction but somehow I guessed it wouldn't even do too well at that. The weather was against it. Some of the stores had sandbags by their doors, kept for the time of the spring tides, when there was a danger of flooding.

I drove as far as I could, as far as the road would allow me, and walked on the shingle to the sea. A tug was pulling a logging boom along the coast, down to Oregon, or California, and I watched it until it passed out of sight, then the horizon was empty again. There was nothing blue above it. The sea was grey and the sky was very low as though a bank of cloud was brushing my hair. It was cold in that desolate way that damp and low temperatures create together. The surface of the water was sluggish. I looked at the town's twin across the mouth of the bay. There could have been a ferry connecting them but there wasn't, which I put down to jealousy. Inside a restaurant I ate a crab sandwich and thought to buy a bag of shells or a greeny-blue glass float from some fishing boat, but I was used to travelling light and I did not know what I would do with such rubbish if I had it.

People are always asking you where you were when you heard that Jack Kennedy had been shot. What I remember is where I was when I heard that they'd executed the Rosenbergs. Friday 19 June, 1953. My twenty-ninth year.

I was in a rectangular motel room, narrower at one end than at the other, like a coffin. There was a plywood dresser and a washed-out blue counterpane to cover the unravelling blankets on the bed, and an army cot pushed up against a wall. A sour window looked out on to a line of cars, a few lights in the distance and everything under the shadow of a dusty sky. I woke out of a short, heavy late-afternoon sleep induced by the fortification of too-early a drink, a stupor sleep when your eyes snap open and your face is covered in cold sweat and you look about and don't know who or where you are. Memory has gone AWOL. You think, for a moment, you are losing your mind. A Gideon Bible was on a three-legged table next to me, unopened. I could hear the TV in the lobby and the murmur of other guests gathered round its light. The room smelled of camphor balls and someone else's sweat.

Voices came past the window. 'They fried,' someone said. There was laughter.

'Like eggs.'

A slower, more stupid mouth asked, 'You think they were spies?'

'Sure, they were foreigners.' An emphatic clog of opinion, thudding down on the skull with a crack.

'I thought they were American-born.'

'Nah, he was a Jew-boy. His wife, her too.' A sigh of understanding.

'I never heard their given names.'

'Julius. And Ethel.'

When I heard they were gone, I ran to the sink and threw up bile and a thin milky stream of gin and lettuce.

I always stiffened when I heard their first names, I mean his name. It could have been Julius. It could have been me. It's the luck, good or bad, of being where you are at whatever moment. I do not believe that our lives are willed by any external forces, other than chance. It's whether we survive or not that matters.

I used to drive with my crocodile vanity case (which had seen too little use since I'd lived in Minneapolis), a couple of pieces of luggage, and a box of beauty samples. I also had a framed photograph of some guy. I really had no idea who he was. He had come in and had the picture taken at a studio in Chicago early on in the war and had never returned to claim or pay for it. He was drop-dead handsome and if I was stopped he was my husband who had been killed at the Sicily landings (which, for all I knew, he had been). I was a widow who made my living selling cosmetics door to door. That was the story.

I remember the first day I left home. After driving for about eighty miles I reached Rochester, where I had business to carry out, though not, I should say, at the Mayo Clinic. What I had to do there detained me for two days, then I circled round the city for about a week, spending the night in small towns: Northfield, where Jesse James failed to hold up the town bank in 1876; Harmony, near where the Amish people live; New Prague and New Ulm, where the Sioux lost their war with the US government in 1862. They were places where wild animals had once roamed (and for all I knew still did), the skins of which made up the inferior sorts of coats such as possum and squirrel and beaver.

Then, very cautiously, I came back into Rochester. I made a call from a pay phone outside a drugstore.

A voice I knew answered. 'Yes?' she said, and I understood very well how much effort it would have taken to keep that voice flat and devoid of terrified inflection.

'Is your house clean?' I asked.

'No,' she said. 'It's filthy.'

I got into my automobile, heard the door slam heavily, experienced the rush of heat that had built up inside while it stood in the sun, smelt the hot pearl-blue leather of the upholstery, and drove sedately out of Rochester, closely observing the speed limit. The car behind trailed me for twenty or thirty miles until its occupants seemed to get bored and turned into a roadhouse, for hamburgers, I assumed. I wasn't shaking, my skin wasn't clammy. I hummed a tune then I broke out into song. The gas pedal thrummed under my feet and the engine also kept its cool. I turned on the radio and someone was talking about crop prices and I was still driving through this alien world which was once again under my control, though I was a fugitive. I still had high hopes. But after I had been driving a further twenty miles I noticed that I dripped cold sweat, stopped at the side of the road, got out and was sick by a water tower. I threw up a glass of Coca-Cola on to the ground. At the next town I stopped and bought a pint of gin and drank long swallows from the bottle and was sick again. I was a prisoner of a tender stomach in those days.

In 1951 we had panicked. The Foley Street trials had finished, our leadership was in prison, where we thought they were going to be tortured and executed, and we ordinary members would be rounded up across the country and held in internment camps. We looked ahead and what we feared was this: that fascism was on its way to America. So what we decided was to send two thousand of our comrades underground, a second-tier leadership in exile in order that if the top cadre were wiped out there would still be a functioning organization. We had a name for them: these were comrades who were 'unavailable'.

I too was unavailable. I had got away from Minneapolis at last. I had been sent underground because the Party found something for me to do, a job for someone with greater experience, more trustworthy, a longer record of service, but the tasks that were involved were so ideally suited to my very limited skills that reluctantly they let me take it on. I had a good car. With Julius gone I had no ties. And I suppose someone might have noticed my capacity for turning myself into something different at any opportunity, which in itself could be a danger since it was possible that I could go wrong once I was on the road. But they took that risk.

Just as I was beginning to find some secure foundations for what we call the 'self', I had to junk it, or drive it underground and brush off the tricks I had learned at my mother's knee. It has been the story of my life – belief and pretence, being my father's or my mother's daughter. My whole existence now was essentially theatrical. I had a role and props and my script, and this acting came easily to me, naturally. If I had stage fright, it was always, like the first time, after the event. The constant trauma of imminent capture was mitigated by the childish delight I found in the endless choices for re-invention, without the censoring attention of some man I was involved with. I could please myself and be anyone I wished: I was a market researcher for a New York advertising agency; the wife of a Mormon minister; a rancher's sweetheart, an Air Force wife, a Pan Am air hostess. Boundless possibilities, eh? Oh, yes, I was my mother's daughter. I had had a good schooling in keeping up appearances.

My territory was of very minor significance, the empty places west of the Great Lakes: the Dakotas, Nebraska, Kansas and Iowa, where you could really hide someone if you had to. I was to set up safe houses, a foolproof telephone code system, courier schedules and a network of non-party messengers – dupes, boobies. There were any number of ways of recruiting these people, but I used the method that came easiest, sexual attraction. Had they been nailed by the FBI their lives would have been ruined, but I didn't care, it was all the same to me. In the balance of things, how could they be as important as a man like Julius, who had given everything for the new world we were being punished for trying to bring into being? I toured through the region, staking out towns, seeing which factories were hiring, buying and selling houses for comrades to live in while they were on the run. I transported them by night, sometimes in the trunk of my car. On the whole I was always afraid, but my nerve held.

Someone asked me once, about that time on the road, did you never want to give yourself in? The answer is obvious. The middle lands had caught and contained me. There was no way out but the most treacherous abandonment not just of myself but of countless others. Of *course* I wanted to give myself up, but then again didn't wild animals consider, when they were being hunted, that survival was the point? Would a mink turn round to its pursuer and put up its hands and say: 'OK, I give in. Take me'? Did a mink cry, 'Let me die so I can go into the other world and join all my furry ancestors in animal heaven'? No, the mink ran for its life. There was no stopping it. It ran until it was worn out and even then it had all kinds of ruses, like playing dead. In a trap an animal would chew off its leg to escape. Sometimes this is what you have to do in this existence, sacrifice a portion of yourself so the whole remains alive. The mind does everything it can to avoid death or madness. The mind wants to remain whole, the senses want to go on apprehending.

In my motel room that night, the night of the day they murdered the Rosenbergs, I saw that dust was falling, dust falls everywhere, throughout the world, for all eternity. Outside there might be snow or a meteor shower or an eclipse of the moon, some wonder that we are supposed to like to look at. What I don't care for about being beyond the gates of cities is the vantage point. Out here I can see how the landscape swallows us up. We are nothing in the universe, not even pinpricks. Once, I recall, we burned an old comrade and watched his ashes fly away, vanishing into the prairie. There is nothing but death and Creation. If there is a spirit world it has never been revealed to us. Our dead comrade was reassembling his molecules into the organisms in frost that break down ploughed soil, a blade of wheat, a worm. We'd shit him out of ourselves in time to come. Be, become, survive. What choice do we have?

Soon the Rosenbergs would be dust. I don't know if they were spies, maybe they were. I don't know if American boys died in Korea because of the secrets they were supposed to have passed on. I don't even believe they were in the Party. If they were, nobody ever told me. It doesn't matter to me whether they were innocent or guilty. Surviving is what we're put here to do, and they didn't manage it.

Meanwhile I was trying very hard not to think of Julius. But why? Who else did I have? The dread and the flight were over; I was coming home or to whatever home we made for ourselves. I wondered if he had changed in his years in Soviet Russia. I wondered how I had changed. I looked in the mirror as little as I could these days except those times when expediency demanded it. I hardly ever considered what I wore. I thought of myself as a reptile on a rock you wouldn't even notice if you sauntered past.

I drove back along the road, hurrying when I saw the day shift drive out of the cranberry canners, through a town, past a sawmill where a line of men were walking out with their lunch buckets and another line of men were walking in. Our rendezvous was on a street corner and his car was waiting for me. I pulled up on to a vacant piece of kerb behind him and flashed my brights at the back of his head. I had never liked that part of his body. Men cut their hair very short in those days and Julius had a roll of fat on his neck like a grunting sweating brow where a razored line of curls stopped, though there was little other sign of corpulence on his body.

I saw his hand on the shift on his steering column, heard the engine come to life and I took off behind him.

I followed him along Main Street until we turned and drove

down past some goods yards by the Union Pacific tracks, when we reached a shaky yellow house built of shingles. From time to time someone had added a lean-to here and there and its gable ends had windows set high in them. Beyond the fence at the back was a pallet piled with tyres, a broken-down outboard engine and some other junk and above us ran the overhead track which passed across the mountain range of wood chips, transporting them to the ships below. The water was fawn and silver and mottled steel and the clouds obscured the tops of the trees on the hills across the river. The air smelled of rot and industrial chemicals. Inside the house it was neat but it lacked a woman's touch. Three pairs of steel-toed work boots and a fourth pair with metal tongues were lined up in the hallway and part of a motorcycle was disassembled on the floor behind the couch.

We stood and looked at each other.

He wasn't so different, a little older, a little heavier, still handsome. Shabby clothes, no change there. But also not the same at all. The whites of his eyes had turned yellow and the irises had sulphur-yellow lights. His fingers were still, hanging by his sides. There was a kind of silence about him. Silence hung like heavy folds of linen from his shoulders, a thickening, stiffening silence. I wanted to touch him but there was no point in stretching out my hand because he was standing behind plate glass. He was muffled and numb.

'So,' I said.

'Well,' he said.

I could not move a muscle. Like a lethal virus, the sickness was spreading from him to me.

Finally he turned towards the kitchen. 'Coffee?' he asked me.

'Yes.'

He came back from the kitchen with two cups and handed one across.

'Aren't you going to sit down?' he asked me, but he was still standing himself.

I sat and he sat next to me. The thin smell of engine grease was in my nostrils. The windows were smeary. A single blue-bottle buzzed against the pane, cannoning into the glass over and over again.

'Whose house is this?'

'A comrade. Works at the sawmill.'

'Where is he?'

'In hospital. He has an injury.'

'I see.'

'Why here? This town, I mean?'

'I don't have a passport any more. I came in on a Soviet tanker three weeks ago. It's a good place for jumping ship. There's no immigration post.'

'So how was the Soviet Union?'

'Wonderful. A worker's paradise. No race chauvinism. People welcome you wherever you go.'

'I suppose you speak Russian now.'

'Yes, fluently.'

'Say something.'

He said a few words and smiled acidly to himself as he said them, but of course I did not know what he was talking about.

'Wow,' I replied.

We lurched into silence.

A train was whistling along the track and the slow rumble of its boxcars was approaching. The house was shaking like Julius's hands as he lit a cigarette. I also took one from my purse.

Remembering our first night together, I waited to see if he would remember too and reach over to light it. But my cigarette stayed in my hand, dry, unflaming. I let it rest in my fingers, as it was.

I wondered what would happen if I reached over and tickled him. It was not a moment for laughter but my hand crept towards his belly, holding his gaze. He caught my hand and put it aside. Then he took it up again, raised it quickly to his mouth and kissed it. 'You always were a bad woman,' he said.

I smiled.

'Want to go to bed?' he mumbled.

'Say what?'

'I said, do you want to go to bed?'

'OK.'

I think that a mechanism somewhere deep inside Julius had been broken, perhaps not beyond repair, maybe it could be mended, but something was wrong with him. Skin his colour can pale, the pallor is not healthy. Bad food, maybe, lack of light. What puts out passion? What extinguishes that? He climbed the stairs slowly. His hands now had a perceptible tremor as he slowly unbuttoned his pants. His penis was flaccid. I walked over in my underwear and took it in my hand and tried to give him life. Nothing, nothing.

'It'll come,' I said.

'Maybe,' he replied, indifferently.

I kneeled and took it in my mouth. The skin was dry.

'This is premature,' I said.

He said, 'Hold me.'

We got into bed and I tried to extend my reach to encompass him. His heart was a slowing pump. He reached beside the bed and lit another cigarette and smoked it in silence. We lay there for about an hour. The smell of engine oil had penetrated the sheets and blankets. He dozed for a while, his lids coming down and extinguishing the yellow lights in his eyes, and when he woke they had gone.

We got up later and went out to dinner and his mood changed, not back to the arrogant autodidact I had once known but to another person, moody, given to abrupt fits of laughter or quick, morose silences that lasted only minutes before he became businesslike and calm.

'Are you happy, Julius?' I asked him as we ate a celebration steak with fries and salad washed down with a bottle of sweetish white wine.

'Yes. Why shouldn't I be?'

'No, I mean happy as a state of being.'

'I see. No, I'm not happy. Who could be happy with this? These petit bourgeois who are preventing what is inevitable, the dictatorship of the proletariat. Their minds must be washed out and replaced with correct ideas.' He waved his hand at the street with its comfortable people walking up and down or, like us, drinking coffee and eating pie.

'You won't be happy until after the revolution?'

'No.'

We rumbled on, along the well-worn wheels of our doctrine.

'You sure dumped me,' I said. 'Two fucking years in Minnesota.'

'There was work to be done. You afraid of hard work? You worried about getting your nail polish chipped or something?' The old flash of his sarcasm had returned.

'Oh, come on, you hated it as well. You couldn't wait to get out.'

'Not true.'

'Not true?'

'I chose to go to Minnesota. I *fought* to go there.'

'Fought?'

'Miss Echo again. They were trying to send me down to the South and I didn't want to be sent. They wanted all the Negro comrades down there. It was race chauvinism. It looked to me like we weren't good enough to wage the class struggle any place except among our kind.'

'Shit. You bastard. And you never told me.'

'What you don't know don't hurt you.'

'So you thought I wouldn't have stayed if I knew. You thought you could put one over on me.'

He shrugged. 'Sure, why not? It worked, didn't it? I didn't think you liked my cock well enough to follow it anywhere.'

'What made you think I wouldn't have gone to the South with you? If that was where you had gone?'

'You wouldn't have been able to take it. You couldn't have taken the pressure.'

'Oh.'

'You ever heard the word miscegenation? You would have heard it enough.'

'I know more about miscegenation than you think.'

'Don't see how.'

'There are things about me you don't know, that I'll never tell you.'

'In your dreams.'

I left it at that. Ships' horns were sounding on the river, the sound of a tug's engine, hauling like a tractor, the whine of the pilot boat.

'It sounds like something big is coming into port.'

'Could be,' he said without interest.

We were managing to pass the evening, and I at least was dreading the night.

It was late fall, early winter.

'Do you have any idea when it starts getting cold here?' I asked him in one of our silences.

'It doesn't get that cold, I believe. A little snow, not much.'

I remembered a garden we had once looked out on, and the zucchini and tomatoes and the magnolia tree. I tried to picture babies rocking in a summer yard.

'I'm afraid I don't have the portable phonograph you gave me,' I admitted. 'I had to leave it behind when I left Minnesota. All the discs, too.'

'You never liked be-bop, did you?'

'No.'

'I used to play some of Parker's riffs over and over again in my head. I can remember every note. They were very complex, those improvisations.'

'I don't know what you find in it. It's meaningless.'

'Find in it?' He looked at me as if I was a being from an alien land who does not recognize the everyday sounds and smells and clamours in the streets that the native takes for granted. 'Freedom,' he said.

'I'm too close to the river here,' he pointed out as we drove home.

'Why?'

He told me about tsunami, earthquakes or landslides on the bed of the ocean which caused tidal waves. 'They can give you warnings now,' he said. 'When you hear that a tsunami's coming you just abandon everything and get out of town.' I thought of the silent disaster under the sea, fishes swept aground and burrowing creatures driven from their holes, ship-wrecks cast up, the coastline broken, roads flooded, houses and churches under water. What could a sandbag do against that?

Chapter Eighteen

What was the wave that would overwhelm us? What could possibly drown us now?

The next morning Julius got up and while I was in the kitchen fixing breakfast he asked me to marry him by shouting through from where he sat, reading the *Daily Worker*. He did not go down on his knees, he did not offer a ring. He just said, 'I think we ought to get married,' and I replied, 'OK, when?'

He said, 'I don't know, not now. I have to get my papers in order. I have to get myself above board again.' It was a time when the reign of terror was petering out, when certain decisions made by the courts were exonerating us, bringing us back from the margins of illegality. It was no longer enough merely to incite revolution, one had to actually commit an act of treason to be prosecuted. A bit too late for the Rosenbergs and a bit too late for the Party, which was all but wrecked. I was surprised at how dead my feelings were when I heard Julius's question. No volcanic joy, but no sudden certainty that I should decline. Simply an acceptance of an inevitability. Only surprise that he had come back to me.

'Were you unfaithful to me when you were in Moscow?' I asked him, handing him a plate of toast and jelly.

'Of course,' he said. 'You too, I bet.'

I had been unfaithful in Minneapolis a few months after Julius left, with Comrade Foy Fellowes, first glimpsed by me at the Wallace convention, who had last year been unmasked as an FBI agent. Papers were found in his car to prove it, indicating he was involved in a deep-cover operation and had been for years. He denied it, said they had been planted as a way of discrediting leading cadre. How could you tell, one way or the other? You couldn't. It was like one of those optical illusion pictures. You look at it and you see a pair of vases, you look at it again and you see an old lady with a feather in her hair, or whatever. I don't know how you can work out the truth in such circumstances. You had to wait for the FBI to open its files and that was going to be never. Someone asked me if I could tell when I had slept with him; had he given himself away in some manner? I said no. All cats are grey in the dark.

There was also a cowboy in North Dakota and a gas jockey in the same state.

'Of course,' I replied. 'We always said no strings, no commitments.'

'That was how you wanted it.'

'I thought that was how you wanted it.'

'I don't know how you get that idea.'

I looked at him, eating his toast, butter on his chin. 'You never said you loved me,' I said.

'Love is a bourgeois delusion, a pathological nightmare. There is no such thing as love.'

'Why are we getting married, then?'

'To fix things.'

'Fix?'

'Between us. I want to make it legal.'

'Legal in whose eyes? The state's?'

'I don't care. I just want a piece of paper with your name on it and my name on it.'

'Why, Julius? Why me?'

He shrugged. 'You happen to be handy.'

So we sat and waited for someone to come and get us. Julius did not leave the house. He smoked and read. He wrote on yellow legal paper, long treatises on colonialism and revolutionary movements in West Africa. I got his cock working again by a few tricks I had picked up here and there.

It was strange to be with him after so long apart, but I was more than thirty years of age and a portion of my youth had been stolen from me by the Federal Bureau of Investigation. I made it my priority to return to normality. I acknowledged to myself that I could not be without a man. All the widows and divorcees and separated wives that I had been on the road were fictions. I bought a cookbook at the five and dime and made stews and baked cakes. I was going to be Julius's wife. Like he had said before, once he started something he liked to finish it. I still did not love Julius, not the way they talk about in romances. My heart did not skip a beat when I saw him, I did not daydream about his handsome face. But I had no will or desire to get away from him. I owed my moral identity to him, my very self.

A week or two passed while the Party bickered about what to do with us. One faction wanted to bring Julius back to Washington to drag what was left of our union work back into the CIO, to defy the CIO Red-baiters, and I guessed they had some kind of super-secretary's job for me at head office, which I thought was fine for I was not ambitious and I still saw myself as serving others, however humbly. A second group was keeping its eye on the segregation struggle in the South where the Montgomery bus boycott was in its first month and to which we had begun shipping Party workers. Who fought hardest and longest for the Scottsboro Boys? our comrades asked the people we met there. We did. The communists.

We spent Christmas together with a bird I roasted and presents for him of books specially ordered from headquarters and, surprisingly for me, a pair of silver earrings in department-store good taste. It was years since I'd had anything expensive and pretty and when I opened the box the first thing I saw was that they were not what I would have chosen for myself.

'What happened to the dog?' he asked me, suddenly, pulling a drumstick from the cold carcass, later that evening.

'Oh, yes. The dog. I had it destroyed after you left.' Before I turned away I saw that his eyes had welled up with tears.

'Julius,' I said. 'What's happened to you? What did they do to you?'

'They didn't do anything,' he said. 'I don't know what you mean.'

New Year's Day, 1956. I did the dishes, vacuumed, took a pair of shoes to be re-heeled under a muggy sky. I could have driven these few streets in my sleep. I was thinking about how I'd probably never get to California now and remembering, with regret, the picture I'd once clipped of the beach and the palm tree and the figure with rolled-up pants walking in the surf. Perhaps there were a couple more hours of watery daylight left before the rain became indistinguishable from the darkness. But my shoes would only take an hour to be mended. 'Come back and I'll have them for you as good as new,' the guy in the store said. Second-hand shoes adorned his window, samples of his craft.

'Are they for sale?' I asked doubtfully.

'Sure. They're shoes people bring me and then they never come back. Can you believe it? My good work they waste, my time. You can't get nothing for them these days, not like years ago. Now everyone has to have new shoes, just for their feet.'

The shoes in his window were indeed individually feet-shaped, the leather stretched to accommodate corns and bunions, heels worn down on one side or the other. Here was a pair of two-tone court shoes, white with liver-brown toecaps and white saddle stitching. What floors had they danced on? Had they walked pavements other than these? Ah, but they were shoes to wear in the city, shoes to walk Seattle in. There were little children's shoes, too, a pair of red leather sandals. 'Lady brought those in for a new buckle,' the shoe-repair man said, 'but the little girl took sick and died. I told the lady, you have other kids, pass them on. But she didn't want them. Difference with her and these others is she paid me just the same, even though those little kids' shoes were no good to her no more. So that's why I always ask for money up front. That'll be a dollar. But don't go far. See that coffee shop over there? They do good cinnamon buns. Have a cup of coffee and a cinnamon bun. Call back and they'll be ready.' The wrecks of shoes.

I knew this coffee shop. The waitress recognized me and

nodded. 'I'll be right over to take your order!' she shouted. She was really moving. She got over to my table panting. 'My shift's just got ten minutes to run so I'll give you your check now.'

'That's fine,' I said. 'I'll have a coffee.'

'No cinnamon bun?'

'No. I'm trying to lose a little weight.' Years behind the wheel, years of hamburgers and donuts, had seen me spread.

She looked at me carefully. She was about nineteen and as slim as I had once been. 'I've got a great diet-sheet at home. I'll copy it out for you and you can have it next time you come in.' I went red. I wanted her to say that, no, I didn't need to lose any weight, why, there was hardly anything on me. But maybe she saw me as a fat middle-aged woman with untidy hair and nondescript clothes.

I drank three cups of coffee in an hour thinking about the night before. Julius taking a long drink from a bottle of Russian vodka he had wrapped up in paper among his things. His eyes becoming muddled. How he began singing an old sophisticated song about not getting a kick from champagne and raising his glass to say that he got a kick out of me. And laughing. Singing the Internationale as the clock struck midnight.

> 'Tis the final conflict
> Let each stand in his place.

'So what do you know about miscegenation?' he asked me, bringing his face close to mine. 'Are we going to make babies together? Will you give me a son, Sybil? A little soldier for the Red Army? For old Julius's army? Are we going to have an off-white baby together? Coffee-colour? You can give me one any colour you like, I don't care, I'll give him my name. How come you never say anything about yourself? Tell me about your mom and dad. Spill the beans, Sybil. There should be no secrets between man and wife.'

'You're drunk,' I told him. 'I've never seen you like this.'

'Good Soviet vodka is talking. A worker's paradise. Heaven on earth. Come here, why you got so many clothes on?'

That was life with Julius, whom I would marry, come what may, so many years after we had first met when one night I went to East 52nd Street on impulse, an honest woman made of me at last. But now my coffee cup was empty, my bladder was full.

I was being directed down the steps to the ladies' room with my bag in my hand and my coat still upstairs on the coat stand. At the bottom there was no sign to point the way. To my right was the open serving hatch of a dumb waiter and the serving hatch on the other side of the shaft was also open. Through it I could see that my off-duty waitress was leaning against the edge. She was cut off at the shoulders but I recognized the sleeves of her red dress and her voice. She was talking about last night, what a great time she'd had and how she would be free again later that week. Her arm was resting next to another, touching it, a man's arm, also cut off at the shoulders. The man's sleeves were rolled up and his knuckles were dusted with clotted patches of dried dough. He had a pinkie ring on the little finger of his left hand, which she reached over and twirled, and above his hand a line of freckles that formed the shape of the Plough.

I didn't say a word. I'd said nothing. There was only the sound of my heart banging against my ribs. So why had they left the kitchen and why were they standing there looking at me, and why was she telling me to pipe down?

He said, 'Piss off, Marge. Give us a minute, Syb. I'll wash up and get my jacket.'

We were walking out of the coffee shop with the manager yelling at him, hey you, where the hell do you think you're going, you just get here, get back in the kitchen, you lousy . . . and past the shoe-repair man standing at the door with the *Closed* sign behind him, waving my shoes at me.

I walked automatically to my car. He looked at it. 'This your motor?'

'Yes.'

'Right, then. We'll go for a spin.'

I drove down towards the sea. He was next to me on the bench seat, not even a stick shift between us. I changed gear on the steering-wheel column. He was wearing an Italian-cut gun-metal grey mohair suit, with narrow trousers and shoulders, narrow lapels and a skinny little pearl-grey leather tie. He was still losing his hair but it had been receding slowly since I last saw him. He was thirty-six and of course his looks were all gone but he still had something around the eyes. He was examining the gadgets on the dashboard. 'What's this?' he asked.

'It's a cigarette lighter.'

'Great.' He took out two cigarettes, lit both and handed one to me. I choked at the first draw. 'Real gaspers, eh? They're French.'

'Where have you been, Stan? Where did you go?'

'Where are *we* going? Have we left town?'

'I'm driving to the beach.'

'What, at this time of year?'

'I'm not thinking.'

'Go on, then. Let's see where we get to.'

Nothing was open at the resort. We stood on the edge of the pier looking at an invisible sun sink over the Pacific Ocean and smoked another cigarette. Clouds were in our hair. A dead cat was lying on the beach, stiffening.

'What a dump,' he said. 'What an armpit.' Then he saw that I was trembling. 'Shit, it's cold. You must be freezing. I know I am and you haven't got a coat on or nothing. Come here.' He put his arm round me for a moment. 'No, it's too cold. Let's get back in the car. You got a heater?'

We walked back to the road. 'Strictly speaking,' he was saying as we opened the doors, 'us meeting again like this calls for a drink. Does this automobile come with a built-in hip flask?'

'Of course not.'

'I'd never have taken you for a scouser if I'd met you now, for the first time.'

'I never used to sound like one.'

'No, I mean I'd have thought you were an American.'

'I must say your American accent has gone.'

'I could never make my mind up if it really suited me. But you know what we were like about the Yanks before the war.'

The car warmed us up and my hands were still. I turned to him. 'Please tell me. Where did you go?'

'That night? New Year's Eve?'

'Yes.'

'Nine years ago.'

'Is it that long?'

'Must be. Didn't you ever find out what happened?'

'No. I never heard another word. You just vanished.'

'Not a clue?'

'No.'

'Jesus, Sybil, think. I got deported. Slung out.'

'The immigration . . . You got busted?'

'No, it wasn't that. In fact you could say it was your fault. What they were on to me for was working without a permit, me being a wetback. It was you who told me to take that job down in Washington, that union job. Well, someone snitched. The second time I went down there they came for me, drove me back to New York, let me go back to our place to pick up some stuff and tell you what's what and then they put me on the next boat. And where were you, by the way? I was hopping. I didn't write for two months and when I did the letter was sent back, not known at this address. So what's your story?'

'I went to 52nd Street.'

'That couldn't have taken you all night. It was four in the morning when we got there.'

It slipped from my lips, like all the other lies I told. It was like a lemming, it wanted out of there. 'Oh, Stan, it *was* New Year's Eve. And you were away. Can't a girl have a little fun?' I smiled at him

He nodded. 'Quite right. I was out of order there.'

'But if I had been home? What would you have said to me?'

He hesitated. 'That's water under the bridge now.'

'So what have you been doing all this time?'

'Went back to sea. Knocked about a bit. The usual. Jumped ship last month. Fancied seeing America again. When I've got a few bob I thought I'd get down to California. Do you think I'm too old to make it in pictures?'

'Just a bit.'

'You?'

What was I going to say? I couldn't say anything. If ever there was a loose cannon it was Stan. We were no longer underground but that didn't mean there was no danger. I concocted a story about how I had married in New York and how we'd moved out to the Midwest for a few years then my husband had got a job at Boeing in Seattle. He'd gone out first to set things up but he'd met a woman. He'd left her and now we were making a last-ditch attempt to patch things up.

'Here?'

'He has a brother who lives here. We're staying at his house for a while.'

'So how does he get to work?'

'He commutes.'

'Bit of a way, isn't it?'

'That's his business.'

'All right. Got kids?'

'No.'

'Me neither.'

I remembered what someone had told me once. 'I heard that you had a child with a coloured woman in Tryon Park. Is it true?' I had watched that child grow up in my mind's eye, sometimes a boy, sometimes a girl.

'No, that wasn't me. Someone else.'

My hands were on the steering wheel like a child playing at driving his daddy's car. He looked at them. I had worn a phoney wedding ring since I left Minneapolis. 'It's fucking cold,' he said. 'Should we head off?'

I started up the engine. 'My husband won't be back until late tonight,' I said. 'He won't be starting out from Seattle for a couple of hours.'

He looked at me and flashed a smile so dazzling that my heart contracted. 'I've got a place. Want to come back there?'

'What about Marge?'

'Who's Marge?'

There was a side street I'd never driven down and on it was a three-storey brick apartment building, the only one in town, built some time in the thirties when there was an idea that the place was going to amount to something. Along the pediment, in the daylight, you could see a frieze of dolphin heads like waves above a line of scallop shells, and a plaque depicting an old-fashioned sailing boat on a white and foaming sea.

'Most of the flats are empty,' he said as we reached his door. 'Everyone wants houses. Me, I haven't lived in a house since I was in my mammy's arms.' He didn't turn the light on but took my hand and guided me into the bedroom.

'Where are we going?' I asked.

'You know.'

I felt I had been watching him undressing for half my life and each time something was different. Now, no stainless-steel identity bracelet but a thin gold chain around his neck. The inverted nipples softer, pulpy. The scant black hairs were drifting across his chest, and his skin, when I touched it, seemed to come away from the bone as if there was no muscle to bind it to his frame. A little device, like a curly horn, was tattooed on his upper arm next to the anchor. I ran my fingers over it.

'What's this?'

'Nothing. A bit of malarky.'

He took out a rubber and put it on. 'Better safe than sorry,' he said, and he came inside me and then lay still for a long time, just looking at my face. I wondered if he was willing himself to fuck me, or willing himself not to, but there was no need of anything, I felt complete. After a while he fell asleep and then I did. When I woke a few minutes later he was flaccid, but I touched the nape of his neck and he opened his eyes and hardened again.

'Syb,' he said. 'You are my woman, aren't you?'

I nodded.

'OK, let's go.'

Afterwards he went for a piss and came back and sat on the edge of the bed. 'The only thing is, you'll have to smarten yourself up a bit.'

'What do you mean?'

'You look a bit rough to me.'

'Even with my clothes off?'

'No, you still look all right without your kit. Bit flabby round the middle, though. You must be getting on. We all are. I can't stand your hair. Do you have to wear it in a bun?'

I reached back and felt it. 'Should I wear it loose?'

'Yes, or have it properly seen to.'

'I'll tell you what I have got – a pair of cowboy boots.'

'Have you? What do you wear them with?'

'One time, with a dress.'

'And nylons?'

'Yes.'

'I'm not sure, I'd have to see it.'

'I'll go shopping anyway. I'll drive into Seattle tomorrow.'

He got back into bed. 'I'm going to take a kip now. Do you have to be somewhere?'

'Yes, I'll have to go in a bit.'

'Come back tomorrow. You'll sort something out with your feller, will you?'

'I'll think of something.'

What *was* I thinking of? I wasn't thinking of anything at all. Thinking didn't come into it.

Stan had never been such a great lover. Julius had . . . size and stamina, and we were comrades and had braved years of danger to be together again. But an old tune plays and before we know it we are singing the words.

I went back that night to my marriage bed. Julius was asleep with beer on his breath, snoring. I turned on the side light and stared at his face. Time erodes us or it silts us up. Julius was dry and time was hollowing him out from within. Yet as I looked at him I knew that the afternoon and evening had been a harmless interlude, a finishing-up of business interrupted so long, long ago. I would not see Stan again, or, if I did, only to say goodbye, to explain half truthfully that I was a married woman and our hours together had been a temporary lapse in an otherwise blameless marriage. And as I thought of it, I did not even *want* to see Stan. What a child he was. The sex had cleaned him out of my system, that urge for lawless encounters that had begun in the years of travelling, and he was no more now than one of the cowboys I had mounted and mated. I felt light and sweet until I remembered further back than my time as a courier, to Julius and even to Stan himself when he was nineteen and I was fourteen and I was a girl with my own chinchilla coat and he was little more than a con-man. But I put that idea out of my head and fell soundly asleep.

Julius awoke late the next day and as soon as I heard him stirring, I put on an apron and began to fix him the finest

breakfast I could muster. The only smells now were of polish
and laundry soap. I put bacon on the griddle, took down a
package of pancake mix and dropped yeasty little rounds on to
the pan. I broke eggs into the bacon fat and watched the
whites turn first cloudy then opaque. It was an act of terrible
love, this, for I loathed eggs and the sight of their yellow
hearts reminded me of pus coalescing around a wound. Finally,
English style, I fried some bread. I slid the contents on to a
plate, poured coffee from the percolator into a cup and
brought it in to Julius, who was sitting in 'his' chair, smoking,
staring into space. He looked at the plate as if he was seeing
through it but he took it from me and put it down on the floor.
Twenty minutes later it was still there, untouched, and he had
smoked another two cigarettes.

'Aren't you hungry?' I asked him.

'I never did like breakfast,' he said.

I took the plate away and scraped the contents into the
garbage, my throat gagging as I watched the fried egg's yolk
break in the air before it reached the place where it would fall,
on top of the pancake-mix package and a mound of still-
steaming coffee grounds.

After I had washed the dishes I came back and sat opposite
him on a hard upright chair. I took out my lipstick from my
purse and began to paint my lips. Julius watched me. 'Soviet
women don't smear that garbage over their faces,' he said.
'Where did you get to last night?' His knees were covered in
ash.

'I went for a drive to the coast and had dinner. I needed
space.'

'Yeah. Sure.'

'Don't you believe me?'

'I don't care either way.'

'I've been used to spending a lot of time alone.'

'I believe you acquitted yourself well. I have been told. It seems you did me credit. I made something out of you, after all.'

I understood then why he wanted to marry me. I was his project, the Red Pygmalion, and he did not give up on anything he had begun.

'I have never told anyone how hard it was,' I said, meekly. 'The kinds of doubts that creep in when you're on your own.'

'I don't want to hear. I have no interest in listening to your doubts. Either you're in the Party or you're not, you're with us or you're against us. You make your mind up either way.'

My doubts. Only in the last months of my life on the road had I been able to admit to myself what we did to those men and women we sent underground, the terrible isolation we put them through, comrades who had drawn politics with every breath and who now lived for years in one-horse towns where they were terrified to make a remark about the weather lest it implicated them. Those boys and girls who were the sons and daughters of the old Yiddish Bolsheviks dumped in some place like Cedar Rapids, Iowa, and sent to work milling Quaker Oats, they went slowly nuts, cut off from culture, from conversation, from good food, from intelligent thought, from newspapers where they could mainline detailed reports of victories, like the Viet Minh's humiliation of the French at Diên Biên Phu, and then argue for hours what this might mean for the rest of Indo-China.

And when they lay awake at night staring into the darkness wondering, 'What the hell am I doing here? What the hell *are* we doing?'; when they could not call or lay eyes on a mother or a father or a wife or a husband or a son or a daughter for four years; when they could never make a single friend for fear it would endanger them; when they had to hold their tongues in the factory when the union was going about a dispute all the wrong way, or when there was no union and the workers had to endure terrible conditions, never knowing how they could fight to change them; when they lived through these blackest years, then I was there to shake them and tell them, 'No! You can't think those thoughts. Those thoughts are not permissible. Those thoughts will deform you and betray us. Pull yourself together.' I said all this without shame or pity.

Someone had been two years in a factory making doll's eyes. Two years in silence.

'There was a comrade in a town outside Omaha,' I said. 'While he was underground his wife left the Party and was living under an assumed name in Texas.'

He was thinking about how his parents had come from Russia to America when he was a tiny child and how they had wound up living in the Projects where they bred communists like rabbits. He was wondering about how, if they'd stayed on the Lower East Side in poverty, maybe his father would have worked just that bit harder and saved some money and they would have moved out to Brooklyn or Queens. 'And would I have gone to high school there and on to college and got a profession? Who would I be now if that had happened, Sybil? Would I have become a communist anyway because I would have known it was *right*? Or am I just a product of my environment, of my times? What d'ya think?'

But I told him not to think.

'Later he asked me to go to bed with him,' I said to Julius.

'I would have, I needed the sex.' I needed to be held just as he did, both of us, alone, needed the temporary complicity of what we call 'intercourse', the pretence that two are one.

'You should have fucked him,' Julius said. 'You got an itch, scratch it.'

I told Julius how I had noticed how some of the most thoughtful comrades took to painting or playing a musical instrument or reading books they had never read before – poetry, novels, new books about existentialism, old books about female emancipation, books from beyond the pale by men long ago denounced, such as Trotsky. They turned inside themselves away from action. They found there something that no one in the Party had ever possessed before – an inner life. In exile from America, they saw that they had to choose between going into internal exile from the Party or internal exile from themselves. 'What could they do, Julius?' I begged. 'The second way led only to madness.'

'*I will not entertain doubt*,' Julius said, and he threw a motor-cycle part at me. It hit the wall and bounced greasily to the floor.

'Tell me what happened to you in Russia. Tell me.'

'I don't know what you mean,' he said. 'It's a worker's paradise. No race chauvinism.' His whole body was still. 'There is no hope, no hope at all for the American Negro without the leadership of the worldwide communist movement. No one will stand by the Negro, apart from the communists. I was treated like a king in Russia. I was mobbed on the street. People thought I was Robeson.'

I said, 'I don't believe you.'

'Then you can go to hell. I am not entertaining traitors.'

Something had happened to him in Russia, something that

he would not tell me. He was denying intimacy, denying a life of the spirit, denying any kind of inner life. Action is almost but not quite all, I thought, so quickly that I had to clutch the idea from the air before it dissolved into nothing.

'And I can't live with someone who keeps secrets from me,' I said. 'I'm sick of secrets. I want a normal life.'

'OK. You want to hear?' he cried, half raised up from the chair. 'You want to know? This is what it was like. I wasn't mobbed. No one thought I was Robeson. Kids on the street used to scratch their hands under their arms like apes in the jungle when they saw me. They called me jungle man. The whole place was white. White buildings, white snow, white faces. There was some fuck-up and they put me in prison. A mistake. So what? Five weeks with no books, no paper, no pen. Nothing. I spent all day playing Charlie Parker riffs over and over again in my head. Then they let me out. Oh, sorry. Wrong guy. Not you. Some other coloured fellow. Because of course we all look the same. But it does not matter. Because *there is no hope for the Negro without communism*. It's all we've got. Now let's hear your life story, then. Come on, spit it out. Let's hear what makes you so special.' But I turned away.

He ran across the room and grabbed me by the hair. 'I want a secret, Sybil. Give me a secret. An eye for an eye, a tooth for a tooth.'

'No!' I shouted. 'I'm sorry about Russia, I'm—'

He rammed me against the wall and was holding my throat. 'Secret time, secret time.'

I pulled his hands from my neck and held his face in my hands. 'Julius. What do you want from me?'

'You took my essence, man. You stole my soul, you fucking

bitch. You made me tell you something I'd have given my life to keep buried in a pit some place.'

'I can help you, I could—'

'I don't need no help. A secret, Sybil. Tell me a secret. Let's get our marriage started out right. You belong to me and I belong to the Party.'

'Says who?' I cried. For I was sobbing.

Chapter Nineteen

I walked out of the house. I left it without looking in the mirror to see my swollen face and ravaged eyes, without brushing my hair or putting on lipstick. And I drove to Seattle, according to plan.

At once, behind the wheel, I fell back into a kind of familiarity and content. No one belonged in this car but myself, it was a car to be alone in. As I drove, I would glance at the seat beside me and try as I might to recollect Stan sitting there or the leather upholstery still warm from his behind. And I kept checking in the rear-view mirror. I was getting muddled up. Though the route was clearly marked to Seattle, I was neither here nor there, neither one thing nor the other, neither fish nor beast.

On the way I stopped for gas and picked up a couple of

magazines from the rack. One of them was *Ladies' Home Journal* and I sat in my car and turned its pages while the gas jockey filled my tank.

'*It will be a gay, colorful spring – fabric tones are the loveliest ever,*' I read. '*Your coat might be a lovely lemon yellow or one of the beautiful new reds – both cheerful colors. Your suit could be a heavenly sky blue or a soft turquoise, both so flattering.*

'*Your hat is your personality quotient, as well as the topping off of your silhouette. Small hats have new charms. Witness – the field-flower turban, brilliant straws wound with tulle or chiffon, little toques with showers of spring blossoms, brims covered with rose leaves.*'

The names of the designers – William Bass, Ben Reig, Hannah Troy, Leonard Arkin, Herbert Sondeim, Arthur Jablow – were unknown to me.

Looking ahead to summer, it was apparent that the sheath dress was passing out in favour of a return to small-waisted, full-skirted printed cottons in mouth-watering sugary pinks and pale blues. I did not have one shift dress in my wardrobe, although the arrow silhouette had always suited me better than the New Look.

Next I looked at a photo of a young matron, Mrs Frederick H. Davies of Cedarhurst, Long Island, who was married to a broker for the Cuban Atlantic Sugar Corporation. She said she preferred a slim sheath, that she approved of beige and subdued colours all worn with white (especially the cleanest, whitest gloves). She was pictured in an Italian silk dress-and-bolero costume with a white collar, white stocking hat and a black patent-leather purse. A bunch of white tulips was carried stiffly under her arm.

I drove into Seattle, parked and determinedly trod the streets until I found a department store. Looking up at the sign at the intersection, I saw I was at 6th and Pine. America was full of cross-streets with precisely the same two names. In some I had had coffee, in others I had stayed the night, in more again I had sat down with a realtor or inspected a house or made a call from a pay booth. Sixth and Pine had no special fix on me, no more than 6th and Main or 6th and Maple. But on 6th and Pine in Seattle were the premises of Frederick and Nelson and I walked through their doors and they swallowed me up. As if an enchanter had poured magic oofle dust into my eyes, I wandered through the aisles, eating what I saw, and even though I dimly remembered that this far west the stock would be dated, the new modes from New York (let alone London or Paris) months or even years away from shipment, I found myself drawn into a world of wonder, my pace slow, time immaterial. Occasionally my steps routed back near the doors and quite clearly I saw the buses and cars pass and people walking, and I was seized with nausea. There might be a strike up the street with its little picket line treading the sidewalk in a trudging circle, arms heavy with picket signs, the uniform chant, the slowly diminishing pile of flyers given out to everyone who passed. This person or that might be hungry, on benefit. A cripple with a stick could have been a millworker, denied compensation. Behind me, in the store, was all the burden of *things*, what they cost, how useless and unserviceable most of them were.

None the less, I looked at everything. Nothing was too cheap or inconsequential for my attention. Breck shampoo. Miss Clairol Color Bath. 'Certainly Red' lipstick by Revlon. Helene Curtis Spray Net lacquer. Ropes of beads by Coro. A cuff bracelet with a honeycombed surface at $2. Tortoise-shell-framed sunglasses at $5 in their own case.

I found myself in the swimwear department, examining swag-strap swimsuits.

I picked up a pair of dust-grey suede shoes and held them in my hands, puzzled. Attached to the front was a sloppy, floppy, slippery grey satin bow and they reminded me of shoes my mother had, kept in her wardrobe and never worn any more for they had been in vogue years before, in the twenties. They were shoes for a flapper to wear in a matching cloche. They were antiques, junk, rubbish. There was nothing 'now' about them. But what did I know about now? I didn't know anything. I could not try those shoes on. I could not place them because I'd lost my place. *Who made the shoes?* I asked myself in a panic. What were they paid? Were they union? How did they do in their last contract?

In time to come the shoes with the grey bows would reassemble themselves and stop floating about in the deep space of my mind. I would see something else, another pair of shoes somewhere else, and recognition would follow. It would not be enough, not ever again, for me to say 'She came towards me in a red dress of some clingy fabric'. It must be blood-red or maroon or pillar-box red and the material had to be crêpe or crêpe de Chine or satin. And the dress must be on the bias or A-line or New Look. It's a Patou or a Jean Muir or a Westwood. An Ossie Clarke that I bought in 1968 on the King's Road defines me for that very moment. I look down at my bare knees in it and I know who I am. Even the velvet shirts stinking of patchouli which I retrieved from a soukh in Morocco in 1972, made to an ancient, timeless design, sewn as like as not by the fading eyes of child labour, tether me down to history. I put them on and become their age, my only stake in the present tense.

I was looking at a pale beige cashmere suit, pared down to

sheath slimness. In another department I noticed that purses, that year, were large. Finally, I came across a bow-back jacket with a slim, panelled skirt in a colour not unlike the coral pink of my Digby Morton costume of so long ago.

An assistant approached me. 'That's definitely your shade, ma'am,' she said. 'Won't you try it on?'

I looked around at the sales staff in their black pencil skirts and white blouses and I saw that those who would have been my contemporaries, ten years on, were nowhere in evidence. All the assistants were younger girls or women older than myself. I supposed that my own generation was at home, like Mrs Frederick H. Davies, looking after their children.

Out of the window traffic hummed. A coloured man sat beneath a perch shining shoes and the sight of his indignity made me break into a sweat. 'Are you union?' I asked the sales-girl. Her blonde hair was drawn back in a French pleat and her lipstick was very glossy. She had a hare's face, all eyes and no chin. Her uniform didn't make the most of her; she'd have done better in pastels, blues and pinks that didn't drain the blood from her face. She needed outfits that would make her seem fragile, not sallow.

'We don't have a union here. But if that kind of thing is important to you, a lot of our cheaper lines are union-made. They have the label in them.'

'But the textiles aren't union. None of those textile mills in the South are organized.'

'Maybe you'd be happier in another kind of store,' she said. 'There's a . . .'

Then a woman in a haze of scent passed by and my nostrils dilated and sent a message to a pleasure centre in my brain which decoded the mingled chemicals and sent back a message:

Nina Ricci. L'Air du Temps. And I was dragged back to those expeditions with my mother along Bond Street and Audley Street, to Fenwick's and Cresta and the White House, where we lunched on egg mayonnaise as a mannequin slithered past on bottle-green lizard feet.

The coral suit was far beyond my means, but I found a sky-blue sheath dress and I bought it. Next I went to the store's beauty salon and asked them if they had a free appointment.

'For a cut,' I said.

The receptionist looked at me and visibly winced. 'If you'd like a permanent, we could fit you in,' she said.

I sat obediently while they lathered my head with cold wave and twined my hair around the tiny curlers. I asked them to style it into a helmet of waves, that were swept up to one side. Finally, back in the cosmetics department, I bought myself a bottle of L'Air du Temps.

When I left the store the temperature had dropped and soggy snowflakes were falling fast, sleet not snow, and the wind whipped my dress box against my legs. Icy water coursed through the gutters and soaked my shoes as I crossed the street. In a store window I caught sight of my reflection, my smooth, swept-up hair heavy with hairspray, and I wasn't sure. But the Negro on the shoeshine stand was saying something. 'I beg your pardon?' I said.

'I'll tell you again. You sure look better now than when you went into that store a few hours back.'

And I sat on his perch anaesthetized by beauty and he knelt and I let him shine my shoes.

When I arrived back in town I went straight to Stan's apartment and dressed myself in my new costume.

'What do you think?' I asked.

'Big improvement, but there's something about the hair,' he said. 'I don't know what it is. It just makes you look old. Your face is heart-shaped but this makes it square – square like a box and square old-fashioned. I don't think it's really you. I reckon you should cut it all off, short, like you used to have it in New York. I'll do it if you like.'

'You? What do you know about cutting hair?'

'I can cut hair. My cousin Peggy was a hairdresser. She taught me. I've got the proper scissors and everything. I used to do the lads when I was at sea. I'm a proper teasyweasy.'

'A proper what?'

'Never mind, let's have a go.'

I ran to the window, holding my hands lightly over my helmet of waves, and Stan followed and caught me. He was looking out, over my shoulder to something on the street.

'I've just paid for this,' I told him. 'It took hours.'

'No,' he said. 'I think you should let me cut it.'

I let him lead me to a chair and I sat while he undid my blouse, took it off and draped a towel around my shoulders. He went into the bathroom and came back with a comb and a jug of water.

He worked away for so long that I began to drowse and it was then that I felt the first peace I had known in many years, lulled into a calm deeper than the time of bovine stupidity, before the war, before my mother's betrayal of herself, back to the Saturday mornings at my father's feet when the world was quiet and only the sound of a fly buzzing in the cloakroom disturbed the blue satin rest of my daughterhood. I sat patiently, being shorn.

When he'd done, Stan brought a mirror. He'd cut my hair to

two or three inches of my scalp, as if I was a man. And yet he'd been right. It took years off me; it redefined my jaw, brought out my eyes, made me look fashionably gamine with a hint of bohemianism. I was a woman to look at, a woman out of the ordinary, chic and special, in the thickest flow of the new and the becoming, the present tense.

He carried the mirror over to the window, to catch the disappearing light of the winter's afternoon. He glanced again down into the street.

'That's it,' he said. 'There's some feller who's been sitting out there all fucking day. I'm going down to tell him what's what.'

I followed his eyes. The anonymous car and the young, upturned face, smart in a pressed coat and dark tie. The closed, watching face that was prepared to endure such long hours of waiting, the monotony broken only by the occasional taking of a note. The cold, the thankless cup of coffee. May they rot in hell, all of them.

I said to Stan, 'I know what that's about. It's the immigration people. They're after you again.'

'Oh, shit!' he cried. 'What am I going to do?'

I walked over to the opposite wall and thought about it. I looked at his panicky face. I ran my fingers through my boyish hair. All day the choices had eddied around me. In the department store I had been in utter mental disarray. Like cheap clothing, I was coming apart at the seams. Julius or Stan – which was it to be? It was obvious. There was no choice. Julius needed me. I needed Julius. I could heal the terrible damaged centre of him. In turn he would take me at last to my rightful place at the centre of the world. I could always think of a secret. I was sure I could invent dozens.

'Listen,' I said. 'You can't go on like this. It will always be the same. You'll never be able to stay. But what about Canada? It's not so far away, only three hours' drive. You don't have any record there, do you?' He shook his head. 'Do you have a passport?'

'Of course.'

'You can get in legally. You could apply for immigration. It would be a fresh start.'

'I want to stay in America,' he replied, with a stubborn look appearing across his always rather vacuous face. 'It's the land of opportunity. I've not even seen a cowboy yet and I'm thirty-four.'

'Thirty-six. Don't you think you're a bit old for cowboys?'

'I'm the man, I make the decisions.'

'Oh, for God's sake, use your brains. Think, think. What's your future here?'

'I've never been interested in the future. I just take life as it comes.'

'That's your trouble.'

'You and me?'

And then I said what I did not expect to say because I no longer knew what I thought until I heard my own words in the air, propelled by my treacherous breath. 'Yes. Both of us.'

He was looking at his shoes. 'Want a smoke?' he said in a small voice.

'OK,' I replied. But he didn't get out a pack of cigarettes, instead he sat down and began to roll a joint. When I saw that I was filled with fear. Screw Stan, no one gave a toss about him, least of all the FBI. I watched him smoke the reefer and shook my head when he passed it over. He drifted away from terror into passivity. I walked over and drew him to the bed and there we lay, in each other's arms, exchanging soft, deceptive little kisses until eventually he hardened and we made love.

So I had been faced with a choice. Should I betray the world, my ideals, my comrades? Should I abandon Julius in the hour of his need? And for what? So I could pick up once again a sordid little affair that had now gone on half my life? Or should I leave Stan to his fate, to his diminishing future?

And given the greatest moral dilemma of my life, I had chosen the worst course. You know what was good about Stan? He never asked me anything, he never wanted anything. We could paddle around in the shallows with each other. I would commit to communism but I could not commit to Julius. He would not tolerate treachery? I had it in my very make-up. I could not believe that this meeting was just coincidence; how could it be? I had crossed that great continent, driving all by myself from one coast to the other. I had witnessed the heart of America. I had made every effort, *every* effort to belong somewhere or to someone. The land had held me down and imprisoned me and I had accepted my fate, I submitted myself to the loss of my freedom. But when I reached the edge of things again Stan was there, waiting for me, as he had always done, accepting and unquestioning. We were meant for each other and meant to be. How could I kid myself? It was just as the man had told me, I was a surfer, my place was on the margins, where no one demanded anything of you except that you keep your balance, that you survive upright, where you could stand back and not be involved in the great noise and clamour of the world. The great forces of Fate had driven his ship to that little port and sent Julius there for me to join him so Stan and I could meet once again. The world was ordered and arranged by giant hands. You could not determine your own future. Stan's presence had shown me that.

Of course in my heart I knew that all of this was nonsense. There was nothing odd at all in Stan being there; after all, ships docked everywhere and coming into land was his work, his trade. It was bizarre for *me* to have showed up, not him. A coincidence that two men should have chosen that out-of-the-way port to make their concealed entrance back into America. But I had to tell myself there was a reason other than selfishness for my great act of treachery. I tried something else. As we drove away from that godforsaken lumber town, I decided that my mother's bad blood had made me do it, though I did not believe in blood any more, only materialism.

Chapter Twenty

Our drive over the border into Canada was uneventful. We showed our passports. I'd never seen Stan's so I snatched it from him when it had been returned and looked at the photo. The light in the photographer's studio made him look exceedingly foreign, with eyes like two black sucked sweets, and the small cleft in his chin cast its own shadow. His lips were slightly apart, as if he'd just finished saying something, some bit of back-chat, I guessed. He was a few years younger, an inch or so closer to the New York Stan, and I was jealous of the people who had known him when he had that tie and was wearing out the armpits of that shirt, in those mysterious years of his knocking about, his this and his that.

'Where was it taken?' I asked.

'I dunno. Somewhere on London Road, I think. Let's see

yours.' My picture had been taken at Burrell and Hardman on Rodney Street, a few days before Christmas 1945. 'Oh yeah,' he said. 'I remember you when you looked like that.'

I stared at my passport photo, at the unfamiliar girl who lived between the four straight lines of a celluloid world. The corners of my mouth were turned up in a little smile. My face was a small, fashionable blank. When I glanced into the rear-view mirror I could only see my green eyes and a faint frown line was drawing itself between them. There were lilac shadows under my lashes and the right eye was a little puffy. I looked at my hands on the steering wheel and found they were smooth but there was a tiny smudge on my manicure. I hadn't waited long enough for the polish to dry before making some move-ment of which I would have hardly been conscious.

Stan was still holding my passport between his own long brown fingers with their waisted thumbs. He was making a study of me. 'Was that a spot?' he said critically. 'Old spotty-face.' I thought how gauche and young he could seem at times. 'This is going to expire any minute,' he said. The passport had arrived only a couple of days before I'd sailed from Liverpool.

I drove away from the border and the flag was flying high over Canada with a small square of the Union Jack on it. We'd left America and come to this strange no-man's-land between the new world and the old. The FBI couldn't get me now. There *was* no FBI, only Mounties in red uniforms astride horses singing duets with Jeanette MacDonald, and who could take that seriously? I felt comforted by the Union Jack. I thought I'd left behind the brutality of America and of life on the run. I was heading towards the Middle Kingdom and my middle years.

'I've been here before,' Stan said. 'I was on a ship once that docked at Vancouver.'

'What's it like?'

'Not bad. Dead, but not bad.'

We drove through an Italian neighbourhood and then a Chinese one. 'This is skid row,' Stan said, as we passed hotels with men sitting outside them clutching bottles wrapped in brown paper. The men were ruined hulks who hobbled when they walked. Stopped at the lights, I gave way to a one-eyed man who waved a hand with only three fingers on it.

'What happened to them?' I asked.

'They're loggers. Maybe miners. Winos, anyway. The camps use them up very fast. That feller's probably no older than forty.'

'You're heading that way yourself.'

'What way? A drunk?'

'No, forty.'

He didn't say anything else as we drove down a short street of department stores. One was called the Hudson Bay Trading Company, so I thought it must be a furrier's but the windows were full of clothes and furniture. The other was called Eaton's. The street looked as if it amounted to something but if you went a block in either direction there was nothing.

'Keep going,' Stan said.

We crossed a bridge and drove along Fourth Avenue. Stan told me to pull over to a side-street, where I parked.

'Which direction now?' I said.

He sniffed twice and jerked his thumb to the right. 'The sea's this way.' We walked three blocks and there it was.

'Is this the Pacific?' I asked, watching ships sail past in the distance.

'No, that's on the other side of the big island.'

'What's this, then?'

'Dunno. But it's not bad, is it?'

The sun was shining and although it was still winter it was possible to imagine people doing what they do on beaches: sunbathing, throwing balls to each other, paddling in the surf, eating picnics, sleeping. I could see that the point of it all would be enjoying oneself in an innocuous manner and it would be hard to identify the harm in it. The beach was not empty outside my imagination. Men and women walked their dogs or threw pebbles into the tiny waves that wriggled on to the shore. Everything was pleasant.

A ship's horn sounded and Stan screwed up his eyes to identify the flag and the markings. 'Polish, I reckon,' he said. 'Wonder where they're off to.' But he put his arm round me, just the same.

We sat down on the sand and though it wasn't hot we did what you're supposed to do – take your shoes off, let sand spill between your toes.

I dug a trench and made Stan lie in it and covered him up until only his face was showing. He stuck out his tongue. I moved my face nearer and touched it with my own.

'Get my dick out,' he said.

I dug down and found his pants, unzipped them and pulled it out.

'You still don't wear shorts.'

'What for?'

People were looking. I dug out his hands, then his feet, and he heaved out of the sand that lay on his chest. 'Time for my dinner,' he said.

We walked back up to the street and just before we reached the car I noticed a sign on an apartment house. There were apartments to rent.

'Do you think they've got one with a view?' Stan said. 'I mean where you could see the sea?'

My mouth was full of water, I didn't know why. This was it, what I'd always wanted. I laughed out loud for the sheer pleasure of it and he winked. On the drive up to Canada I had noticed that he squinted a lot. I thought perhaps he needed eye-glasses but was too vain to admit it.

The super took us to the top floor. 'Two rooms plus bathroom and kitchen,' she said. She opened the drapes. 'English Bay.' She pointed to the beach we had just sat on and beyond there were mountains.

'What's this little room?' Stan asked.

'It's a walk-in closet.'

'There you go, Syb. Plenty of space for all your outfits.'

'And yours.'

'We could pay you two weeks' rent on the nail,' Stan said. I was amazed. I'd never seen him be businesslike and decisive, but I suppose you couldn't get by as a hustler without having some idea of how to make a deal.

'Where are you living now?' the super asked him. She ignored me.

'We just got into town. We've come up from . . .'

I cut him off. 'We've motored across Canada,' I said with no trace of an American accent. I would get the plates of the car changed. 'We emigrated to Toronto but we didn't like it there so we decided to set out for the west. Now we want to settle.'

She nodded and turned back to Stan. 'Can you keep the rent up?' she asked him.

'Oh yeah, no trouble. We'll both get jobs.'

Jobs. Plural.

The woman told us she would lend us some sheets and blankets.

When she'd gone I hung my clothes up in the walk-in closet and Stan took out his shoes and polished them.

'I'll give your cowboy boots a scrub too,' he said.

He breathed on the leather and buffed it with his sleeve when he'd finished. I came out of the bathroom after a long soak, pink and smelling of bubble bath. After only a few days with Stan I was getting thinner; he was watching my diet for me, ordering me cottage cheese plates and black coffee. 'Step into them,' he ordered.

I paraded up and down in nothing but my cowboy boots, feeling like a burlesque queen, not feeling all that happy, stunned by recent memories of proletarian morality. Outside, it had begun to rain heavily and it was to keep this up for the next three or four months.

Stan was getting his camera out again, looking at me through his glass eye, turning what would shortly be the past into the ever-present.

'Where are all the other pictures you've taken of me over the years?' I demanded.

'Safe,' he said.

I struck several poses, then we went to bed in the middle of the afternoon in our new home. I was feeling over-confident. I was babbling. I was telling him he had finished with the sea.

'Oh, no, I haven't,' he said.

'What's all this with you and sea? I'd have thought you would have had enough of that life at your age. It's nothing but rum and sodomy from what I've heard.'

'When you can get it.'

'Tell me about being at sea. Tell me about the war.'

He sat with his arms crossed behind his head. He began to talk in a monotone. 'My clothes were wet most of the time. You could never get your boots dry once they'd got a soaking. The flour was damp. You couldn't get a proper washing and the hold stank. Some of the officers were right nutters. You see weird stuff at sea. You don't know the half of it.'

'How far inland have you ever been, Stan?'

'I went to Nuneaton once. You can't get much further inland than that.'

'What for?'

'A wedding. We didn't get enough to eat.'

'People say the prairies are like the sea.'

'Come off it, you can't get sunk on a prairie. You can't drown in the middle of a field, can you?'

'Oh, I don't know.'

'It's a rough life at sea. You don't know what goes on.'

'So why do you go to sea?'

'It's my trade.'

'Surely baking is your trade. You could open a fancy pastry shop in Vancouver. Why don't you do that?'

'I can't do fancy pastries.'

'What about those French rolls you told me about once. I still haven't had one.'

'That's just showing-off stuff, like my pal who can carve a swan out of ice. It's not what you *do*.'

'Selling narcotics isn't your trade.'

'It's nobody's trade. That's just for readies.'

'Well, I think your vocation is taking pictures.'

'My what?'

'Your talent.'

'What's your talent?'

'I haven't got one.'

He got up from the bed and walked across the room to fetch a package of cigarettes. He shook the pack but it was empty. 'You got any smokes?' he said.

'In my purse.'

He carried it over to the bed and handed it to me. I took out two cigarettes and he reached over and withdrew them from my fingers. 'Light?' But I had left my lighter at Julius's house. He got up again and rummaged through his pockets. The two or three books of matches he found there contained only stubs of torn cardboard. 'I'll take it from the stove,' he said. I heard him go into the kitchen and I supposed he bent, as we have all done in the past, over the filament that turned from black to grey to glowing red and held the cigarette against its burning surface until the shreds of tobacco caught and glowed first orange then turned into ashy worms, and he pulled it away and held it to his mouth and drew on it to get it going. He brought it back to the bed and lit a second cigarette from it, which he handed to me. There was no ashtray; he held his hand cupped to catch the ash which he threw down on to the floor and later rubbed in with his heel. 'It's good for the carpet,' he said. 'Or that's my theory.'

The windows were full of rain and steam and clouds and the breath of ships.

He watched the cigarette burn down to the filter, which began to char and smoke.

'When you sign on a ship and it sails – goodbye. You're no longer human, you're finished, dead. You're not alive until Allah delivers you safely ashore.'

'Allah?'

He closed his eyes. 'Yes.'

We went out the next morning and were both home by lunchtime with jobs. Stan had found work in the kitchens of the Hotel Vancouver. I was taken on by Eaton's selling scarves and gloves. The first thing I bought with my staff discount was an imitation Hermès square and the next week Stan came in and picked out some initialled handkerchiefs for himself.

The papers were still churning out the old Red Menace stuff. A few days later, while Stan entertained himself with John Hazard and Rex Morgan MD and Kerry Drake and Dot Dripple in the comics section, I read an article by Tom Alsbury, president of the Vancouver Trades Council, which proclaimed REDS FOUND IN ALL RANKS OF SOCIETY, and I made a note of the organizations it helpfully provided as being infiltrated by or controlled by or purely communist: the BC Peace Council, I wrote. The Civic Reform Association, the Vancouver Folk Singers, the United Jewish People's Order.

One might think that my membership of the Party was purely a matter for rational thought but on that subject I was quite irrational. I am quite well aware that others saw me as the frivolous, sex-mad, self-deluding little fool I undoubtedly am but my membership of the CP was central to my sense of who I was. It was the only thing that stood in the way of the deep pit of moral depravity I believed I would fall into, a pit dug the night I was conceived. Despite my spectacular defection, going AWOL not just from my future husband but also from the Party, I knew I had to fight my way back in. Of course I would be expelled, but having chosen the Party it would not be allowed to desert me. I had not abandoned communism in principle, the communism that was a way of giving myself an identity I could live with: I had abandoned Julius.

I had no excuses. I did not even bother to think of a story. I assumed that after a period of massive disapprobation I would be accepted back, given the most menial of roles, never again to be trusted with responsibility of any kind, and I didn't care. I would stand on cold corners selling the press. I would type and make stencils. They could not deny for too long my desire to be useful. We were in a cramped office, by a closed roll-top desk. Uncle Joe stared gloomily down at us. I inhaled and smelled the familiar odour of duplicating machine fluid and saw thick piles of uncut stencils stacked in a corner. All this was as old to me as the brown stains on the cups, the slovenliness and disorder, the batches of *Daily Workers* waiting to be sold. As much as I felt distaste for these objects I loved them for the way they had pinned down the corners of my life and with them in my hands I knew that once again I could find my purpose and meaning. *They* had not let me down, far from it. I had a deep longing to pick up a stenographer's notebook and sit methodically taking notes, quiet and purposeful and untraumatized by the strange thing my life had recently become. I thought that there might be a middle way, that I could preserve the two sides of my character.

I was taken to one side. 'You were on your own for a very long time, on the road, weren't you?'

I nodded.

'We shouldn't have trusted you.'

'No. I lacked the necessary iron conviction that would have helped me withstand errors of thought,' I agreed.

'But mainly it was a sex thing, I mean romantic. Personal?'

'Yes.'

I endured much more of this and many hours later I stumbled out into the street. I was expelled for my own crimes and I stood there and told them that they had not seen the last of me.

Four days later, the puzzling headline appeared, RUSSIA DENOUNCES STALIN. I shared with many the initial disbelief and I thought that what at first appeared in the capitalist press was propaganda, until I read the transcript of the Twentieth Congress. I made up my mind to accept what purported to be the truth. I had to, on behalf of all of those I had transported at night, the ones we'd buried alive. I owed it to them.

Who was Stalin? A murderer, a savage, a butcher; he was halfway mad and a torturer. A Jew-hater. I had given up my best years for a deception, a trick – as I say, I loved treachery, I was good at it. I could not contemplate what this would do to Julius. But he had known, of course he had. He must have seen with his own eyes. But he couldn't face it. Julius had pinned the hopes of centuries of oppression and segregation and humiliation on a force that would free the Negro. What would he have left, without the world communist order? What movement could possibly rise up now, in our Eisenhower years, to speak for his kind? What Negro leader was there to part the Red Sea and bring his people out of slavery? Where could Julius turn?

Then again, how convenient for me. I was a premature anti-Stalinist, without even knowing it. In the months to come when everything collapsed and Stan was all that was left, it turned out that I had made a good move to cast in my lot with him.

I no longer believed that revolution was around the corner.

When I was with Julius I was at the centre of the world and the Party lay thickly around us like armed guards. Beyond was a thin, depopulated region, consisting of the barely visible 'thems', the extras that made up the People, the working class. But life was full of Stans, unorganizable, ignoble. Or guys who mended shoes for a living. Or women who tried on silk roses. They too knew that life was shit but you could make it great; the problem was that they wanted to make it great in their own way, which wasn't ours, and who were we to tell them they were wrong? I thought back often to the New York Jews with food between their teeth, talking about big ideas, and I remembered how the soul swelled to listen to them, people who wanted to make life the greatest of all, the grandest, the best. And then you wound up in a mill town in Washington with Julius and this was who you had to make their dreams come true. The Rosenbergs were just two dead people. It was all impossible, impossible. Waste. The revolution was never coming to America. The next generation of kids, the ones born before and during and after the war, who were coming up now – what was going to ignite them to action? Nothing would. What would they have to remember about the Depression years and the years of fighting and the bombing? Look around you; they were growing up with everything they needed. Only kooks like me, fuck-ups, bitter in my Nazi half-hell, needed this crutch of communism to make me feel I was worth more than shit.

Nothing changed in anything I thought, nothing at all, it was just that the power had been suddenly turned off at the mains.

I could easily, *rationally* have stayed outside of the CP after my expulsion. I did not need to force them to take me back. It was the best time in the history of our century to walk away from politics and yet I stayed, I clawed my way back in. Listen, I wasn't on the edge of things when I was in the Party, I was right in the centre, in the middle of history and the heart of my times and the struggle to humanize the human race which had to be the sweetest thing about being alive. No one knew the inner lands better than I did, the places as far away from the edge as you could get. The longer I was outside the Party the more I was sickened by my own actions, how I had run away, not because the Soviet Union had lost its claim to the moral leadership of the world socialist movement, not because of the countless dead, not because the hope of the world had been extinguished, not because I had been betrayed by the Party. But because I was sick of Julius. I betrayed myself.

This was my guilt, to have had the world, even a tarnished one, and thrown it away. So I chose a price. My penalty for abandoning the Party was to return to the Party in its dwindling, twilight, moribund days. If I'd walked out just a few months later when we knew I could have been gone for ever, no need of an excuse, but it was disappearing when I did that condemned me to more years in a back room turning the handle of a Gestetner machine, numb to the faction fights that killed communism from within, atoning for the vast sin of my superficiality. What dreck we were, those of us who were left, what moral slop, what toerags.

Perhaps I could have lived with the knowledge of my own treachery and surely that little betrayal had been wiped out by the very much greater one of Stalin's. But there was also this: in Eisenhower's America, as one looked around, did knowing what we did about Russia make the poor of America any richer? Did they have seats now on the bus in Montgomery?

Could they eat their soup and sandwich at a lunch counter in Mississippi? Did the blacklisted actors and teachers and public servants have their jobs back? Were the Mob-controlled locals returned to the hands of the workers? Who had their rights? Could you raise a silk rose to your hair without fear of humiliation?

Chapter Twenty-One

For the first months that we spent in that languid backwater of the continent, its climate so moderate that it was known elsewhere in Canada as Lotus Land, Stan and I were thrown together with little but each other's company, and we wrestled with each other, trying to find out the truth of the years we had spent apart, but neither of us succeeded and for the first time I heeded my cousin Jasa's advice and attempted to live in the present tense.

We began afresh. Stan said nothing about marrying me but my wedding ring, purchased out of Party funds, which would have seen further duty with Julius, remained on my finger and Stan would always refer to me as 'the missus', even to my face. He worked nights, I worked days. I didn't know what he did at midday when he was woken by the city's noontime hooter, calling to workers to lay up and have their lunch; when he yawned and stretched and I was gone, folding a pair of emerald suede gloves in tissue paper and sending them along the shoot to gift-wrap.

It took some time for us to acquire company. He met people, of course, he always did, but they were not my kind of people, for he needed his supply of dope and he quickly found the insubstantial tracks that would lead him to it. I would not join him in these pleasures any more, but I accepted that in order for him to get them for himself he would have to hang around not our own waterfront, our strip of Kitsilano Beach with its bathers and sun umbrellas and ice-creams, but the place where the ships docked, which wasn't in any country but its own.

He also found a boozer but that was not a place for me or for women at all (apart from the usual types who made their living from being where men always are). In those days men drank in beer parlours, full of guys from the mills smelling of cedar and hemlock, drinking pale ale and tomato juice, the logger's cocktail, while women were limited to drinking their mimsy little brews in the bars that were attached to hotels (the only places permitted to serve hard liquor), and Stan and I particularly liked the lounge at the Sylvia, where you could sip away at a Brandy Alexander only yards from the beach, watching people throwing coloured balls at each other and eating picnics. There was nothing to do on a beach but enjoy yourself, a *marvel* that such places should exist at all, really, when you think about it. Everyone reclines, neither here nor there, all the old rules overturned and replaced by new ones governing only these little strips between the water and the land. An entire branch of the fashion industry is dedicated to dressing beach-goers, and what would then have passed for promiscuity or near nudity on Granville Street – brief sun-dresses or tiny shorts or those assemblages of brassière and panties that were called biki-nis – here were normal attire, even though it was obvious, looking at them, that they were underwear masquerading as something else. But however undressed you were, as long as the fabric was correct (not silk or satin or lace which belonged in the boudoir) and nothing, on a man, resembling jockey shorts, then identical garments that would be scandalous elsewhere were permissible as long as they were cotton and patterned with palm trees and fruits and blowsy roses.

We didn't stay in the apartment long; we rented a two-bed-room house even closer to the beach, which I set about transforming with a 'look'. Come in, let me take you on a guided tour.

Your shoes are clattering on my hardwood floors and you see I have barely covered them with just one or two undyed sheep-skin rugs – skins, really – scattered about. The walls, you'll notice, I have left off-white. Over at the window my drapes are tan imitation silk, some miraculous new artificial fibre made out of wood-pulp or plastics or petroleum, oh, I don't know what. And look at my Swedish furniture of pale varnished pine – have you ever seen anything like it? And while I am not myself an artist, I could tell at once in the store how 'now' this painting was (in reproduction, of course), just splashes of white and khaki and brown hung in a plain frame. Breathe. Not a mote of dust stays a moment in my house. Purity and simplic-ity are my bywords when it comes to interior décor. Forget it, there is nothing, absolutely nothing here that you could call middle-European. Nor any sign of my mother's 'colours': her eau-de-Nils and golds, her Wedgwood and asters. There are no flowers in my house, only oatmeal hand-thrown vases, filled with colourless dried grasses, Nature's death. But I can see what has caught your eye, my conversation piece, my collection of bleached driftwood and brittle shells collected from the beach: great branches of broken, whitening wood and luminous, mother of pearl carapaces that have once housed soft creatures that fed off tiny things that swam.

Light, you see, light, it was a place full of light. And in the summer the salty, fishy smell of swimsuits drying in the hall, for every morning, before work, I went for a bathe, even in the cold early fogs of our Julys and Augusts, when the sun had not yet burned them back into the sea. My body responded to this exercise and soon I was more lithe and tanned and firm than I had ever been and I ventured to bronze my hair with a colour rinse from the pharmacist and let it grow straight, to my shoulders, which saved hairdressing bills. Though Stan always preferred it in that cropped style he had done himself, so, once a year, on the anniversary of our arrival in Vancouver, I let him cut it again and it had the rest of the year to grow out.

Stan was handy round the house. I didn't realize he had it in him but he said that on a ship you had to be able to do anything in a pinch. He could fix broken appliances, build shelves. We hauled slabs of slate back from a builder's and under my instruction he constructed for me a rough, unhewn fireplace that was the 'feature' of my living room. He took to domesticity very well. To my astonishment, I discovered he could knit. He bought himself a futuristic hi-fi system in blonde wood and stainless steel and on it he played his be-bop and sometimes Elvis Presley and I played Nat King Cole. He knocked up a special cabinet for our discs.

He continued to dress impeccably. He did not own a single pair of blue jeans; 'I've got my standards,' he would say. He bought ties like he bought packs of cigarettes. He had hundreds. He made up for the loss of his looks. 'I'm like a dummy in Lewis's window, me,' he often said. 'I can't help it, it's my nature.'

We joined the public library but he never managed to wean himself off the comic books and westerns that had always been his companions, on ship or on shore. Then we rented our first television set and he stopped reading altogether. He would watch anything, game shows, Ed Sullivan, he even enjoyed the sponsors' messages. In later years he would have been diagnosed as an addictive personality but I knew my Stan better than that by now. Underneath the sharp lines and edges of his outfits, his Slim Jim ties and shining shoes, his deliberate cultivation, his *cool*, Stan was deeply passive. He loved inertia, he liked to drift and daydream. I thought he went to sea so he could float, it was his natural condition. Of course, he couldn't swim; most sailors can't. 'The water's so fucking cold you wouldn't stand a chance,' he always insisted. But he could tread water – that was a proper survival skill – and when we went to the beach he would wade in through the gentle waves, submerge himself to his shoulders and make those occasional wandering motions of the arms and legs that would keep him afloat for as long as he wished. I would see him from the beach, his dark head bobbing, pushed back and forth by the current as he directed his gaze out to sea. He loved to sleep, too, he loved dreaming. I used to watch his face and discern his eyeballs moving about beneath the lids. He did not talk in his sleep, he gave no clues about the worlds he entered alone, without me. But we always fell asleep holding hands. It was our way. Of course we only slept together, properly, at weekends. During the week he lay in our bed alone, when he returned dusted with flour and smelling of ovens and yeast and butter and egg glaze to an empty and silent house.

I did not stay long at Eaton's. One day a woman came in to look at gloves for a wedding. She was chic and foreign, Belgian, with darting little black eyes, pointed ears and a smile that could be at once replaced with an expression so disagreeable when she was crossed that you preferred not to have seen the smile at all. A woman of fifty who was a widow and frequently smoked tiny black cheroots. She was black not in her skin (which was rather brown and mottled) but in everything else. Her clothes were never in any other shade. She was the colour of night and had the disposition of night. She terrified and excited me.

I showed her grey and white gloves but she asked to see black kid ones. I withdrew them from the showcase without comment. She asked me what I thought of the store's gown department. I wrinkled my nose and she produced again that smile that seemed as if it had been acquired secondhand, or as an unwanted legacy. She ran, she said, a little dress shop on the North Shore where the rich people lived, and she sold exclusive costumes which she designed herself. 'I can't get staff,' she said, leaning across the counter. 'These people are barbarians. Won't you come and work for me? Be my salesgirl. Together we can redistribute wealth. From them to us.' I looked at her hard. Where had she come by such a phrase? I never found out. She offered an advantageous salary plus a generous commission and so every day I drove across the Lions Gate Bridge to arrive at Madame Evelyn's (or so it said on our bags and the shop front). It was easy work. Madame never consulted me on what she made. She did not need to. Her taste was absolute. She had magazines sent over from friends in Paris and she simply copied what she found there. She had a marvellous seamstress and I would be fitted with the *toiles* that formed the foundations of the garment's design, to see how it would hang on a real woman. Madame travelled twice a year back to France to see what was being worn on the boulevards and in the cafés, and this way the three of us built up a terrific business. Dressed by her hand (me, she would permit to wear colours), to Stan's eyes I was perfect.

We did not meet socially. She never enquired about my private life. I knew nothing about hers except that she had been married to an elderly husband whom she had met as a young girl in Bruges in the twenties. He had left her well provided for, but restless. She was a woman of energy as well as ambition. Like me, she was childless and this *salon du modes* was her baby, her life.

What did the Party think of my position? What could they say? There were barely five thousand members in the whole of America then, and only a handful in Canada; our influence in any workplace was nothing. They were not going to send me back to some factory, I had served my time. The stench of lard and rotten potatoes still lurked in the recesses of my lungs. And still I went to the Party offices one evening a week and turned the handle of the Gestetner machine.

At home I kept a file of newspaper clippings about the bus boycotts and the lunch-counter sit-ins in the South and one day I was very happy to see Julius's name amongst those who had been arrested in Montgomery; I treasured that clipping for many years.

So this was my life throughout the 1950s. Sybil Ross who had travelled so very far, came to rest here in this sybaritic place.

Time erodes us or it silts us up and me it was filling in with dry land or at least a marshy sludge that resembled it from a distance in my dry house full of bone-dry things reclaimed from the sea. I was laid low by requited love but what a little bitch I really was, who could not keep her hands off another woman's man.

We're at the beach, Stan and I, with our friends Laurence and Margaret from the Party, and their two young children, Chris and Heather. Laurence was a salesman; he specialized in fancy furniture. 'I'm the greatest salesman in the city,' he would say. 'I can sell those greasy bourgeoisie anything.' Laurence had a simple line on the revelations of the Party Congress. 'Joe Stalin was the right man for the job at the time,' he said. 'He kept the goddamn country together. Hitler would have been all over the place if it hadn't been for him. *Then* you could have started counting the dead.'

'I just believe in peace,' Margaret said. 'I just know that the Soviet Union is not imperialist. They have no reason to go to war. Hungary, that's different. That's nothing to do with what we're talking about.' Imbeciles, I thought. But friends are always hard to come by, I find.

Stan got on with Laurence because he'd been at sea, like him. As far as Stan was concerned Laurence was a guy I knew through the retail trade. 'He's a commie,' he said. 'But I won't hold that against him.'

While Margaret and I are working on our tans, staring into the Cyclops eye of the sun, Stan and Laurence are looking at the surface of the water. They're talking about waves. Have you ever noticed that about a beach, the way everyone sits facing the sea, watching it, when there's nothing much *to* look at?

They're sitting with their legs stretched out, Stan in little blue bathing shorts with red piping and a drawstring waist that outlined what he called his package. Laurence has cut off an old pair of khakis which Margaret has hemmed for him. It's the first time I saw anyone do that. She and I are in our best and sexiest swimsuits. Mine is called 'Riviera' and it is red and gold and green with a halter neck. We're both dieting together and I have lost eight pounds with only two or three more to go. Our diet is easy. We eat a lot of grapefruit, like the movie stars, with a teaspoonful of cider vinegar mixed in water before every meal. You don't want to eat much after such appetizers.

'What's a wave?' Laurence is saying. He's handing Stan a bottle of beer in a brown bag. Stan swallows a few mouthfuls and rubs a few drops on his forehead. It's August, it's hot. Our nostrils are full of sea-water and sweat. In the sky there are a few clouds but they're moving very quickly down to Washington and I wonder if a cloud can begin in the Arctic and pass longitudinally down the whole of the continent, to its very tip, to the Antarctic waters of Patagonia, or if a cloud is too insubstantial for that and would get blown full of holes, into nothing, before it has passed more than a dozen miles. But I have no idea.

Stan is looking at the foam on the water's edge. 'It's a ripple,' he says. 'Everyone knows that.'

'Good,' Laurence says, smiling. 'Always a ripple?'

'No, it's born that way but it grows up.'

'Like into whitecaps.'

'Yeah, then chop, and wind waves, and maybe a storm sea.'

'Then it dies down, gets old, turns into swell.'

'Swell can travel a long way.'

'Half a continent. What happens when it reaches some land?'

'It can make surf.'

'The most exciting part of the ocean.'

'Then it bashes its head against the beach and it's had it, it's dead. It's gone.'

'The brief and happy life of a wave.'

'Not so brief.'

'Do you know what's going on on the bottom?'

'No, what?' Stan's reaching for the beer again. He holds his fingers over the top of the bottle and shakes it and then sprays it over my legs. Margaret and I scream and flail and giggle.

A man is carrying a curious long board down to the water's edge. He propels it out into the surf and tries to stand up. The water bears him into land again. Pointless.

'When the wave changes, the ocean bed changes as well, but when the bottom changes, so does the wave. The sand is always being rearranged. The land below has its effect but so does that transient foam have its effect.'

'That's deep,' Stan says. 'It's deep, isn't it, Sybil?'

But I know what Laurence is getting at; I know what he is saying about the surfaces of things. The wave lasts only a moment, then it spends itself but it leaves the ghost of its form on the ocean bed. The ocean floor's terrain seems fixed, yet it creates the wave, that transient moment. Funnily enough this is how I think of fashion, that transient moment which somehow endures, the kind of present tense I can live in.

We glance at each other, Laurence and I. He's forty and his hair has gone prematureiy white but he's a good-looking guy.

Even with Margaret, my so-called best friend, I was able to lie. I could lie on her children's heads, when her husband's sperm was still inside me, still damp in the walls of my unused birth canal and my diaphragm hurriedly dusted with talcum and hidden in a secret place.

Laurence said he would leave Margaret for me, but I laughed in his face. Me, walk out on Stan? *That* was a joke.

We lay in bed one evening at my house, when Stan was out at work and Margaret was visiting her mother in Nelson. As a lover, Laurence was full of 'go'. He was not imaginative and really rather prudish, but he was good at pumping away, delaying his own climax until I came and one must never treat such gifts lightly. Stan had entered a period of premature ejaculation in which the beginnings of my own orgasm, the contraction of certain muscles in my vagina, would excite him intolerably and he would ejaculate suddenly when I was only partway there.

I did not tell Laurence this when we lay in my bedroom, which had its mattress on the floor as a sentimental attachment to the days in the room in the meat-packing district in New York.

'What are you doing with the guy?' he asked. 'How did you wind up with that loser?'

'I've known him half my life.'

'So?'

'He's my fate, my destiny.'

'We're Marxists, we don't believe in such nonsense.'

'Normally I don't, but in this instance I do.'

'Is it true you were with that Fellowes character?'

'Yes.'

'Jeez, you can choose 'em.'

'He's still fighting to get back in.'

'Well, he would, wouldn't he? I heard he was down in San Francisco.'

'Yes, he's got right back into organizing.'

'What do you think – could he have been framed?'

'I don't know, I just don't know.'

'Ah, come on. If anyone would have the picture it would be you. And your main squeeze was our former Comrade Harris. The biggest Red-baiter in Mississippi, using everything, all the organizing skills they taught him in Moscow, against us. So you go from one maybe louse to a definite louse. Then there's this one. He's brain-dead, I mean you can talk to him about a few things but ideas? That baffled look he gets on his face when you change the subject too fast, like he doesn't know the time of day. There's nothing there; nada. My kids have got more sense than him. He has no idea what the war was about, he doesn't know what's going on in Suez, he's barely heard of the hearings. He reads nothing but garbage. He reminds me of a slug, no, a leech, suck, suck, suck.'

'Which is more than you do.'

'I beg your pardon?'

'Never mind. He's not a leech, he makes money, he's never out of work. And he is, after all, a worker, which is more than can be said for us.'

'Don't tell me you go for him because he's a member of the Masses?'

'He's a very fine photographer.'

'*Pictures.* Who needs a brain to look at pictures? I have a Box Brownie. I can take photographs.'

'Stan's an artist.'

'You wish. Some artist, a grown man with two hundred neckties. What does he want with them all? How many neckties can one person wear?'

People were always putting Stan down. I'd grown used to it.

Julius had thought nothing of him either. It had to be a form of sexual jealousy in men who sensed his ambiguity and were frightened and attracted by it. I was feeling cool and louche, in command, with two men at my beck and call.

I lit a Marlboro and blew smoke rings.

'You know my mother is German,' I said. I don't know why it came out. I told Laurence to shock him, at a singular moment when I did not care one way or other what he thought. I didn't give a fuck. I can get like that.

'So what? Both my grandparents on my mother's side were German. The country is full of German immigrants. None of that baloney matters over here. Scots, Irish, Ukrainian – who cares?'

'Yes, but my father is Jewish.'

He paused and thought about it. 'I still don't really see the problem. Everyone comes here to make a new life for themselves. How long have you been in North America? Ten years? More, thirteen, fourteen? Yet you're not an immigrant, are you? You're a foreigner, like you're here on a visit. Your accent changes according to who you're talking to. You're great at pretending to be Canadian, but it's a put-on, isn't it? You won't commit. Where do you belong, anyhow?'

'With Stan,' I said, remembering our time together in New York. 'He's my country.'

And so my big secret fell flat after all those years.

We went on a little vacation once, Stan and I, in Laurence's van, to the interior, to the Okanagan Valley where they grow the fruit and try to make wine. He hated it. All that we liked there was a house a man was building out of embalming fluid bottles. I think he was a retired undertaker. It made us laugh.

'Get us out of this dump,' Stan said. 'Let's go back.' We spent one night at a camp site on top of a mountain in the drenching rain. Periodically he hung his penis out of the window to relieve himself but I was not so lucky and had to crouch behind a bush with my panties around my ankles. 'What's the *point* of this?' we asked each other in bewilderment. We returned after three days. Laurence asked us if we had had a good time and Stan and I laughed. I had passed through many similar kinds of places, so I did not share Stan's bewilderment, but I understood it. Laurence was raving about the view of the Rockies in the distance, the grandeur of mountains and the geological fascination of rock formations and glacier valleys. He belonged anywhere, that Laurence did, I'll give him that. He was a real survivor, the very spirit of the pioneers.

We were indissoluble, Stan and me, a fixture, an item, a combined entity. Finally we found a vacation spot we liked, Long Beach on the far side of Vancouver Island, where the west coast of Canada properly gave out to the Pacific and the surf was heavy and the sea full of swell. We stayed at a little hotel and spent all day tanning, lying there for so many hours each day doing nothing, bidden by no one but ourselves.

All our most intimate conversations took place at the beach where the wind blew our words away and made them less material, uncommitted. 'You're not my little girl any more, are you, kid?' he said.

'When have I ever been that?'

'Don't forget, I knew you back when,' he replied. Suddenly he began to describe our first encounter. 'Such a fucking know-it-all. Mouth full of marbles, fourteen going on thirty. That lilac outfit you had on, and your hair like Veronica Lake. I couldn't keep my eyes off you. I couldn't keep my hands steady on the camera, wondering if I was in with a chance, wondering if I'd get a knock-back if I tried it on.'

'*You*, nervous? Come off it, you never were.'

'That's all you know. I didn't have much experience with . . .'

'Women?'

'Yeah.'

'You seemed to know what you were doing that night in that house off Smithdown Road.'

'I'm not saying I hadn't read *books*.'

'Books?'

'You know, dirty books.'

'Was I your first, first woman? I mean, would I have been if we'd done it that night?'

'No, not the first, but the first I hadn't paid for.'

'Why me?'

'I told you.'

'But why did you come back?'

'I wanted someone on shore. It was too hard getting that kind of thing started with a feller and when you did they were always married. You couldn't keep it up for more than one shore leave. You left it for when you were at sea.'

'Do you still think of yourself as bisexual?'

'Me? You're joking. I put all that behind me years back. It was just a phase.'

'Good.'

I could not persuade him to wear any underpants – he thought they were in some way not manly – but then I caught him trying on my own black lace panties and from then on he sometimes wore those. What little secrets we hid in our West

Side home that was so full of sun and beige surfaces it seemed never to harbour any shadows.

I was on my way to complete depoliticization, an occasional silent presence in the branch, when the Cuban revolution came along and here was Fidel Castro, a man of my own generation, young and vital and perhaps beneath that beard even good looking. It was something to make a revolution now, after all the mistakes of the past had been learned, and right on the doorstep of the United States of America. I did not even worry about the Bay of Pigs; I did not believe for one moment that Fidel would let those missiles off and allow anyone to come to harm. In the stagnant fifties who would have thought that there would ever be a new decade full of hope and promise? And from far away who would have thought that our old home town would prove to be at least one epicentre of the new world order?

When I was thirty-eight my periods became erratic and I would go for two or three months at a time without one. Then they stopped altogether. It was uncommon, the physician said, for the menopause to begin so early but that was what had happened to me. The oestrogen factory had ceased production, forced into involuntary and permanent lay-off. The last egg had hit the runway and taken off into the usual oblivion, missing, as usual, its mark.

Chapter Twenty-Two

As far back as 1957, when we got a telephone installed, for want of anyone else to phone I placed a trunk call to my parents whose number and exchange emerged, intact, from my memory. I hesitated for many minutes before I rang the operator. I pictured the house on Queen's Drive, our house of secrets. It had been empty of me for many years. I wondered what had happened to my room, to the ottoman which when I sailed for America still contained my old toys: the golly, the celluloid dolls, the childish lamp with its wooden goblins. Just before the war the room had been repapered in a Regency yellow silk stripe with curtains and pelmet of the same pattern but in a contrasting shade, and I had been given a kidney-shaped dressing table, skirted in the curtain fabric, very like my mother's, on which lay my matching set of hairbrush and mirror. It was the room I returned to, creeping in through the front door after those passionate courting sessions with Stan, my neck covered in love-bites. It was the room in which I dreamed of my future life and fell sleep with a fashion magazine still between my fingers. And out of the window the gardens of Liverpool ran down to the sea.

The line connected, there were those familiar double rings, and after some time I heard my father's voice, as heavy and ornamental as a carved mahogany dining-room table lustrous with French polish.

'Hello? Who is this?'

'It's me. It's Sybil.'

'Who?'

'Sybil.'

He was saying *something*.

'Daddy, what is it? I can't hear you properly.'

'I'll put your mother on.'

There was a muffled pause and now my mother's voice came on the line, also like furniture, but this time a blonde maple cocktail cabinet, bright and glassy, mirrored inside and lit by concealed bulbs, and she was saying, 'Sybil, my darling, it's been so *long*.'

We talked about this and that. And as usual I concocted some tale or other which I'd forgotten as soon as it came out of my mouth. My mother listened, carefully. 'Yes,' she said. 'Yes, yes. I see.'

'What's the matter with Daddy?'

'Wait a minute,' she said. 'Talk about something else.'

I told her about the shop. She was pleased. 'What are your gowns for this season?' she asked. We were discussing Balenciaga copies when she broke off. 'Don't blame your father.

He's crying, darling. He's sitting in the dining room crying his eyes out.'

'Why?'

'Oh, you don't understand him. He loves you but he also hates you because you went away and left him.'

'Hates me?' It had never occurred to me that I was in any way diminished in my father's affections. I thought that time, on the other side of the Atlantic, was frozen.

'You're his own flesh and blood, he has no one else. He felt it very badly when he had his illness.'

'What illness?' I clattered my fingernails on the telephone table, they beat out a little tune and to my irritation my polish chipped.

'Sybil, he had a heart attack, three years ago. He hasn't been the same. The doctors told him he must not worry, he must not let anything distress him. But how could he not be distressed? We had no idea where you were. You could have been dead, for all we knew. We rang the American consulate and asked them to find you and then they began to ask us so many questions. We thought maybe you had become a criminal, a prostitute, even.

'Your father is not what he was. Everything must be his own way and if it is not, he tells me I'm trying to kill him, I'll give him another coronary. My life is . . .' My mother spoke into the room into which my father had returned. My father came back on the line. He was a different man.

'Your mother tells me you're working in a gown shop,' he said in a hearty voice. 'What have you got this season? Do the women dress well in Canada? Do you think t-strap shoes are making a comeback?'

I asked him how business was. He said it wasn't bad. But you couldn't sell anything but mink. 'That's all anyone wants, mink. It's a nice fur but you get bored working with it after a while. I'm doing a Persian broadtail for your mother with just a little white mink collar and her initials in the lining – the same as yours, of course. I could make one for you and send it out.' We discussed import duties while I turned this offer over in my mind. I wasn't sure what I wanted. All through those terrible winters in Minnesota and the West I had often thought of owning a fur again, but now it was offered, in a climate where there was no real need of anything but a waterproof, the gift had come too late. And in truth I was not even sure if I would feel comfortable wearing a fur. Good clothes were one thing, they were a mark of your femininity and your taste, but fur was symbolic of the capitalist system that I still secretly despised in all its full-blown excesses. The Party had bred instincts into me that were as deep as those my upbringing had nurtured. I could no more cross a picket line, then or now, than I could leave the house without powder on my nose and lips coated in Estée Lauder or Helena Rubinstein.

'A woman is nothing without a fur,' my father was saying. '*Nothing*. Every little *shiksah* on Scotland Road has her bit of cony to hang round her neck. You know in the war, when we couldn't get the skins from America, people made fur coats out of *cats* rather than go out with nothing on their backs. You have no fur coat? How are you a woman?'

To placate him, I said I would consider his offer. He changed the subject to 'that bastard Nasser'. I told him what *I* thought, that I had rejoiced when I heard the news of the nationalization of the Suez Canal, that Britain's disastrous loss spelled the end of its imperial past. That I was not, like him, a Zionist. I did not think of Israel as my country. I did not believe it was calling me home. I spoke approvingly of Tito. My father was beside himself. 'Are you a socialist? Do you love that son-of-a-whore Attlee, who sunk the boats of our refugees from the camps in Haifa harbour? The man who hung our freedom fighters?' He began crying again. 'I brought this on my own head,' he was saying. 'Hitler has come back from beyond the grave to strike me down, to finish off what he started . . .' He did not understand, and I did not know how to explain to him, that I had learned from his own mouth and his own deeds to believe without being able to help it. We ended the conversation with both of us sobbing.

We had become like two fists, my father and I.

That my father's personality had continued its deterioration, begun, I was certain, after he received Jasa's letter, accelerated by his zealous support of Zionism, deeply upset me. He wrote me letters with little cartoons in them in which Nasser was depicted in one of those bath-towel head-dresses that children wear in school nativity plays. Nasser's trousers were down and flies buzzed about his bare and hairy arse. A donkey stood nearby. My father's drawing style had developed a savage and satirical bent since the days when he had exclusively sketched his willowy ideas for the upcoming season's line. Then letters would come from him, which would slip behind the radiator and lie unopened for months until I threw them away, still sealed. What is there between fathers and daughters? What is the bond so deep and so sexual that it leads to this, to the struggle we daughters make to break free of our authoritarian lover?

I wanted him to die. I willed his death, but before that I was to have granted my wish, to get my old daddy back, for, not long after, he developed another illness, and he would not remember that I had come to America at all and to him I was still his little girl, sitting apart from him on Saturday mornings when the *shofer* cried out and his head was bent in worship. He would speak on the phone of my little patent leather shoes and my frocks and my helmet-like hair and urge me to make some minor change in them. Or he would suddenly think I was seventeen and make arrangements for my chinchilla coat to be taken into cold storage. But then he forgot who I was altogether, that he had ever had a daughter, and my mother said he spoke only of Belgrade, of his own father and mother and of his sisters, whom he still believed to be alive, and when any post came he always opened it eagerly, in expectation of a letter from home. They had moved down south, to Bournemouth, early on in this illness and he spent his time, my mother told me, sitting on a bench above the beach watching the parade of fashionable women walk past, until one day he began to descend the zigzag path and enter, fully dressed, the sea, crying out for his mother, and (understandably) my own mother had to have him put away in a home.

In the summer of 1964, the year I turned forty, Stan and I took another trip to Long Beach and lay on the sand watching the clouds. The world had become an exciting place.

'We were born at the wrong time,' I said. 'Don't you think? The war took away our youth. Wouldn't you like to be young now?'

'I wouldn't wish the thirties on anyone,' he replied. 'You didn't know the half of it where you lived.'

I had never mentioned the conversation I had with the man in Central Park. 'Was the war fun or was it awful?'

'It was fucking awful,' he said.

When I was on the road, many is the time I stopped my car in the middle of nowhere and got out to stretch my legs and light a cigarette. Sometimes I would come across the wreck of a house and a piece of fence with tomatoes and squash and roses growing wild, the tomatoes ripe and rotting on the ground, their seeds spilled everywhere, starting new plants. Once I saw a wild sunflower and other times feral cats scratching among human bones, and you understood that here there had been a town that failed and had died and been swallowed up again by the prairie. Or there would be a house or two and a gas pump with a store, a town that had tried to grow but turned out small and stunted and had all but failed.

I found a town that nearly made it in Nebraska. A hundred yards from the main street was a burying ground surrounded by a picket fence that had been white once but now was grey. The markers started in the 1880s and they recorded the usual infant deaths, fever deaths, childbed deaths, a few deaths of old age. Then, in 1918, there was a sudden rash of war graves, three, four family names repeated over and over again: Chalmers, Blackthorn, Wright. Then a space of years and just a few graves. The newest graves were also military, twenty-five of them between 1941 and 1945. George Chalmers, aged nineteen, at Normandy. Frederick Chalmers, his brother, aged twenty-two, at Iwo Jima. William Blackthorn, aged eighteen, at Salerno. Thomas Blackthorn, twenty-five, also at Normandy. Samuel Wright, twenty. Michael Wright, twenty-seven.

It must have been something in the water, an old man at the store told me, but that town reared a lot of boys, always more boys than girls, and it was just the damnedest luck that the biggest crop always came of age when there was a war on. And they would go sign up on the first day. So I remembered those boys in the graveyard in the dead town on the Great Plains. I felt sad for them, sent off to foreign lands where they did not speak the language, to die so far from home.

'You're lucky to be alive, really.'

'I think about that all the time.'

'*Do* you?'

His eyes were closed but the sunlight was so strong he still shaded them with his hand. 'More or less every day.'

'What do you think about this war in Indo-China?'

'What war's that?'

'America is involved.'

'What for?'

'To prevent the spread of communism.' I explained the domino theory.

'Well, you've got to go to war for something, I suppose.'

'What did you go to war for?'

'Fuck knows.'

'To save the Jews?'

'If I hadn't met you I'd never have even heard of the Jews outside the Bible.'

'Which do you believe in – God, Allah or nothing?'

'Mainly nothing, but when I'm on a ship, then Allah. I think I'm getting a bit burnt here. Is it time for my dinner?'

We moved into the shade and I unpacked our legs of cold chicken and pieces of fruit.

When we got back to Vancouver the phone was ringing as Stan turned the key in the door; the sound bounced about between the hardwood floors and the white walls and the bleached driftwood, more of which filled the trunk of the car.

I caught it before it stopped, while Stan was carrying in our cases. It was my mother. My father had died while I was away. It was too late to come home for the funeral. He had been in the ground for over a week already. My mother did not sound upset. 'You must remember, darling,' she said. 'I'm still a young woman. I'm only sixty-one. I have my health.' We agreed that I would return eleven months later, for the unveiling, the erection of his tombstone. 'Your father left me very well provided for,' she continued. 'And of course there is something for you, for the moment, though you will not receive the residue of the estate until I die.'

I stayed up very late that night trying to make myself cry, but no tears came at all. Stan left me to it. When I came up to bed he squeezed my hand. 'The tears will come, Syb,' he said. 'Don't force it. They'll overtake you when you're least expecting it.'

For almost a year I forgot about my father's death. Intermittent letters arrived from my mother describing her progress with solicitors, and I wrote punctually back.

In 1965 an aeroplane ticket was sent and I prepared to make the long flight back to England, a country that I had not known for so many years that I could scarcely imagine it without rationing, coal fires, the powdered debris of brick dust and the blackout. Stan came to the airport to see me off and we held each other for a long time before I passed through the no-man's-land of the departure lounge. It was the first time we had been apart for nearly a decade. 'Send my love to the Pierhead,' were his last words, and when I turned back for a last look he was still there, smiling and waving, in a pink button-down shirt, elastic-sided Cuban-heeled boots and one of those collarless Beatles jackets.

The air, I found, is not my element. It's too abstract. Clouds are theoretical entities from below but inside them you find nothing at all, you pass right through them. I don't belong up there. I break into a cold sweat and panic during turbulence which I find unnatural, as if one was driving on a bumpy road and not suspended thirty thousand feet in the middle of nowhere. Throughout most of that flight I clutched the sick-bag in my hands, though I did not need to make any use of it for I kept my stomach resolutely empty, refusing the in-flight refreshments. I thought we had arrived when at last we landed to refuel at Gander but we were only halfway there. For hour after hour I stared down at the ridged surface of the Atlantic below. In the air it is impossible to perceive motion or colour; the brain's functions are stopped. We were over Dublin, then we were crossing the Irish Sea, then a moment or two later the pilot instructed us to avail ourselves of the view of the Mersey on the aircraft's left and people in the cabin began to cheer and sing 'Yeah yeah yeah'. Then in another moment we were there. We had crossed from the Republic to London in less time than it had taken me to drive from the coffee shop where I had met Stan again to the coast; a lot less. England had seemed irreducible, but here it was, contracted, a blink in time. A short pause in history. I wept in relief and panic when at long last we dropped from the air on to the runway in London and I gingerly descended the steps, my smart BOAC bag over my shoulder, waved off by the stewardesses in their Hardy Amies uniforms.

Of course it is a truism that everyone who comes to England for the first time or after a long absence wonders at how small everything seems, and I did question the taxi driver about why he insisted on plotting a course entirely along back streets when we were, he pointed out, idling in traffic in Tottenham

Court Road. I saw objects like milk bottles and telephone boxes as if I was on some of Stan's queer drugs that made them at once both familiar but out of perspective, as if seen through the wrong end of binoculars. The city came to me as a series of colours and abstract shapes, which my brain was unable to compose into objects with any function. Some squat, dun-coloured structures on the south side of the Thames, where slums and warehouses used to be, made no cognitive sense until I was told that they were theatres and galleries and concert halls, the whole a 'complex' of buildings constructed to mark the hundredth anniversary of the Great Exhibition. And yet to me they resembled a dunghill. The giddying effect of the Post Office tower with its revolving restaurant was almost more than I could bear.

But if London only approximated to the city I had known before the war, at least some of my map references were still there. My mother had booked me into a room at the Cumberland Hotel for a couple of nights and I found, when I arrived, a note from her explaining that she had arranged a line of credit for me at Fenwick's in case, she mentioned delicately, I had nothing suitable to wear. I smiled when I read it. Did she expect me to arrive dressed as a lumberjack? The Art Deco lifts at the Cumberland were gone and so were the checkerboard bedspreads. A carvery had been started up. People were talking about afternoon tea at the Hilton Hotel at 7/6d a head. I had forgotten how the money worked. There was a new cinema on the corner of Edgware Road. A Negro was walking past it in silver lipstick. The city was full of tiny, pale girls in sleeveless mini-dresses, and the names above the gown shops had been replaced by the word boutique. Our young queen, whose coronation with its mystical clap-trap I had watched with such derision in a bar in Iowa, was now middle-aged and had teenage children of her own, and those dinosaurs, the aristocracy, showed no signs of lurching to extinction.

Little girls and long-haired boys were wearing stinking old rabbit coats and Boer War military jackets. There was *no order* to any of it. You almost had the sense that they were wearing what they liked. None of this was smart. It was dishevelled. I could not, under any circumstances, envisage myself in this season's modes, if these were what they were. I found myself in Carnaby Street and looked in the window of John Stephen for something to buy for Stan. I'm sure he would have known exactly what he wanted, but I didn't have a clue.

I retreated to the hotel, went into the bar and ordered a stiff drink. The past was rushing away behind me, like the dark road my car had once sped along. For the first time it dawned on me that my father was actually dead. Who was administering the will? What had the estate been worth? How vigorous was my mother? And then I thought to wonder, what the hell was I doing over a quarter of a century later with a layabout I'd picked up in Sefton Park when I was so green I could barely feed myself?

At Fenwick's I bought a very expensive imitation of an Yves St Laurent dress and matching jacket in black bouclé wool, and the next day I climbed aboard the Bournemouth Belle as I had done so many times in my childhood. Bournemouth, at least, was little changed, a travesty of the Mediterranean with its pines and deceptively balmy air and its deep shadows in which, of course, night-time skirmishes took place between respectable men and those they could find who, thrillingly, were less so. From the station my taxi took me a short distance to a great white-painted mansion block running at a right angle to the choppy sea and once I had passed the porter at his desk I found myself face to face with my mother after nearly twenty years.

She was as thin as a stick. Her hair was blown up into a platinum blonde bouffant shell through which you could see her scalp. She was wearing a short, cream Chanel suit, braided in brown, and gold chains hung from her neck. Her long spiky eyelashes bore no resemblance to the short, pale ones I remembered, so I supposed they must be false. Her narrow mouth was painted in a frosty, pearl pink. To be honest, I thought her entire appearance was unspeakably vulgar.

We stood at the door of her flat, looking at each other. I was surprised to find that she was as shocked in what she saw as I was myself. 'Sybil, darling!' she cried. 'Your body, what has happened to it? You look like a football player. Those muscles!'

'Aren't you going to invite me in?' I asked.

The flat was cavernous and decorated in the same eau-de-Nils and golds as the house on Queen's Drive. I asked her if she had had it redone but she said it had been like this when they'd bought it. 'We could tell at once it was for us,' she said.

She showed me to my room. 'Your father wanted a one-bedroomed flat,' she told me, 'but I said no, what if Sybil wishes to return home? At least we could give her a roof over her head until she settles.' There were twin beds with matching royal-blue satin coverlets and fitted wardrobes entwined with gold curlicues. None of the things I left behind were there, not my ottoman, not my schoolgirl novels. I asked what happened to them. 'Darling,' she said in surprise. 'We threw them away when you left. You didn't want them, did you?'

We had tea in the lounge from her white and gold porcelain

cups and talked of this and that. The flowers in their Wedgwood vases were irises. My mother, as we know, loved beauty for its value and its expense and I doubted if she could find any affection for the brown, lean woman with strong shoulders from a daily riding of the swell, that she found before her, albeit dressed in an approximation of the art of the most exciting young designer of the day. I had bought something for myself in Fenwick's, with my own money: a patent leather handbag with a gold chain strap. Only at this did my mother look with feverish, envious eyes.

In the afternoon we took a turn along the front and she seemed so fragile that I thought the Channel breeze would bear her away. We tottered past beach huts on our stilettos, my mother's higher by far than my own. The sea was taupe-coloured with ivory waves. Then we returned and she fell asleep in her chair.

While she slept I went through her wardrobe. There were some good things, some very good indeed, but most were copies. She had thrown nothing out. The dashing Schiaparelli suit from before the war was not, in fact, a Schiaparelli but a Susan Small. A boxy evening bag in dove-grey suede with a pristine cream satin lining lay next to rather a lot of stuff that was no better than Swanky Modes. Some of her diamonds were paste and much else was marquisite. The forgotten, unopened parcels containing yellowing sheets and towels from the White House were just second-hand bed-linen at the end of the day. I suspected that her silver Georgian coffee set might turn out to be reproduction. My mother, I saw from the labels in her wardrobe, was not all she cracked herself up to be. She was not quite the thing.

The unveiling was well attended. Several of my father's pals had also moved to Bournemouth on their retirement, but others motored down from Liverpool for the occasion. They were not the Jews I had known in New York that jabbered and sweated and hungered for the Messianic age of brotherly love and equality for all. They did not quote Ralph Waldo Emerson or Turgenev or Spinoza.

My father's coffin had been lowered into the ground a year before, his shrunken body shrouded in first his *tallis*, then the Israeli flag. It was the deepest mark of respect. He really was all tied up with those Zionist terrorists, of course, I found out later. He'd had the police at his door and not just about me. My own father had been a kind of revolutionary, or at least a nationalist.

The wind was whipping about the cover over his stone. It was removed and I saw his name carved in gold on the pinkish marble that looked like potted meat. Half of it was in Hebrew but there was his name, the inscription in its entirety:

SYDNEY ROSS (IZIDOR ROTH)
Born 1893 died 1964
Beloved husband of Sonia and adored father of Sybil
May his soul make aliyah at last

The moment I saw my own name there a stone broke in my chest and my heart poured forth its waters. And, like the Red Sea, once parted came together again, drowning all that was left within.

And they looked on me, uncertainly, whispering, 'Who is she?' The daughter, the daughter. So then they came over and shook my hand. 'Long life,' they said. 'Long life.'

My mother stood in black silk, a gold Star of David around

her neck, looking most unconvincing among the graves. No one kissed her or held her hand. I thought that she must be very alone but I didn't feel sorry for her. In none of the pictures in our photograph album was she depicted holding or touching me. I have no recollection of ever sitting on her knee while she read me a story. Though I suppose she had kept her love up, all these years, until she had seen how I had turned out.

A left hand grabbed my own left, sideways, like an arm wrestler and it would not let go. 'You don't remember me, do you?'

The mouth was lopsided and without its cigar but I knew him at once. 'Mr Kauffman, of course I remember you. Thank you for coming such a long way.'

'It's no distance. I live here now. Your dad and I used to go to the bookies' together.'

'I didn't know my father gambled.'

'Oh, no, no, he wasn't a man for throwing his money around. He just liked a little tumble now and then. He was a wonderful fellow, your father. He had furrier's hands. He could tell the quality of a skin just by feeling the point. We won't see his kind again; they broke the mould, my dear, they broke the mould. Now you?' He looked me up and down and one red watery eye managed a wink. 'You turned out very nice. Lovely. You married?'

'Yes.'

'Who's the boy? Anyone I know?' He glanced down at my ringed finger, at the old ring the Party had bought for me. 'Not rich.'

'No, someone I met in Canada.'

'Yes, yes, you live out there now, don't you? I used to do a lot of business in Canada. Your father told me about you when he still had his faculties. Thank God you weren't here to see him lose them.'

'What did he tell you?'

His ruined mouth began to say something then thought better of it. 'That you were a lovely girl, always, a lovely girl.' He still gripped my hand and he was squeezing so hard that my knuckles were showing white. 'Long life, my dear, long life. Come and see me some time. Will you promise?'

I promised.

'Ah, lovely. Give me a kiss, dear.'

I planted one lightly on his cheek and he grabbed my shoulder. Then my mother came up and took my arm in rescue and we proceeded slowly through the graves to the waiting car. 'Horrible man,' she said. 'Horrible. I don't know how your father could stand him.'

'Do you see him much?'

'Him? Never.'

After everyone had left the house and we had soaked the cloths that had been stained with sweet red wine and brushed away the crumbs of almond cake from the carpet with the Ewbank, and my mother announced that the event had gone off very well, she began to talk of travel over a light supper of fish fingers and frozen peas which she produced from the ice compartment of her refrigerator with a flourish. 'Have you tried these?' she asked with excitement. 'You'll find they're very good.'

We ate this meal in five minutes, accompanied by a small dab of mayonnaise. I washed up and made tea. All the food in her cupboards smelt old. I wondered if she was grooming me to be her companion.

'Your father never took me anywhere,' she was complaining.

'Once we went on a holiday together after you left us. Once! And do you know where he took me?'

'I don't know. Where?'

'The Isle of Man.'

'Wasn't it very nice?'

'Nice?' She stared at me. 'You don't understand.'

'No, apparently not.'

But of course I did. I just wouldn't let on. The Isle of Man was where they interned the fifth columnists during the war.

'I thought he went to Israel.'

'Yes, he did, with a group. I didn't go with him. Naturally, he wanted to be with his own kind.'

'Oh.'

'Now I think *I* would like to pay a similar kind of visit.'

'To Israel?'

'No, you're being silly. To Hamburg.'

'Whatever for?'

'To see my brother.'

I was dumbfounded. 'How do you know he's still alive?'

'Oh, he is,' she said. There was a little blue shadow brushed over her eyelids and her frosted lipstick was bleeding into the cracks above her mouth. She had changed from black into a bitter-lemon jersey Jaeger suit with matching kid court shoes. 'Karl-Heinz was always—'

'Karl-Heinz! What a name.'

She looked at me, surprised. 'What do you find strange about it?'

'It's so . . . German, I suppose.' I watched her take this in.

'But you know, darling, I *am* German.' And she began to reminisce about her early life. I listened, fascinated. I wondered if her mind was becoming very slightly disconnected, pulling apart to enable her to live in two distinct historical dimensions. One moment, it seemed, she was the widow of Sydney Ross, stalwart of the JNF, then she slipped away, back to the turn of the century, when she and her brother played in a garden near a park in which they heard the news that their father, a master mariner, was lost at sea somewhere beyond the Baltic. She was a child of the Schleswig-Holstein, a proud daughter of the free port.

'And of course you are half-German too.'

'Don't remind me.'

'I beg your pardon?'

'Are you affronted?'

'I am, certainly.'

'For God's sake, Mother, don't you realize what you and Father did? Don't you understand the shame? I had the shame of being German and also the shame of being a Jew, of knowing what was done to us in the camps.'

She said, 'I don't know what you mean.'

'Mother, the Germans killed six million Jews.'

'Did they? I don't remember.'

I stared at her. There was absolutely nothing to say.

Her old face was turned away from me in pride. There was a small tea-coloured stain on her jersey jacket. What do we have to jettison to preserve ourselves? Does a mink that is hunted turn to its captors and surrender? Of course it doesn't, it goes on running. There are animals that will shed their tails if necessary, to lighten their weight.

'Where is Karl-Heinz now?' I replied, after a long time.

'Still in Hamburg, of course.'

'How do you know?'

'Don't bully me, Sybil, you're not a prize-fighter.'

'Still, tell me.'

She looked at me scornfully. 'What sort of woman are you, without manners of any kind? What have you become?'

I deferred for the time being, but later, when the side lamps were lit and we were watching television, I brought her a small glass of Noilly Prat and a long, rather stale sponge-finger biscuit that I found in a tin. I had forgotten she was supposed to be a diabetic and so, it seemed, had she. I set them down on the smallest table of the nest and drew it next to her.

She sipped and nibbled. We watched to the end of 'her' programme (*Coronation Street*, which despite its vulgar players she found highly amusing) and when the commercials came on I walked over and turned off the set.

We looked at each other.

'Karl-Heinz?' I said. She saw no escape.

'Many years ago we got back in touch. He found me through the German consul.'

'When was this?'

'I told you, a long time ago.'

'After the war?'

'Of course. How could it be otherwise?'

'In the fifties?'

'Yes, around 1954 or 1955. It wasn't so difficult. I had written when I married.'

'Did you say who you had married?'

'Of course, a furrier.'

'A Jewish furrier?'

'There was no particular reason to say so.'

'You were ashamed of marrying a Jew?'

The sponge finger was in crumbs. It was all over her skirt.

'If I was ashamed I would not have married Sydney. He was

openly a Jew, he had nothing to hide. I simply never thought to tell Karl-Heinz.'

'Did you tell your mother?'

'She was dying, it was Karl-Heinz I wrote to.'

'Does he know now that you married a Jew?'

'No.'

'I see. What did he do during the war, this uncle of mine?'

The phone rang twice, then stopped. Immediately afterwards the ormolu clock on the mantelpiece chimed the quarter. My mother was paper thin. I could have torn her in two, easily. We looked at each other. She looked at the floor.

'Do you think this pattern of carpet is dated?' she asked, smiling brightly. 'I can never make my mind up about this ultra-modern Scandinavian furniture. At first I thought it was frightfully ugly, but now I can see it has a certain chic.'

'You're mad,' I said. But of course she wasn't, or at least only as mad as she absolutely needed to be.

I had often fantasized about those Nazi relatives of mine and in my dreams of course they always held the doors open to the ovens. Now I was in a position to find out exactly what they had done during the war. Well, Karl-Heinz was too old to fight. He had a bureaucratic job, carrying out the administration of supplies to the cities. Like Stan, he had kept Germany fed. His son, Dieter, however, had seen active combat in the Luftwaffe and I dare say he might have bombed Liverpool during the Blitz, though he was too polite to admit it. I met them years later. We took coffee together in a sinister grand hotel on the Neuer Jungfernsteig and he assured me that they had known nothing of what was happening to the Jews. Believe it if you like, thousands wouldn't. It gave me some satisfaction, however, to find that his daughter later moved to

Berlin and formed that group of radicals on the outer perime-
ters of the Baader–Meinhof gang and, after their arrest, she
was smuggled into the Eastern sector where she works, to this
day, with a children's theatre company.

Chapter Twenty-Three

I had been left five thousand pounds with the promise of much more to come if my mother did not live long, and my father had invested his capital prudently. There was the prospect of my becoming not rich but, as we said in Jewish circles, 'comfortable'. What was I to do with my prospects? I was sufficiently a Leftist still to believe that such amounts of unearned wealth did not belong to me, and I made up my mind that most of it would have to be given away carefully to selected causes. I would send some, for example, to Cuba. There were such people as communist millionaires and I laughed to think of myself as Jewish financier who would bankroll a revolution. But first I would permit myself this considerable windfall which, after all, my comrades in the Party need not know much about.

What to tell Stan? Not the whole truth. My fortune would make him financially dependent on me and I was not sure what he would think of that. He could be very traditional. He sometimes took on overtime if he thought my income was overtaking his, though I had long since despaired of him having a career.

For the remainder of my time in England I did my duty and accompanied my mother on a shopping spree in the West End, which she went at with great gusto, parading along Bond Street as if she was Lady Muck with a flat off Park Lane, instead of a furrier's widow from the kosher belt of Bournemouth. I don't know what she saw when she looked in the mirror: perhaps those withered arms seemed fresh and young to her. She had her wrinkled years before the age of facelifts got going, or she would have been the first to go under the cosmetic surgeon's knife. Poor Mother. I don't think of her much. When she died I had her cremated in accordance with her wishes. She told that old joke about wanting to have her ashes scattered in Fenwick's, so I would come and visit her, but I arranged with the undertaker to have them thrown into the English Channel. I was out of the country at the time.

Meanwhile, back in 1965, when she was still very much alive, we went to the theatre, dined out, took day-trips to stately homes and made conversation about the furniture. I remember her glancing around the garish interior of the Royal Pavilion in Brighton. 'If your father had had his way, we would have lived like this,' she remarked.

But then I had performed all my obligations and I was able to book my flight back to Vancouver. I rang Stan with the details of my arrival and he picked up the phone almost at once. I liked him on the phone, I liked that slightly metallic voice of his, as if he were always swallowing silver polish or mercury. He gave his usual joke telephone greeting:

'Speak to me.' And then, 'Oh, it's you.'

'Who did you expect?'

'Nobody. What's up?'

'Guess what? I've inherited some money. I'm not saying it's a huge amount, but we could do quite a bit with it and there's more to come one day.' I was sorry I said it as soon as I spoke. I had been too impulsive, too keen to share my good fortune.

'Well, we knew it was on the cards. So how much did the old feller leave you?'

'Only five thousand for the moment.'

'Not bad, not bad at all.' Stan wasn't bothered about money. Easy come, easy go. It was all readies to him. He seemed to be taking it all right so I pressed on.

'We could use it to buy the house.' —

'What house?'

'Don't be daft, the one we live in.'

'Who lives in?'

'Us, you and me.'

'Oh, I get it, yeah, that's a thought.'

'Or is there something else you can think of?' Was this going to be another nail in the coffin of domesticity for him? What could he have in mind? Some kind of boat?

'Not offhand, no. Is it burning a hole in your pocket?'

'I thought you'd be pleased.'

'I am, sweetheart, honest. We'll look into that business of the house when you get back. I can ring the landlord tonight if you like and make enquiries. See what he wants for it, if he's selling.'

'Then you are pleased.'

'Sure, thrilled to bits.' But that's not how he sounded at all. His voice was hollow, like an old tin mug.

'What are you wearing?'

'What I usually wear when I've just got in from work. What do you think?'

'I'm sorry, are you tired? I know it's not a great time to ring.'

'I'm just in a mood, that's all.'

'Why? What's the matter?'

'Nothing. You just get that way sometimes.'

'Are you missing me?'

'Oh, aye, yes, don't worry about that.'

'What are you up to?'

'Nothing much. Blown a bit of weed, watched a bit of TV, the usual.'

Sometimes the heart turns cold for a moment. In my mother's flat, surrounded by shopping bags, our greedy purchases arranged on hangers, Stan seemed a dead loss. Maybe, I thought, I have grown out of him. I can do better than this, I said to myself, considerably better. I thought of his swollen fingers with their long nails feeling inside me and I shuddered. No one could have been more surprised at this reaction than myself. I dismissed it from my mind for the moment; I would think about it later.

'You sound depressed,' I remarked.

'Do I? If you say so.'

'What's that supposed to mean?'

'Oh, for fuck's sake, let's not have an argument. How are you getting on with your mam? Have you killed her yet?'

I laughed and forgot that I no longer loved him. 'Not quite, but nearly.'

'How did the funeral go?'

'It wasn't a funeral, I told you. But it was fine, fine. It passed off very well.'

Seagulls were crying at both ends of the line. My mother's ormolu clocks were chiming seven in erratic sequence and a dog began to bark in the flat below.

'That dog,' my mother said from the bedroom. 'That terrible hound.'

'What did you say?'

'I said I'll see you next week, then.'

'Yes, I'm—'

The operator came on and told us we had thirty seconds left.

'What was that you were saying?'

'I was going to ask whether you'll be able to meet me at the airport.'

'No, I'm sorry, love. I've got to go to work, I can't get out of it, big do on. But I'll wake you up the next morning. How about that? I'll bring you breakfast in bed when I get off.'

'Be seeing you, then.'

'Yeah, be seeing you.'

I said goodbye to my mother and I did not expect to see *her* ever again. I did not need her and I didn't see why she should need me. I formally dissolved the Ross family.

On the plane I tried to decide what I wanted to do about Stan, but good fortune had seated me next to a young Negro and I flirted with him for most of the journey. I bought him highballs and he showed me his scrapbook. He was a nightclub singer bound for a series of dates in Calgary and I wrote down his name and said I hoped I would see him perform some day. We both laughed but actually I think he found me a bit long in the tooth.

I ate my steak and green beans and little potatoes and salad. I watched the cabin darken and people find a door into sleep. I saw how the stewardesses applied their smiles, touching them down at each corner with tiny dabs of glue. I gave myself an entire manicure. I left my crocodile beauty case on that flight; I never saw it again. It had done good service down the years, although half the bottles had been smashed at one time or other and the chromium tops were missing or tarnished. The lining was stained with many spillages. Where does unclaimed debris go? Is my crocodile beauty case buried deep in some landfill site? Was the crocodile's skin allowed to decay a quarter of a century after the flesh that once filled it? Was it rendered into gases or metamorphosed into some kind of solid fuel made from fallen luxuries that will warm whoever is here in a million years?

Thirty thousand feet below me Arctic foxes and wild mink and snow leopards were going about their very limited business, hunting, feeding, reproducing, being hunted. I supposed that you couldn't use the underbelly of a she-creature, or the pelt would be marred by its nipples. I thought about fur in all its forms. I thought of a fur lampshade and instead of being sickened I found the notion quite alluring, light shining through the pelt, imparting a dense, dim glow.

I did not expect Stan to be there to meet me at the airport, for he had never gone in for surprises of that kind.

Our house was on the verge of being consumed by twilight when I turned the key in the door. I sat for some time admiring my cool white and beige surfaces. 'Home,' I said aloud.

After a while night came down over the mountains. I changed into a pair of linen slacks and in bare feet I walked out into the yard where the corn and zucchini I had planted had done very well in my absence. The cherry tree which hung over the boundary of our neighbours' property into ours was giving fat morello cherries for the first time in many seasons and the fruit lay, hardly mottled, on our grass. There was a lustre to all the surfaces that came from polishing by hand or by wind and the mysterious shadows in the corners of rooms harboured no ghosts but invited you to rub your cheek against their soft dark nap. The air was scented with peaches: a bowl of them, only a few wrinkled, was on the coffee table next to this month's editions of 'my' magazines and the afternoon's paper. In the kitchen the refrigerator was stocked with all the things I liked to eat and drink when I was tired: cool water-ices, bottles of soda, slices of pumpernickel and sweet butter. A new photograph of an overcast beach brushed with sagging rain clouds hung framed in the hall. There were two matches in a smoked glass ashtray on the telephone table underneath it and the blackened stump of a cigarette.

I turned on the hi-fi and played a number of records, mostly from the sugary throat of Nat King Cole. While I was listening I did a few yoga stretching exercises. I found a new disc that Stan had bought while I was in England, which consisted of nothing but bongo drums.

And then I found that I was tired in a different way and I climbed the stairs to bed. The linen had been drawn back to welcome me and the sheets were faintly scented with my perfume. In the bathroom I washed my face, remembered with a disappointed cry that I had left my beauty case on the aeroplane and found a jar of cold cream in the cupboard to rub into my face and neck. I stepped on the scales to discover that I had gained no weight while I was away and then once in bed I drifted off into a fine, natural, easy sleep until ten the next morning, when the house was as empty as it had been the night before and Stan was not there.

This time I had been deceived by his closet, for while most of his clothes were still hanging in colour-coded ranks, not all were, not quite. *Some* suits were missing, a few favourite ties and three or four pairs of shoes. Two suitcases, one top-coat. The most portable of his camera equipment (not his tripod). A number of discs, all be-bop.

I went back to bed and stared at the ceiling. Nothing, nothing. Then I laughed and thought, 'Oh, so what? Who cares? It doesn't matter, there's nothing to cry about.' Nor did I cry. I caught a little moth with my bare hands from the air, the kind that eats clothes and flour and rice. The sun went and came back and went again.

I dressed myself up in one of Stan's suits, one of his shirts and a tie, and I pushed my feet into a pair of his shoes, pale tan leather loafers. I looked grand, in the mirror, not a bad likeness at all. I went back to bed like that, still in his shoes.

Eventually I tried everything on that he'd left. Everything was a mess, his clothes were all over the place. Ties wound about my feet like creeper and I tripped over, falling heavily to the hardwood floor. Over the next few days huge multicoloured bruises grew over my knees and elbows, as lush as tropical flowers. Another tie sent me banging into the edge of an open wardrobe door, catching me on the side of the head at the hairline, which took on the appearance of a pelt, matted with bloody hair.

I found his toenail clippers and clipped off my fingernails as close to the quick as I could, and I removed the polish from them with acetone. I found his haircutting scissors in the dressing-table drawer and I cut off all my hair. A trail of his clothes tangled through the house and it got so that whatever I tripped on I would exchange for what I was wearing.

He was my skin, my pelt, my country.

After Madame rang and, getting no reply, drove over, found me wearing a summer-weight sharkskin jacket and dressed me like a woman again in clothes from my still unpacked baggage, I went down to the beach, poured petrol on Stan's garments and applied a match. It was an incredible conflagration, a stellar bonfire ringed in myriad sparks. Flames shot up and caught on branches of overhanging trees, igniting them. Pieces of charred worsted ascended in a column then blew out to sea. A crowd gathered and the fire brigade was called. I was arrested but let out with a caution. I came home and found one suit remaining that had fallen from the banister to lie unnoticed behind the front door. I buried it in the garden.

They had always been very nice to me at the Hotel Vancouver and now they showed me Stan's letter of notice in his childish hand and his receipt for his last paycheque handed over to him in person the morning of my arrival.

'He was a good worker,' the boss said. 'You couldn't wish for better. He didn't need yeast, he could make the dough rise just by looking at it. He knew his trade and I can't say fairer than that.'

I have often wondered what went through his mind, whether he intended to leave me a note, whether or not he'd started one and abandoned it. If I had called again just before I left whether his mind would have been altered. Whether I had tempted Fate considering if I should leave him, when I should have known I would never have done anything of the kind. I saw him turning down the covers of the bed for me, stocking the ice-box, collecting the paper from the hall and placing it neatly on the table. Was he wearing my panties when he went?

I don't know what he meant about the suitcase because I can't imagine that he could have forgotten it was there. He might have left it by mistake because he was in such a hurry or, more likely, I think, he wanted me to find it. But I don't know how he expected me to do that. It was only because I dropped an earring six weeks later which rolled off and fell under the space behind the steps of the house that led up to the porch that I saw its familiar brown handle sticking out almost from within the timbers of the building itself. I recognized it immediately, that case he had always kept locked in New York, where he kept his most important possessions, his signed photo of Dixie Dean, his seaman's discharge book and a picture of a bread rabbit he had baked for a child's birthday party on a liner crossing to Burma before the war.

I took the case inside and forced the lock with a chisel.

Most of the contents consisted of photographs of me, collected in batches and held together by rubber bands, some on the point of perishing. After many years I saw again the picture I had had taken at the automatic photo booth in New York when I was starting to look like an American, and there was another I had sent from Liverpool to his ship docked in New York harbour a few months before he deserted. Here were all the pictures of me naked in New York looking like a pet, the first he'd ever taken of me, I thought, but older still were little snaps of me in Liverpool standing at the Pierhead with half a ferry steaming out of the edge of the frame to New Brighton. There was another tiny one with deckled edges in which I posed with a cigarette, half my face obliterated by a brown mark. On the back he'd pencilled: 'Syb on the Cazzy.' The cast iron shore. I ran to the kitchen for scissors, my heart pounding, and came back and snapped all the rubber bands, and pictures fell out in random disarray and I snatched them up then threw them aside as soon as I had glanced at them. Me in our old apartment on Fourth Avenue in nothing but my cowboy boots. Hundreds of photographs of me on the beach, me cooking or mending or gardening. Me out at sea breasting the waves in my early-morning swims. His glass eye had missed nothing. I'd hardly noticed he was there. And deeper still, like geological strata, digging down into glacial valleys, were more pictures that I had never known existed. Me through the windows of the furrier's on Fifth Avenue, modelling stoles and jackets. Me and Thelma walking in Central Park. Me and Marvin eating ices on Coney Island. Everywhere I had gone he had been. Weeks later I still found ones that had gone astray to fall, unnoticed. Pictures of me and Julius through the window of his railroad shack. Pictures of me stumbling out of Party headquarters on the day I was expelled.

Never had a woman been so photographed, through every stage of her life from the age of fourteen on. In those pictures was a history of fashion in the second part of this century and a history of how age takes us unawares, how decay eats away at us. There I was, in every gradation of the grey scale, for none of the photos were in colour. I sat with my life all about me and wept, knowing in my heart that it ended here, with the last photo.

The suitcase had another secret. Sewn into its inside lid was a pocket of torn grey silk and in this I found several sheets of paper.

It took some evenings of pondering before I understood the code that they contained. They were a listing of a dozen or so post office box numbers across the country and I wrote away to all of them.

The replies arrived first in ones and twos from the nearest places (none of them were in Vancouver), then in batches several days apart until the last one arrived from Newfoundland a full three weeks after I had the first tragic envelopes. Roughly half contained pornography, though a few were innocent catalogues of men's underwear.

The rest were pictures of Stan himself, never alone, taken on board ships; of course they were, you could see the portholes. I could date each one by the clothes he wore. There was a calendar of the fifties and sixties in the width of his ties alone, and the rate his hairline had receded. He sat among them like a father. They were all the age he was himself when I first met him, teenagers being hugged by their dad. Sometimes they were clearly merry and raising glasses to the camera and sometimes they all sat, their flies unzipped, showing what they had. Or he grasped their penises in his hands, smiling. But in every picture he looked at them with such affection as if he only really wanted to pet them and kiss them and buy them nice things to wear. What struck me most was how old he looked, next to those boys.

I thought I was a chameleon. I had prided myself on my capacity to deceive and dissemble and pretend but I had been a fool. It was always me who had been deceived. I'd understood nothing about life at all, nothing. Everyone who had ever been close to me had turned out to be a stranger.

You think you can bear pain better when you are older, but you can't, it's worse. The heart is a resilient and plastic organ when you are young but when you get to the age I was then it's been through the fire and hardened, and when it takes a blow like this it cracks. I remember doing the dishes, my hands in soapy water holding a yellow coffee cup, looking out of the kitchen window to the bare leaves of the morello cherry tree and thinking, in six months' time you will have forgotten this. But six months later, when the tree was hung with another crop of fruit, like a *déjà vu* I held that same cup and the pain was worse. I wandered through the wilderness like Job, through the devastation and destruction. The soul has its Shoah. And six months on after that, the same thing, until I threw the cup out because it doesn't matter any more, it's just your life.

PART FOUR

Chapter Twenty-Four

For many years I have risen early and, dressing in navy linen slacks and an ecru cotton sweater, I have walked the streets of my own neighbourhood for exercise, keeping time at bay. Since the momentous events of the autumn of 1989 a thought has often recurred as my small stride paces the pavements of Holland Park: of an item I heard on the radio one morning in the shop a week or so after I returned from Saigon, while I was examining a 'diamond' choker through a jeweller's lens (on closer inspection marquisite glued on to a velvet band). It seemed that a day or so after the first breaches appeared in the Berlin Wall, and overloaded Trabants drove with unnecessary haste through those promising gaps to freedom, a man was found wandering just a few metres on the FDR side.

'Are you a refugee?' a reporter asked him. 'Are you escaping to the West?' The man spoke into the journalist's microphone. No, he explained. He had just come out for a stroll. The street he lived on in East Berlin ran down to the Wall and he had always wanted to know if the numbers continued on the other side.

I laughed at that, wouldn't you? But I put the choker down and began to think (or what passes for thought these days). At first I supposed it could be interesting to speculate about whether one of the two Berlins had a road beginning with, say, number 87; there again, had the city officials decided to rename it number one? On the whole that is a question for town planners and geographers. What I find really attractive is the banality of such an enquiry on a day when 'History' was being made, right there where he stood. The fact is, and let's accept it, some people couldn't care less. Or rather they tailor history's cloth to suit their own coats. The days and weeks after the Wall came down you saw such individuals on the news, freshly liberated, standing at market stalls pointing at kiwi fruit. I suppose that for thirty years or so this man lived out his time, trapped behind a sheet of deteriorating concrete, and when he gets his chance to escape does he take it? No. He goes and looks at the numbers, then, having satisfied his curiosity, he returns home and has lunch. Then what?

We were talking about all this at my cousin Jasa's funeral, as you do.

At the end of his life my cousin Jasa had been trying to weave all the disparate threads of it into a blanket to cover him in the coldness of the grave. After he returned to Yugoslavia he managed first to get his old job back on the Party newspaper in Belgrade, then he became its London correspondent. He did a little freelance work for the BBC and, rather mysteriously, I thought, they gave him a regular position and finally he found himself comfortably settled with a house in Hampstead, two passports and a young second wife.

We spent much time together and he became my closest friend, for it was only with Jasa that I had a history. He was the only person left in the world who knew me when I was young, who remembered when I had a heart-shaped face and my hair was cut in a curly page-boy crop and I wore ballerina dresses that touched my ankles in the days before my skin became as creased and coarse as linen. He knew of my old penchant for men of colour. He even knew (how could I keep it from him?) of my secret years of wandering across the American plains. He understood why my accent was so unplaceable, how it was that in certain circumstances I could speak as if I was a Kensington beauty from before the war and at other times I seemed indistinguishable from a lifelong citizen of the United States. Whatever was called for. He rang me on the telephone for long chats whenever I went off to a spa or a health farm to do what I could to keep, if nothing else, my figure.

We were political, Jasa and I. We did a little human rights work together and I was secretary of my local anti-apartheid group.

It was in his company, in the colder months, that I wore my mother's furs. They needed no alteration and her embroidered initials, the same as mine, did not need to be unpicked from the satin linings. I lived in her skins. When she died I took the best of her wardrobe, keeping the genuine Chanels and Molyneuxs, discarding the Susan Smalls. A few outfits were of such value that I sent them to the salerooms and two were purchased by the V&A, where you can see them to this day. So my mother was at last preserved for posterity in exactly the manner that she would have wished. She is part of history now.

Perhaps I was too harsh on her. I read recently of a countess in France during the Occupation who was denounced by her maid for having harboured a member of the Resistance at her chateau. She was taken off to Ravensbruck where she survived, and returned to Paris at the war's end, looking glamorous. It seems she had met up with a woman there who had worked for Schiaparelli and she had remodelled her camp uniform for her. What to think about that, I'm not sure. Some people have no darkness in them at all and maybe they're the better off for it. I myself have done as much as I can, all my life, to skate along on the surfaces of things. Isn't that what most of the world is, a surface, whether on land or on sea? Don't we walk on surfaces, don't we sail on them? Like the man who had just gone out to find if the numbers on his street continued on the other side of the Wall, perhaps you should do without heartbreak, if you can manage it.

Sometimes, if Jasa was not wanted at home or at Bush House, I took him with me to auctions where I bought antiques cheap, later of course to sell them dear. I had little interest in Victoriana. The baroque and the rococo or *moderne* were my specialities, having sickened years before of those bleached-out styles I used to like, and Jasa looked at the gilded furniture with nostalgia and approval. The cold days in which we sat in freezing salerooms, me wrapped in a fifties mink, reminded him not only of the winters of his youth but of that brief time when, with his family, he worked in the skin trade and sat at home on

Friday nights around the mahogany dining-room table covered with its snowy damask cloth, the room flickering in the light of the Sabbath candles' glow.

I accompanied him, occasionally, to the synagogue on Dean Street in Soho, where once a year he said *yiskor* for the souls of the dead, me peering down on to his shrouded shoulders and thinking of my own dead parents, and the special and strange love we had all once felt for each other.

'Do you know, Sybil, we are the only religion,' he told me, 'whose new year begins with the autumn equinox, before we go into the darkness?'

At New Year it is written, and on the Day of Atonement it is sealed, how many shall be crossed out and how many created, who shall live and who shall die, who by fire and who by water, who by sword and who by beast, who shall be rested in his home and who shall be wrested from his home. There is no life after death but this, a chance once a year on the first day of creation to give an account of yourself and be examined. I am an atheist. I cannot appeal to God, only my fellow man. I set out my life before you, for judgement.

Three injunctions. Self-awareness, social justice, the longing of every Jew in exile to find a home. Have I succeeded in any of it? You know my story now. You decide.

Jasa had known he would die soon. He could feel his heart giving out. 'I'm glad I'm dying now,' he told me. 'There are terrible times to come, Sybil. When the East collapses every little place is going to want its own flag. They've got long memories, those people. And listen, it's going to be bad for the Jews, very bad. People like us with two passports, with no allegiance anywhere – I tell you, we're finished. It's the end of the road for us. People are going to ask us who we are, where do we belong, and what are we going to tell them? What are we going to say? That we don't belong anywhere? We're going to need to keep our wits about us to get through this one. Light me a cigarette, will you?'

When I lay in bed that morning, on the day of the funeral, having been woken by a car alarm out of my dreaming (a grand reverie about silver accessories), I was thinking that I wasn't sure what to wear. As Jasa had told his second wife, the former Yugoslavian Airlines hostess, that he wanted a Jewish burial, it was taking place only two days after his death and I had no time to plan and little in which to shop. I wasn't certain who would attend and whether those who did would have a wardrobe of garments suitable for such an occasion. We are all getting on. We're not as young as we used to be. A black suit or coat is a necessity for our social lives these days. Normally I don't go to funerals as a point of principle but I was making an exception for Jasa, the only relative, apart from my parents, that I have ever known. My black outfits tend to the casual – loose trousers and velvet shirts from the time I spent in North Africa twenty years ago, when I adopted a local dress then temporarily fashionable amongst the young. I was not young myself but I do not believe I looked ridiculous.

But I am past that phase now. I revert to my own youth, a nostalgia not for the years before the war but for the fifties, a time when my fashion sense was temporarily in abeyance. To watch me, to catch my eye, to look at me walking about my neighbourhood later, after my morning constitutional is done, and I am bathed and dressed more formally, carrying something from Harvey Nichols or manhandling a small gilt mirror, you would understand at once that I am the sort of woman who favours French navy and white with matching bags and shoes and belts, though of course only some prehistoric creature would wear gloves these days, at least when the weather is mild. I am short, so I wear a Chanel suit well and a handbag on a gold chain. But of course I am sixty-seven and no one *does* look at me or consider my appearance. What do they care about the expense undergone to have a little tuck in the fold under my eyes or the collagen inserted in the line between my brows?

I know exactly what I am. A vain and shallow woman, though as far as I am concerned, it could all have been so much worse.

To return to that man and his numbers. Did he vote for reunification, for the reuniting of numbers 87 and 89? Are they together now? After so long apart, did the road divided have two quite separate names? Was something restored? Is it possible to go back into the past and set it right? I'm sure the man voted. He seems a conscientious soul. But what a capacity to live in the present, never burdening it with some sense of momentous grandeur! With one important exception, when it comes to the world of fashion, I've always lacked it. This is one of the first things Jasa said to me: that we Jews are only interested in the past and the future and we don't know how to live in the here and now.

It gets worse as one gets older. A crust has hardened over my mind and I think old ideas are better than new ones. Last week I walked past a demonstration of animal rights protesters. Sentimental imbeciles. I was handed a leaflet which I folded, unread, and threw in the next litter bin, though I could not avoid seeing other discarded ones on the pavement showing creatures mewling in leg-hold traps. Torture. What *I* could tell them about torture, with my membership of Amnesty International and my diligent letter-writing campaigns to various dictators. Little did these bleeding hearts know that I still pay for my remaining furs to be kept in cold storage each summer. Let the children worry about animals with their simple little personalities; I take care of my own. I am loyal to those men and women who earn their living in the skin trade and they shall not go without a roof over their heads for want of my Persian broadtail coat or my ocelot jacket.

I never wear them. I'm not afraid of the hooligans with their spray cans but I don't have the occasion. I would definitely have worn the Persian broadtail for Jasa's funeral, but it was late August, it was too warm. My cousin Jasa died on the day of the coup against Gorbachev and by the time he was buried it was all over. Jasa's heart condition closely followed events in Eastern Europe. His first coronary thrombosis occurred the day the Germans voted for reunification.

I ran out to Fenwick's and bought for the funeral a black gabardine coat-dress with a double-breasted row of gold buttons, the reveres piped in cream, its skirt reaching just below the knee. There is nothing worse than seeing the bones of an old woman's legs. And when I got to the cemetery I was glad I had made the effort. There were a lot of mourners, more than I had expected. The few who were young were probably from the embassy, while the men in dark macs, their strands of hair coloured an indistinct shade by Grecian Formula, were his former colleagues from the BBC, old Balkan hands from the old days we have all lost. There were also proprietors of two pâtisseries in Hampstead which Jasa had patronized for many years, checking in daily when he was in town, to spoon forks of *linzertorte* and Black Forest gâteaux into what he had idiomatically learned to refer to as his 'cake hole', that red succulent cavern beneath a moustache customarily dyed orange and yellow with nicotine. Jasa always smoked. He never tolerated the kind of lapses of loyalty to his packets of cigarettes that I did. Though he deplored smoking by women for aesthetic reasons, his own face was seldom seen without a fat white tube whose glowing coal he regularly ventilated so that it combusted into tiny sparks that flew about his head.

And there were numerous children from each of his two marriages, and of course his second wife, the one thirty years younger than he, who used to be an air hostess.

It was a nice warm day. Very dry. The ground was compacted. Birds twittered and tweeted in the trees. Jasa in his box was lowered six feet under. I thought of him there and realized that I had never seen him horizontal; even in illness he was always raised up on his pillows, nibbling the corner of a forbidden syrupy pastry, puffing at a clandestine cigarette, talking, talking. He was not a man to shut up, Jasa. Above ground, the air was sweet, though the stones in this Jewish cemetery were bare of wreaths or bouquets or those little vases into which a grieving widow can stick a weekly tired bunch of cheap daffodils. Cut flowers mock the dead.

The men filed by, each shovelling a spadeful of earth into the grave, as it was their *mitzvah* to do, one of those innumerable acts which are supposed to give pleasure to God and make us more human. I saw my cousin disappear beneath their charity. Then they washed their hands at a cold-water tap, to be purified against death. We women looked on.

Is life shit or is it great? Or can you make it great? This was the argument Jasa and I had with each other all our lives. Well, I said to him in his hole. The jury is still out.

Back at the house we ate cake and drank glasses of red wine that tasted like cough mixture, though the second wife had also provided spindly glasses of cold white Chardonnay. Not one of Jasa's drinks. The room we stood in was decorated to her taste. A tiny pattern of sprigged rosebuds on lavender ground, her idea of Englishness. I don't know how Jasa put up with it. I shook hands with all the children. The eldest boy, in an Italian suit of three or four seasons ago, the underside of his tie slightly marked by a razor, his one fastidious concession to the rending of his garments. He had not allowed his beard to grow as he should, as the chief mourner. But why bother? He is not a real Jew. The old, dead first wife was – what? I can't remember. Well, not a Jew and of course in the Party so an atheist. This boy (he must be forty, more) is the one who stayed on in Belgrade and made his living driving to Germany, stealing a Mercedes or a BMW, dumping the car he came in, and driving back to sell the stolen vehicle on the black market. Anything you wanted, he could get it for you. He accepted orders as a night-club crooner takes requests. He had a number of rackets. I know Jasa thought him a fool. He had made no attempt to leave Yugoslavia, to establish a foothold elsewhere. Like all Jews of our generation, Jasa and I always preferred to retain two passports.

Three, four, five o'clock. The house rocked on through the afternoon. Shadows were forming in the spaces where guests had stood, shaken hands, drunk their sweet wine, crumbled their cake and departed. Jasa's widow could not empty and wash the ashtrays fast enough. The air turned blue and grey. A cut-glass tumbler fell to the carpet and only made a thud, did not shatter. The rabbi came over to wish me long life.

We could relax when he was gone. The old cronies sat together and before long a small group went off into another room to make up a party for a game of cards. The sweet thick wine was put away and we were drinking whisky. The widow went upstairs for a while and came down again, her make-up refreshed.

To be married to an old man, to live with an old man's stench, I thought as I watched her. Fuh.

I crossed and uncrossed my rather good legs in their dark stockings. The men looked at them. I stayed there because I was appreciated. My glass was refreshed, enquiries made about my comfort. 'Sit here, Sybil, better for your back.' 'Cake?' I shook my head. 'Sybil is still watching her figure, she does not let herself go.'

So now we were talking politics. 'Chaos is coming,' someone said. 'Chaos. We're going back to barbarism. Europe will be laid waste by tribalism. It'll be worse than Africa, worse. Everyone wants to be a nation now, a street wants to be a nation. A fire on them, a fire.'

The widow sipped her drink and said nothing. The oldest boy (not her son, you'll remember) said that this sounded bad for business. Everyone nodded. 'Communism was doomed from the word go,' he said. 'How could any of you think it would ever work?'

The widow said, 'It could have worked but no one ever thought that Russia would have to struggle by on its own. They thought there would be an alliance with a communist England and a communist Germany. It was the isolation that caused the military build-up.'

We turned to her, astonished. 'Who told you that?' I asked. 'Your husband?'

She looked at me and did not like me. There were two or three beads of sweat engorging themselves in the cleft between her lower lip and her chin. On her very jaw-line there was a mole with two black hairs growing from it, one long and silky, the other short and coarse. 'I have been educated,' she retorted. 'I have been to meetings.'

'A lousy Trotskyite,' an old voice uttered in a stage whisper.

We discussed Berlin. I spoke of museums in the newly opened sector and what treasures I had seen that are contained there. I described unknown paintings, Lalique, Fabergé, artefacts from Charlottenberg that found themselves stranded on the other side of the city. It is well known that from time to time I keep a shop, to which customers are invited only by appointment. That I own some flats which I do up, sell, move on to the next, living like a nomad. I always make a profit. I pride myself on that. If you don't make a profit, why bother being in business at all? You might as well live in a workers' co-operative.

The room was full of the smell of old men's bodies and the perfumes they wear to conceal their stench and the smell of cigars and foreign cigarettes and the lingering almond scent of cake. The black patent leather shoe with its square grosgrain bow on my right foot strained uncomfortably past a bunion. There are other pains. I have a trouble about which you will hear nothing further. I hate illness bores.

My body still has other aches. Four years ago I was walking along the Strand when I passed a young man, a boy, I mean, in a leather jacket, crouched in a doorway, one of the homeless. He was so handsome that I dropped a ten-pound note into his lap. I had retreated several steps up the street when he caught my shoulder, turned me about and kissed me on the cheek. I shuddered with pleasure at his touch. I do not wish to remember how long it is since I last made love. Ten pounds for a kiss.

I had made the best of the bargain. He smelled of nothing at all unless it was rain.

I am a carapace of confidence. I live in its superior tower.

'The country is on its knees.'

'The government won't last a month.'

'The race was fixed, I knew it the minute I got to the track but I never act on my instincts.'

'A glass of lemon tea should not be a difficult thing to make.'

'Gorbachev is a gonner.'

'I saw a swastika on a grave.'

'Everything depends on the oil you fry your *schnitzel* in.'

'No, you're wrong, it's the quality of the veal. The flesh must be white, not off-white, shite-white. Dead white.'

'We're all being kept in the dark.'

'So, *nu?*'

'I knew nothing about racism until I came here. Back home, I thought everyone was the same.'

'They were the same. When did you ever meet a *schwarze* in Belgrade?'

'When? The military academy was just along the street. We trained every fucking terrorist in the world on my street.'

Later, the speaker, Jasa's eldest son, came and stood with me by the window.

'So,' he says. 'You are my father's cousin. I hear all about you. You are good capitalist.'

'Not quite.'

'He said you are.'

'I make money, sure. I make a profit. No more than I need.'

He looked at my clothes. 'You buy that dress in Italy?'

'No, London.'

'It has an Italian look. I like Italian clothes.'

He examined his fingers and I had the chance to take in his square handsome face on a red neck, the washed-out denim eyes, the tortured points of his shirt collar, the pink hands.

'Strictly speaking, you are now my only relative,' I pointed out.

'Nothing on your mother's side?'

'Not really.'

'Well, then, we stick together.' He took my arm in his and we stood by the window, facing into the room. I came up to just beneath his shoulder, my mouth smiling round my own gathered-in face, what streams away from the gathering centre of a knotted handkerchief.

'Yes,' I said. 'That's what we should do.'

'All these old men,' he remarked, 'all talking about the past. Who cares? The past is nothing. Me, I live in the present.'

'Then you have no bad memories to run away from.'

'The past is finished with. Communism is all finished.'

'That's true.'

'Nobody thinks about it any more except a few old women and a few old men.'

Here comes Yeltsin on the news. What a peasant, what a drunk. Is this where it all ends up? I put on a linen jacket and go for a walk in Holland Park. I run a finger along railings and they leave it covered in black sticky dust. It's one of those London days in early March when nothing much is going on with the weather: the usual grey mottled sky, some shivery-looking cherry blossom. I pass a gazebo in which a little child is sitting completely alone but his chin is resting in his hand and his elbow and arm are parked, like an umbrella, on the bench next to him. He looks so blasé sitting there: someone ought to give him a packet of fags and the *Daily Mirror*.

I walk over to him. 'Are you all right?' I ask. 'Are you on your own?'

'Nooo!' he replies, as if such an idea was absurd, as it would be if you were three, or thereabouts.

'Where is your Mummy or Daddy?'

'*I* don't know.'

I look about and here they are, coming towards me, smiling. 'We were just there,' they say. 'On the grass. We could see him.'

So I walk on. The family is complete behind me, the child cuddled in his mother's arms.

Back home. Tea. I spend the rest of the afternoon doing nothing, thinking nothing. Time rocks on without me. I put my cigarette out in a ridiculous Wedgwood ashtray. Where did I get it? Don't know. Why haven't I thrown it away? Don't know. You wake up one day and wonder what you are doing in this alien landscape full of all the things you have accumulated and can't remember why or how. And it is not just the space you are living in which is strange. I look down now at my hand and see at once there is no way that it could be mistaken for that of a young girl. Oval nails, painted coral, crisp half-moons, tidy cuticles, yes. But skin like crumpled silk. The veins and bones show. The hand is the first place from which we lose fat as we grow older. Even if I had a rump as broad as a pig's arse and thighs corrugated with cellulite, my hands would be elegant wands of sinew and cartilage.

It didn't take long to think *that*. My hand is still busy in the ashtray. I used to have a habit, once, of leaving my cigarettes upended on their filters, like little columns, but I don't do it any more.

Morning coffee with Jasa's second wife at Fortnum and Mason. Try as I might I can never manage to arrive after her. She has being late down to a fine art. She made her little entrance from the street door like a poached pear in oatmeal linen and caramel accessories and the gold chains on her chest swinging from side to side when she walked. Myself, I think she takes up too much space in the world. She exuded a kind of uncomplicated blown-rose sex appeal. Her unnecessarily large lips were as usual a sticky sugar almond-pink, the colour of dragees. Her blonde hair held back from her forehead by a black velvet Alice band. I suppose she thinks she resembles Marilyn Monroe. As if.

I nodded as she approached. Does anyone wear heels so high these days? Does anyone left in the country have court shoes with little *bows* at the back of the ankles?

'Sybil,' she said, air-kissing my left cheek. I air-kissed back and the scent of Calvin Klein's Obsession overpowered my own L'Air du Temps. Force ten gales of her perfume were gusting across the room.

The waitress – one of those dour foreign little women they always find jobs for here – came and tried to tempt us with a tray of patisserie, stiff little pastry tarts stuffed with a mound of confectioner's custard on which strawberries sit on their fat backsides. Vanilla slices trying to be airy. Jasa's widow pointed to a wedge of *sachertorte* and gave the waitress one of those little-girl looks, a moue of 'I know I shouldn't be *naughty*'. The waitress gives her back a thin-lipped smile. I shook my head and masked my plate with my hand. 'Coffee for me, black.' It's all the same to the waitress.

'And for me, café mocha. With whipped cream? You have it? Yes, thank you.'

The waitress laid down a pastry fork on the other side of the table. Two pairs of hands, both plumper than mine, which I placed under the table and felt the linen's folds that could stand up alone like a screen if you needed them to.

'Do you mind if I smoke?'

'No, go ahead. A light?' She brought out a little silver lighter and leaned forward to click on the flame.

'I didn't know you did.'

'Not for years. Jasa gave me this when we were first married. I carry it in my bag, you hardly know it's there but you can never tell when you might need to set fire to something.'

'Such as?'

'I don't know. I didn't mean anything.'

Our coffee came. The *sachertorte* reminded me that Jasa and I used to have coffee and pastries together, once, long ago in a place full of steam and foreign accents back in the days when he was still with his first wife, that girl from near the coast, near Split, I think, who went on to become a devoted Party functionary. I liked her on the occasions when we met in New York, though I had been frightened of her at first. I couldn't pronounce her name so I called her Dru. She gave me books to read sometimes and was patient with me, more patient than anyone in the study group. In return I took her shopping and she giggled and said she was pleased to have a fine dress. But she died some time in the sixties, of one of the cancers women get.

A moustache of cream was on her successor's mouth. She licked it off with a round, very red tongue. Something was bringing the blood to her face. A little drink or two at lunchtime, alone in her chintz bedroom? Or not alone? I took out my glasses to get a better look at an array of open pores across her nose and chin.

'Widowhood suits you,' I said, smirking. 'You're blooming.'

'Do you think so? Would you say I had lost a little weight?' She shifted around in her chair as taxis passed along Jermyn Street behind her head. The surfaces of things here are matte and thick with their quality. There is a lack of cheap gloss. The coarseness of linen, the dullness of men's suiting, the powdered noses.

'Maybe a pound or two,' I said, meanly.

'I go to aerobics classes twice a week. Do you exercise?'

'I do yoga stretches.'

'Really! Do they work?' Her mouth was a hole down which cake disappeared endlessly. She went at it in tiny forkfuls. She was like a workman with a spade, endlessly transporting a brown mound from one place to the other.

'I've been doing them since the sixties. I hardly think about them any more. It's just a habit, like brushing your teeth.' My coffee finished, I took out my compact and reapplied my lipstick. I powdered my nose. I avoided looking at my eyes.

'You've always taken care of yourself, haven't you?'

'I do my best. Do they know at your aerobics class that you eat cake?'

'Oh, a little something doesn't hurt now and again.'

'Really? I have never given in to self-indulgence, not that kind, anyway.'

I didn't know why I was doing this to her except it was as much a habit as doing my cobra stretches. She finished her torte and put her fork down.

'You have always thought I am a very trivial person, yes?'

I was embarrassed for once.

'Because I worked for an airline, a waitress in the sky.'

'It's a job.'

A smiling job. You have never had smiling jobs. Neither did Jasa. He always got what he wanted by his will. Sometimes the rest of us have to smile to get our way.'

'You don't have to tell me what we need to do to survive. I'm a past master.'

'Oh yes, we all know you are very strong. You don't live like the rest of us. When they made you they broke the mould. You're iron. I know about all your little adventures.'

'I doubt it. You don't know much.'

'You were a member of the Party.' She laughed. I suppose she thought me either naive or an opportunist. Probably both.

'Yes, I was, and it made me better than I should have been. Believe me, it could all have been a lot worse.'

'You never had a husband?'

'Yes, but no, not the way you mean.'

'Jasa was always very unhappy if he didn't have a woman. He liked something to rub between his fingers.' There is plenty of her own flesh to knead.

'I'm sorry he's gone. I'll miss him. He was like a brother to me, sometimes a father.' I was trying to imply a superior closeness.

'Enough, Sybil,' she said. 'Were you jealous of me? Did you want Jasa yourself?'

She would think that, wouldn't she? The truth is (which I was not going to tell *her*), I was jealous of my cousin, not his wives. Life came easily to Jasa, I'd say. After the war everything worked out for the best; that guy always landed on his feet. A job always came up for him – look at the way he suddenly arrived in London with the BBC. He was never short of women, he had how many children? Three, four, is it? When Dru died, at fifty, he could start again. This little twerp had given him back his youth, but who was going to give me back mine? He had everything, *everything*. He died in his wife's arms. A lump formed in my throat, a yeasty mass of self-pity. I poured myself another cup of coffee to dissolve it.

When I could speak properly, I said, 'Jealous? Of you? Of a former air hostess?'

'All right,' she said, moving her plate away from her. The sugar-pink lips were setting themselves into a new and unusual pattern. 'OK, you win. Listen, I didn't ask you to come here today for this. I have a need from you.'

'From me?'

'It's Jasa's son Nebojsa, from his first marriage. You met him at the funeral. He's coming to London and he needs a roof over his head.'

'Which you can't provide?'

'No. I'm selling the house and moving to a little place. Jasa's pension wasn't so hot. I have to liquidize my assets. I haven't the room. You have. You have property all over London.'

'I don't, I just have my own flat.'

'That's not what I heard.'

'Then you heard wrong.'

'But anyway, the flat you live in is huge. You have three, four, bedrooms?'

'Yes, I have spare rooms.'

'Then you can take him in.'

'Why should I?'

'He's your own flesh and blood. Isn't that enough?'

'Does he have refugee status?'

'No, but you will sponsor him.'

'I will?'

'Yes.'

We looked at each other across the table. Her soft pink flabby face had now completely lost its expression of vague good nature. And though I sought with all my might to say no, I found that in my heart I wanted very much to say yes. For to have a man about the place filled me with such delight that when I thought of Nebojsa's clothes hanging in the closet and his razor in the bathroom and the male smell of him on his skin, passing through my rooms, I felt green and young and giddy and I walked back to Holland Park swinging my handbag in the sunshine as the buds on the cold trees warmed and curled and stretched and opened. The early cherry blossom was no longer shivering and, noticing window-boxes full of narcissi and tulips, I stopped at a flower stall outside the tube station and bought two bunches of freesias, which I arranged at home in a gold vase embossed with fleur-de-lis. I opened the windows in my bedroom and, taking off all my clothes, I did my yoga stretches, a double session.

Chapter Twenty-Five

When Nebojsa came to me he was in a such a state of mind that I thought he would do nothing for the rest of his life but watch daytime television and drink Jack Daniel's from the bottle. The war didn't suit him. 'War is bad for business,' he said.

He didn't like London, either. He thought it was dirty and disorganized. He admired German order. 'Düsseldorf,' he said; 'there's a city. Clean. People work hard, they buy good things. Very nice.'

'How long will the war go on?' I asked.

'Years. The Serbs will not rest until they avenge the blood spilt at the Battle of Kosova.'

'When was that?'

'Thirteen eighty-nine. We just had the anniversary.'

'The Serbs seem to be on the wrong side in this. The press is making you out to be monsters.'

'Yes, we give the Croats a taste of their own drink. Filthy fascists. Tudjman, a fascist. That's what they say back home. Sure, probably. But all in the past. Who cares? Two years ago I got big money selling video machines. Now look at us. We're fucked. Video machines probably fucked too. Because of some wars, some defeats no one remembers except people with nothing better to do.'

We went out sometimes to a bar or pub, to Soho. We passed an animal rights march once, winding its way from Hyde Park down to the Houses of Parliament. I explained what it was about.

'Some people want to live their lives like flowers,' he said and, clearing his throat ostentatiously, he spat into the gutter.

Later a beggar came up to us and asked Nebojsa for a pound.

'For what do you want pound?' Nebojsa asked him.

The beggar, a reeking, peeling drunk, really, with dripping eyes and mouth, said he needed to buy himself a beer. Nebojsa reached into his pocket. 'I give you ten pence,' he said. 'Now you find nine other people and get them to give you ten pence and you have pound. Put some effort into your life.' The beggar stared at the coin in his palm.

'What's this shit?' he asked.

'You don't want ten pence?' Nebojsa asked him. 'Good. I take it back.' And he picked the coin up from the beggar's hand. 'You are in business,' he told him. 'In your line you cannot get what you want to have but what the customer wants to give you.'

In a pub we sat at a table and he got out his cigarettes. He would only smoke Marlboro; he distrusted other brands, could only recognize ones that were a known currency, and had to know what they were worth. There were many young girls around and his eyes darted about, looking at them. There was a girl in a maroon leotard – or was it what they call a body? Her breasts were carried in front of her like two mounds of pink blancmange on a serving dish.

'Are you looking at her cleavage?' I asked him.

'What is cleavage?'

I pressed my own two small breasts together beneath my navy dress.

'Ah, cleavage.' He repeated the word. He was now around forty but he ran his life, I thought, like a teenager. He had a girlfriend back home in Belgrade and a child of fifteen from an ex-wife and he rang both of them once a week from a phone box. He did not bring girls back to the flat, but two or three nights a week he didn't come home at all. He said he had been at parties with the other Yugoslavians he knew through hanging around certain bars where they gathered to watch satellite football on giant TV screens. He thought I did not know that he smoked cannabis and did some cocaine when he could get it. I told him that he looked like Paul Newman. 'Not Steve McQueen?'

'No.'

'OK. Is not a prize but it's a win.'

I failed to mention that I meant Paul Newman as he looks now, not how he appeared in my day when he was young and blonde and gorgeous.

My second cousin had no trade. He had discovered that the black market as he knows it can only exist in communist countries where consumer goods are controlled or unavailable. My second cousin is a product of a particular moment, of societies in the process of disintegration. Unfortunately, his had now actually collapsed and he lacked a role.

I paid for the drinks. Nebojsa ran through his social security cheque in a day or two. I was planning to find him some work decorating, which he regarded as menial, fit only for peasants. This made me cross. 'Your father always knew how to play the system,' I said. 'He could survive in any regime.'

'Better not to ask who was paying him.'

'What do you mean?'

'Just don't ask. Don't make my father out to be anything more than what he was, an apparatchik. That's a good memory of him. He never believed in anything.'

'You've got to believe in something. I took that in at my father's knee. It's a necessity of life. All meanings are not equal, you know, some are better than others. I believe that to this day. I believe it as I sit here talking to you now. One person's opinion is not as good as the next man's. Some things are true.'

'No, everything is the same. You take, I take. No difference.'

'You must have believed in something once.'

'I grew up in a communist country. What they taught me in school I believed. Only later I find that it is nonsense.'

'I was a Party member, did you know that?'

'Cleavage, cleavage,' he said.

'Pardon?'

'I just remember the word you told me. I repeat it to fix it in my head.' Which he pointed at. 'Yes, I hear you were in the Party. How come?'

'Oh, you know. The worker's struggle, blah blah, commitment to pacifism, blah blah, fighting against union corruption, blah blah, pitting ourselves against segregation, blah blah.'

'You believed that?' he said, pityingly.

'Yes,' I said. 'You know I did.'

'Tell me what you believed,' he said, laughing at me.

OK, I thought, I'll tell you. I dredged my memory. 'I believed that by study, following the guidance of the leadership and then the fullest possible democratic discussion in debate, we arrive at the correct position. By the greatest possible unity in action, we succeed. This is the essence of democratic centralism.'

'History knows only one imperative – forwards,' he said, stabbing a finger in the air.

'Even the history of capitalism itself is the history of Progress, for without a bourgeoisie there is no working class, only a peasantry,' I responded. We were both laughing now.

'And without the great revolt by the working class there is no workers' dictatorship. And without a workers' dictatorship, there is no socialism.'

'And without socialism there is no chance for the state to wither away and for humanity at last to be free.' It's like a fluency we both have in a dead language. *Did* I believe it at the time? Of course. What else should I have believed in?

But perhaps how things were and how you recollect them aren't the same. Could it be possible? All this was such a long time ago, more than forty years. Maybe those preposterous words are only a clumsy way of concealing something more important, in the human heart.

Nebojsa lit another cigarette and also lit one for me, which I took, burning, from his fingers. 'My father said you went crazy for a while. He said you got caught up with some people, like you had a temporary madness. He said he tried to warn you away, but you wouldn't listen. He said there was some man involved.'

'There always was, with me.'

He looked at me, surprised. 'You like men? Perhaps I can find you one. An old man it would have to be. A man likes a woman who is younger than himself. Tell me, cousin Sybil, tell me why you believed in these absurdities, that man is good.'

'Well, partly it was the times, though only a complete imbecile like me would have joined then, in America, right at the beginning of the McCarthyite period, the witch hunts. Did you hear of those?'

'Yes, I see a film about it, with Robert de Niro, made for TV movie, I think, not so hot.'

'Ha, that was about Hollywood. I was never there, I don't know about that, only what you read. But listen, those guys got off lightly, they were just fellow travellers. What they did to the real communists was something else again, I can tell you. Talk about harassment, they were busting us, they were even beating us, peaceful crowds with kids, just sitting on the grass listening to music. The Klan was there at one place with clubs and the police stood by and did nothing. I bet there was nothing about that in your movie. Your father, as you say, thought I was an idiot. You're right, he always knew which side his bread was buttered on. He told me I was swimming against the tide, but that's not how I saw it. I was propelled into the Party by circumstances. I didn't feel I was rebelling against anything or anybody – except him, as it happens. Of course I just didn't realize what a long shot all of it was. You cannot imagine anyone as naive as myself back then, at the end of the forties.'

We sat in silence. I was trying to remember how the CP had been on the point of destruction, under assault from the lousy Red-baiters, crumbling from the inside, from the inner core of its FBI spies and informers and stool-pigeons, about to launch a series of bitter purges as the leadership turned from its wartime consensus and its hopes for Wallace back to a hardline Bolshevik vanguard. Had I refused to go with Julius and stayed in New York I'm sure I would have been no more than a fellow-traveller for a few months until fear, and Morris's ridicule, drove me back to a more suitable existence: one in which, through Morris's influence, I would be found some job on a magazine where I would have come, once again, under the spell of couture and forgotten my brief political past so far as to confine it to the occasional signing of a petition to protest against the treatment of the Negro in the South or the execution of the Rosenbergs.

Or perhaps I would have fallen into some other way entirely that I could not imagine, for I had not in fact taken the path that would have led me there. If I had stayed in Greenwich Village would I have found, as my next lover, a painter or a poet or a writer? Would I have become his Muse or would I have even found in myself some latent talent that had so far gone unrecognized? (And, I should say, still has – I have never located any stifled artistic longings beyond a good eye for colour.)

Nebojsa was looking at me, perplexed. I don't think he took me seriously as a former communist, and who can blame him? Still, I was.

'You get an American accent when you talk of these things,' he said. 'I am surprised. I thought you were an English lady, very English.'

'There's nothing English about me,' I replied. 'Neither of my parents was English. I spent twenty years of my life in the States. I had very good teachers, you know, the best. There was someone who really opened my eyes for me. He made something out of me, out of a pretty little fool.' I was remembering something Julius said once. 'It was this . . . person who convinced me that there are two ways of changing the world. Either you can first make it work, then you can make it just. Or you can make it just and then make this just society work. Everyone on our side of the family, except maybe your father, when he was younger, has always taken the former path. Myself, for a while, I believed that you could take the latter.'

'Very nice idea. We tried it in Yugoslavia. Look at us now.'

Nebojsa was saying that there were many contradictions and paradoxes in life. He had thought himself about all these things but for the moment all he wanted was to get drunk and sleep with a woman. He was looking meaningfully at his empty glass and so I handed him some money and he made his way to the bar to order another Jack Daniel's for him and a Cinzano with soda for me.

Having my second cousin Nebojsa living with me had come to involve a number of inconvenient questions.

London in the summer. Who is stupid enough to stay here? I, for one. I have to remain close to the specialist at the hospital for my *ailment*. I have an appointment every week. Anyway, I don't like being outside capital cities. Nebojsa and I sat on my little balcony high above the traffic with drinks and he laughed when I told him my stories of my days as a communist. He thinks I am a dope to have turned myself into a worker.

'We romanticized the working class,' I said. 'They were icons. Look at what you're wearing, your jeans and your T-shirt and your leather jacket. Don't you know that was practically the uniform of the American working man? Not until the sixties did the middle classes wear that kind of stuff, when the student protesters began to dress that way.' In Belgrade, he replied, any smart person made sure they had a job in the bureaucracy and wore a suit. Unless they were really smart, like himself, and kept work to a highly profitable minimum. But I was not smart, I pointed out. I was not an intellectual.

'So you spent how long in some dump?'

Nebojsa knows only two Americas. New York and Los Angeles. Skyscrapers and Hollywood. He doesn't know there is something else. He thinks you can pass in a moment between the two coasts. He does not know that it took me years.

Nebojsa wanted to go to the famous English countryside so I took him. We went to Yorkshire, to the Pennines. This was deliberate on my part. He looked around in horror. 'Very nice,' he said. We had a northerly cream tea and came straight back again; we did not even stay the night.

I share his mystification. When I look at Nature, I don't really see anything, just the nondescript colours of grass-green and earth-brown and various shapes in the landscape. Even after all that time on the road I can't identify the name of a tree or a flower and many animals look the same to me unless I can get up close to them and inspect their fur. A cat is smaller than a dog and a sheep is bigger than that. Sheep on distant hills sometimes look like maggots. Cows can often be confused with horses from a distance but their bodies are thicker and their legs are shorter. A wasp has a narrower body than a bee. I've never seen a pig in real life. Ants are very small. I don't recognize foxes or mink when they are running around, before they are made into coats and jackets and stoles and hats and trim. I take after my father in that respect: he considered himself a judge of horseflesh, by which he meant that he would motor to the races at Uttoxeter and come back the poorer but with shield-shaped passes hanging from his binoculars.

'I am city boy, you are city girl,' Nebojsa said, as we returned, thankfully, to the flat.

For the past five years I have been writing a little book on colour. I have been attempting a study of the spectrum which would allow interior decorators to make a more educated assessment of tonal variations. After the invention of the first brilliant white paint, titanium white, in the twenties, my generation got rid of colour in the inside of homes; white was a symbol of architectural purity. There is no white in nature apart from snow and a few flowers. Nature is pretty colourful on a good day; that's about the most you can say about it. Colour is one of the few luxuries in life. Anyone can open a tin of paint and spread it on the walls. A good coat of yellow ochre is one of life's great surfaces.

The flat I am living in currently has been finished for two and a half years and I really should sell it and move on. The longer I leave it, the more the décor will wear and it will lose value. I am slightly worried that my colours will have dated. These very hot strong shades are coming in; everything is supposed to look like some Spanish *casa*, which is a bit of a joke in London. The problem is that I am quite comfortable here and really there is no financial incentive to leave. If my dividends fall, I can just sell one or two of my better pieces. Like my Venetian painted bed, large enough for a palazzo, large enough for a nobleman to practise debauchery in. Another joke. Or my chinoiserie, the collection I brought back from Asia. There are eight occasional tables in my sitting room alone.

Nebojsa went out and got himself a little job in a shop that sold chandeliers. He had to stand on a ladder wearing a white coat and white gloves and every morning he washed the chandeliers in a solution of warm water and vinegar. Then he went to the back and read the paper until called upon for his next duty. When a customer bought a chandelier, the proprietor had a little ceremony in which they were served a glass of cheap champagne. It was Nebojsa's job to open and serve the champagne in perfectly washed glasses.

What a job for a grown man. But, oddly, Nebojsa is quite decorative in his way and his foreignness makes him exotic.

I don't cook any more. I used to, but there isn't much point unless you are cooking to fill a man's stomach. Nebojsa never came home to find me peeling and chopping. He sent out for pizza, I made a salad for myself.

He kept promising to find me an old man. I had an old man once, though not as old as I am now. On the whole, though, I prefer young boys. I like to look at them. I watch them from my window. My eyes caress their bodies. At twenty they are like wild animals. That is the age I like them.

'What about 1956?' Nebojsa said. 'What did you do then?'

'What about what came immediately before it?' I reply. 'What do you know about that?'

'Nothing. I was a tiny baby. Crap time, the fifties. Very repressed.'

He watched the news but did not discuss with me what he saw there. Sometimes he had nightmares and woke up screaming; when I asked him what was wrong he said that he had been dreaming about his period of national service in the army.

People would ask Nebojsa where he was from and he would say: 'From Yugoslavia.' It would have been enough once, but now they were know-it-alls. 'Croatian, Bosnian?'

'From Belgrade, Serbia,' he would tell them. It was as bad as being a Nazi. I told him to get smart and always say he was from Sarajevo.

'Actually,' he said, 'as far as I'm concerned I'm Yugoslavian. If Yugoslavia doesn't exist any more, too bad. That's not my problem.'

But it was his problem. He had a completely useless passport in the name of a non-existent country and even then he lost it, which was a disaster as he had it in mind that he would go to America, to the land of free enterprise where his talents would be better appreciated.

'It's fine,' he said. 'I buy a passport.'

He went round building sites trying to persuade Irishmen to exchange their passports for cash, without success.

'Get me passport!' he cried out to me. 'I got to have bloody passport.' I pointed out that I was doing everything I could. His application for residency was making its excruciatingly slow way through the Home Office but why so slow? he wanted to know.

'Because that's how these things work,' I pointed out.

'You give someone money, you find the right person, they do what you want.'

'Not here.'

'This place. You're a number, not a human being. At home, you want something, you find someone you know. You take them a bottle of whisky, you have a little chat. Something happens. Here, no one knows you, you're nothing. Nothing happens.'

'It's our famous sense of English fair play,' I said, sarcastically.

Then he had the idea that we could go to a Jewish home for idiots, mental defectives. We would identify someone around his age, apply for a copy of their birth certificate and get a passport in their name. 'It has to be Jewish because then the name just sounds strange, not English. This person will never have applied for a passport. It's perfect. It will work.'

'No,' I told him.

So this is my old age or approaching it. You know about Julius, or you should do. His book sold well in certain bookstores and he was constantly on TV, narrating some documentary on PBS or being interviewed sitting in his house on Sugar Hill, a wall of volumes around him, still a lifetime pedagogue, even more so after he got his honorary professorship at City College. He was very telegenic with his venerable white Afro, his Nigerian robes and the Yoruba greeting he always offered in his grave, tendentious voice. I heard him once talking about the race chauvinism in the Party, about the absence of proper debate. They used him as an errand boy, he said. The secret I dragged out of him who hasn't heard him tell it? Even in the twilight years of the Cold War he could still be seen giving his account of his time in Moscow, the coldness that tormented, white faces against the white snow in winter and in summer a life lived in greyscale. I received a small mention in his autobiography: 'Around this time I slept with quite a few white women,' he wrote. 'They were girls from Greenwich Village who wanted to hop over the race fence for the night. I even lived with a couple for a while. The last one, I remember, I rescued from a dope dealer. She worked in a department store and, hell, was she dumb. But pretty.' It was surprising to me that Julius could turn out so shallow. He had transformed himself into a master-piece of public relations. He got a huge obituary in the *Guardian* when he died in 1987.

Stan? I don't know. I have no information. There's nothing I can tell you.

Chapter Twenty-Six

I was in the hairdresser's undergoing my usual treatment, which attempted to restore to me the dark helmet of hair with which I began my life, when I picked up a supplement from one of the newspapers left by a customer before me. On the cover was a black-and-white photograph. It depicted a young girl dancing the lindyhop with a black man. She was dressed in a silver-flecked skirt and a white blouse that made a kind of wide tableau of her breasts. She was so very young and pretty and she seemed to be possessed and transported so that she did not notice the crowd gathered around her and her partner, the men laughing and smiling, the women with sullen faces. She was a creature from another time and you could not but want to know who she was and what had become of her.

My hands were shaking as I opened the magazine. There were three more pages of pictures inside, all of the same young girl as she danced and twirled, was thrown about from limb to limb.

A short article accompanying the pictures explained that they were from an exhibition at the Bluecoat Gallery in Liverpool and had been taken by a local amateur photographer, retired baker Stanley Maguire from the Wirral who had briefly lived in America after the war and had many interesting stories to relate of the dance halls of Harlem and the jazz clubs that once lined a street or two that ran between Fifth and Sixth Avenues. The pictures were, it seemed, a remarkable record of a vanished age and shed light on the character of all those white girls who defied the conventions of the day by experimenting with interracial relationships.

'The young girl here is a symbol,' the article told me, 'of a time when the Beat generation was creating the syntax of what was to become sixties youth culture – its slang, its music, its experimentation with drugs. Who was she? Where is she now? Mr Maguire cannot or will not tell.'

I travelled up to Liverpool on the train and walked the short distance from Lime Street Station to the Adelphi Hotel. Lime Street was semi-derelict. The shops were mostly shut up. Seagulls screamed overhead. The heels of my black suede shoes clicked up the steps. I was carrying my overnight bag, dressed in my mother's Persian broadtail coat, with our initials embroidered into the lining in turquoise silk thread. The white mink collar warmed my throat. A hall porter ran down to take my bag from me. 'We'd better get you straight to your room, love,' he said. 'You're not thinking of going out in that coat, are you? Well, if you do, don't carry much money with you.'

'I won't be going out at all,' I said. 'I'm just meeting someone this afternoon for tea in the lounge.'

'Not going to see Liverpool?'

'I've seen enough already.'

The doors along the corridor all opened outwards, like the doors on a ship. I removed my coat and hung it on a satin hanger that I took from my bag. I bathed and changed into a lilac Jaeger suit and repaired my make-up and then I lay down on the bed for a little while and closed my eyes. When I woke, I put a gold chain around my neck from which hung a small clock. I strapped my Omega watch around my wrist and went down to the ground floor with my Persian broadtail about my shoulders.

The deserted lounge was much as I remembered it, vaster than the ballrooms of the heavenly infinite, low wicker chairs and a solitary waitress in an old-fashioned black-and-white uniform. I found a table precisely in the centre, ordered a pot of tea for two and a plate of biscuits. I sat and waited.

For seventeen minutes no one came or went; I smoothed a finger along my neck.

When I looked up again he was walking slowly towards me dressed in a grey leather bomber jacket, the kind wives buy for their husbands at C&A or Marks and Spencer. His trousers were a nondescript grey also. A maroon pullover did nothing to conceal the girth around his middle. His hair had receded to a few strands slicked back with hair oil. I felt tears well up at the sight. Who had done this to him?

He sat down heavily in the chair next to me, out of breath.

'Well, here we are, Syb. Beautiful coat. You're right back where you started, aren't you, on top of the world.' His voice was thick with catarrh. He would keep coughing into a hand-kerchief. 'Mucus,' he said. 'It'll be the death of me.'

'Thank you for coming,' I said.

'It wasn't any trouble.'

'Did you have to travel far?'

'Over the water. I live in Wallasey now, near the sea.'

'We used to go there when I was a child. We used to drive to Parkgate.'

'Oh yeah, that's still going. We pop along there on the odd Sunday for potted shrimps.'

'Yes, we used to do that.' I poured him a cup of tea and he reached into his pocket for artificial sweeteners.

'When did you arrive?' he said.

'At lunchtime.'

'So you've not been out at all? You'll have needed the rest after your journey.'

'Just the walk from the station.'

'Terrible, isn't it?'

'What happened?'

'Well, that's easy. It was when the docks finished that we were finished off. The only reason for Liverpool being here was that we were a port for the Atlantic trade. Being on the sea bred us different. We were always bloody narky because you could always get away. We had our freedom. When ships stopped coming we were stranded. It turned us in on ourselves. It made us an inland place but we weren't brought up for it.'

'When I was a child we used to think that the Mersey would bring us prosperity for ever. That's what my father always said.'

'Yeah, it was an easy mistake to make. We didn't see what was coming.'

Time either erodes us, or it silts us up. There is no cast iron shore.

'So what have you been doing all these years?'

'This and that. I've got a daughter. Her name's Ella, after Ella Fitzgerald. Do you want to see a picture?' I nodded. He took out his wallet and passed over an image of a girl. She was ordinary. Nothing like him. I wondered if he had been deceived and was not the father.

'She's done a YTS in hairdressing,' he said. 'She must get it from me. Do you remember I used to cut your hair?'

'Yes.'

She s a lovely girl, isn't she?'

'Yes.'

'Not your class, of course. Just ordinary, but she has a very loving nature. She takes care of her old dad.'

'That must be comforting.'

He ate a biscuit. 'I see you're still flush,' he said between the crumbs.

'What do you mean?'

'You had some money due to you, didn't you?'

'Oh, that, yes. I gave a lot of it away.'

'You what?'

'South Africa, that sort of thing.'

He patted me on the shoulder. 'Oh, that's good. Very nice. They got rid of those bastards in the end. We had a drink on that when it happened, the day old Nelson Mandela got out.'

'I never thought of you as political.'

'That's not politics, is it, it's just fair dues.'

'You loved jazz, didn't you?'

'Still do. I've got every recording Charlie Parker ever made. That was something, to have seen the Bird in his heyday. I can still get bought a drink on that story.'

'Still smoke dope?'

He smiled. 'Gave it up when it came into fashion. You can't see me in a tie-dyed T-shirt and one of those coats they used to wear like old dogs.'

'No, not your style.'

'It was the end of cool, all that, for years. I was a dinosaur. I couldn't be bothered in the end. I just let the wife get my clothes now. She's very keen on M&S. I can't even drink much any more, just a half-pint on my birthday and Christmas.' He patted his stomach. 'The wife's got me on a diet, but I keep telling her not to hold her breath.' He paused. 'Shame we didn't know about keeping out of the sun, eh, Syb? You'd have skin like a baby's bottom now.'

'We didn't know. Can I pour you some more tea?'

He looked at me and held a hand over his cup. 'I'm sorry,' he said. 'For backing out. I never knew if you were the making of me or the death of me. I couldn't figure it. I never meant for us to go on that long, all those years but every time you turned up it would be back on again, *we* would be back on, without me ever deciding. I just looked round and there you were.'

'You always said I was your woman.

'I know. You were.'

'The ground under your feet.'

'The ground under my feet. Did I say that?'

'Not to me.'

'I don't remember.'

People don't remember things, do they? You have to remind them all the time. 'I found some stuff after you left. Pornography and pictures. Of you.'

'Did you?'

'You told me being bisexual was just a phase.'

'Phases.'

'Oh, I see.' It was cold in the lounge. I put my arms into the sleeves of my mother's coat, for warmth.

'I was never faithful, you know. I was always running around.'

'I didn't know.'

'No, you were too wrapped up in yourself to notice.'

'I wasn't faithful either. I slept with Laurence, for one.'

'Yes,' he said.

'He told you?'

'We were mates.'

'That's not the impression he gave me. He wanted me to leave you.'

'No, that didn't work out, did it?'

'You mean that's what you wanted?'

'I was having it off with Margaret. It would have been handy.'

'Margaret. I never thought . . .'

'You were never much one for talking to women, were you? You weren't exactly an early women's libber.'

We were silent for a long time. The waitress came over and asked if we wanted some hot water for the pot. I sent her away.

'What a sham,' I said.

'No, no, Syb, it wasn't. I did love you, I just couldn't take you.'

'And are you faithful to your wife?'

'Who'd have me now?'

'You took all those photographs of me. Why?'

'You were easy to light. Your skin's very contrasty.'

'That was it?'

'More or less.' He looked at me and his eyes were moist and bright.

'I was in the Communist Party,' I retorted. I didn't need *his* pity.

'*Were* you? I never knew that.'

'I really fooled you, then!'

'We fooled each other. Would you say you'd had a good life? Mine's not been bad.'

I turned to look at him, to hunt for any trace of the man I had loved for so long and I willed myself to find it. 'I wish I'd belonged somewhere. I wish I hadn't spent so much time on the edge of things.'

'You belong, all right.'

'Who to? What?'

'To yourself.'

'That's not enough.'

'But it's had to be, hasn't it?'

I was so cold, even in my mother's coat. My teeth were chattering. 'I wish I'd never come here.'

'What?'

'I said I wish I'd never come here.'

'No, you don't, sweetheart. It'll be the making of you.'

'It's a bit late in life to be *made*.'

'People who are blind have fantastic hearing, did you know that? The brain makes it up. You're like that. You're not all there but you've adapted. You're a fully signed-on member of the human race.'

'Oh, go fuck yourself, Stan. What do you know?'

The waitress cleared away our tea-things and my uneaten plate of biscuits. The door seemed very far away.

'Have you got a room here?' he said suddenly.

'Yes.'

'Can we go up there? I'm feeling a bit rough. It's come on all of a sudden.' He was very grey, his breath accelerated. Alarmed, I took hold of him and we made our excruciatingly slow progress across the floor, up in the lift and into my room.

'I'll lie down for a bit if you don't mind,' he said. He pushed his shoes off and fell heavily on to the bed. He was there for some time, his eyes closed until his breathing became more regular and some colour came back into his face. I made him a cup of tea from the tray of packets on the dressing table.

'That's lovely,' he said. 'Just the ticket.'

'You look better.'

'I feel it. Bit of a moment, that.'

'We're getting on, aren't we?'

'Yeah, I'm seventy-five next birthday.'

'Christ, so you are.'

He lay with his arms behind his head against the pillows, looking at me. 'Listen, love,' he said. 'I'll let you in on a secret. Until I met my wife you were the only woman I ever really wanted, from the moment I saw you in Sefton Park. The rest was just going through the motions. And it was a good hunch, wasn't it? I mean you're pushing seventy and you've still got loads of class. The thing is this. You talk about love, but there's different kinds. My wife Kay was twenty when I met her and she was so gorgeous I thought I'd drop down dead. A stunner. Remember I was over fifty at the time and I thought I had no chance. I couldn't believe it when she went for me. I felt twenty again myself with her on my arm. She was so young I knew I'd have to look after her. I'd have to be a man. You always stood up for me, you stepped right out of your class. You looked out for me, you wanted me to make something of myself. You were like a mother who'll dive into the river without thinking after her baby who's fallen in. But what you gave, you took. I wanted to be a man and you wouldn't let me. I left because you didn't need me. In fact I know you looked down on me. You made me feel thick. You'd have been much better off with Laurence, anyone could see that a mile off except you.'

'You sound very grown up all of a sudden.'

'It does that to you, having responsibility for a family.'

'I got everything wrong. I thought it was settling down that scared you. I thought you didn't want to be trapped. You were a free spirit.'

'Syb, sweetheart, that wasn't me, it was you.'

'Me?'

'I always had somewhere to go back to and here I am. I knew who I was and where I was from. I was Stan Maguire from Toxteth, Liverpool born and bred. Son of a sailor and son of a sailor's son. You never knew who you were or what you came from. You were free. What did you do all those years before we met up again?'

'I was on the road for the Party. I was an underground courier.'

'Well, then. No, sweetheart, don't cry.'

'My cousin Jasa said we were dinosaurs, people like us who didn't belong anywhere. It's the age of nationalism.'

'He's talking through his hat, tell him.'

'He's dead, we buried him two years ago.'

'Listen, the world will always be able to use the likes of you. You're neither one thing nor the other and that drives people mad, but we've got to have you. It wouldn't do if we didn't.'

The light was going. A ship's engine sounded on the river, or maybe I dreamt it because there are no more ships.

'Come here,' he said.

'No.'

'Come here,' he said again.

But I had already turned and was looking out of the window. Across the top of the city my gaze sped, to the river as it widened and narrowed and met the sea. My thoughts were rushing down to the sea, and the brass and the ivory horns and the trumpets were sounding on the water, where ships sail on the surfaces of things to the very edge of our burning world.

Still Here

Linda Grant

'Blunt, honest . . . often beautiful and bitingly funny'
Rachel Seiffert, author of *The Dark Room*

Two middle-aged people meet in Liverpool, once the
embarkation point for nine million future Americans, now a
dying port. Alix has returned to her birthplace for her
mother's death and to receive her dying wish. Joseph, an
American architect, is there to build a hotel on the
waterfront. Both are hiding a great deal – from others and
from themselves.

'It's a testament to Grant's skill that she can create a novel at
once so serious and so readable' Maggie O'Farrell,
Independent on Sunday

The Clothes on Their Backs

Linda Grant

Shortlisted for the Man Booker Prize 2008

Vivien spends a quiet childhood encapsulated in the present, sealed off from the past by her timid refugee parents. She's ten before she finds out that she has a relative: to the horror of her father, her glamorous, dangerous uncle appears at their door, dressed in purple mohair with his leopard-print-clad mistress upon his arm. But why is Uncle Sándor so violently unwelcome in her parents' home?

'If you read only one novel this year, make sure it is *The Clothes on Their Backs*'
Sunday Express Magazine

'Richly imagined . . . it is a joy to welcome such a vibrant and thought-provoking book' Michael Arditti, *Independent*

You can order other Virago titles through our website: *www.virago.co.uk*
or by using the order form below

☐	Still Here	Linda Grant	£7.99
☐	The Clothes on Their Backs	Linda Grant	£7.99
☐	The People on the Street	Linda Grant	£9.99
☐	The Thoughtful Dresser	Linda Grant	£11.99

The prices shown above are correct at time of going to press. However, the publishers reserve the right to increase prices on covers from those previously advertised, without further notice.

———————————— 🍎 ————————————

Please allow for postage and packing: **Free UK delivery.**
Europe: add 25% of retail price; Rest of World: 45% of retail price.

To order any of the above or any other Virago titles, please call our credit card orderline or fill in this coupon and send/fax it to:

Virago, PO Box 121, Kettering, Northants NN14 4ZQ
Fax: 01832 733076   Tel: 01832 737526
Email: aspenhouse@FSBDial.co.uk

☐ I enclose a UK bank cheque made payable to Virago for £ . . . .
☐ Please charge £ . . . . . . to my Visa/Delta/Maestro

Expiry Date [| | |]   Maestro Issue No. [|]

NAME (BLOCK LETTERS please) . . . .

ADDRESS . . . .

. . . .

. . . .

Postcode . . . . Telephone . . . .

Signature . . . .

Please allow 28 days for delivery within the UK. Offer subject to price and availability.